D1439189

Cardiff, by the Sea

JOYCE CAROL OATES is the author of over
seventy books and the winner of a host of
prizes including the National Book Award and
a Guggenheim Fellowship. Oates is Professor
of the Humanities at Princeton University.

Also by Joyce Carol Oates

Cardiff, by the Sea

JOYCE CAROL OATES

A Mysterious Press book for
Head of Zeus

First published in the US in 2020 by Mysterious Press,
an imprint of Grove/Atlantic, New York

First published in the UK in 2021 by Head of Zeus, Ltd

These stories were previously published in different forms: 'Cardiff, by the Sea'
first appeared in *Ellery Queen*; 'Miao Dao' was an Amazon original; 'Phantomwise: 1972' first appeared in *Ellery Queen* and was reprinted in *The Best American
Mystery Stories* 2019; 'The Surviving Child' first appeared in *Echoes: The Saga
Anthology of Ghost Stories* and was reprinted in *The Best Fantasy and Horror* 2020.

A catalogue record for this book is available from the British Library.

ISBN (HB): 9781800241398
ISBN (XTPB): 9781800241404
ISBN (E): 9781800241411

This book was set in 11.5-pt Scala by
Alpha Design & Composition of Pittsfield, NH

Printed and bound by CPI Group (UK) Ltd, Croydon, CR0 4YY

MIX
Paper from
responsible sources
FSC® C020471

Head of Zeus Ltd
First Floor East
5–8 Hardwick Street
London EC1R 4RG

WWW.HEADOFZEUS.COM

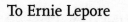
To Ernie Lepore

CONTENTS

CARDIFF, BY THE SEA

I.

1.

In the dark smelly place beneath the sink. Behind the drainpipes. She has made herself small enough to hide here.

Strands of a broken spider's web sticking to her skin. Her eyes wet with tears. Hunching her back like a little monkey. Arms closed tight around her knees raised against her small flat chest.

She is just a little girl, small enough to save herself. Small enough to fit into the spider's web. Smart enough to know that she must not cry.

Must not breathe. So that no one can hear.

So that he can't hear.

The door to the hiding place is opened, she sees a man's feet, legs. She sees, does not see, the glisten of something dark and wet on the trouser legs. She hears, does not hear, his quick, hot panting. With a whoop of wild laughter he stoops to peer inside. He has discovered her. His face is a blur of tears. His mouth moves and is talking to her, but she hears no words. But then the door is shut again and she is alone.

In this way, it is determined. In the spider's web she is allowed to live.

2.

Phone rings. Unexpectedly.

Not her cell phone, which Clare would (probably) answer without a second thought, but the other phone, the landline, which rarely rings.

Seconds in which to decide: Should she lift the receiver?

Seeing that the caller ID is not one she recognizes. Calculating that the call is likely to be a robot call.

Yet this rain-lashed April morning—out of curiosity, or loneliness, or heedlessness—she lifts the receiver. "Yes? Hello?"

One of the shocks of Clare's life.

For it seems that a stranger has called her, introducing himself as an attorney with a law firm in Cardiff, Maine. Informing her that she is the beneficiary of an individual of whom she has never heard—"Maude Donegal, of Cardiff, Maine. Your grandmother."

"Excuse me? Who?"

"Maude Donegal—your father's mother. She has passed away at the age of eighty-seven . . ."

Not sure what she is hearing. Thinking it might be, must be a prank, her first instinct is to laugh.

"But I don't have a grandmother with that name. I don't know anyone with that name—did you say Douglas?"

"Donegal."

A pause, and the voice at the other end of the line continues, disembodied and matter-of-fact, as a voice in a dream: "But Donegal is your birth name. Didn't you know?"

"Birth name! But—where is this place"

"Cardiff, Maine."

Clare has never heard of Cardiff, Maine. She is sure.

Having lived in Minnesota for much of her life—at first St. Paul, then Minneapolis. A very long distance from Maine.

In more recent years Clare has lived in Chicago, Brooklyn, Philadelphia, Bryn Mawr (where she is living now). Still a considerable distance from Maine.

". . . any questions?"

"N-no . . ."

"I hope I didn't upset you, Ms. Seidel."

Of course not! You have only torn a rent in the fabric of my life.

Clare thanks the attorney. The conversation ends. She has been too distracted to ask Lucius Fischer what the *bequest* from Maude Donegal is, how much money, or property—whatever. Now she is too embarrassed to call him back.

He'd asked for her address. He will be sending her a document via UPS that should arrive the following afternoon.

Also, he will be including, at their request, the phone number of Donegal relatives in Cardiff. If Clare comes to Cardiff, they have expressed the hope that she will stay with them.

Relatives! But these are strangers, and Clare can't imagine herself staying with strangers.

She values her solitude, privacy. Her aloofness might be mistaken for shyness, her reticence for secrecy. She is not by nature a suspicious person, but she is (certainly) not naïve and so wonders if this sudden "good news" is to be trusted.

If it is a ruse of some kind, she will soon be enlightened: someone will want money from her.

Clare is not familiar with wills, bequests—"probate court." Never in her life has she been a *beneficiary* of anyone's will; it has not even crossed her mind that her adoptive parents have (possibly, probably) named her in their wills, as she is their only child and their only likely heir . . .

So taken by surprise when the attorney called, she'd failed to express regret for the death of Maude Donegal. She fears that she has forgotten the name—no, here it is written down: *Maude Donegal.*

How callous Lucius Fischer must think her, unmoved by a grandmother's death.

But she isn't my—grandmother! I have no grandmother.

Clare's (adoptive) grandparents are no longer living. And when living, they had not figured much in her life.

How strange it seems to Clare, such syntax: *Grandparents are no longer living.* As if *not-living* were something the grandparents were doing at the present time.

Clare had envied classmates who'd spoken casually of their grandparents. Totally taken for granted—*Grandma, Grandpa.* What did these tender words mean, exactly? Both her mother's parents and her father's parents, elderly at the time of the adoption, had not much warmed to their granddaughter, it seemed.

Clare scarcely remembered them. Strangers, staring at the little mute adopted child across an abyss.

(Oh, had Clare been *mute?* Surely not. Not most of the time. Only dimly she remembers—something . . .)

(A kind of net, or web, over her mouth. Sticky threads against her lips, caught in her eyelashes. Breathing in, in shuddering gasps, the broken cobweb is drawn horribly into her nostrils.)

Clare scarcely remembers at all. That is a fact.

Too young at the time to realize that if her parents had been able to have children, probably—well, certainly—they would not have adopted her. Their love for her, their intense *interest in her,* would never have sprung into being if they'd had children of their own.

In high school biology Clare learned that DNA is everything. Individuals care for their own—offspring bearing their DNA. Male animals in many species are prone to destroy the offspring of other males, mating with the mother animals to replicate their own DNA. A desperate mother may try to hide her young from a predatory male, but once she comes into estrus, she is compelled to mate with the male animal bent upon killing her young to make way for his own.

Compelled to mate. Why?

Her parents' parents hadn't warmed to their (adopted) grand-daughter, for that reason perhaps. Clare was not *one of theirs.*

But how unnatural it must be, then, for biological parents to cast off their young . . .

That is the mystery. Clare has not liked to consider it.

Now, having turned thirty, she considers herself too old—that's to say, not sufficiently young, naïve, hopeful—to really care about biological parents—ancestry.

Why risk being hurt (again)? She hasn't fully acknowledged that she has ever been hurt, in fact.

She looks up Cardiff, Maine, in a book of road maps. Very close to the Atlantic Ocean. Nearby towns of Belfast and Fife suggest that this (eastern) part of Maine was once a Scots settlement. She wonders if her (paternal) ancestors were Scots, or Irish. Until that morning she'd had little thought of ancestry.

(Though she has felt, undeniably, a tug of interest in Celtic history—art, music. Hearing, by chance, an Irish ballad on NPR while driving somewhere, so overcome with a sensation of loss, longing, she'd almost had to pull onto the shoulder of the highway . . . Detecting a Scots or Irish accent, however faint, she is immediately riveted.)

But why should origins matter? The adopted one knows that only now, here really matter.

Clare sees that Cardiff is not one of the larger cities in Maine. Only nineteen thousand people. Seventeen miles north of Eddington, on the coast, which looks as serrated as a knife.

Strange to suppose that she might be from there—a mere dot on a map.

But, well—we must all be from somewhere.

Clare chides herself, don't be hopeful. Don't give in to expectations. *Hope is the thing with feathers*, the poet has warned. Easily injured, because vulnerable.

She has never wished to believe in genetic determinism— "fate." As an educated person, as the child of professional educators, she understands that it's the environment that shapes the self, essentially.

People, places. Quality of life, education. The air we breathe— is it clear or is it contaminated? The immediate environment that surrounds us, this is what matters.

In this, Clare has been lucky. The sentiment is, adopted children are lucky. Plucked out of obscurity, chosen, therefore cherished. She has been well educated, she has never gone hungry or feared for her life. (Has she? Not within memory.) And now she is living in a quite nice one-bedroom rental apartment a short walk from the ivied Bryn Mawr Humanities Research Institute, where she is a postdoctoral fellow, engaged in a study of nineteenth-century photography.

Her work, which involves visiting the excellent photography archives at the Philadelphia Museum of Art, is entirely self-determined. The institute has a policy of allowing its research scholars to work in solitude, in privacy, for years, without having to report to anyone.

You could die, Clare has thought, bemused, and the institute wouldn't know for months. Such freedom from scrutiny is thrilling yet also unsettling. *You could die from loneliness*—has crossed Clare's mind.

Too restless to work today. Peering at slides in the high-ceilinged archival reading room at the museum, preparing footnotes on her laptop—Clare is too distracted. Instead, she spends hours at home, scrolling the internet, researching Eastern Maine, the rockbound Atlantic coast. Historic eighteenth-century settlement of Cardiff.

There are distinguished (male) artists associated with Maine: Winslow Homer, Rockwell Kent, George Bellows, Frederic Church . . . Surely there are talented women artists whose work has been overlooked, undervalued.

Women artists rarely survive their generation, no matter their talent and originality. No matter the awards their work receives, no matter even the male artists with whom they are associated. As soon as they die, their work begins to fade and die. Clare has felt the injustice and is determined to help remedy it.

In Maine, she will embark upon a new project. Perhaps.

Beneficiary. Estate. Grandmother—Donegal. The deep-baritone voice of the Cardiff lawyer echoes seductively in her ears.

Clare wishes she could share her good news with someone. But there is no ideal friend here in Bryn Mawr. She has always been cautious about speaking too openly with anyone, even a lover. Especially a lover.

Intimacy with another entices us to reveal—too much. Unclothed, we are vulnerable. Once a secret is shared, it can never be retrieved.

Also: Clare hasn't told anyone that she was adopted. That is her secret. So now she can't tell anyone about the happiness she feels as an heiress.

Proof that someone cared for her. A grandmother.

But why did she wait so long to acknowledge you, Clare?—this grandmother of yours . . .

And what about your (birth) parents? Are they alive? Will you try to contact them?

Questions Clare has no wish to hear. No idea how to answer.

Trying to focus on the computer screen. Scrolling through a website devoted to Winslow Homer in Maine. Badly distracted by rushing random thoughts . . .

Within a day or two you might meet them. Whatever awaits you in Cardiff.

Clare has tried not to think of them—mother, father. Even as a child she hadn't allowed it. Assumed that neither parent was living, for otherwise why would their daughter be given away to strangers at the age of two years, nine months?

No one would do such a thing voluntarily. An unmarried girl or woman might surrender an infant out of desperation, but a toddler is a different story.

Yes but you might have been sold. Not only didn't they want you, they wanted to make money from you.

Not possible. Ridiculous! Clare would never believe this.

And now, having learned that her father's mother has left an estate, that the Donegals were not impoverished . . .

As a child, Clare had known children who'd been adopted. Middle school, high school. Astonishing to her that such an intimate fact, such a *shameful* fact might be shared with others. One of her college roommates became (exasperatingly) obsessed with seeking out her biological mother. (Clare hadn't encouraged her in the search and hadn't sympathized when the mysterious birth mother turned out to be a disappointment.) Even to these girls, Clare had not declared herself. She'd never made any effort to explore the legal process of seeking out biological/birth parents.

When you are adopted, it is not in your best interest to ask questions why.

To know that you are adopted is the answer to any question you might ask about your adoption.

Phone rings!—this time Clare checks the caller ID before recklessly answering.

Seeing with dismay that a friend is calling—a (male) friend, not (yet) a lover, but a (seemingly) romantic prospect—with whom she'd made plans, she realizes now, to have dinner in Philadelphia that evening. Her friend is a fellow postdoc at the institute, whose research brings him to the Free Library of Philadelphia. A day ago Clare was looking forward to this evening and would have been sharply disappointed if her friend had canceled; now she has forgotten all about it and will have to invent a plausible excuse for not meeting him at the restaurant.

So sorry, Joshua! I was hoping that I'd have time to call you— but—there's been a family emergency—I must be away for a while, unavoidably.

3.

Her personal identity has always been simple enough—*adopted*.

Blank slate. Washed clean. No memory.

Very young, not yet three, when she'd been adopted by a (childless, older) couple in St. Paul named Seidel.

That was all she'd needed to know about that phase of her life: she'd been adopted at a young age. All she'd wished to know.

A tabula rasa, it is. Adoption.

Her (adoptive) parents did tell her that her birth name was Clare—that is, her name was Clare Ellen when she'd come into their lives, and this was a "very charming" name that they saw no reason to change, as (of course, officially) they would be changing her last name now that she was their little girl.

A matter of property, possession. A child is delivered to an adult or adults—delivered by birth, sometimes delivered by an agency.

Maybe she'd seen that name—Donegal—on her birth certificate. So long ago, it made no impression on her and (in fact) she has forgotten.

Every adoption is a mystery—*Why?*

Why was I given up, given away? Why was I not wanted?

By whom was I not wanted?

But Clare Seidel was/is the perfect (adopted) daughter. Clare did not/does not ask.

A grateful child does not ask why.

The Seidels were older parents. Might've been their adopted child's grandparents. Both were teachers with a mission—educators. Over the course of seventeen years of marriage they had not had children, though (Clare has gathered) they'd tried. Not long before Clare was adopted, a beloved dog belonging to the Seidels had died. Clare has seen pictures of this pert, brush-haired Airedale flanked by its adoring master and mistress and has felt a stab of jealousy, fear. (If the Airedale hadn't passed away at the age of twelve, at precisely the time he did, would the person identified as Clare Seidel exist?) The Seidels did not wish to think that life had cheated them. They had combined incomes, two cars, a house with a reasonable mortgage. For two weeks each August they rented a cottage on Lake Superior. They were grateful for the orphaned child Clare, as Clare would come to be grateful for them.

Don't hurt Dad's feelings! Don't ever make him think he isn't your Dad, because he is.

Because there is no other Dad, or Mom, for you. There is—just us.

Instinctively Clare knew. She understood. She was their (adopted) little girl who would never ask why.

For instance, an (adopted) child never asks, *Why did you want me?*

Couldn't you have children of your own, was that why you'd adopted me?

Of course, never ask! Unthinkable.

An (adopted) child never asks, *But where did I come from? To whom did I belong before I was given to you?*

16

Later, in school, Clare felt a swell of pride when the smiling teacher pronounced the very special name that meant her: *Sei-del.*

Such pleasure it gave her, when at last she could write, to write

Clare Seidel

Clare Seidel

Clare Seidel

in her notebook.

But all that, that part of her life, her very early life, hardly seems hers any longer.

4.

Next day the UPS delivery from Lucius Fischer arrives. Clare discovers that she has inherited twelve acres, a house, and outbuildings at 2558 Post Road, Ashford County, Maine.

Property! Better than mere money, which has no historic value, property is something Clare can possess.

Several times she scans the lawyer's accompanying letter but discovers no new information. No warmly scribbled personal postscript—*Congratulations, Ms. Seidel!*

Indeed, a properly formal letter on stiff stationery with the letterhead

ABRAMS, FISCHER, MITTELMAN, & TROTTER.

Fischer's signature is all but unreadable. She'd felt such a curious rapport with him the previous day . . .

And that was how we met. Over the phone.

Over the matter of my grandmother's will.

Smiling to think of how it might be narrated from a future perspective. How (random) lives intersect with other lives, changing these lives forever.

. . . it was purest chance! The phone rang, I picked it up, and there was Lucius on the other end, saying, Hello? Am I speaking with Clare Seidel?

Totally uprooting my life. And his.

Clare imagines a summer place on the Atlantic coast. Plate-glass windows facing the ocean. Tall hemlocks, a curving country road. Boulder-strewn beach. Crashing waves of the grayish-blue Atlantic Ocean, too cold to swim even in midsummer. Ceaseless wind.

Sees herself in white clothing, a figure in a Winslow Homer watercolor of dreamlike beauty. Descending stone steps to the beach. Behind her a mysterious figure . . .

Almost, Clare can see the man's face. But as she stares, it begins to disintegrate. Blurs, as if with tears.

But no: She will sell the property. If she can.

Never will she live in rural Ashford County, Maine. Her professional work necessitates her living in large urban areas, near research institutions.

Fischer has informed Clare that she has thirty days to file her claim in the Ashford County probate court. She wonders—how much is the property worth? Is it worth her effort?

Clare could use the money. She is thirty years old, has never had any but temporary jobs, academic appointments. A very small savings account. She has liked to think of herself as a person immune to material things. Though she has a weakness for beauty, she doesn't need to own it.

Landscapes, art. Music. You can take pleasure in these without owning them.

As you can take pleasure in people, lovers—without being owned by them.

She has never wanted to marry, still less have children. Crying babies fill her with dismay. Shrieking children fill her with panic. A (former) lover objected that Clare tended to "drift" when they were together: he never knew where the hell her mind was, but he could sense that it wasn't with him.

Clare winces, recalling. She regrets having hurt another person.

In your web. In your cocoon. Beware whom you allow in.

In each place Clare has lived since leaving her parents' home, she has accumulated a small number of friends, none of whom knows the others. This is crucial to Clare—that her friends don't know one another. And each time she moves to a new city, she is negligent about keeping in contact with these friends.

Yet if one of her friends fails to keep in contact with her, she feels wounded, anxious.

Her feelings for others are transient but powerful. Like a fire that burns hot, then rapidly cools.

Do others feel the same way? There have been men—there have been women—who'd seemed to care for Clare, from whom she'd retreated hastily.

Through her life as an adult Clare has had a succession of lovers. As she has had a succession of friends. Many more friends than lovers, but many more lovers than she has relatives. Until now.

"Oh, fuck. Do I *care?*"

Impulsively she decides to open a bottle of wine. Chardonnay, purchased a few weeks ago when she'd contemplated preparing a meal with wine, for friends, but other plans intervened. To celebrate, Clare thinks.

To fortify her nerves. Just this once.

Until now Clare has never drunk alone. It's a very self-conscious act, drinking alone. Something sad about it. Defiantly, she empties her glass.

Time to call home in St. Paul. Her strategy is to call at a time when it's likely that her father won't be home, but her mother will be.

Not that Clare doesn't love Walter. But speaking with her (step) father is sometimes awkward. Clare has always been able to speak more openly, more warmly, with Hannah than with Walter, though it can't be claimed (Clare supposes) that she has ever been able to speak to Hannah without a sense of—is it unease . . .

Clare is in luck, Walter isn't home. Hannah answers the phone on the first ring, sounding eager, lonely.

Yet there's an air of subtle reproach in Hannah's greeting. Clare tries to remember—does she owe her mother a call? Has she failed to call back when Hannah has left a message? Inadvertently, Clare often erases messages from Hannah in her voice mailbox.

Clare has called Hannah with the intention of sharing her good news, but somehow the opportunity does not arise. *Guess what, Mom? Good news!*—these cheery words fail to come.

Indeed, Clare glides over news of her own (private) life. She is grateful that Hannah has a fresh slate of complaints about a nemesis-colleague who has bedeviled Hannah Seidel for what seems to Clare like decades. She doesn't mind at all, as she has sometimes minded, that Hannah doesn't seem to recall having told Clare any of this before. *Within the family, old news is good news*, she thinks in a small attempt at wit.

Then Clare hears herself ask something extraordinary: Does Hannah know if Clare's biological parents are living?—a question that brings their conversation to an abrupt halt.

Biological parents. A clinical and graceless term but (Clare thinks guiltily) preferable to *birth parents.*

"But—why are you asking such a question, Clare—now?"

Hannah's uphill full-velocity voice has shifted to a lower gear. Her eyes, near visible in faraway St. Paul, Minnesota, have narrowed, her mouth has become a small, angry wound.

Clare says she'd been meaning to ask. For a long time . . .

"But why?"

Why, when you have us. Why do you care about them!

"Why? It seems like a natural question . . . I am thirty years old."

"Thirty years old! What has that got to do with it?" Hannah is genuinely perplexed, annoyed.

"I mean—I'm not a child any longer . . ."

"But it was all explained to you, Clare. Years ago. Don't you remember?"

"I—I—I don't think that I remember . . ."

Clare tries to recall—exactly what, she doesn't know.

"We were provided very little information, Clare. And it has been a long time now. More than a quarter century since you came into our lives out of the unknown." Hannah speaks reproachfully, as if it were Clare's fault.

Out of the unknown. A stinging remark.

"Your father and I were told very little about you, and none of that information has changed in subsequent years. All that we knew, we told you years ago."

Clare listens, chastened. She can't bring herself to say, *But I don't remember. I need to be told again. Please!*

"I was just wondering if you knew—if they are living. Or—if . . ."

Hannah's voice is loud over the phone, huskier: "We never knew if there was a *they*, or just a *she*—a mother. There'd been

22

an accident—we were told—but we never knew the details. No idea how old your biological parents were at the time. You have to understand, Clare, this was a long time ago and things were done differently then. There was shame attached to giving away a child to be adopted, and there was a feeling, not exactly shame, but something like complicity in shame, in adopting. Taking advantage of someone else's unhappiness. We had to work with a Catholic agency through the Planned Parenthood agency in Minneapolis. They insisted upon guaranteeing anonymity if either side requested it—the parents who were adopting and the—other . . ."

Clare is stunned by Hannah's outburst. She has never heard her mother speak so openly. Now Clare is beginning to remember. *Anonymity. Sealed records.*

Don't ask. Futile.

"There was nothing more we could do, Clare. We couldn't push for information to which we had no legal right. We had no idea what we were doing, really—adopting a baby was totally new to us. It was a very emotional time. We'd assumed we would be adopting an infant—of course—but we were very grateful to adopt you . . ."

Hannah's voice trails off, as if she realizes what she is saying. "Clare? We wanted only what was best for you."

An odd thing to say. What was *best* for—who?

Numbly, Clare assures her mother yes, she understands. Of course.

Everyone wants the best for an orphaned child they have never seen before.

Clare understands that she should end the conversation. She is upsetting Hannah. But she isn't able to end it. Her curiosity is like a rabid thirst, parching her mouth. "What part of the country did they live in, did you know? My parents."

My parents. This is a mistake, Clare has misspoken.

Hannah says curtly that she doesn't know. If she'd ever known, she doesn't remember.

Then, relenting: "Well, maybe—I have the impression they'd lived in New England."

"Not the Midwest?"

"Why is it important where they were from? Has someone tried to contact you?"

"No!" Clare is quick to reply. "But do you think you could send a copy of my birth certificate, Mom?—I would appreciate it."

At Clare's age, *Mom* has become an awkward term of endearment. Even as a girl, Clare had had difficulty pronouncing *Mom* clearly.

Dad, she calls the other parent, less awkwardly.

Trained from an early age, encouraged by the (smiling) (step) parents, Clare has not felt comfortable with such generic terms of endearment.

Nor has she called any lover by a term of endearment. *Darling, honey. Dear one.*

"You don't have a copy in your possession? That's odd."

The Seidel family's legal documents are kept in Clare's father's filing cabinet in his home office, in scrupulously marked folders. Clare has inherited from the (step)father a certain fanaticism about neatness, clarity, boundaries. When in doubt, file. File away.

Clare feels a pang of shame. She has never fully moved out of her parents' house and brought her personal documents with her—never having acquired a home of her own, in her unsettled life.

A vagabond life of the mind. An undefined life, like a Polaroid print that has only partially filled in.

"Thank you so much, Mom! I need it for—medical insurance . . ."

Not an obvious lie, Clare thinks. Hannah will never suspect anything like the truth: that Clare will be presenting the birth certificate to a probate court in Cardiff, Maine.

Through a windowpane she has been observing an enormous spider's web just outside. A masterpiece of intricately connected threads of varying lengths, damp with moisture, quivering and awaiting insect prey. At the center is a fat-bellied black spider, motionless now, as if exhausted by spinning out its guts in such splendor.

At last the conversation ends. Hannah will say goodbye abruptly, with a sighed *Well!—love you*, and Clare will respond, as if prodded in the chest with a forefinger, *Love* you.

Never do mother and daughter quite bring themselves to say *I love you*.

Exhausted, Clare hangs up the phone. Badly needing another drink.

The trouble with being adopted is that you are always provisional. No matter your age, you are at risk of being sent back.

Next, Clare prepares a more challenging task: to telephone the Cardiff "relatives" whose number Fischer has provided.

Elspeth, Morag—surviving sisters of Maude Donegal, the phantasmal grandmother. Fischer described them as "younger sisters," but surely they must be elderly, in their eighties at least.

For this, another half glass of wine is required.

Never before the other day has Clare known of blood relatives. And now she has great-aunts.

On the first ring, Clare's call is answered.

As if the vigilant great-aunt has been breathlessly awaiting the call. Clare thinks—*My new life!*

The (female) speaker's name is—Elspeth? At first Clare can barely understand her: the woman speaks with a pronounced Maine accent and punctuates her words with curious little syllables—*um, eh?* She is formal in her manner and (seemingly) hard of hearing but surprisingly friendly, Clare thinks, for a Maine native; very curious about Clare, but not seeming to hear what Clare tells her, for she asks Clare when she is coming to Cardiff more than once and breaks off the conversation abruptly, as if someone has called to her. "Well, then! That's settled. You will stay with us, Cla-re. As long as you wish."

"You will see, dear—there is plenty of room in your grandmother Donegal's beautiful old house."

5.

Three days later, Clare has arrived in Cardiff, Maine.

Ringing the doorbell of a shabbily dignified old cobblestone house at 59 Acton Avenue, which is very sparely lit inside.

Like a storybook house, it is. An artifact of the Victorian era, on a street of similarly large, stolid, graceless private homes set back from the street amid tall hemlocks and overgrown privet hedges.

The Donegals must be well-to-do, Clare thinks. At least they'd been well-to-do in the past.

Cardiff, Maine, is a decaying nineteenth-century mill town, not yet fully converted to the tourist trade like other towns in this part of Maine. It is still picturesque along the waterfront, as decay often is, with long-shuttered mills and factories, a scattering of discount outlets and "antique" stores, boutiques selling arts and crafts.

Acton Avenue is clearly one of the prestigious streets in Cardiff, or once was, though near the city center houses like the Donegal residence have been appropriated for commercial purposes. Divided into apartments, professional offices. A dignified old-rose brick mansion has been converted to the Ashford County Historical Museum; another sprawling Victorian bears the humbling sign CARDIFF COUNTY FAMILY PLANNING & SERVICES.

Clare rings the doorbell again. Recalling how, on Halloween evening in St. Paul, as a young child, excited, apprehensive, she and other masked and costumed children had dared to ring doorbells at houses like this one while their parents waited in vehicles parked at the curb; how relieved they were when no one answered. Though there are lights inside the house, she wonders if anyone is home. Evergreen boughs crowd against the sides of the house, obscuring the downstairs windows. On the slate roof are patches of moss, and miniature trees have taken root in congested rain gutters. Clare smells leaf mold, moist dark earth, a subtle odor of organic rot beneath the veranda upon which she is standing. Yet, as gentle as an intimate caress comes the sudden thought. *Is this home? Am I in the right place now?*

To be orphaned is to be never in the right place. Though you would not wish to acknowledge it.

Clare's heart is beating rapidly in anticipation. She should know better, she tells herself: she is no longer a naïve child, practiced in batting down her hopes as you might bat down an over-affectionate dog.

No! This is certainly not your home.

Four hundred twenty miles from Bryn Mawr, Pennsylvania, to Cardiff, Maine. Approximately six hours by interstate, too long to drive in a single day yet too short to break into two driving days. If Clare had a companion . . .

Clare doesn't have a companion. Wisest to break the drive into two days, as she has done, and drive with caution. Blessed with an inheritance, the first in her life, Clare made herself into one of those infuriating drivers who hugs the right lane of the interstate, whose vehicle others pass in an unending succession.

Since the call from Lucius Fischer she has been thinking obsessively—*grandmother, will. Bequest.* And now she is here.

Inside the cobblestone house, voices. Inset in the stolid oak door is a round oriel window through which Clare can see only a muted flash as a light is switched on inside. With a flourish the heavy oak door is opened, and two elderly, oddly dressed women greet Clare as effusively as excited parrots.

"Here you are! Oh, you look like—"

"—like *him*. Your daddy—"

"—our Conor—"

"Ohh—she *does!*"

Tremulous voices. Eyes shimmering with tears. The taller of the women presses her hand against her flat bosom, panting.

"Well—thank God!—you are *here*—"

"—safely—*here*—"

"Welcome, Clare—"

"Come inside, dear. You must be—"

"—exhausted!"

"—famished!—I was about to say, dear, when this rude person interrupted me—"

"She interrupts me all the time, Clare—nobody is ruder than *she is.*"

"—famished after that long drive—"

"—and exhausted—"

"—come inside, dear—"

"—it is Clare, isn't it?—"

"—have been waiting for—"

"—for you. For—"

"—years."

Amid the flurry of greetings Clare is feeling light-headed. The women are plucking at her eagerly. She is hugged, and hugged again. And again hugged by surprisingly strong, thin arms, the breath squeezed from her rib cage.

"—like *him*! Your daddy—"

"—your poor, poor daddy—"

Brushing at their eyes. Brushing at their cheeks, where tears sparkle. The taller exudes a sweetly stale talcum-powdery fragrance, the shorter a gingery-medicinal smell of aged skin.

"My dear, I am Elspeth—"

"I am Morag—"

"—Maude's younger sister—"

"—Maude's *younger* younger sister—"

"We spoke on the phone, dear—"

"*She* grabbed at the receiver before I could lift it, and then—"

"Shall I take your suitcase, dear—"

"—she didn't let me so much as say hello to you." Morag, the shorter of the two, is especially vehement, reproachful. "*She never does.*"

Clare allows herself to be led into the house by the great-aunts, Elspeth and Morag, into a foyer with a stained marble floor. The odor of leaf mold and damp earth mingles now with the sharper fragrance of the elderly women and the airless air of the old house. Like soft-feathered birds, the women—the great-aunts—crowd against Clare. She could not have said which was Elspeth, which Morag (impressive Scots names!). One of them tugs Clare's suitcase from her fingers, but the suitcase falls at once to the floor, striking Clare's foot—the suitcase is too heavy for the elderly woman to lift.

"Oh—*you!* What have you done!"

"Not a thing! I was just trying to—"

"Always interfering and spoiling things. The poor girl has not been here five minutes and you are dropping her suitcase on her *foot*. Let me take it, Clare—*I* will not drop it, I promise."

"Excuse me! I am perfectly capable of carrying her suitcase—"

"No! You've demonstrated that you *are not*—"

Clare stammers that she can carry her suitcase upstairs herself. It isn't heavy, it's no trouble at all . . .

"Why, we wouldn't hear of it, dear Clare—"

"You have journeyed so far, you are our guest—"

"If only Maude were here—"

"—except, if Maude were here, there'd be no—will . . . And no Clare."

"Oh! That is not a *hospitable* thing to say to our guest. *Shame on you.*"

"Shame on *you!*—for even *thinking such a thing.*"

Clare smiles awkwardly. She has had little experience with being so fussed over by "relatives" who are (in fact) strangers to her but are not behaving with the conventional restraint of strangers.

Trying not to think that this might be a mistake, agreeing to stay with these great-aunts.

In fact, why had she said yes to the invitation? How much simpler it would be to stay in a hotel nearby.

Enticed by the idea of family. These elderly women are the only blood relatives Clare has encountered since her adoption, and she can't remember her adoption.

Is the taller and more animated of the two women, Elspeth, addressing Clare warmly? Or is that Morag?

Both great-aunts are staring at her avidly. Hungrily.

Both women are shorter than Clare, who is of moderate height at five feet seven; the shorter of the sisters is considerably shorter, with a seemingly misshapen spine. The taller and presumably younger sister has an ivory-pale, scarcely lined face upon which a "glamorous" cosmetic mask has been rouged, drawn, and powdered—arched eyebrows, blushing cheeks, a rosebud mouth; her bouffant hair is an unnatural tangerine color, of the airy texture of cotton candy. The shorter, presumably older sister with the twisted spine has a pushed-in pug face, a low forehead, pasty-pale skin, scanty eyebrows, and no eyelashes. Her mouth is thin-lipped but broad.

Elspeth, the taller, is festively attired in an electric-blue satin dress, a black lace shawl over her thin shoulders; Morag, as squat-bodied as a fireplug, wears what appears to be male clothing—shapeless dark pants of some soft fabric like jersey, not very clean, and a cable-knit pullover sweater with a stretched neck. Her hair is not dyed, like her sister's, but a mixture of stone-gray and chalky-white, somewhat coarse, though thin enough that Clare can see the pale, vulnerable scalp beneath. The taller, more stylish Elspeth wears silver-framed glasses; Morag's are chunky black with plastic rims.

Clare has a vague, unnerving sense of someone standing in the background, or at the periphery of her vision, looking on. Another great-aunt?

But when she turns, there is no one. A dim-lighted hallway leads back from the foyer into the somber interior of the house.

The great-aunts are standing very close to Clare, as if guarding her. They insist that she have tea with them. "It will restore your color. You are looking pale as a ghost."

"As if she has ever seen a ghost." The other sister laughs scornfully.

"It's a manner of speaking. *You* wouldn't know."

"I know this: you are the only silly person who has ever seen a ghost and brags about it."

"I do not—*brag!*"

"Well, if Clare sees a ghost, it will be your fault—for putting the idea in her head."

"*You* don't know everything."

Clare isn't sure if she should laugh at the sisters' bickering or try to ignore it. She understands that the brusque exchanges are for her benefit, and she doesn't want to make a blunder, to offend by laughing with one of her great-aunts at the expense of the other.

Elspeth is the wittier, and crueler; Morag is not so quick-witted but has a bulldog way of flaring up, incensed. It would seem at a glance that Elspeth would be stronger than Morag, as she appears to be more able-bodied, but in fact Morag is sturdier, heels flat on the ground.

Yet both behave in a very kindly way to their guest, and they seem to be genuinely concerned for her.

"Please come in here, Clare, and have a seat—you've been under a strain. We've had the tea things ready for some time . . ."

"That isn't a very nice thing to say to a guest! 'Ready for some time'—that's rude."

"I only meant—"

"—just ignore her, Clare; my sister so rarely has company, she has lost her manners."

"—only meant the tea will be getting *cold.*"

"Then—we will *reheat* it . . ."

Like young children or dogs eager for affection, the great-aunts are competing for Clare's attention, which is embarrassing to her. She has a vague idea that another person, a third great-aunt perhaps, a wraithlike figure, is somewhere close by, preparing to bring out the tea.

In a drawing room crowded with heavy antique furnishings, carpets and tapestries, Clare is urged to take a seat on a velvet settee that creaks slyly beneath her weight. The smell of mold is strong here, as well as an earthy, gritty odor she guesses might be rodent droppings, which she has smelled before in her life, in places not so very clean.

"We know you're tired, dear Clare, and only want some privacy in your room, but—we have so much to talk about first!"

"How d'you know the girl wants *privacy*? She is famished, look at her! She wants her *tea*."

"—*high* tea—"

"—except we only have Pepperidge Farm cookies, not hot buttered scones and clotted cream, every kind of jam and jelly, like they serve at the Ritz, but—"

"Oh, that Ritz! She wants you to ask, 'Which Ritz?' so she can say '*the* Ritz, on Piccadilly.' You know—London."

Elspeth speaks scornfully. When Morag protests, Elspeth says, with the air of one delivering the pièce de résistance, "And I don't mean London, Connecticut."

"*New* London, Connecticut—"

"Oh, just *stop*! She goes on and on about it! We were taken just once as girls by our father to high tea at the Ritz, and she never got over it—"

"—*she* never got over it—"

"—and d'you know what, Clare?—the tea was English Breakfast and wasn't even steeped in the pot, it was *tea bags*."

Clare laughs, uncertain why this is funny, if she is meant to laugh. It seems cruel to her that the taller, more attractive, younger-appearing Elspeth should speak with such scorn, intending to belittle her dwarflike sister who speaks so earnestly; also, there is something missing about Morag, one of her hands perhaps—Clare is sure she has seen a smooth-skinned stump . . . But when she dares to look more closely, Morag seems to have two hands of more than ordinary size, manly hands, with the broken nails of a laborer or a gardener.

"—so much to talk about, dear!—we have been waiting and *waiting*. Since our poor dear sister passed away last week, and we were informed of the shock of the will—"

"—not that we are badly shocked, oh no—"

"—*no*. Not at all *badly shocked*. We'd known that—"

"—our dear Maude had many 'interests'—"

"—charities—"

"—St. Cuthbert's—"

"—relatives scattered all over New England—"

"—quite a shock, but not a *bad shock*—"

"—dear Maude has left us this house—"

"—*jointly*, us and her son—Gerard—"

"—oh yes: Gerard—your bachelor uncle—"

"—she looked after us—and a few others in the family—"

"—our dear nephew Gerard, you will meet—"

"—*we* didn't marry, as Maude did; she was very brave—"

"—she so grieved for your father, she could not—"

"—could *not bear*—"

"—even to think of—"

"—for years, to think of *you*."

"Yet she was aware of you—"

"She was! We all were—except—"

"—the years flew by—"

"—flew by . . ."

Amid this exhausting chatter, an elaborate tarnished-silver tea tray is brought into the drawing room, set ceremoniously on a low table in front of Clare. A rattling of cups, spoons. Chipped but beautiful, fragile Wedgwood china, ornately patterned silver spoons just slightly tarnished. Whoever has brought in the tray isn't visible to Clare, for her—his?—face has been obscured by a cloud of steam rising from the teapot.

"—I will pour. Here, Clare—"

"—your cup, Clare—"

"—*your* cup, we have selected carefully—"

"—rosebuds, dear Maude's favorite—"

"—and this spoon!—actually it is a baby spoon—"

"—*your* spoon—"

Clare rubs at her eyes, tired from the long drive, and sees that the great-aunt who is stirring the tea is Elspeth, unless it is Morag . . . And who is the other person in the room? Clare glances nervously about; her strained eyes detect no one.

There follows an interlude of merciless chatter. Like sharp-beaked birds peck-peck-pecking at her. Of course, Clare thinks, her elderly great-aunts mean no harm; they mean well; they are lonely, perhaps, for company; they are excited to meet her, as she is excited to meet them.

Clare, a finicky eater, chronically underweight, has more appetite than she'd have imagined for lukewarm English Breakfast tea diluted with rancid-smelling cream. And Pepperidge Farm ginger cookies, not fresh, that crumble in her fingers, causing her mouth to water, they are so delicious . . .

"—(She is too thin, isn't she!)"

"—(We will remedy that!)"

Curious, the great-aunts speak of Clare as if she isn't in the room with them.

Her eyelids begin to droop. She is so very tired suddenly. With glittery eyes behind their polished bifocal glasses the great-aunts observe her closely.

"—time for bed, dear? Your room is awaiting you—"

"—aired out and freshly made up just for *you*—"

"—(Oh! Take the cup from her, before it falls—)"

"—(*You* take it, you're closer!)"

Not yet nine p.m., very early for Clare to go to bed. Yet it feels much later. Midnight.

Clare is so very tired, she can barely keep her eyes open. How rude she is to be falling asleep in her great-aunts' presence . . . Barely can she rise to her feet from the velvet settee. Barely can she articulate her words, to apologize.

(What has happened to her? Clare thinks, *They have poisoned me!*—but the thought passes in and out of her consciousness like a short thread pulled through the eye of a needle.)

There is a moment, a juncture in time (like the moment before Clare answered the telephone back in Bryn Mawr, when she might have chosen not to lift the receiver), when Clare might have escaped the great-aunts, might have pushed her way out of the drawing room, stumbled into the dimly lit foyer and out onto the veranda and the shock of fresh air, and from there to her car parked at the curb. But she does not, for the possibility never occurs to her. She is so very sleepy. There is a childish comfort in sleepiness and in the passivity of sleepiness. And the great-aunts are so kind.

Not sure what is happening but she will obey: upstairs! A room awaiting her for days. (Years?)

Weakly, Clare lifts her suitcase to carry it up the stairs. But the suitcase (which had not seemed heavy previously) is heavy now. (She'd brought with her only a few articles of clothing, several books, an extra pair of shoes, toiletries in a plastic case—nothing heavy.) Short, squat, misshapen Morag laughs affectionately at Clare— unless it is scornfully. "Let *me*"—managing with just a stump of an arm to secure the suitcase against her thigh, carrying it in triumph up the stairs.

Clare rubs her eyes, stares. *Is* Morag missing part of an arm? Clare can't quite see.

"—inside, dear Clare! Here—"

"—awaiting *you*."

Elspeth, the great-aunt with the pale flame-colored hair, sweeps before Clare, leading her into the guest room. Clare has an impression of the glamorous great-aunt brandishing a torch aloft—but of course there is no torch.

Astonishing to see that the guest room in this strange house feels familiar to her—one of those places in which details like walls, ceilings, floor coverings are not yet defined, but rather sketchy, cloudy. *I have come too soon, the dream is not prepared for me. Will there be oxygen to breathe?* Yet she isn't frightened. On the contrary, she feels as if she has come to a familiar place, a place that has been awaiting *her*.

"Off!—with the shoes—"

"Off!—with the socks—"

38

"Loosen this—"

"Loosen this—"

"And this—"

Like ether, lethargy lifts from the stiff, sun-faded satin coverlet of the four-poster bed to embrace Clare. The mattress is very hard—horsehair. (How does Clare know this? Clare knows.) Upon a goose-feather pillow her head rolls as if it has become unfastened from her body. All her limbs are limp, unresisting. Her thoughts come broken, jagged. And then they are vaporous, like clouds. High, scudding clouds blown by the Atlantic breezes.

Busily, happily, the great-aunts tug at her clothing, cooing over her as if she were a great, helpless baby. From a distance she hears (to her embarrassment) how she is "no great beauty," but at least "she takes after *him*, not *her*. That woman was *so plain*."

6.

Low thrilled voices waft upstairs.

> *She doesn't remember.*
> *She must remember!*
> *No. I think she doesn't . . .*
> *She's pretending not to remember.*
> *No. I think she actually does not remember.*

There is a pause. You are not sure if you are fully awake or captive still in this unfamiliar bed with its hard, unyielding mattress beneath a thin, frayed sheet amid bedclothes that smell of mildew in a dream that has gone on and on and on, like wading through murky water that sucks at your feet and threatens to pull you down, and so you keep your eyes shut tight as a child might do, in dread of what you might hear next.

> *She doesn't even remember us—who found her.*

Sudden laughter. Hilarity like small glassware shattering.

7.

"Clare, dear?—breakfast time."

"—time for breakfast, dear Clare!"

Wakened by voices calling from the foot of the stairs.

These are elated voices, slightly chiding: Clare has overslept, it is past nine a.m.

Staring at her watch in disbelief. Nine fifteen a.m.! Usually Clare wakes before dawn, is out of bed by seven. Astonishing to her, she has slept a stuporous twelve hours in the four-poster bed in her great-aunts' guest room. Even now her head is heavy, her vision blurred, as if, instead of sleeping heavily, she has spent the night trying to read a text too close to her eyes.

At the door, voices are daringly intimate, thrilled.

"Are you hungry, dear?"

"We have prepared a special breakfast for you, dear . . ."

Teasingly, the doorknob turns. But—at least!—the door is not pushed open.

Clare has been staring at the turning knob. Hairs stir at the nape of her neck in childish terror.

Quickly she calls to her great-aunts that she will be downstairs as soon as possible. She is so sorry she has overslept . . .

"No hurry! No hurry—"

"—our little *sleepyhead.*"

Laughter like glassware breaking. Clare shudders.

Disoriented, groggy from sleep, she tries to wash herself in the bathroom attached to the guest room. Here, everything is too bright: stark white tile walls, floor. Overhead, a white glare. In a corner of the ceiling, the remains of a broken cobweb, stirring just perceptibly . . .

Clare shudders. She will get rid of the cobweb, later.

In an antiquated mirror above an antiquated sink, a pale face, matted hair. Bare shoulders, breasts that look abashed, vulnerable— nipples as hard as small pits, alert and wary.

Underarms! Clare scrubs with a washcloth, fiercely.

No idea how to use the antiquated shower inside an enormous white tub. Faucets that turn reluctantly, causing ancient pipes to groan. Showerhead like a leprous sunflower.

She will have to ask the great-aunts how to operate the damned shower. No time now to draw a bath—to fill the tub with hot water, climb slipping and sliding into it as into a Roman sarcophagus.

(Also, the tub isn't so clean. Stains like cobwebs, loose hairs.)

A night of exhausting dreams! Shaking her head to clear it.

Why has she come here? Where exactly is this?

Back in the bedroom, dressing with childish haste. You fear being surprised when you are not fully dressed. Bare feet! Impossible to run with bare feet . . .

Clare's fingers move numbly. There is a strange disconnect between her brain and her fingers, her limbs. The way she has felt occasionally in the past after having taken a drug to help her sleep—not a powerful barbiturate, only just Benadryl—but the morning-after effects were unpleasant. *Of course—you know you were poisoned. Last night.*

Breathing through her mouth, trying not to panic. Out of her suitcase (which looks as if it has been shaken, its contents jumbled) she manages to pull clean underwear, clothes. *The great-aunts! They want to remove me from their sister's will before probate court, they want my inheritance.* Driving to Cardiff the previous day, Clare wore a sweater, jeans, her usual running shoes. But she has brought more formal clothes to wear to her appointment with Lucius Fischer this morning.

"Lucius. *He* will be my friend."

Clare's fingers are so numb; it requires many minutes for her to dress herself properly. Even then, she has forgotten her hair—stares at her reflection in a bureau mirror—a stunned Medusa.

Shame!—under ordinary circumstances she would have taken a shower, washed or at least thoroughly wetted her hair and combed it out. Too late now.

Hair like a wild scribbling. Dilated eyes, registering bafflement.

No escape except down the stairs. Drawn by friendly-seeming voices. Clare enters a room, a breakfast room, shading her eyes against sunlight from a wall of windows. Her mouth is very dry. Her eyes feel oversized, exposed. The great-aunts turn to their guest, smiling eagerly. Elspeth's preposterous flamelike hair lifts from her pale-powdered face; Morag's muscular fireplug body roots her firmly to the floor. It seems that they have been speaking of Clare to someone, but who this is, a third party at the farther end of the breakfast table, Clare can't determine. The elderly sisters' eyes are bright-glittering in a way that discomforts Clare.

"Breakfast is porridge—"

"—prepared the proper Scots way, with steel-cut oats."

"—a dash of milk—"

"—brown sugar—"

"—raisins. Hurry!"

Clare is urged to sit at the closer end of a long table covered in a mustard-yellow plastic tablecloth.

Porridge! Clare has not eaten porridge for many years. She remembers liking it as a child; more recently, not so much. The great-aunts have prepared a particularly thick, gluey oatmeal, already beginning to congeal around the edges of Clare's bowl. She picks up her spoon: it's the tarnished silver "baby spoon" of the previous day.

Clare is determined to eat the breakfast her great-aunts have prepared for her, as if to demonstrate to the elderly women that she is grateful for their hospitality, their kindness. She does not dislike them, and she does not fear them—that would be absurd.

Though she sees, in her bowl, that the raisins seem to be moving in the gray-gluey porridge.

"She doesn't care for our porridge, Morag!" cries the great-aunt with the tangerine-colored hair.

"She doesn't care for *your porridge*, Elspeth!" cries the great-aunt with the twisted spine.

Embarrassed, Clare grips her baby spoon harder. Of course the raisins are not moving. Steel-cut oatmeal with a dash of hot milk is her favorite breakfast.

"Now you've embarrassed our dear niece—she feels she *must eat*."

"Well, she needs to eat. She's a growing girl—and growing girls *must eat*."

As Clare struggles to lift the tarnished baby spoon to her mouth, to chew, to swallow a gluey clot of porridge, avoiding the raisins, the great-aunts hover close about her, fussing and fluttering. Is there something sinister about them, or are they simply concerned for Clare, fascinated by her, as one might (plausibly) be fascinated by a stranger who has turned up in the guise of a relative?—a beneficiary?

Clare has prepared a crucial question to ask the great-aunts: Why was she given away for adoption when the Donegal family is clearly well-to-do? Didn't anyone in the family want her?

But—how does she dare ask such a question? Her voice cracks when she begins to speak. Her throat closes up.

The damned porridge is as thick as taffy! Pouring hot milk into it hardly helps.

"Is it too hot, dear? Or—"

"Not hot enough?"

The sisters' solicitude seems genuine. Clare wonders if they have ever had a houseguest before in their lives.

Elspeth is wearing a taupe silken dressing gown with a wide sash. It might be a ball gown of some antiquated sort or a costume appropriate for a festive occasion; bizarrely, the top slips open if she moves carelessly, revealing a bony upper chest. Also, Elspeth has powdered her face lavishly, so that she resembles a ghostly clown; her arched eyebrows, which had seemed to Clare glamorous the previous evening, have been shakily penciled onto her face this morning, as her red-orange lipstick has been applied with a shaky hand. The pug-faced, squat-bodied Morag, hair disheveled and uncombed, appears to be wearing practical flannel pajamas beneath a dressing gown of some coarse material, like denim. Her eyes are gleeful, fixed upon Clare.

"*We* don't like our porridge," Morag says slyly. "It isn't porridge of the quality they serve at the Ritz."

"Well, it would be more palatable for our guest if it were hot, at least. Someone has let it get cold and congealed . . ."

"*Someone* turned off the burner on the stove."

"*Someone* has to be vigilant, or we'd have the fire truck rushing up the street to our house—again."

Clare smiles uncertainly. She has given up on her oatmeal but continues to hold the dainty little spoon so that her elderly relatives won't suspect her of disliking their food.

Taking time now to notice the fourth figure in the room—a man—of indeterminate age—neither old nor young, neither smiling nor frowning, seemingly indifferent to Clare as well as to the chattering great-aunts, leaning forward at the table, on his elbows, wielding a spoon in his left hand while his right hand rests on the tabletop, the fingers as stiff as claws.

Astonishing. This person, a stranger, seems to Clare somehow familiar—his features resemble her own, obliquely: something about the set of the eyes, the nose . . .

He has a pronounced widow's peak, dark hair threaded with silver, a sharp-boned face. He is not very friendly. Yet observing Clare through half-shut eyes, covertly. Beside his porridge bowl, a newspaper folded lengthwise.

Disconcerting to Clare, this person resembles her enough to be, recognizably, a relative, yet the more she regards him, the less certain she is that this is so.

He has coarse, even pitted skin, putty-colored. She is fair-skinned, with a smooth complexion.

He is surly-mouthed, ungenerous. She is quick to smile, flatter.

It appears that eating is a challenge to this person, who grips his spoon awkwardly in the fingers of his left hand, but the great-aunts don't annoy him by offering assistance, Clare has noted.

Nerve-damaged, Clare thinks with a twinge of pity. And perhaps he is brain-damaged as well. There is a stony, shut-off look in his eyes.

"Gerard, dear! Here is a niece of yours—Clare—"

"—a niece who is *new to you*, dear. New to all of us—a surprise . . ."

Gerard frowns at Clare without seeming to acknowledge her. She represents an intrusion, it seems; an interruption of his breakfast and newspaper. Grudgingly he nods, mutters what might be *h'lo*.

Unless it's an enigmatic mutter—*eh*.

"Clare, dear—our nephew Gerard, who lives in this house—with us—since his mother passed away—"

"Your father's younger brother, Clare—"

"No. Gerard was *older*—"

"He was not. He was *younger* . . ."

"Younger than Conor—at the time. But now Gerard is older."

"Well, he has become older. Every year older."

"That's what I said, exactly! Every year, *older*."

Gerard is a lean wolfhound of a man, sunken-cheeked, suspicious, uncomfortable with being discussed as if he were not present. His expression suggests the vexed anguish of the martyred Saint Bartholomew in the seventeenth-century oil by Casolani. Clare has the idea that the elderly great-aunts are deliberately testing their nephew's patience with their banter, under the guise of being friendly and protective.

"And yet, you know—Gerard is *not old*. Gerard is—"

"—to us, still a boy."

There is something disfigured about Gerard, Clare realizes. His eyes, disconcertingly like her own, are yet deeper set in their sockets, rimmed in shadow. His jaws sprout wispy hairs, and there are tiny cuts, dully gleaming with blood, on his cheeks, as if he has shaved hastily or carelessly. His left ear appears subtly mangled, and both his ears are flushed. He wears mismatched clothing, a brown tweed jacket that fits him loosely, a black T-shirt, corduroy trousers. The tweed jacket is old and frayed at the elbows but seemingly of a high-quality wool; the black T-shirt imparts a slovenly, priestly air.

"Hello! I'm very happy to meet you—Gerard."

The name sounds too intimate—*Gerard*. Clare wonders if she was expected to call him Uncle Gerard.

Though she is feeling ill at ease, Clare manages to exude a warm rush of optimism, enthusiasm. When in doubt, it is wise for an attractive youngish woman to play the ingénue. She wants to be liked!—badly. For is Clare not a long-lost relative of Gerard's, mistakenly given away as an orphan? Should Gerard not be smiling at her with an expression of wonder, welcome?

Should not Gerard leap from his chair, hurry to her, hug her?—his strong arms threatening to crack Clare's ribs?

Should not Gerard kiss her cheek, laugh in delight at her, with her?

But glowering Gerard merely shifts his shoulders in the tweed jacket. Clare hears him murmur what might be *yeh*, or *uhhh*. No doubt he is annoyed at being distracted from the newspaper folded beside his bowl of porridge.

"I'm Clare. I guess—your niece? I mean—a niece of yours . . ."

How absurd! Clare feels her face burn, embarrassed. When you're a child, you are vulnerable to individuals like Gerard, usually slightly older children who intimidate you with their inscrutable, seemingly hostile behavior; you can see that they feel disdain or dislike for you, yet you can't imagine why, when you have done nothing to antagonize them. Not knowing why, you persevere, smiling until your face aches, hoping to entice a cool smile from the other even as you know the effort is hopeless.

But Clare is not a child now. Clare Seidel is thirty years old. Indeed, she is a much more attractive individual than putty-skinned Gerard Donegal, at whom she wouldn't have glanced in another setting. Clare should have long outgrown that treacherous childhood terrain, in which you can't escape your tormentors because they are classmates at your school and you are thrown together with them, as in a particularly congested circle of Hell, through the machinations of well-intentioned adults.

The great-aunts are lightly chiding, provoking: "Clare is your niece, Gerard. We told you about her just yesterday. Don't you remember? She is the daughter of—"

"—you remember: Conor."

Gerard frowns severely. Shakes his head *no.*

Clare wonders how to decipher this. Gerard doesn't remember his deceased brother, Conor, or doesn't wish to remember? Or perhaps he doesn't believe that the young woman to whom he has been introduced, who continues to smile hopefully at him, is indeed his niece.

"Clare is Conor's youngest child, Gerard—"

"*You* remember—I am sure."

Clare is distracted, hearing the name Conor uttered so frequently, and so casually.

It is the first time that she has heard "Conor" spoken aloud, she thinks. Unless Lucius Fischer had spoken it on the phone.—She can't recall.

A magical sound to the name that makes her want to cry yet smile happily. *My father.*

As a woman named Kathryn was her mother. *My mother.*

Overwhelming to Clare, a riddle she has no idea how to solve, the realization that the three strangers in this room, in her presence, are not only related to her by blood, but they once knew her father, and they might speak casually of him if they wished—*Conor.*

For all of her conscious life Clare has accepted her situation—*orphan.* No relatives. And now . . .

Clare has been studying the birth certificate her mother Hannah sent her by priority mail. An official document that Clare had surely seen in the past but with so little interest she'd forgotten it.

Why should I care who I'd been? They gave me away, they didn't give a damn for me.

The names of her (birth) parents hadn't seemed to Clare to signify actual people, as the names of remote places don't seem altogether real. She'd become accustomed to thinking of these strangers as deceased since her birth, as if her birth had initiated their death(s); but she had no reason for thinking such a bizarre thought. She has always known, or should have known, that she was given up for adoption at the age of two, nearly three. Not as a newborn.

"Clare is our guest, Gerard! Your guest, too."

"Clare is here to visit Mr. Fischer, Gerard—our attorney."

"Your attorney, too!"

"She drove all the way from Philadelphia, isn't that impressive? In her car, alone."

"Because of the will—your dear mother's will. You remember—"

"*She* is a beneficiary, too. Your niece Clare."

"It's the old farm on Post Road, dear. I'm afraid—yes . . ."

"You know, you might drive Clare out there sometime soon to see the property she has inherited—"

"—an opportunity for you and Clare to become acquainted—"

"—unless—"

"—unless, of course—"

"—you would rather not."

These words hang provocatively in the air. *Rather not.*

At this Gerard rises abruptly from the table. Skids his chair along the hardwood floor.

He makes a grunting noise, as of disdain, derision. He bares yellowish teeth in an angry grimace. His eyes swerve in their sockets, but he doesn't look at Clare—he has not looked at Clare once. With his left, good hand he snatches up his cap and the folded newspaper and noisily exits the room by a rear door.

An ashy odor in his wake, unwashed male body, hair. Not even a sidelong backward glance.

The great-aunts are taken by surprise, wide-eyed with a sort of ostrichlike thrilled alarm. Their mouths make *tsking* sounds. Clare wonders if they aren't gratified that their interrogative chatter has driven the scowling man from their presence.

"Oh, dear! We are so, so sorry, Clare—"

"Our nephew Gerard is not usually so—"

"—rude—"

"—*shy*. He is not at ease with strangers—"

"—even strangers who are relatives—"

"—backward, unsociable—"

"—headstrong, stubborn—"

"—terrible shock—trauma—"

"—he'd once been *bright*—"

"—as bright as Conor—"

"—no!—not nearly—"

"—indeed yes. When he entered the seminary—"

"—*not as bright as Conor*—no—"

"—more diligent than Conor, really. More—"

"—devout. Obedient."

"Well, God looks after him now—"

"—God *should!* After what God did—"

"—shhh! D'you think that God isn't listening?"

The great-aunts confide in Clare that her "bachelor uncle," Gerard Donegal, had once intended to be a Jesuit. He'd been a seminarian at Saint Joseph's Seminary in Portland, Maine, until he'd had to drop out for "personal, family reasons" and return home to Cardiff to make a home with his parents.

Since his father's death, he'd been responsible for driving his widowed mother wherever she'd needed to go, in recent years primarily to medical appointments and to mass at St. Cuthbert's Church. Everyone agreed—Gerard had been a devoted son. He'd helped with the maintenance of the house and the grounds and supported himself now with odd jobs in the neighborhood.

Yet he has continued to pursue his religious pilgrimage on his own, to this day.

Really!—Clare had to wonder. The pained grimace, yellowed teeth, and averted eyes hadn't signaled, to her, what you'd call a religious disposition.

"Oh, indeed—yes. Gerard is not a very sociable soul—as you have seen!—but he is a very reliable worker. He mows lawns, trims trees, rakes with an actual rake, not one of those terrible leaf blowers—a huge, *huge* rake of the kind you can't buy any longer. He will dig, dig, dig wherever you request. He will clear driveways of snow. He will work in the rain—in the *snow*. He can clear underbrush. He can repair roofs, chimneys. He can replace broken windows. He can *paint*—as good as any professional, and much more cheaply. Of course, Gerard can use a gun—rifle, shotgun. You can hire him to shoot groundhogs, raccoons—pests that destroy gardens. (Gerard will not shoot a deer—though Cardiff is overrun with white-tailed deer. It is against the law to hunt deer within the city limits, but Gerard will scare them away at your request.) Indeed, there are ladies up and down Acton Avenue who depend upon him—'What would we do without Gerard Donegal!' they say. He'd entered the seminary at nineteen, wanting to serve God by becoming a priest, and for a while he was happy there. His mother was so proud of him—we were all so very proud of him—but then . . ."

"Well, you see—nineteen was *young*—"

"Nineteen was *not young*. Not for a first-year seminarian."

"Nineteen was young, for Gerard was young—naïve, some said. Too devout."

"The strain of working so hard, learning Latin, trying so hard to be worthy of the priesthood—"

"—being *so good*—"

"—a vessel to be filled with God—"

"—with *Jesus*—"

"—just too much for poor Gerard—we think . . ."

"And then—our family tragedy . . ."

"Poor Gerard! It all ended so—abruptly . . ."

"Oh, what are you saying? You mean poor *Conor*?"

"*Conor, Gerard*—our dear nephews!—God have mercy on us all."

Clare has been listening closely. She feels like a child in the presence of malicious adults speaking so rapidly in a kind of code. She cannot absorb the meaning. She must listen with every atom of her being. What are the great-aunts telling her?

Clare hears herself stammer weakly: "I guess—then—they are—are not—*living*? My parents, I mean."

A startled silence. Elspeth and Morag exchange the most fleeting of glances, but do not reply, as if their naïve young relative has uttered something obscene.

Of course your parents are dead. No one will even speak of them.

What did you think—they've been alive all these years, waiting for you?

Clare doesn't want to look at the great-aunts, to see how they are regarding her—with pity? sympathy? indignation?

She thanks them for breakfast and offers to help clear the long table covered in mustard-yellow plastic, but Elspeth hisses for her to stop.

"Please! We wouldn't hear of it, Clare. You are a guest in Maude Donegal's house."

Morag agrees vehemently. "Indeed, yes. *I* will clear the table. I believe it's my shift." She heaves herself onto her foreshortened legs, snorting with laughter as at an obscure joke.

The great-aunts are taking turns at housekeeping, it seems. They tell Clare that until probate court and the settling of their sister's estate, they are obliged to downsize the household staff.

"'Taking turns'—listen to her! *I* do most of the housework." Morag laughs genially.

"You do not! That is a slander."

"Slander, is it?"

"*I* do all of the finances and mental work, which is a far worse strain . . ."

As the sisters bicker, Clare drifts to a window to glance outside. Where has Gerard gone? She can see only a slovenly privet hedge trailing across a cracked flagstone path, dripping rain. It seemed that Gerard had departed in that direction, but there is no sign of him.

"Gerard lives in this house with you?" Clare asks.

"Gerard lives in his mother's house, as we do," Elspeth says. "*We* are not Donegals, you know—Morag and me. Our family name is Lacey."

Elspeth speaks with an air of pride, as if the name Lacey might impress Clare. Morag amends, "Our maiden name, it is—Lacey."

"Don't be ridiculous! Lacey is our family name, not our maiden name—*since we are not married.*"

"Of course we are not married! *I* certainly am not." Morag laughs again, heartily.

"And so, we can't have a 'maiden' name if we are not married. We have only our own surnames. Sometimes I feel that I'm speaking to an obstinate idiot who will not understand the simplest facts." Elspeth laughs in exasperation, rolling her eyes at Clare.

But Morag is determined to claim Clare's attention. "Maude was the Lacey sister who dared to marry. She had the courage others lacked. To 'reproduce the species'—for some, this challenge is too much."

"And she married very well. An older gentleman—"

"—Le-land—"

"But she never turned her back on us—not for long."

"What d'you mean by that—not for long? Maude was generous to her family, always—"

"—almost always—"

"—and once tragedy struck her life, she needed her sisters close beside her."

Tragedy?—this must mean the automobile accident, Clare thinks. But she doesn't dare ask the great-aunts about this sensitive subject.

The great-aunts tell Clare of how Gerard had to drop out of the seminary just a few months before he was to be ordained. A terrible tragedy for the young man, he'd worked very hard for five, six years. "However long it takes to become a Jesuit. A very long time. He'd been so devout—spiritual—nothing like the way he is now. In fact, Gerard had been the one to discover—the accident."

Clare stands very still, listening. *The accident?*

"Seeing such a sight was traumatic for Gerard. He never recovered. He had what is called a nervous breakdown—never recovered from *that*."

"And what a tragedy for the Church, losing such a devout priest! Everyone who knew him said how it was Gerard's destiny to be a priest—you could see holiness in his face when he'd been just a young boy."

"He sang in the choir—the purest boy-soprano . . ."

"Not like Conor—*he* wasn't the type to give up the world for God, as Gerard was . . ."

"Oh, Conor! He paid a terrible price, too—for loving the world too well."

"For loving *her* too well."

"Ah! God bless his soul."

"God bless all their souls."

Clare listens avidly, gratefully. *Her?* Was this her mother, Kathryn? She believes that in their maddeningly oblique way, the great-aunts are telling her crucial information. "The accident—do you mean the accident my parents died in? A car crash?"

Elspeth catches Morag's eye as if to warn her—*Don't say a word.*

But this is so overt. Clare surmises that she is expected to notice, and to inquire.

"You said that Gerard 'discovered' the accident? Do you mean—on the road? On a highway? Did he drive out to see where they were? Is that what you mean?" Clare feels herself flailing like a drowning swimmer. But the great-aunts merely gaze at her like observers onshore, curious, not so very kindly.

Elspeth sighs again, vexed. Morag's slit of a mouth puckers with the effort not to laugh.

"Whoever said that Gerard discovered anyone on a highway? Certainly not. Gerard was the one who—(we never knew the details, the details were kept from us)—discovered the—"

"—the bodies . . ."

"—the *remains*, I was going to say. *Remains* is the proper term, I believe."

"*Remains* is a terrible term! You just stop."

"*You* stop. You are being ridiculous."

Clare is feeling light-headed, disoriented. It's an effort to continue to smile sweetly at the elderly women who glare at each other and not at her, as if she isn't their intended audience.

They have sent a volley of small arrows into her heart. She has no idea how badly she has been wounded, just yet.

"Excuse me! Enough," she says before she retreats upstairs to her room. There, in the antiquated bathroom, she succumbs to a fit of gagging, squatting over the ancient toilet, sweating and miserable; she succeeds in vomiting up only a thin, rancid-smelling liquid. But whatever is making her ill has hardened into a gluey little ball in her stomach, not easily dislodged.

Do they hate me because I am a beneficiary of their sister's estate?

Because I am not one of them, I have no right to be here?

And have they poisoned me—again?

8.

Resolutely, throughout her life she has not thought of them—her (birth) parents.

Now she thinks of them obsessively. Thoughts like ticks that have burrowed into her very flesh.

Tiny, loathsome insects you dare not try to remove with tweezers, lest their black bodies break into pieces, irretrievable.

Desperate to know whether her parents are alive or dead. If dead, how? Why? And why was she given up for adoption when the Donegals were well-to-do?

Clare will ask where her parents are buried. (If indeed they are buried. Anywhere.) A visit to a cemetery here in Cardiff. As in a dreamy photograph by Julia Margaret Cameron, the day will be gray, ghostly, overcast, pelting rain.

With childish tenacity and defiance, not allowing herself to think. *But maybe one of them is alive, at least. That is possible.*

How relieved Clare is to leave the heavy-browed cobblestone house on Acton Avenue!

Outside, the air is much fresher. She can breathe more deeply. The overcast sky seems to be opening in layers of translucent cloud.

She glances about, wondering if she might see—who? A limping figure . . .

But no. No one.

Driving to Lucius Fischer's office in downtown Cardiff. Her appointment is at eleven a.m., and she is anxious not to be late. Her thoughts are disorganized, distracting. No idea what to think of the great-aunts—if they are on her side.

She tells herself not to be ridiculous. Of course the elderly women mean well. They are annoying, exasperating—but essentially, they are her friends.

Yet—it has seemed to Clare that the two of them are sometimes mocking her. Laughing at her, evilly.

When she tries to recall what they'd told her about her parents, she cannot. There is a kind of scrim close against her face—through which she can't see and can't hear.

Are they living, or—not? Please tell me.

She is still feeling shaky after the fit of vomiting. Most of her nausea has faded, though the gluey nugget of oatmeal remains in her gut.

She thinks that she will move out of the Donegal house that afternoon. Following her appointment with Fischer. Can't risk another meal there. Even if they are not trying to poison her, the food they give her may be tainted, spoiled.

Depending upon what Lucius Fischer tells her, she may decide to return to Bryn Mawr the next morning.

Forfeit the inheritance, just possibly. Yes.

A sudden decision. Like snatching up a knife, slashing her own throat.

As she'd once told a lover—abruptly—*That's it. Enough. I think we are through.*

Her only inheritance. Her only connection with blood relatives. Her connection with her (deceased) parents.

Still, she might forfeit it. She doesn't need the Donegals in her life. She has lived most of her life without them, why should she be vulnerable to them now?

The way Gerard Donegal shoved back his chair, heaved himself to his feet, turned his back on her, walked out. *My father's brother. No connection between us. Why should there be? Nothing.*

Though Clare left the house on Acton Avenue with more than enough time to drive a mere two miles, she finds herself late for the appointment after all. To her astonishment it is nearly eleven by the time she locates State Street, the main street of Cardiff. Then she is caught in a maze of narrow one-way streets downtown and in a long stream of vehicles, as slow and somber as a funeral procession, routed onto a single lane through an endless construction site. Then, on foot, having parked her car, she can't locate the address she has been given, running desperately along a sidewalk in a neighborhood of razed buildings surrounded by rubble . . .

Late! She will be late after all.

Goddamn. Why'd you do it? Answer a ringing phone without knowing the caller.

That was the original mistake.

9.

"Ms. Seidel! Please take a seat."

Lucius Fischer shakes Clare's hand briskly. Releases it in virtually the same instant. So matter-of-fact, regarding her with bemused eyes, Clare understands in an instant that there can be no rapport between her and this middle-aged lawyer, no special bond. Something that has been bunched and tense in her chest sinks, slides down in a trickling heap, like sand.

What a fool she is! Over the phone Lucius Fischer's deep-baritone voice had cast a sort of spell over her. As if she'd expected, in remote Cardiff, a place of which she'd never heard until recently, to discover some sort of (improbable) romance, sexual intrigue.

A friend, at least. Someone who might care for her.

Fischer had seemed to be confiding in her on the phone. She hadn't imagined that—had she?

He'd seemed to be promising her—*I will guide you through this, Clare. You can trust me.*

Carefully, Fischer explains that he is the executor of Maude Donegal's estate as well as the lawyer who'd drawn up Maude Donegal's will. He explains that the will is unusually complicated, asit had been rewritten several times over a period of twenty years.

"There was an original will, drawn up by an older partner in this office," Fischer says, naming a name that means nothing to Clare and makes no impression upon her, "but that original will has been changed of course. And after Leland Donegal's death, again changed."

Clare wonders why she is being given this information. Is there a mystery of some kind involving her grandmother's will? Some sort of legal irregularity? She is intrigued as Fischer speaks of the Lacey sisters, Elspeth and Morag—"your formidable great-aunts— spinster sisters of a bygone era." Both Elspeth and Morag earned degrees in education from the University of Maine in the 1960s. Both had careers as public school teachers. Elspeth was a middle school principal, much admired (and feared). Morag taught math and advised the school archery team. Both women were active in their parish church, St. Cuthbert's. Their nephew Gerard—Maude Donegal's younger son—had been a Jesuit seminarian in Portland in his early twenties.

"As a young man, Gerard was very promising, it's said. Of course, I didn't know Gerard then—I only became aware of him afterward."

Afterward? Clare notes this.

Fischer tells Clare that he'd known the Donegal family initially through Leland Donegal, who'd become his client upon the retirement of an older partner in Fischer's law firm. Leland had inherited the Donegal family lumber business—"one of those old Maine families whose fortunes were made by cutting down Maine forests"—and was very well-to-do by Cardiff standards.

As it turned out, Leland hadn't cared for business. He'd wanted to be a renowned philanthropist, like the Carnegies and the Rockefellers. He'd given away what must have been millions of dollars in all—scholarships for local high school students, museums and colleges, hospitals, the Church—until at last the money began to run out.

"Evidently there was some 'awkwardness.' Leland had pledged to give a million dollars to the Jesuit seminary where Gerard was a student, but—he had to break the pledge, which was humiliating to the family. And some other pledges, as well."

Clare would like to know more about the young Gerard: Had he been so unsociable at the time, in some way handicapped, disfigured? Or had something happened to him afterward? But she doesn't want to impress Lucius Fischer as an inquisitive person.

"And—my parents? Are they . . ."

Clare speaks hesitantly. For surely she knows the answer.

If Fischer is startled by Clare's question, he is too gentlemanly, and too professional, to let on.

"Your parents, Miss Seidel? Certainly you must know—I'm afraid they are no longer living."

No longer living. An odd phrasing.

"They died, my dear—have been deceased—since January 6, 1989."

"Oh. I see." Clare smiles inanely. Wipes at her eyes. Even now she isn't sure she has heard correctly. "Did you say—both of them? I mean . . . *both?*"

"I'm afraid so, yes. Both."

"On that one day? Both—at once?"

"Hasn't anyone informed you, Miss Seidel?"

"I—I—think so, yes. But . . ."

Of course, Clare knows. Has always known. Must have known. The Seidels had told her. (Hadn't they?) But years ago. She is sure, many years ago.

What a pathetic fantasy of hers, that one or both of her parents might be living and that she would be "reunited" with them in Cardiff, Maine. She has a sudden impulse to laugh, harshly.

Please help me. I am so lonely. Please.

Clare shakes her head to clear it. What on earth has she been thinking! Blood rushes into her face, and she fears that the (embarrassed, disconcerted) lawyer can read her thoughts.

Stiffly, apologetically, Fischer says, "I'm sorry to upset you, Miss Seidal. If I can be of any . . ."

"Yes. You can tell me: How did my parents die?"

"How did your parents *die?* Why, I think—it was never exactly confirmed. I'm not familiar with the details because I wasn't living in Cardiff at the time . . ." Fischer speaks guardedly, reluctantly. "The best advice I can give you is to read their obituaries, Ms. Seidel. And other public records. You probably can't access the obituaries online, but you can find them in the *Cardiff Journal,* on microfilm in the main library. That would be the most practical approach."

"They died in an accident? A car crash?"

"It may have been an accident of some kind. That is possible. But you must read about it, I think. That's what I would advise."

"What kind of an accident was it?"

Clare imagines a flaming holocaust on the interstate. An eighteen-wheeler, an automobile pulverized. It occurs to her to wonder why she wasn't inside the vehicle with her parents. Where had she been at the time?

"I've tried to explain, Ms. Seidel—I didn't live in Cardiff, and I wasn't professionally associated with your grandfather Leland Donegal at the time."

There is a pause. Too much has been uttered too swiftly to be absorbed. Clare has felt like a captive in a rushing vehicle on a downward curve, unable to steer the wheel, unable to apply the brake.

Meaning to deflect the subject, Fischer asks Clare if she would like coffee. "Our receptionist can bring it, if you like."

Clare declines, with thanks. In her fragile mood, small kindnesses are much appreciated.

Still, Fischer is intent upon deflecting the subject of Clare's parents' deaths. Asking her now, with exaggerated courtesy, how she has liked Cardiff. Her great-aunts? And how was the drive along the coast from Bryn Mawr?

Clare hears herself stammering replies. With part of her brain she is engaged in what's called making conversation.

"Did you know, Cardiff was originally called Cardiff-by-the-Sea. But no one calls it that any longer, and most residents have forgotten."

Personal questions follow, of a friendly nature. Fischer is preparing her, she thinks. Wary of upsetting her in the close confines of his office.

Clare tells Fischer that she has a B.A. from the University of Minnesota and a Ph.D. in art history from the University of Chicago, but she has not often taught art history. Rather, she has applied for research fellowships to allow her to work uninterrupted on a project: her first grant was a Guggenheim, freeing her to complete a monograph on the life and work of Gertrude Käsebier, which was published by a distinguished art-history press and well reviewed in small professional journals; her second grant is a fellowship at the Bryn Mawr Humanities Research Institute. So stated, Clare's life—which seems to her spare, minimal, even monastic—somehow expands in significance. Fischer smiles at her, impressed. Indeed, there is a kind of romance in a life so obliquely presented.

"Well! I envy you, Miss Seidel. Surrounding yourself with beauty, not—law."

Clare only nods silently. Yes.

"In art, even the ugly is beautiful somehow. Yes?"

Clare agrees. She has often thought so herself. The more defiant and mysterious the ugliness, the greater the beauty. *Yes.*

"But I think you've come to see me today to find out the terms of your bequest—yes?"

It seems that Clare is but one of a number of beneficiaries in Maude Donegal's will. The situation is more complicated than usual, Lucius Fischer acknowledges, since Mrs. Donegal had in her keeping several wills, two of which were executed by a law firm in Portland, not Cardiff. As beneficiaries, including Elspeth and Morag, slipped in and out of favor, and back in favor, their names were excised and then added again; again excised and added, often by Mrs. Donegal herself in her own small, spidery hand. There were not proper witnesses much of the time. The most recent will, executed by Fischer himself in November 2017, which names him executor of the estate, takes precedence over all preceding wills, of course, but individuals who'd stood to inherit from previous wills can be expected to make claims against the estate and will very likely receive settlements if their claims are reasonable.

The situation is further complicated, Fischer tells Clare, because her name didn't appear in any will prior to 2015. A bequest had been made to "surviving daughter of Conor Donegal." Only in the most recent will had Maude Donegal provided the name Clare Ellen Seidel.

How strange this is, Clare thinks. *Surviving daughter of Conor Donegal*—as if Clare had had no mother . . .

Also, *surviving daughter* seems to suggest that there may have been another daughter, or daughters, who had not survived.

However, Fischer assures Clare that there is no ambiguity about her inheritance: twelve acres of farmland and woodland, a farmhouse and outbuildings in northern Ashford County, on a road called Post Road.

Yes: property. Clare is suffused with happiness at the thought.

"Unfortunately, I don't have a photograph of the property to show you. Nor have I ever seen it. Northern Ashford County is sparely inhabited, I think. Beautiful landscape, hilly—along the coast. I'm told that the property has been allowed to become derelict . . . There are back taxes owed on it, which you will be required to pay, I'm afraid. That's the law!"

Lucius Fischer utters *That's the law!* in an almost gleeful manner.

Also, Clare will have to wait at least three months before she can take possession of the property. If she knows much about the intricacies of probate court . . .

Clare shakes her head no, she knows very little about probate court. Very little about wills. She is feeling dazed, disoriented.

No longer living. Surviving daughter.

However, Fischer tells her that the law allows her to borrow money against the claim, if she wishes.

"Is that something people do—borrow money against their inheritances?" Clare is amazed.

"Yes. Often."

"Really! Well, I would not."

Someone loved me. After all these years.

It's a fact: Clare's grandmother made an effort to learn her name and to locate her. After so many years, adding Clare's name to her will.

"People do unexpected things," Fischer says, as if he can read Clare's thoughts, "as they approach the end of their lives. Sometimes it's the influence of conscience—like a half-buried deity waking."

What an odd remark! Clare thinks. She is made to realize that Lucius Fischer is not so conventional as he appears.

"Mrs. Donegal wasn't a particularly eccentric person, so far as I know, but her will turns out to be a somewhat eccentric document."

Fischer has prepared a copy of the section of the will that pertains to Clare, for her to take with her today. Though the entire will runs to more than thirty pages of dense legalese, most of it doesn't involve her.

"Thank you! This is—well, astonishing . . ."

Clare feels such elation, she wishes she had someone to confide in.

At my age. Out of nowhere. Someone cared for me after all.

Fischer is on his feet. It is time for Clare to leave. If she has no further questions . . .

She realizes she has forgotten something . . . But what has she forgotten?

On the wall behind Lucius Fischer's desk is a diploma in a shiny mahogany frame: LUCIUS M. FISCHER, UNIVERSITY OF MAINE LAW SCHOOL.

For a disorienting moment Clare wonders if the diploma is real. If any of this is—*real*.

As if her personality were evaporating. Like dew as the morning sun beats hard upon it.

Wanting to ask in the plaintive voice of a child—*Are my parents alive or dead?*

Also: How did they die? And why was she given up for adoption? Was there no one in the Donegal family who wanted her?

She might ask too where her parents are buried. If indeed they are buried.

In her professional life Clare is a highly articulate individual, rarely tongue-tied, rarely shy, but in the presence of Lucius Fischer she is stricken with dread for what she might be told if she asks crucial questions.

Fair enough, Clare thinks. She has had her opportunity, and she has failed.

In farewell, the lawyer's handshake is less brusque than it was in greeting. He has warmed to Clare to a degree; he has become fatherly.

He reminds her to learn more about her parents' deaths by consulting the Cardiff newspaper in the library—"Just down the street." Indeed, he will call a librarian friend of his, to prepare microfilm for Clare.

"The public record is always preferable, Ms. Seidel, to what individuals might tell you. Put your faith in objectivity."

10.

Died. No longer living. Have been deceased. Since January 6, 1989.

Clare steels herself for what she will discover in the Cardiff Public Library.

Still, it's heartening to her that one of the librarians greets her so courteously. "You must be Ms. Seidel, yes? Mr. Fischer just called."

"Yes! Thank you."

Clare is escorted into a small room at the rear of the building. Here she is provided with rolls of microfilm, a projector with a hand crank. The friendly librarian shows her how to turn the hand crank, with care. "Remember, this microfilm is *old*." Clare Seidal, an art historian who is accustomed to accessing much older microfilm, is grateful for this courtesy.

Boxes of microfilm preserving issues of the *Cardiff Journal* for 1989. She wonders if the original newspapers still exist or whether they have been allowed to molder and crumple into dust.

Thinking that it is obituaries she seeks, Clare is astonished to immediately discover on the front page of the *Cardiff Journal* for January 8, 1989, a banner headline:

SUSPECTED HOMICIDE-SUICIDE IN DEATHS OF 4
Two Adults, Two Children in Ashford County
Family Shot to Death

Clare freezes in horror. Quickly skimming the article. *Did my father kill his family and himself?*

Her eyes fill with tears. There is a hot clammering in her head.

What she has discovered is scarcely to be believed. Newsprint quivers in her vision. A man bearing the Donegal name, a man alleged to be her father, shot to death his wife, daughter, son. In their house in rural Ashford County, on a road called Post Road.

It will take some time for Clare to read, reread. It will take time for her to comprehend. Her fingers have gone numb, she can barely turn the crank, scrolling ahead to a continuation of the article past columns of blurred newsprint. National news, international news, Maine news, local news . . . By degrees, the lurid story unfolds, but at its core is the simple—terrible—revelation that sometime in the afternoon of January 6, 1989, a man named Conor Donegal, thirty-four, shot to death his wife, Kathryn, thirty-one; their daughter, Emma, six; and their son, Laird, nine, in their home on Post Road and then turned the gun, a handgun, on himself.

Clare forces herself to read, reread more carefully. Wiping at her eyes to clear her vision. *What is missing? Who is missing?*

Belatedly the realization comes over her. *My father killed his family and himself—did he? But not me?*

That Clare is alive is evidence that she was spared. This terrible carnage, wife, two children, murderous husband—all of them struck down, but the youngest child, a girl, two years nine months old, must have been (miraculously) spared.

Spared. But why?

Eventually Clare learns that Clare Ellen Donegal, the youngest of the Donegal children, was found unharmed, not by police officers searching the house, but by relatives of the deceased who'd come to the house after the bodies had been removed, to look for the missing child.

("Unharmed"—except badly dehydrated, traumatized. The little girl had crawled into a small space beneath the kitchen sink, presumably to hide from the gunshots.)

Clare scrolls ahead to further articles on the subject of the Donegal homicide-suicide in the *Cardiff Journal*. Fast-forwarding through a blizzard of headlines, news, photographs—international crises, ravages of war in the Mideast, heavy snowfall along the Atlantic coast, political stalemate in Congress . . . How trivial, the events of the great world! For beyond the self, when the self is sick and assailed, what is there that matters? Eventually Clare pieces together a time-line for January 6, 1989.

In the late afternoon, at the probable time of the shootings, neighbors of the Donegal family on Post Road heard gunshots coming from the Donegal property, assuming that the shots were those of hunters, for hunting was common in rural Ashford County. When the family failed to show up the next day at a gathering at the home of the elder Donegals in Cardiff and calls to the house went unanswered, Gerard Donegal, Conor's younger brother, drove out to investigate and found the bodies. Gerard called police, who came to the house at once. In the confusion of the bloodied crime scene, which involved several of the downstairs rooms of the house, police officers failed to find the missing two-year-old who'd crawled beneath the kitchen sink to hide from the slaughter, less than six feet from the bodies of her slain mother and sister.

Only later, after the bodies were removed and taken to the county morgue, were relatives allowed to enter the house to search for the missing Clare Ellen. Even then, the terrified child remained hidden, too weak or traumatized to answer the relatives' cries for her; only after some time, when they were about to give up the search, did they hear the child whimpering "like a hurt animal" and find her hunched beneath the sink, behind a garbage pail, in a space "so small, you'd think a cat could not have fit in it."

By this time, Clare Ellen had been hiding for approximately eighteen hours.

Semiconscious, badly dehydrated, in a state of shock and exhaustion, the two-year-old was brought by ambulance to the Cardiff hospital, where she was, at the time of the newspaper account, on the critical list . . .

But is that—me? How can that have been me? I have no memory of any of this.

Appalled, fascinated, Clare cannot stop reading. Scrolling through columns of newsprint. Was there a suicide note? (Yes, it seems so: but its contents were to be kept confidential by police for the time being.) Was any reason offered for the slaughter? (Yes, it seems so: but again, this information was not available to the media.) As the lurid narrative loops back upon itself like a sinister roller coaster, repeating crucial facts, accumulating peripheral details, Clare feels as if she is disintegrating, in a miasma of despair. What a shock! Why had no one warned her! Lucius Fischer obviously knew that her father had murdered his family, but he'd been too cowardly to tell her.

In a trance of horror, she studies the photographs of her parents, reprinted several times in the *Cardiff Journal*.

Conor Donegal. Kathryn Donegal. So young! In fact, Clare's age now.

Each is very attractive, smiling at the camera. Conor squints as he smiles, a dimple in his left cheek, like a wink. He is boyish, confident, a rascally glitter to his eyes. Wavy dark hair, thick and swept back from his face, a widow's peak at his hairline. (Clare stares in amazement: she too has a widow's peak, not quite in the center of her forehead and not so prominent as Conor Donegal's.) Kathryn is wanly pretty, her smile more guarded. A popular girl in high school, you'd suppose. The kind of girl Clare might have observed at a distance, intrigued by her air of composure and self-sufficiency.

(Clare is incensed on her mother's behalf. Why on earth had the great-aunts called Kathryn *plain?*)

At least Clare knows what they look like now. *My father. My mother.*

She is relieved that no photographs of her lost sister and brother are printed in the paper. Emma, Laird—only just names to her. Heartrending names. For Clare has no memory of these children.

No memory of any of them: the lost family.

And here in the January 10, 1989, issue of the *Cardiff Journal* it is revealed, somewhat casually, that the "rescuers" of the missing Clare Ellen Donegal were Elspeth and Morag Lacey, identified as aunts of the deceased Conor.

Clare reads the terse little paragraph several times.

75

So I owe my life to them?—the great-aunts?

She wipes at her eyes, shuddering.

Recalling that morning in the horsehair bed when she'd overheard the sisters speaking at the foot of the stairs like ghost figures in a dream. Marveling, gloating—*Oh she doesn't remember! Not even us—who found her.*

II.

11.

In blinding sunshine, she has lost her way. She has lost her balance. And then she seems to be on the ground. Heaviness in all her limbs, a sharp ache on the side of her skull.

Someone stoops over her, concerned. *"Miss? Are you all right? Can I . . ."*

Fresh air revives her. Fresh air is all her feverish face requires.

". . . help you? Call an ambulance?"

Unable to answer. The roaring inside her head has returned, deafening.

Ninety minutes have passed since Clare arrived at the library. Ninety minutes since (she recalls, stunned) she'd hurried up the stone steps, eager to learn the worst.

Exhausted. Turning the hand crank, peering at microfilm. Strain in her neck, shoulders. Feeling as if she has been dragged across a rock-strewn landscape by her hair.

Beneath her feet the concrete walkway slides away. She has fallen heavily. A sidewalk, grass growing beside it. Smell of damp earth. A stranger is stooping over her, hesitant to touch her, to lift her.

So heavy! Clare weighs less than 110 pounds, but her knees, her legs have not the strength to support her.

But then she is seated on something stony, a low ledge, trying to breathe. An iron band around her chest.

There is a person speaking to her, a stranger. He is concerned about her, asking if there is someone he should call, but Clare insists no—no one . . .

"No! Really, I am fine. I *am*."

"You're sure I shouldn't call an ambulance? You're looking very pale . . ."

"Thank you, but no! No."

Clare doesn't face him. Whoever this is. Wisest strategy is not to lock eyes with any stranger. When she is vulnerable, distracted. A stranger who may then perceive how truly in need of help she is.

No, no!—the last thing Clare wants is to be taken to an ER in this city where she knows no one. Hospitalized against her will—a nightmare. In the confusion of the moment she could not have named Cardiff, Maine. Could not have explained where she is coming from and where she is going.

By now she is much recovered from the fainting spell. She *wills* herself to recover. Walking away, steady on her feet, so that the stranger will not persist.

But why are you walking away? Is this not the intersection with another? Another life, whose web you have blundered into.

But no, there's no time. *Must keep walking.*

Eventually she locates her car, a compact metallic-gray sedan that looks more battered than she recalls. Even then, Clare stares at the license plate as if she has never seen it. Has someone altered the numerals? Or—isn't this her car after all?

(It is. She checks the interior, the back seat where she has left some clothes. Of course this is her car.)

Not sure that she should be driving, still weak-kneed, light-headed. Though chiding herself—*Ridiculous. They died so long ago. You have lived so long without them. And you have no memory of them.*

The spell has lifted. Must be, blood has returned to Clare's brain, bearing oxygen, clarity.

Strong enough then to unlock her car, drive out of the lot.

Strong enough to return to—where?

Needing to escape now. To drink, get drunk. Curl into a ball. Disappear.

So alone! Devastation.

Plan is, return to the house at 59 Acton Avenue, hurriedly re-pack your suitcase, leave. If the great-aunts call after you in surprise, hurt, reproach, you will tell them, *Thank you for your hospitality. But—goodbye!* You will not pause, you will not linger at the foot of the stairs like a hurt child. If pressed to explain yourself, you will not burst into tears. At the front door you will tell the great-aunts politely—*I don't want anything here. It was a mistake for me to come here. Take the "bequest"—it's yours.*

What relief it will be, driving south! Out of rockbound Maine, where thin mists drift across the roads like wraiths.

You want the property on Post Road. *That* house.

On the drive north to Cardiff you'd been enthralled. Hadn't wanted to distract yourself from your billowing euphoric thoughts by listening to an audio book or music. The possibility of an inheritance—any inheritance—had captivated you. The possibility that you have relatives—living relatives—had captivated you. Not for a moment had you stopped to think what these possibilities might mean.

On Acton Avenue (which has not been easy to find: unfamiliar street names, unfamiliar houses, several times your mind goes blank, no idea where the hell you are or what is so urgent that propels you to be doing this) Clare parks her car in front of the cobblestone house. On this chilly April day the house and grounds appear to be bleached of color, like a faded photograph. Clare can almost see cracks in the photograph, a smudged fingerprint at an upper corner.

She wonders if the great-aunts have spied her from the upstairs windows. Fat, dimpled spiders lurking in their web, waiting for their spindly-limbed insect prey.

What a very long time is required to climb out of her car, make her (careful) way up the front walk, place her (shaky) foot on the first step of the veranda. She is feeling defiant, yet a moment later is seized with dread. *But why am I here? Why did I come back?* A dream in which Clare is both herself and a detached and bemused observer.

Somewhere between the first and second steps, she collapses.

Somewhere between one breath and the next, she feels herself extinguished.

. . . but waking then, dazed, sick with dread, lying on the hard-mattressed bed in the upstairs room where she'd been carried. Only dimly has Clare a memory of being lifted from the sidewalk, a man's blood-darkened face, averted eyes.

Grunting as he'd carried her. Kicking open a door.

Close by, the great-aunts are hovering, murmuring and cooing like startled birds. Whoever carried Clare up the stairs, dropped her onto the bed, has departed. Only an ashy smell remains, and the dull ache of fingers gripping her.

12.

"Why didn't anyone tell me?" Clare means to speak sharply but sounds instead plaintive, wounded.

It is hours later. Already the day has begun to wane.

Downstairs in the great-aunts' parlor. Wine-dark velvet wallpaper, frayed in the lamplight. A smell of dust, cobwebs, furniture polish. On a marble-topped coffee table in front of the Victorian settee on which Clare is numbly seated, someone has placed a tarnished silver tray bearing chipped Wedgwood plates, and on these plates are crustless cucumber-and-cream-cheese open-faced sandwiches on white bread, Pepperidge Farm oatmeal cookies, radishes as large and red as bovine eyeballs. A beige-laced arm, long, slender fingers with "frosted" nails, steam rising to subtly distort the features of Elspeth Lacey as she ceremoniously pours tea into three delicate teacups.

Clare stares at the little sandwiches. Suppresses a shudder. As if she would eat any more of the great-aunts' poisoned food!

"But of course, dear Clare—*we did.*"

"Certainly, Clare—you *were told.*"

Clare protests, no. No one told her; she'd had to discover it for herself in the library. On microfilm.

"Not at all, dear. Morag told you, I'm sure—"

"—well, *hinted*. We didn't want to shock you."

"—didn't want you to run away when you'd only just arrived."

"Not bluntly. Not rudely. *I* would not, of course—"

"When you called the other day—"

"An unexpected call—"

"A *welcome call*. It was then, when you identified yourself, the granddaughter of Maude Donegal—"

"*The* granddaughter of Maude Donegal—as if you'd known that you were the single, singular one—"

"Well, I'm sure that I prepared you—"

"For the worst! Elspeth is very good at that."

"Not *for the worst*. Morag, will you stop? You are embarrassing yourself and confusing our dear niece, who has had a great shock . . ."

"—except Elspeth chooses her words with such care, like an executioner choosing the very sharpest instrument, you might—almost—if you didn't know what to listen for—"

"—Morag, stop! You are not amusing."

"—might misunderstand."

"I am not like that at all. Not at all. And in any case, there was Luke Fischer. *He* certainly explained the situation to the poor child."

"And if he did not, shame! As the executor of Maude's estate, Fischer is being paid enough to be more responsible."

"Paid entirely too much, in my opinion. Lawyers!" Elspeth snorts in fastidious exasperation.

Clare is overwhelmed by the great-aunts' rapid voices. Like birds' beaks peck-peck-pecking at her head.

She manages to protest. No one prepared her. No one warned her. Not even Lucius Fischer that morning, who'd been too cowardly to tell her the circumstances of her parents' deaths but sent her to the library down the street to discover that her family had been murdered, that her father was—had been—the murderer . . .

"Oh, my *dear*. Must you."

"Indeed. After—a quarter century . . ."

"Some things do not need to be *uttered*."

Elspeth winces, fluttering her skeletal-thin fingers in a gesture of repugnance. Morag grins and shrugs her shoulders, one of which seems subtly misshapen; she leans forward to offer one of the teacups to Clare, who hesitates before accepting it.

"Sugar, dear? Milk?" Morag leans discomfortingly near, smiling so forcefully that Clare can see tiny trilobites of creases in her cheeks.

"Thank you—no."

"Don't intimidate the poor child, Morag. You have a way of *lunging*."

"*You* have a way of—of—plunging."

Elspeth laughs in derision, clearly having won the exchange of witticisms.

Clare would like to set the teacup down somewhere unobtrusive. She is feeling light-headed, uncertain. Vaguely she realizes that she hasn't eaten for hours, and after she'd eaten breakfast, she'd been sick to her stomach.

"It's just that I—I would have liked to be warned. Before I—read about it in the newspaper . . ."

"Well, of course! *That* would be a shock."

"—preventable, one might have thought." Morag shakes her head vehemently, as a bulldog might.

Strange, how Clare seems to lose her *selfness* in the presence of the elderly great-aunts. As if the very molecules that compose her neural being begin to shudder and shake, on the verge of disintegration.

Is this me? What has happened to me? Must concentrate . . .

In a corner of the parlor a tall grandfather clock with a glittering glassy face begins to solemnly chime the hour—*one, two, three, four, five* . . . Something crucial about the time, Clare thinks. Hadn't she meant to leave this house by now? Though she concentrates on the chimes, she soon loses count and has no idea what time it is.

"Drink your tea, dear! Before it gets cold."

"Before you spill it, dear! Your hand is shaking."

Using both hands, Clare lifts the delicate chipped cup to her lips. Fragrant steam, like a caress.

Bitter tea! Clare swallows with difficulty.

"Darjeeling. It can be strong. And possibly, Morag has let it steep too long."

Is it some comfort to observe that the great-aunts are drinking tea, too? Clare wants to think so.

Always it is easiest to please. Clare recalls how, as the little orphan child, she'd been particularly eager to please.

Indeed, the great-aunts are pleased. Elspeth claps her beringed fingers together lightly in the sort of simulation of applause one might make to a very young child.

"Well, dear! I hope you realize it will do you no good to brood. Twenty-five years ago the Donegals wasted far too much time brooding over the—the tragedy—and some of them never recovered."

"But they persevered—"

"God, yes! They persevered."

"I think you mean *we*."

"Well, he was not *our son*, you know. He was Maude's son."

"He was *our nephew*. And his children were—"

"Never mind! Why are you dwelling upon it!—I beg you, Morag, *just stop*."

"I am merely pointing out that—"

"Stop! Have the common decency to refrain from picking at old wounds, will you? Are you so obtuse, so willfully ignorant, you have no awareness that our dear houseguest Clare is—was—*is* one of those very children?"

Morag stares at Clare, aghast. For indeed she seems to have forgotten. Clare was the surviving child.

A family massacre, mother and two children, father. And the third child hidden among cobwebs beneath the kitchen sink.

Clare wasn't there, yet Clare remembers.

But no: Clare doesn't remember. But Clare *was* there.

Morag says hotly, "*You* stop, Elspeth! You are a bully. All my life you have bullied me. I refuse to be censored and straitjacketed in my speech as I have been in my pathetically truncated and expurgated *life*. I merely said—"

"And I have said *the Donegal tragedy is past tense now*. Very *past*."

Elspeth's unnaturally youthful unlined face has been powdered a starker white than usual. Her brown-penciled eyebrows are arched in distress, no less genuine (Clare thinks) for being theatrical; her rosebud mouth is puckered. And Morag, staring at the floor, her wide, thin mouth grimacing, seems genuinely moved as well.

Since breakfast Elspeth has changed into dark silken trousers, a tunic of beige lace, high-heeled black patent leather shoes. Her silver-rimmed glasses perch at the end of her narrow, pale-powdered nose. Morag seems to have thrown on clothes carelessly: shapeless gray jersey pants with a prominent elastic band, a V-necked argyle sweater with frayed elbows, high-top sneakers. Her chunky black plastic glasses have been shoved against the bridge of her pug nose, the lenses visibly smudged.

Elspeth's hair is puffy, airy, glowing with tangerine-bright luminosity; Clare wonders if she'd looked this way when she'd been a middle school principal. Morag's metallic-gray hair, bluntly shorn, swings about her jaws as she shakes her head with dogged vehemence.

"*I* say—(please do not interrupt, Elspeth!)—that the past is not ever *past*. We just can't see it."

"Oh, just *stop*. You are upsetting our dear niece, and you are not amusing."

"*You* stop. Clare is interested in what I'm saying, I am sure."

"She *is not*. Will you have a cucumber sandwich, dear?" Elspeth holds out a platter to Clare, who stiffens.

Shakes her head curtly, *no, no thank you*.

There's a dull ache at her left temple where her head must have struck the concrete walkway.

"You must keep up your strength, dear! You are looking quite pale, isn't she, Morag?"

"Best not to bully *her*, Elspeth."

"I am not bullying her, I am caring for her. *You* can't see beyond the end of your own—very short—nose."

Elspeth laughs daringly. Morag glowers.

Clare laughs, startled. How like a *family* this is! The relentlessness of intimacy.

If she'd grown up in Cardiff, the great-aunts Elspeth and Morag would have been family. She'd have known her grandmother Maude Donegal. Frequently, she'd have been brought to this house.

And others she'd have known—her closer family . . . Her mind goes blank, as if she has come too near to a hive of buzzing bees.

Elspeth again offers the platter of sandwiches, and this time Clare accepts with a murmured "Thank you."

Out of politeness. Courtesy. Doesn't want to appear rude. Her great-aunts have gone to the trouble of preparing a tea tray for her.

Hesitantly, Clare takes a small bite. The cucumber is overripe and limp, but the cream cheese has a peppery tang. The white bread is so stale it has the texture of a cracker.

Clare is made to realize in wonder—*Why, these are the women who found her. The little girl beneath the sink.*

And—*without these women, the little girl would have died.*

But who was the little girl? And when was this?

A profound revelation. Clare might turn this revelation in her fingers like a precious gem.

For she has learned that on that afternoon the sisters had driven to the house on Post Road to search for the missing child. *God was guiding us*—they were quoted as saying.

Clare feels a wave of gratitude. So powerful she might drown in it.

"Aunt Elspeth, Aunt Morag—I owe my life to you, I've learned today. The two of you . . ."

Impulsively Clare stammers, "Thank you!" She wants to say more, much more, but her brain seems to have gone blank.

The great-aunts are surprised. Visibly startled. Elspeth presses a beringed hand against her lacy chest; Morag stares and blinks. Each shimmers in delight, like shaken foil. Clearly Clare's unexpected words are pleasing to them. But Elspeth reaches out to touch Clare's wrist gently.

"Well! That's very kind of you, dear. But—"

"—surely someone else—"

"—*someone* else would have thought to—"

"—eventually—"

"—but yes, if we hadn't come along—"

"Which we did! We did! For such was God's will."

"—if we hadn't come along when we did, perhaps someone else would have come along, but—"

"*But but but!*"

"—too late."

Clare shudders. What does it mean—*too late?*

She wonders how close little Clare Ellen was to death. Exhaustion, dehydration, terror. How precarious, the surviving child's life: a candle flame that might have been blown out by a gust of wind.

Yet *God's will* had ordained otherwise. These women who are her great-aunts, who she never knew existed before a few days ago, are responsible for her very being.

The thought comes to Clare—*Maybe they don't want to poison me. Maybe they love me.*

Vaguely she recalls that she'd intended to leave the Donegal house by now. In fact, by now she'd planned to be on the interstate headed south.

She can't remember why. Such a drastic decision. The afternoon is rapidly waning, soon it will be dusk. Though the month is April, the cold feels like winter; in Cardiff, there are strips of aged soiled snow against the foundations of buildings, in shadowy places. Remnants of icicles. Slow to melt.

Too late to leave today, but possibly tomorrow?

Yet why tomorrow? Her great-aunts have made it clear that Clare can stay with them, in this house, for as long as she wishes. She must file a claim in probate court, the lawyer has said. She will need to make another appointment with Fischer, perhaps.

She will want to visit the cemetery where her family is buried. Definitely, she will want to visit the cemetery and take photos.

She will want to make inquiries: mother (Kathryn), father (Conor), sister (Emma), brother (Laird). She will want to see photographs of the lost family; she will want to make copies of these photographs. She will not (yet) want to ask, *Why did my father do such a terrible thing?*—for the question is too bright and blinding, like gazing into the sun.

Indeed, Clare's eyes are dimmed by tears. She is feeling a wave of something warm, soothing—gratitude.

She'd fallen on the walkway in front of the house. That sudden sense of helplessness, dread—*falling*. Suddenly your knees buckle, your legs cannot support your weight, you strike the ground like a tree falling.

The second time within an hour, Clare has fainted. And before Cardiff, Clare Seidel never once fainted.

Then there were cries, the great-aunts' cries *Oh oh oh come help her! Help her!* And someone was stooping over her and she was being lifted and carried up the veranda steps and into the house, as a child might be carried—unresisting, in utter trust, wonder.

A man's strong arms, an ashy smell. Yet try as she might, Clare can't see the man's face.

"Was it—Gerard?" Clare is hesitant to speak the name of her uncle for what will be the first time.

Elspeth laughs, startled; spills tea onto her beige lace bosom and wipes at it irritably with a napkin. Morag stares blankly at Clare.

"Was it Gerard—*what*?" Elspeth fixes Clare with a look of incredulity.

Has Clare mispronounced the man's name? Or, in her confusion, has she uttered the wrong name?

"—the person who carried me upstairs? Laid me on the bed?"

Quickly Elspeth tells her yes. Of course: Gerard.

"At our direction, Gerard did so. Seeing you fallen—"

"—*so fallen*—as if from a great height—"

"—lifeless—"

"—poor girl! This has been such a strain for you—"

"—right there on our sidewalk—such a shock to see—"

"—it was I who saw, fortunately—"

"—indeed, yes! Morag is sharp-eyed as an owl—"

"—and so I saw, and summoned Elspeth—"

"—and Gerard was summoned, from his bachelor quarters on the third floor—"

"—though we have been made to know that we are not welcome on the third floor, calling up the stairs to Gerard is allowed—"

"—in an emergency, that is."

"Very reliable in emergencies, our nephew. You would not think it from seeing him, but—"

"Oh he is! He *is*."

"Priests are expected to step forward in times of crisis and give aid to others; they are trained not to think of themselves, but to think of others, as Christ did. Gerard is quite remarkable in an emergency—"

"But in ordinary life—daily life—"

"—in ordinary life, Gerard is not so adept. Or rather, Gerard is not so *engaged*. Sometimes the poor boy forgets to eat, he is so—disconnected . . ."

"—so *mournful*—"

"So we are particularly grateful when Gerard helps us out, as he has done more than once when we've needed him. And for years, when his mother needed him. And today—"

"Gerard rarely shows it, but he *feels*."

"He certainly does! Not like most men . . ."

"Just a shame, Gerard is so—shy—"

"—antisocial—"

"—not really *anti-*, more just *nonsocial*—as his mother used to say."

"Well, Gerard has trouble making conversation. It's as if his tongue is too large for his mouth. He tries, but the words don't come. And so he becomes anxious. He becomes excitable. He avoids even us, who are his closest blood relatives!"

"My goodness, imagine—our nephew avoids even us."

"We prevailed upon him to have tea with us today, but he ran away—of course. He's particularly shy of you, Clare."

"—not at ease with girls. Never was."

"—why, he'd have made an ideal priest, when you think about it—a vow of poverty, chastity, and obedience would have been quite natural for him."

"Oh, he was selfless—he *is*. He did not deserve such cruel treatment at the hands of his father—virtually disinheriting him by running out of money before he could donate to the seminary. Gerard never complained, but—you could see, his heart was broken."

"Yes. Leland has a good deal to answer for—in Hades."

Unexpectedly, the great-aunts burst into laughter. Like young girls, knowing that they are being naughty.

Clare notes that Morag has been eating cucumber sandwiches, hungrily; Elspeth is daintily sipping tea and nibbling at an oatmeal cookie with quick, furtive bites, like a mouse.

Clare's headache has lessened, the bitter black tea seems to have numbed the pain. She has eaten several cucumber sandwiches, her hunger has been assuaged, and she is feeling less anxious. No idea why she'd been so insistent upon leaving the Donegal house this very day . . .

"We will ask Gerard if he'd like to drive you to see the property on Post Road," Elspeth says, "when you're ready to see it. The old farm would be difficult to find for someone unfamiliar with northern Ashford County."

"Difficult?—impossible!" Morag snorts.

"Like a maze—unimproved roads that get washed away over the winter, and nobody has thought to establish a detour. Bridges that are out. Yes, an outsider would require a guide."

"Indeed! 'An outsider would require a guide.'" Morag repeats these words with ominous import.

"And who better than Gerard? He would know the way far better than we would."

"Well—*we* no longer drive. As you know, *I* no longer drive."

"You were a perfectly fine driver, Morag. It was unfair, it was *sexist*, for them to take away your license. You were not even seventy-five, you were *young*."

"Well. Water under the bridge."

"I am just saying that last time we made the journey—*there*—you were the designated driver. But—not now."

Morag shudders as a dog might do, its skin rippling smoothly.

"Not now, indeed. *Never*."

The great-aunts fall silent for a moment, considering. Then Morag says provocatively, "Maybe Clare doesn't want to see the property. Her inheritance. Maybe she'd rather not."

"Well, if she does—"

"You could sell the property without seeing it, Clare. If you wanted to."

"—I'm saying *if she does* want to see it, Gerard might drive her."

"—and I'm saying *if she wishes to be spared* . . ."

Swirl of voices around Clare's head. Hive of humming bees. *Shut your eyes, mouth. No one will see.*

Emma, Laird. Almost, the names are familiar to Clare. Faint, teasing echos.

Mommy! Mommy! Mommy!—a girl's shriek, must be Emma.

Other screams she'd heard. Her own, she didn't hear. Tottering on weak legs, falling. Crawling on hands and knees across sticky linoleum. The door beneath the sink is not fully shut. Clawing to open it as deafening thunderclaps erupt behind her.

95

But in the shadowy place beneath the sink, there is quiet. Behind the filthy drainpipes, spider's webs.

Raised voices, heavy footsteps. More screams. Gunshots, not hurried, carefully spaced.

But Clare is safe drifting into sleep. In the great-aunts' parlor, on the velvet settee that creaks beneath her weight. No longer light-headed, anxious with hunger. No longer fearful.

Seeing that Clare has fallen asleep on the settee, Elspeth presses a finger against her lips—*Shh!* Morag pulls a mohair shawl over Clare, gently.

13.

Please just tell me—anything you know about them.

Anything you remember . . .

By the end of the week Clare has acquired the names of Cardiff residents who'd known her parents. As adults, as young adults, even as children. She has a list of relatives, neighbors, friends, and classmates of Conor Donegal and Kathryn Thrush; she has a list of teachers, names of Cardiff police officers who were called to the scene of the shootings. Several times she has returned to the Cardiff Public Library reference room to search for more information about what purportedly happened on the afternoon of January 6, 1989, in the house on Post Road. She has become friendly— almost!—with the helpful librarian, whose name is Linda Peele. (In another lifetime, Clare thinks, she and Linda Peele would be close friends; in this lifetime, that will not happen. Clare has no time to cultivate a friendship with anyone, still less has she room in her heart for friendship.) With the zeal and thoroughness with which she'd established herself as a competitive young art historian, she has set for herself the goal of finding out all that she can about Conor Donegal, Kathryn Donegal (née Thrush), Laird Donegal, Emma Donegal.

My father. My mother. My brother. My sister.

Almost at such times Clare feels a thrill of something like elation, joy. For though these individuals are no longer living, they certainly did live at one time.

Repeating, soundlessly moving her lips. A quivering emphasis upon *my*.

My father. My mother. My brother. My sister.

In this family Clare Ellen was the baby. Approximately three years younger than her sister and six years younger than her brother.

Her sister! *Her* brother!

Mouthing the names: "Emma." "Laird."

Both are beautiful names, Clare thinks. And Conor, and Kathryn. Beautiful.

But she remembers nothing of her lost family. A scrim obscures that part of her brain. A gauze curtain, near-impenetrable.

Yet (Clare thinks) she must have played with her sister. At the age of two years, nine months she must have been in awe of her "big" nine-year-old brother.

Six years older than Clare Ellen, Laird would (perhaps) have only tolerated her. Though (possibly) he'd loved her . . . And Emma had loved her, often hugged her. Emma had allowed her little sister to play with her dolls and snuggle with her stuffed animals.

Yes, that must have happened. Surely.

More difficult to remember her mother, her father.

Shimmering, blurred like tears. There Mommy and Daddy would be, tears.

Except yes: she recalls *being held.*

If she makes an effort to push aside the gauzy scrim, she can see—almost—something . . .

Possibly, she recalls Mommy holding her tight against Mommy's beating heart. Almost recalls Mommy's soft, warm body. Hiding her face in that body. Burrowing between the soft, warm breasts.

Sucking milk. A leak of milk. Sweet breast milk, unmistakable smell.

Lying in her crib, wide-eyed, blinking as two tall figures gaze down upon her. Their faces are blurred, uncertain.

Then suddenly the faces are clearer. The scrim has vanished.

Mommy's smile, just for *her*. Daddy's smile that makes a little crease in Daddy's cheek.

And so Clare is made to realize, in wonderment—*I do remember. I was loved, I was not abandoned.*

"Who am I?—a Donegal relative."

Clare isn't eager to reveal herself as the surviving child of an infamous local massacre. Better to claim a little distance as the daughter of a cousin of Conor Donegal who'd never met Conor—(of course: Clare appears too young to have met someone who'd died twenty-five years ago)—who was born in the Midwest, lives now near Philadelphia, and has never visited Maine before.

"Yes, it's beautiful. Driving along the coast—stunning."

In truth Clare finds the beauty of Maine somewhat overwhelming. Views of the Atlantic Ocean from the coastal highway ever shifting, mesmerizing. Where half the world is water, the sky looms too large.

It's the twilit Maine of Winslow Homer that Clare finds most haunting—mist-shrouded, clouded, evasive. Porous boundaries between shoreline and sea, sea and horizon, horizon and sky, as in a watercolor wash.

Conversing with strangers, Clare is at her most hopeful. She is determined to make a good impression. Not to arouse suspicion. Several people with whom she speaks ask her point-blank if she's a reporter, and she quickly assures them no, she is not, certainly not. "I'm a remote Donegal relative curious about the family. But primarily I'm an art historian researching Maine artists of the nineteenth century . . ."

Art is a good neutral subject. If individuals to whom Clare speaks become too emotional, recalling *that beautiful young family*, adroitly Clare can shift the subject to Winslow Homer, George Bellows, Rockwell Kent, Andrew Wyeth. (She isn't one of those insufferable art snobs who sneers at Andrew Wyeth.)

Clare has been sleeping poorly in Cardiff. There are soft bruises beneath her eyes that she disguises artfully with makeup. She has brushed her thick dark hair back from her forehead into a chiseled-looking bun, as a ballerina might do; on her mouth she applies bright red lipstick—an American girl eager to please.

"Oh! My God, you look like—*him*."

One of the mothers of sons who'd been "close friends" of Conor Donegal in high school stares at Clare, hand to mouth in an expression of genuine surprise.

"I mean—your hair, at your forehead. It's beautiful—that little peak."

The woman pauses awkwardly. "Your eyes, too . . ."

A chill passes over Clare, who would like to hide her face from the woman's scrutiny. But she manages to laugh, uneasily.

She says that she has seen photos of Conor Donegal and is sure that she doesn't resemble him.

"I'm told that I take after my mother, who's from St. Paul."

Still, the woman isn't convinced. Clare can see.

In a faltering voice Mrs. Freeman says: "He was an excitable boy, people said. Not that I ever saw it myself. He wasn't ever rude to *me*. But Billy always said Conor had a hot temper and he'd never back down from a fight . . . Him and Billy and some friends of theirs were drinking and hanging out at the Kennicott Bridge, they were underage at the time, and some bikers from Lewisburg came along and Conor got in an argument with one of them. They all started fighting, and eventually the police were called . . . I don't think they were arrested or anything, but somebody might've gotten hurt and had to have stitches. Conor was Billy's best friend for a long time, but Billy said you had to watch out. If Conor drank fast, he'd want to fight with somebody. Some Irish kind of thing, Billy said, how they have one drink and then another, and another, and can't stop until they're blind drunk . . . People mostly said it was 'temporary insanity,' what Conor did, that he'd have never done if he'd been sober."

Clare thinks, *Temporary insanity. That was it.*

So others have suggested. Speculating on Conor Donegal's motives. But of course for such savagery there can be no sane motive.

Gradually a portrait of Conor Donegal is coming into focus. Clare's father is described as having been "a good guy, basically"— "great friend, you could trust"—but a "binge drinker"—"hot temper" (again!)—"never backed down from a fight." Several former teachers recall him as "intelligent but easily distracted"—"naturally inquisitive"—"not a great reader, but good at math." He was a "good, not outstanding" athlete—a "natural team player." He'd liked music, including Irish folk rock. He'd liked Rick James, Lionel Richie, James Brown. He'd taken a miscellany of courses at the University of Maine at Bangor but hadn't completed a degree. He'd worked for his father, Leland Donegal, but eventually quit to go into business for himself—"which didn't work out too well."

An entrepreneur with borrowed money, eventually bankrupt.

Well—some initial success, a few years of rising profits, then setbacks.

Clare steels herself to hear that her (handsome, charismatic) father had been a brutal husband and father, but the consensus seems to be that he'd been "crazy about his family"—"loved his wife, kids"—"would've done anything for them."

How it happened that Conor Donegal had (allegedly) slaughtered his wife and his two oldest children, then turned the gun on himself—"Nobody could understand. Not then, and not now."

A middle-aged woman who identifies herself as Kathryn Thrush's "oldest, closest friend" confides in Clare that Conor Donegal had been a "problem drinker" since his early twenties—that Kathryn had stayed with him for so long, always thinking she could reform him; he made a show of belonging to Alcoholics Anonymous but kept "relapsing"; he'd tried to quit drinking a half dozen times, but always failed.

"She made excuses for Conor because she loved him, so he took advantage of her forgiving nature. A man will do that if you let him—*any man* will do that if you let them." The woman speaks vehemently, with wounded eyes, as if Clare has tried to argue with her; but Clare knows better than to disagree with another's interpretation of the past.

And Clare is thinking, *Maybe Conor hurt her too. Maybe she can't forgive him for it.*

Another middle-aged woman, who identifies herself as having been a neighbor of Conor and Kathryn's when they lived on Mott

Street in Cardiff, confides bitterly in Clare that claims that Conor was a serious member of AA were "bullshit": Conor only pretended to attend meetings, or maybe he went to meetings to placate Kathryn and the Donegals, who were too trusting. Conor was a "master manipulator of hearts"—*she* knew.

Another woman with wounded eyes! Clare thinks. *My father was a collector of hearts.*

Clare learns that after the bankruptcy, her parents, still young, with two young children, decided to purchase a (foreclosed) farm in northern Ashford County. They were both "headstrong"— "reckless"—"willing to take risks." They had "romantic ideas" about country life and trying to make a living by farming—fruit orchards, preferably. Not beef cattle or dairy, nothing that involved animals. Kathryn would say with a shudder, "No animals! Farm animals *die*."

A curious thing to say, Clare thinks. She wonders what her mother meant: that farm animals (like beef cattle) are made to die, or that farm animals are at risk of dying from diseases, prematurely.

When her mother is recalled, Clare listens intensely, very still. Her head is bowed, her eyes half shut. She scarcely dares to breathe at such moments; this feels like forbidden knowledge to her.

"Oh, Kathryn Thrush! She was a *lovely woman*. But—"

But. Meaning—what?

A lovely woman but reckless in love?

Clare is reluctant to ask questions that might provoke or annoy. She does not want to appear overly inquisitive. She understands that her welcome in the homes of strangers is provisional, precarious. But she is hesitant for other reasons as well. When she merely thinks of questions she might ask, her heart beats painfully. *But did Conor Donegal love Kathryn—his wife? Did he love his children?*

Everyone to whom she speaks seems to insist, *Yes*, he did.

Certainly he did! Which is why what he did to them, and to himself, left everyone baffled.

Did he ever hurt anyone before that day? Did he ever threaten anyone?

Was there no warning? Could no one have helped?

No. Clare can't voice these questions. Can't bring herself.

Days pass, a week. In a trance of concentration she makes her way down the list of names. (Initially not very cooperative, Lucius Fischer seems to have decided to help her with introductions.) She makes telephone calls, shyly/boldly knocks on the doors of strangers. In most households she enters zones of loneliness that are virtually palpable—"Oh yes! Come in! Is it—Clare? I was rummaging in the attic and found these yearbooks . . ."

For a young, unmarried woman it is instructive to Clare to observe at close hand how women some years older than she, married women, mothers of (mostly grown) children, seem to be starved for company. (Companionship? Clare cannot offer that, except fleetingly.) She spends hours in Cardiff homes on sofas or at kitchen tables being shown yearbooks by women eager to reminisce about their school years, never failing to point out to Clare their own photographs, along with those of handsome Conor Donegal, very pretty Kathryn Thrush.

Her parents, so young! Long before they were her parents.

In that netherworld before Clare's birth. A world contiguous with the world she is in now, yet utterly mysterious.

Caption beneath Conor Donegal's senior yearbook picture: "*A brave bold man am I.*"

Caption beneath Kathryn Thrush's senior yearbook picture: *"She walks in beauty like the night."*

Clare recognizes the quotation beneath her mother's picture—from a romantic Byron poem—but not the one beneath her father's. An odd yearbook custom, such quotes. As if a human being could be so glibly summed up.

Conor's activities were primarily sports: baseball, football, swim team. Kathryn's activities were cheerleading, girls' choir, Drama Club, Hi-Y.

More than once Clare is shown the same yearbooks, studies the same photographs. She has even begun to recognize faces, names. With gratitude, she listens intently to whatever she is told. For she is grateful, like a time traveler who has been welcomed and not rebuffed in a past time both precious to her and unknown to her.

She asks permission to record conversations on her iPhone. She is never denied permission. And never does she express doubt or suspicion that what she is being told may be misremembered, exaggerated.

The witnesses to the past who open their homes to Clare never doubt their own memories. They are adamant, convinced. Recounting tales of Conor Donegal and Kathryn Thrush has been a ritual for them. Clare's interest is flattering, her interest revives and inflames their memories. For it has been a quarter century since most of them have been questioned so closely.

Clare wonders how they would react if they could hear one another reminisce about their shared past—who was really Kathryn Thrush's *very best friend* through high school? Who was really Conor Donegal's first girl friend in high school?

It would seem that Conor and Kathryn were in the same class at Cardiff High. But this is not true. Conor was several years ahead of Kathryn, and (Clare guesses) might scarcely have been aware of her at the time.

Though most of the persons Clare has contacted are very willing to speak with her, there are some who refuse her altogether. Relatives of Kathryn Thrush: an older sister named Irma, scattered cousins, an ailing mother in an assisted-living facility—none of these will even speak with Clare on the phone, let alone agree to see her.

Identifying herself as a "distant relative" of Conor Donegal's seems to have been shortsighted after all. Evidently there is still bitterness between the families, animosity on the part of the Thrushes over the murders of Kathryn and the children.

Who? No! Nothing to say to you.

Twenty-seven years! Might've been yesterday.

How unfair it is, Clare thinks, to blame *her*. As if guilt could be inherited, like original sin.

And what about the Donegal children, Laird and Emma?— Clare forces herself to ask.

Few of the witnesses seem to recall the children, or are eager to speak of them. The subject of slaughtered children is too painful— exudes no air of adolescent romance. Blinking back tears, a woman of Clare's approximate age confides that she'd been "Emma's closest friend in kindergarten." A man in his early forties reminisces about playing softball with Laird Donegal in seventh grade. (Clare doesn't protest—*Seventh grade? My brother was too young, he didn't live that long.*)

"Emma?—she was very sweet. Quiet. Her mother fixed her hair in such pretty braids. We were all so shocked—scared—at school, when . . ."

"Laird Donegal. That's a name I haven't heard in twenty years. Jesus! He wasn't a close friend but—I can remember . . ."

Voices trailing off, vaguely. Obscure embarrassment, unease. Clare understands that her sister and brother have been lost in time, on the brink of being forgotten.

She will redeem them. If she can.

Of the youngest child, who'd hidden beneath the sink, the child whom a raging lunatic father failed to murder, few speak with certainty. "Not sure what happened to her. The Thrushes sued for custody to take her to live with them, but—after that—it was said they'd put her up for adoption."

And: "Mrs. Thrush got sick. Kathryn's mother. Couldn't take care of a young child. What happened to her daughter and the other grandchildren made her kind of—lose heart, I guess. Lose hope."

And: "Some kind of nervous breakdown. Vivian never got over it, to this day."

And: "One thing Mrs. Thrush didn't want was any of the Donegals adopting the little girl. She hated them all, blamed them for what Conor had done, which people thought wasn't fair—but that's how people are around here—never forget, never forgive."

So that's the explanation, Clare thinks. So simple after all. For years she'd been captivated by the mystery of how she'd been given away for adoption, and this is it.

Never forgive, never forget. A bitter wisdom.

The Donegals, her well-to-do relatives, hadn't given her away to an adoption agency; they'd never had custody of her. It was her mother's grieving mother who'd given her away to strangers out of spite, meanness. Sheer hatred.

In this way, Clare Ellen's life was decided. And who is to say that her life wasn't saved, adopted by strangers in another part of the country who knew nothing of her background, brought up in a place in which she was never identified as Donegal.

He was hotheaded. He was a great guy. He was a great friend. He'd do anything for you—if he was your friend. He never forgot, and he never forgave. Sure, he had enemies. But he had friends. He'd had some bad luck. His father treated him like shit—him and his brother both. He was like no one you'd forget—he was special.

Can't say why, he just was. You'd have to be there.

What happened with Conor, some of us never believed.

Killed his family? Wife and kids? Bullshit. Somebody else did it, made it look like suicide.

Sure, it could be done. If it was done with some planning. The Cardiff Police Department was a joke. Four, five men. Some kind of "senior detective" came over from Portland and didn't give a shit what went on here.

Nothing like these police officers you see on TV. "Forensics"—that's a laugh. Assholes probably walked all over the house tracking blood, getting their own fingerprints on things.

Could they figure out who used the gun? That Conor was the one for sure? Bullshit.

The gun they found at the scene, on the floor beside Conor's hand—not a gun he'd purchased or had a permit for. Just some unknown gun out of nowhere—couldn't have been his. Christ!

Mostly all the township cops do is issue traffic tickets. Weekends, round up the drunks. Drunk and disorderly—creating a public nuisance —kids breaking into 7-Eleven stores, gas stations—fights at the high school.

There's a pretty bad drug problem now in Ashford County—methamphetamine—but back then, meth didn't exist. Anyway, not here.

This asshole they call a coroner—"medical examiner"—probably took one look at the scene in the house and ruled it murder, suicide. Easiest verdict you could come up with.

Though there was a suicide note—they said. But that could be faked too.

Look, I knew Conor in school. You know somebody when he's a kid, you're kids together, it's like you are brothers—you know. Any kind of bullshit they pull, you can call them on it.

This time, must've been middle school, some asshole kid threw a stray dog off a bridge. Looked like the dog was injured, couldn't swim too well. Poor bastard was whining and drowning, so Conor waded out to rescue it, in the river where there's all these damn concrete blocks and rusted wires you could cut yourself on and get—what's it called—tetanus.

Yeah, that was Conor Donegal. Fuck he'd kill his family. Maybe if he was beat down bad enough, he'd kill himself—which I actually doubt—but his family, those kids—never.

Hearing this, Clare is filled with a sudden fierce certainty, joy.

Thinking, *I love him. He is my father, and I love him.*

14.

Final interview. Clare is exhausted, exhilarated! Chorus of voices in her head. Like a jury, for this has been a trial.

The last person Clare visits is a retired Cardiff police lieutenant. Hike Druitt is in his mid-seventies, soft, shapeless bulk slumped in a wheelchair, small bullet-colored eyes fixed upon Clare distrustfully.

"Who'd you say you are? One of the Donegals?"—frowning/squinting at Clare, who nods courteously.

"Yes, sir. A distant cousin of—Conor Donegal."

"'Conor Donegal! Christ."

But *sir* has pleased Druitt, Clare can see.

The elderly ex-cop requires acknowledgment of his authority, though (of course) he no longer has any authority to harass, badger, threaten those he considers his subordinates. Clare won't go so far as to call him *officer*, but *sir* seems plausible and appropriate given his age.

"*That* was a mess. Worst crime scene we ever stepped into. Never got over it, Jesus!—those *children* . . ."

Clare has been allowed to meet with Hike Druitt reluctantly: his daughter-in-law, his caretaker, has cautioned Clare not to overexcite him, for he suffers from a lung condition, a heart condition, high blood pressure, arthritis, asthma . . . He lives with his son and his son's family in a beige brick bungalow at the edge of town; his room is overheated and smells strongly medicinal.

As if he has been arguing with Clare, or with someone represented by Clare, Druitt speaks vehemently: "Well, see. A man is devastated. A man isn't a *man* if he can't provide for his family. People said temporary insanity—anybody who'd do what he did had to be insane. Nobody who knew Conor Donegal would disagree with this."

Clare listens intently. Eyes lowered, thoughtful. Even as her brain spins. *Why do you say that? What do you know?*

In a rambling, aggrieved voice Druitt recapitulates for Clare the circumstances of the "Donegal murders"—so familiar to Clare by now she has become virtually numbed to the account.

Yet of course Druitt's perspective differs from the others, for Druitt was one who'd actually entered the deathly house, seen the bodies—four bodies, three rooms.

Clare can shut her eyes and see: the body of the murdered wife and mother, Kathyn, on the kitchen floor; close by, the body of the murdered six-year-old, Emma.

Blood, you have to imagine. On the kitchen (linoleum?) floor.

In the living room, the body of the husband and father, Conor. In a back bedroom, against a farther wall, as if he'd run there to crouch in terror of his murderous assailant, nine-year-old Laird.

(Clare waits for Druitt to mention the third child, hiding beneath the kitchen sink in a nest of spiderwebs, even as she knows that Druitt will not recall little Clare Ellen, for no one does.)

(*Why is this?* Clare wonders. Because little Clare Ellen didn't die that day, but survived? And disappeared from Cardiff forever?)

The gun with which the four victims were shot to death lay close beside the body of the father. Close beside the father's lifeless hand.

And here too, blood. Glistening pools of blood. And in the bedroom, on the floor and splotched on the farther wall where the screaming child had died.

Each newspaper account of the shooting includes this detail in a separate, terse paragraph of print: the murder weapon, a forty-five caliber revolver, close beside the lifeless hand of Conor Donegal, where it would seem to have fallen from his fingers.

Gunshots at a (close) distance of five to six feet—chest, throat, head. The wife and mother, two shots. Each of the children, two shots. The husband and father, single shot to the head, less than six inches, not the temple, but the side of the head, instantaneous death as the bullet shattered the brain.

From the many accounts Clare has read within the past several days, she has constructed this narrative. Like a Polaroid print slowly filling in.

Druitt isn't recounting these facts, if they are facts. Druitt has, it seems, a cavalier nonconcern for a narrative not his own. Instead he is speaking of his memory of being summoned to the house on Post Road. He and two other officers warily approaching the house. Circling the house. Trying to peer into the windows.

"Anytime you try that, you can get your damn head blown off. Shotgun. We were lucky."

Finally, guns drawn, hands shaking. Gathered at the rear of the house, prepared to kick in the door, which turns out to be unlocked.

(In his thirty-year career in law enforcement, Hike Druitt never once fired his gun. Have to marvel at that, don't you?)

At last, taking a deep breath. Stepping into the "hellhole."

They'd been told what to expect by the dispatcher who'd sent them, who'd been told by the person who'd called 911 what was waiting for them inside. Still, it was a "nasty shock"—"four bodies"—"worst crime scene we ever stepped into."

Druitt is breathing with difficulty now. Panting like a heavyset man climbing stairs.

The person who'd called 911. That would be Gerard Donegal, Clare thinks.

Still, Clare asks. She is polite, methodical. Like one concerned with getting things right. Does Druitt recall who'd reported the shootings?

"Some relative of the family—a priest—somebody said . . . I don't remember who it was. Maybe a neighbor."

Druitt frowns, squinting in Clare's direction. Suddenly suspicious: "You're a reporter—are you?"

Clare tells him no. Not a reporter.

Explains again, carefully, for she guesses that Druitt is hard of hearing, that she is a "distant relative" of Conor Donegal's. She'd never met Donegal. In fact she'd never met any of her Cardiff relatives. She is thirty years old and has never visited Cardiff before. She is a historian. She is concerned with historical fact. And now she is staying in the Donegal house on Acton Avenue because she is a beneficiary of Maude Donegal's estate.

(Why is Clare telling Druitt this? Is she boasting? She is stricken with shame to think so.)

But Druitt isn't following these remarks. He has no idea who Maude Donegal was and no interest in her estate. Like a man seizing control of a steering wheel, wresting it out of the hands of another less competent, he resumes his impassioned story.

Clare wonders if Druitt has told and retold this lurid tale to his family. To anyone who will listen. Who once listened. Retired from the Cardiff Police Department, no longer in contact with the men who'd shared the traumatic experience with him, forced to recall alone the horrific incident, somehow still baffled by it, perplexed and resentful.

"... this kid, rookie kid, takes one look at—well, never mind— ain't pretty—he's stepped right into it!—starts puking up his guts. Chri-st!" Druitt shakes his head, incensed, grinning.

Clare is recording Druitt's words on her iPhone. She is also taking notes, out of respect for the retired police officer. Perhaps she will never listen to the recording, never read the notes. There is no need; she has memorized everything.

I don't need to be told. I was there, I remember. Even what I didn't see, hidden beneath the sink, I knew. I knew everything.

How shocked Druitt would be if Clare revealed her identity to him. How he would gape, uncomprehending.

You never knew I was there! You hardly looked for me. You left me for dead. I died and was dead, but now I am here, I am alive, and I can laugh at you if I want to, you pathetic old man.

But why is Clare flooded with sudden rage? In fact she feels sorry for the elderly, ailing man. The way he gazes at her, tilting his head, blinking his lusterless bullet eyes, Clare wonders if he is half blind. She feels a rush of sympathy for him, sorrow. He is old, he is ill, he will not live long. For the past twenty-seven years he has been haunted by a terrible memory, impossible to shake off.

If Conor were alive now, he'd be only sixty, sixty-one. Not at all old.

If Kathryn were alive now, she'd be in her late fifties. Possibly a youthful woman, still. Clare knows numerous professional women, academics, scholars who retain a radiant youthfulness well into their sixties, particularly if they have never been mothers. Her own mother might have been one of these. Fair-haired, silvery-brown-haired, with a dazzling smile.

"Did you know them, sir? I mean—the family that was killed . . ."

"Know them? No. I did not."

"You didn't know Conor Donegal?" Clare enunciates the name with care. It has become precious to her.

"How'd I know him? Or them? I wouldn't know the Donegals, hardly." Druitt laughs mirthlessly. Clare wonders if she has insulted him unwittingly.

"Sir, did you have trouble finding the house? Out in the country, in the dark?"

"Yes, we had some trouble." Druitt pauses, staring into space. Trying to recall. "But—it wasn't dark, I don't think. No."

"It wasn't dark?"

"N-no . . . I don't think so."

For a moment Clare is confused. Perhaps she is misremembering.

"There weren't lights on in the house when you arrived?"

"Don't think so."

"Was there a car in the driveway?"

Druitt shrugs, irritated. Lights in the house, car in the driveway —bullshit. What's that to him, his story?

Clare persists: "And when you got there, at the house, was anyone else there? Waiting for you?"

"Anyone else there? N-no . . ."

"The person who'd called 911?"

"No. I don't know . . ." Druitt shakes his head like a befuddled dog, jowls quivering. He is becoming distressed, antagonistic. "Miss—are you a reporter?"

"You've asked me that. No. I am not a reporter."

"For somebody not a reporter, you've got a hell of a lot of questions."

But that's why I am here, sir. To ask questions.

At Cardiff police headquarters Clare was told curtly that no one currently on the force had been there in January 1989. They'd all retired or moved away or died. Anything Clare wanted to know was "in the public record." She could find out for herself online or in the library. Their records didn't go back that far, the police chief told her, and even if they did, the records were not open to the general public. She'd have to get a court order—which wouldn't be worth her trouble, he could promise.

Clare was shocked. The police chief seemed to be sneering at her. Yet why would he sneer at *her*? She'd presented herself to him in the small Cardiff PD headquarters (in a municipal building that shared quarters with the township tax collector) as a Donegal relative from out of state, soft-spoken, well-groomed, gracious. She'd made her request quietly and unassumingly. Yes, she'd detected a sexual edge to the man's rudeness, a swaggering *maleness* that in more urban, urbane quarters would have seemed exaggerated, a comic macho cliché. She had not blundered into offending the man, she was sure. And yet . . .

As Clare was about to leave, the police chief relented. Telling her to get in contact with Hike Druitt. "He was on the case. He can tell you about it. If he's still compos mentis."

Clare has learned that Cardiff residents don't think much of the Cardiff PD. Small-town department in a part of Maine in which there is little crime, never a mass shooting. In 1989, the five-man department was totally unprepared for a "bloodbath" like the Donegal case. In a daze of horror, inexperienced officers tramped through the bloody crime scene. They'd missed one of the victims—a traumatized child hiding in a space beneath a sink so small that an adult man would have to squat to look into it, and wouldn't think to look. They'd misplaced or lost evidence. The suicide note was discovered, later lost, later discovered again, and (possibly) again lost. Forensics technicians did not come to the house for several days. No one succeeded in establishing the ownership of the revolver found beside Conor Donegal's body, reputedly stolen from a Bangor, Maine, resident, who'd had a permit for it, in 1986. (Was it even Conor Donegal's gun? Had anyone ever seen Conor with the gun or with any gun? Not even a rifle. No.)

"Temporary insanity—had to be. He was jealous, maybe. Of the wife. People said. She was damned good-looking—people said. He'd been drinking and something snapped, and—whatever happened, happened. Open-and-shut case—people said."

"Did you think so, sir? Open-and-shut—did you think that, too?"

"Well. I guess so. A man losing it, shooting his wife, his kids, himself—happens, sometimes. Up here. In the winter especially. Late winter."

Druitt pauses, remembering: "Also, he'd had money problems."

And: "Also, he'd left a note."

"A suicide note?"

"Left a note on the kitchen table, folded neat beneath yellow glass baby-chick salt and pepper shakers. Later, the note got lost—not my fault, but I remember what it was."

"What—what was it?"

"This kind of big block letter writing, like a child would do, capital letters: '*God forgive me. I will not forgive myself.*'"

Clare shudders. Was this her father's despairing voice?

"Was there a signature?"

"A signature? No. Just the letter *C.*"

"You said—the note got lost?"

"The actual note got lost, but I think there was a picture of it. I think—yes, there'd have to have been a picture. Photo. The downstairs of the house was all photographed, next day."

"Next day? Not that day?"

"Well—no. Nobody to take pictures in Cardiff. They'd had to send some officers over from Portland. Detective." Druitt utters the word *detective* in a derisory tone.

Clare leans over her notepad. Her eyes are filled with tears, not of sorrow but rage. "Sir, did you search the rest of the house? All of the house?"

"What kind of question's that? Of course! 'Course we did. Cellar, too. Garage."

"Did you look in closets? Beneath beds?"

Druitt makes a grunting noise, signaling displeasure. Clare is careful not to insult him and bring the interview to an abrupt end.

"Sir, just one more question. What did the medical examiner report?"

"Medical examiner? You mean, coroner?"

"For the township. A pathologist."

Druitt considers. He is breathing heavily, asthmatically. Portions of the story that don't include Lieutenant Hike Druitt fail to engage him, visibly. Clare can see, in the tilted shelf of his mind, shadowy objects about to fall off.

Then Druitt surprises Clare by suddenly laughing.

"That asshole! 'Open-and-shut case'—like hell."

Clare listens, transfixed. Not daring to interrupt.

". . . like, anybody could leave a suicide note. Anybody could place a gun by somebody's hand. Stage a crime. You see it on TV, but in actual life, in a place like Cardiff, there isn't the science. The resources. And if you have a suicide, you don't have to look for the perpetrator. You've got the perpetrator, he's *dead*."

Druitt pauses, grimacing. For a moment the lead-gray eyes shine with angry merriment.

"Asshole coroner was a junkie, in fact. Morphine. Some of us knew it at the time, and some of us didn't know. Me, I didn't actually know—at the time. But later, it came out."

"The coroner was a junkie? Morphine addict?"

"Even then, he wasn't fired. They let him resign, stayed on the payroll until he could get his pension."

"The coroner's findings weren't contested? After—after this came out?"

"It never *came out*. Never got into the news. In a damn small town like this, you mostly keep quiet. Police chief, scared of his own shadow. Anything that kept a lid on things, kept things quiet. The mayor of Cardiff never asked questions—what they call 'oversight' these days. On the force, any one of us could be fired, anytime. Nothing like in a big city where the union has guts. Still, if you grew up here, you wanted to live here, so there's that. You learn young not to get in each other's way."

"No one in the Donegal family contested the verdict?"

"Verdict—I don't know. Maybe not. Maybe they did. *Me*, I had to take sick leave. My guts just turned to water, like. Like dysentery you get traveling to Mexico. Bad headaches, too. Seeing what I saw, stepping into that hellhole. Christ! I stopped reading about it. Anything came on TV, I'd walk out of the room. Why I took early retirement."

Druitt speaks vehemently, breathlessly. He has become agitated. Clare fears he is overexciting himself.

She sees the anguish in his eyes. She sees that there are short, tough little quills on the elderly man's raddled jaws and neck. Wiry gray hairs in his nostrils, eyebrows. Like his hairless head, his hands are liver-spotted, bruised. The nails are discolored. Ravaged now, a wreck of a man, at one time Hike Druitt had been an attractive man, you could see—a woman had loved him, at least.

Clare feels a surge of sympathy. His *maleness*, so broken, vulnerable before her.

Surprising Druitt, and herself, by coming to stand before him, daring to take his hands in hers. They feel clammy, boneless. "Lieutenant Druitt, thank you! Thank you for agreeing to speak with me." She leans over the astonished man in his wheelchair, gripping his fleshy, liver-spotted hands in hers, squeezing his hands warmly, as a daughter might do.

Druitt is so taken by surprise, he can't react quickly enough to retain Clare's hands in his, as he'd have liked to do, can't prevent her from easing gently away from him in virtually the next moment.

He protests, pleading, "Are you leaving? You aren't leaving—are you? What'd you say your name is? D'you want a beer? Jesus, I could use a beer . . ."

Druitt's excited voice draws the vigilant daughter-in-law, his caretaker, inside; presumably she has been eavesdropping outside the door all this while. She glares at Clare with the look of one personally betrayed. "Excuse me! Time's up. I told you not to excite him—he isn't well, you'll have to leave *now*. I'll show you out."

Druitt doesn't shrink meekly before the incensed woman, but turns upon her with a look of fury. Protests *no*. Goddamn, there's nothing wrong with him, he doesn't want his visitor to leave yet, he has "fucking more" to tell her.

"Dad, she's going. Just stop!"

"*You* stop. Mind your own damn fucking business, you!"

Flush-faced, the daughter-in-law ignores Druitt, pushes Clare out of the room. Back into a narrow hallway, to a door, blinding dull-bright air—"Goodbye! If he has an asthma attack, if he starts to wheeze and choke, you're to blame . . ."

Clare apologizes, feeling sincerely guilty, ashamed. She has taken advantage of an elderly man, just as she'd been warned against doing. Yet, she is feeling triumphant, almost giddy.

Though she is also very tired, dazed with tiredness. Weak-kneed in the chill April air that pierces the marrow of her bones like shards of glass. Behind her, the embittered woman is calling after her, cursing her, but when Clare turns to apologize another time, the door has been slammed shut.

No one there. The windows of the beige brick bungalow are blank, blind in daylight.

15.

Who is it? What?

That night, trying to sleep in the hard-mattressed bed in her room in the Donegal house. In a delirium of exhaustion, yet not able to sleep. For each time Clare sees herself descending, like a deep-sea diver, into inky-dark sleep, she is startled into wakefulness.

Where are you? Hello . . .

At last Clare sees herself daring to approach the slumped figure in the wheelchair. His face is a blur, perhaps it has become rotted, putrescent. Yet she is fascinated. Groping for his hands. Eager to grip his hands.

He lifts his head, reveals his ravaged face. Clare sees—*Father. Are you my father?*

Jolted awake, frightened. Too upset to sleep again until just before dawn. And maybe she doesn't sleep—at all—lying on her back on the horsehair mattress, hearing church bells (St. Cuthbert's?) tolling at a distance like a tolling of the dead.

Sitting up. Alone in the bed. (And where is the man in the wheelchair whose chilled hands she'd gripped? His breath had been foul with the foulness of the grave. Yet Clare had adored him.)

So it has been revealed, Clare thinks. Her father, Conor Donegal, was not the murderer. Someone else was the murderer.

Is the murderer. For surely he lives now, Clare thinks.

And why has no one realized until now?

16.

"But he didn't. He wasn't. It doesn't add up . . . He *couldn't have*."

Clare insists upon meeting with Lucius Fischer. But Lucius Fischer is not so enthusiastic about meeting with Clare.

Once he learns what she wants to discuss, which has nothing to do with the will or her inheritance, Fischer is stiffly reticent, impassive. He isn't rude, for Lucius Fischer is a gentleman, but he makes no comments as she speaks, and he does not ask questions.

"It's obvious—he has been maligned. Not only accused of killing his family, but he's a victim himself, and the real murderer has never been apprehended."

Fischer isn't meeting Clare's rapt gaze as he had the other morning, but he is courteous enough to indicate to her that yes, he is listening.

"The police never looked for anyone else. They didn't seem to care if the 'crime scene' was staged. I spoke with one of the police officers—Lieutenant Druitt. That's what he says. That's what he *thinks*."

Lucius nods, though not in agreement. Just to indicate—he is listening.

125

Clare speaks at some length, trying to keep her voice from trembling. She tells him that Druitt had told her that the county coroner at the time was a morphine addict—not to be trusted; the Cardiff Police Department hadn't the experience to deal with such a crime; there was no "oversight" from local authorities.

Open-and-shut—Conor Donegal killed his family, and himself —the easiest verdict.

By this time, the hellhole in the house on Post Road has become so vivid to Clare, she begins to think that she has seen it. Then she realizes, *of course she has seen it.*

At least she'd seen the interior of the house before it was a crime scene. She'd seen it as a child, a small child, with the eyes of a child that are both seeing and "blind"—for the child brain is blind, lacking the requisite language to comprehend what is revealed to it.

All this she tries to explain to Lucius Fischer. It is frustrating to her, maddening, yet she must bear it that Fischer doesn't respond to the extraordinary things she is telling him, as she would expect him to do; she sees that he is gravely frowning, and he does not lift his eyes to hers.

She tells him, in an aggrieved voice, that she has not been able to contact the Thrush family. They have refused to speak with her because they consider her a "Donegal." She'd realized too late, she should have introduced herself as Kathryn Thrush's daughter.

"Do you think you could help me, Mr. Fischer? If you were to call someone in the family . . . Explain the situation . . ."

Clare's voice trails off. She understands that the lawyer is not going to help. Though he appears sympathetic with her, as one might sympathize with a sick person, reluctant to speak of the sickness out of kindness, or cowardice.

Clare is thinking that she is so alone.

Realizing that she has never seen a photograph of herself at the age she'd died—two years, nine months.

That is, she has never seen a photograph of herself before that age. She has seen cherished snapshots taken by her (adoptive) parents in St. Paul after she'd come to live with them, but she has never seen pictures of Clare Ellen Donegal. She wonders—do any exist?

A picture of herself in her mother's arms, as a baby. Just one! Herself as a baby, in Daddy's arms.

"Ms. Seidel? Excuse me? Is something wrong?" Lucius is looking at her now, concerned.

Clare has been rubbing at her eyes. First with her fingertips, then more forcefully with her fists. It isn't that she is crying— though her eyes may be damp with tears—but she is overcome by a powerful urge to clear her vision, that she might see what it is she cannot seem to see, or to recall.

Quickly she assures Fischer that she is all right. It is always her first impulse—to assure others that she is all right, not to alarm or inconvenience them. Especially if they are male, she does not want their pity, disapproval, disgust.

"I can see that you're upset, Ms. Seidel—Clare. You may be exhausting yourself here in Cardiff. No matter what people have been telling you, repeating rumors and gossip after twenty-seven years, it isn't likely that after so long, anything could be done to reopen a case—unless there was actual evidence that had been mislaid, and found. I can only advise you, it's hopeless."

"No. I don't believe that. How can it be hopeless—is the truth *hopeless*? How can it be too late to clear Conor Donegal's name?

Too late for justice?" Clare speaks bravely, but her voice has begun to quaver.

And what will you do? Exhume corpses? Resurrect the dead? Clare seems to hear a sneering voice close in the room with her.

Lucius Fischer isn't sneering at Clare. But he isn't agreeing with her, either.

Indeed, Fischer is looking wary, cautious. As if he fears that in another moment his distraught visitor will ask him for legal help in her quest.

"Oh! You are on their side, I can see. You aren't even listening."

"Of course I'm listening, Clare. But—I have no idea what you mean by 'on their side.' Whose side?"

"The side of the murderer! The side of the people who don't give a damn that an innocent man was blamed."

In his restrained, gentlemanly way, Lucius Fischer winces. But doesn't deny the truth of what Clare has said.

Clare is furious at the man, her only friend in Cardiff. Knowing that she should be grateful that he'd agreed to meet with her at all. He'd been pointedly kind to her, patient. Hadn't he directed his receptionist to squeeze her into his crowded schedule that day, as the receptionist has made clear to Clare. Now it's three fifty-five p.m., and there is a (paying) client waiting in the outer office with an appointment at four.

"Well. I'm sorry that you feel that way, Clare. It's very distressing to hear."

Fischer accompanies Clare to the door of the outer office and into the corridor outside, to the elevator, where he presses the down button. Clare wonders if he wants to make sure that she is actually leaving, and not intending to linger in the corridor outside his office; or whether he feels genuine concern for her.

No doubt, both. Clare can see through tear-dimmed eyes that Fischer wants to say something further to her, but hesitates.

In that instant she hates him, as one who has betrayed her.

As if, in another lifetime, Lucius Fischer was meant to be Clare's close, intimate friend—her guide to the lost world of her childhood. As if he'd been meant to love her as a daughter.

The elevator arrives. A lifesaver.

Awkwardly, Fischer settles for shaking Clare's hand.

"Well! Goodbye, Clare—Miss Seidel. If there's anything that I can . . ." He begins to recite these perfunctory words, with their air of feigned sincerity, then realizes what he is saying, and the words trail off into embarrassed silence.

Politely Clare says, "Thank you, Mr. Fischer. But I don't think so."

17.

The great-aunts stare at Clare in astonishment and dismay. So agitated by what she has told them, they can barely stammer.

"Why, Clare—why would you say such a thing—"

"—*think such a thing*—"

"—did *he* put you up to it—"

"—Luke Fischer?—how dare he!"

The great-aunts exchange glances as Clare shakes her head adamantly *no*.

"Then—who?"

"—could be so cruel, after—"

"—so many years dredging up—"

"—terrible, tragic past—"

"We have learned to accept—"

"We have learned to *endure*—"

"It is finished now. It is *all over*. Twenty-seven years—"

"—no point in dredging up—"

"—the terrible, tragic past."

Like parrots, the great-aunts repeat their shrill, stammered words. Clutching at each other's hands like frightened children. Clare is surprised by their reaction to her question, which seems to her a plausible one: Why did everyone assume that her father killed his family and himself? Why did no one investigate the shootings more closely? *Open-and-shut*—why was this judgment made so quickly?

Almost, Clare relents her excited words. Elspeth and Morag are looking ill.

"I'm sorry, Aunt Elspeth—Aunt Morag. It's just that for the past few days I've been talking to people who knew my parents, who didn't—don't—believe that my father did the terrible things he's been accused of doing. We must try to reopen the case . . ."

Elspeth stares at Clare in disbelief, pressing a skeletal-thin hand against her chest; Morag shakes her head grimly.

"No, no! Reopen the case—"

"—after twenty-seven years . . ."

"The media will pounce—as they did last time—"

"Vicious, wild beasts—"

"Shame! Shame! Cannot bear it—"

"Our poor dear sister Maude—never recovered . . ."

"Poor Leland—never recovered . . ."

"He'd left a note—you know . . . Your father."

"—that's to say—a note *was left* . . ."

"What on earth d'you mean—a note was *left*—"

"A note was *left*—exactly what I said. "

"What, are you insane too?—*you*—"

"*You* shut up. *You* are not Maude."

"Well, *you* are certainly not Maude . . ."

"A terrible, terrible idea—"

"—media would devour our bones—"

"—no point in dredging up—"

"—terrible, tragic past."

Clare lets the sisters protest like excitable birds, but she isn't going to be deflected by them. Like a driver gripping a steering wheel, she is determined not to relinquish control.

She tells them about Lieutenant Druitt. Called to the house on Post Road, one of the officers who discovered the crime scene. "Druitt doesn't think it was ever really proved, that Conor Donegal was the killer. He told me that the county coroner wasn't to be trusted . . ."

Elspeth is wiping at her eyes with a white linen handkerchief edged in lace. Carefully, one tear-glittering crafty eye, then the other. She is making a concerted effort to recover from her shock and to regain her air of insouciant authority even as Morag continues to shake her head in disbelief.

"Leave things as they are! We have suffered enough."

"All of us—"

"Him, too—"

"Him, most of all—"

"The brother, who'd *seen*—whose life was altered . . ."

". . . stopped the poor boy from trying to kill himself upstairs . . ."

"After that terrible accident on the highway—"

"'Neurological deficit'—permanent."

"So distraught, so *sad*. Like he'd lost his soul."

"Of course he'd lost his soul!—wouldn't *you*?"

"Tried to hang himself. We cut him down."

"We? What d'you mean 'we,' Elspeth? These hands."

Grinning, Morag brandishes her hands with pride, like a triumphant boxer.

* * *

In this way, Clare learns that her father's younger brother, Gerard, suffered a collapse—"not just 'nervous' but 'physical' too"—shortly after having discovered the bodies in the house on Post Road. He dropped out of the seminary, he had an accident on the highway— "skidded his car on black ice, slammed into a retaining wall"—was incapacitated in a hospital for months, then attempted suicide by hanging himself once he was back home. "Except poor Gerard wasn't really strong enough. He'd lost weight, he looked like a scarecrow. He couldn't tie the knot tight enough for the noose—his hands were too weak. You know, there is a hangman's knot—it's tricky. He wasn't up to it."

18.

"*He* is the murderer. Gerard. They know, and they keep the family secret."

So long has Clare been transfixed by sorrow, it is thrilling to her now to be transfixed by rage.

More reasonably, she supposes, of course the great-aunts can't *know*. But they must have suspected, at the time. As others must have suspected. Yet—

"No one cared enough. 'Open-and-shut.' An act so terrible it will never be repeated. And Gerard is a broken man. Maybe he will kill himself—no danger. They think."

In her room at the top of the stairs Clare paces in a trance of emotion, conviction. Her brain is ablaze!—lightly she strikes her thighs with her fists, yet not so lightly (she will discover hours later) that there will not be bruises.

Reopen the case. Clear Conor Donegal's name.

Resurrect the dead.

Clare has come to realize that she was summoned to Cardiff, Maine, not by chance, but by design: it will fall to her, and to her alone, to redeem her father's name.

Then she realizes, *My grandmother Maude Donegal was the one to summon me. Remembering me in her will . . .*

Conor Donegal's mother would certainly have understood—probably suspected—that he might not have been the murderer of his family.

Yet if Maude suspected that her younger son, Gerard, was the murderer, in her desperation she might have wished to protect him—as families do in such circumstances.

The loss of one child is a catastrophe. The loss of two children, unspeakable.

This is the reasoning of the great-aunts, Clare supposes. Not that they would defend Gerard as a murderer (she would guess), but rather, they have no wish to consider that anyone except Conor was responsible. And Maude Donegal would have felt the same way. Devastated by loss. Confused, grieving. Maude Donegal couldn't have been thinking clearly back in 1989—none of the family would have been thinking clearly in the aftermath of such tragedy.

How plausible this seems to Clare as she paces in her room, alone, shivering with excitement, brain ablaze.

19.

Since she'd first been introduced to Gerard Donegal the previous week, Clare has scarcely caught a glimpse of him in the house.

Her father's younger brother. *Her* uncle.

How strange it is, how uncanny!—to have met a blood relative, her father's brother, unknown to Clare, as Clare has been unknown to him.

Gerard's living quarters are on the third floor, Clare has been told. Several times she has stood at the foot of the stairs to the third floor, head inclined, trying to hear—something . . . A murmur of voices from above? A single, pleading voice? Muffled laughter, footsteps? She is certain that she has heard faint music through the ceiling: something rapid and scintillating, like harpsichord music. Another, more solemn rhythmic sound: Gregorian chant? Standing by the stairs, gazing up, Clare has imagined encountering her uncle as he descends the stairs rapidly.

Hello, Gerard!—it's me, Clare . . .

Gerard, hi! Remember, we met last week . . .

Ridiculous fantasizing, as if Gerard wouldn't recall her, still less her name. Of course the great-aunts would have been talking about her to him, preparing him to meet her as well as tormenting him.

Gerard!—here is your niece. Conor's daughter.

You remember—Conor . . .

More than once Clare has nearly encountered Gerard in the house, as he exited limping by a rear door. She wonders if he has been avoiding her even as she has been seeking him out . . . Before she'd understood his role in the murders.

She'd escaped him, hiding beneath the kitchen sink. Gradually the memory has been returning to her, as sight might return to one who has been temporarily blinded by illness or trauma. Soon she will *see again* what she has not seen in twenty-seven years.

Hello, Gerard! You remember me—Clare Ellen.

But he will not face her. Cannot. Now Clare understands why, when they'd first met and Clare greeted him with a smile, Gerard had stiffened and looked away.

Of course you remember me, Uncle Gerard. The child you failed to kill.

He'd wanted to kill himself, it seemed. A pity, Clare thinks, that he hadn't succeeded.

Since arriving in Cardiff, Clare has several times asked Elspeth and Morag if there are family photo albums she might examine. How badly she wants to see photographs of her young parents, her brother and her sister, and herself.

Evasively the great-aunts have said yes, they thought there might be photo albums somewhere in the house; their sister Maude must have kept albums of her children and her grandchildren; possibly these were hidden away in the attic after the tragedy. But neither of the great-aunts seems to have looked for the albums, nor have they been enthusiastic about Clare's offer to look for them herself.

"Oh!—oh dear, *no*—"

"—not in that attic!—why, you'd get *lost*."

"It's vast. It's a Sargasso Sea. It's—"

"—*not recommended*, dear. Truly!"

"We will find the albums for you—"

"—we promise!"

Exchanging sly glances, as if humoring their anxious niece even as they assured her that yes, soon—"tomorrow!"—they would look for the albums.

Clare supposes that the Thrush family would be in possession of photographs, too. Maybe all the children's pictures are in their possession, as they'd taken custody of Clare Ellen after the shootings. But Clare can't seem to make contact with the Thrushes, who resent her as a Donegal relative.

It isn't too late, Clare thinks. Soon she will contact the Thrushes again.

At the foot of the stairs to the third floor, she stands indecisively. The attic would be accessible from the third floor, presumably. She could look for the missing albums in the attic. That would be a very plausible reason for prowling about on the third floor.

The mysterious sounds seem to have abated. Clare remembers that Gerard isn't home. She'd seen him drive away in his pickup truck that morning. Gerard Donegal has become a manual laborer, clearing away winter debris, preparing neighbors' lawns for spring mulching. Once a seminarian intent upon serving God, since the deaths of his brother and his brother's family Gerard has become another kind of servant, one who abases himself, groveling in dirt.

Impulsively Clare climbs the stairs to the third floor. Since arriving in Cardiff she has begun to behave in ways not typical of

Clare Seidel, who has always been watchful, cautious, measured, premeditated. This Clare moves impulsively, speaks spontaneously, sometimes stammering with emotion—as in her outburst at Lucius Fischer. She discovers spittle on her lips, she laughs unexpectedly. Staring at the great-aunts, she has more than once discerned the elderly women's hairless skulls, the ghostly X-rays of their skeletons. Glimpsing the "bachelor uncle" Gerard, she has seen the ropy-blue artery in the man's neck—is it the carotid?

Clare notes that the stairs she is climbing are not carpeted like other stairs in the grand old house. The hallway ceiling on the third floor is lower than ceilings elsewhere, the wall lights dimmer, more antiquated. There is a smell of mildew, subtle rot.

Servants' quarters, Clare thinks. Gerard prefers to live here.

But why didn't you bring a knife?

A knife. Easily, Clare could have found a knife in the kitchen downstairs.

Surely she should be armed prowling the third floor of the Donegal house. If her uncle Gerard is a psychotic murderer, certainly she should be armed.

But it's too far to go, two flights of stairs down. Clare might encounter sharp-eyed Elspeth or mordant-minded Morag, who would be suspicious discovering their houseguest in the kitchen.

Next time, Clare thinks. She will arm herself.

Reasoning that she isn't in any real danger here. Not just yet.

For Gerard doesn't know what Clare knows. Gerard doesn't know that Clare knows.

Cautiously she makes her way along the corridor. Trying doors.

The first door is unlocked, opening into an empty room— small, cramped, with a single square window, bare floorboards. The second door opens as well—another small room, unfurnished and smelling of dust, cobwebs.

A third door, and a fourth—more dust, cobwebs.

Servants' quarters in another era. Clare imagines that in each of these cell-size rooms a woman lived out her life.

She has nearly forgotten what she seeks. Steps to the attic? A trapdoor in the ceiling, a ladder to pull down?

Her hand turns another doorknob, but this door is locked.

Gerard's room! More specifically, a suite of rooms. Clare recalls Elspeth remarking drily that she and Morag are not welcome in their nephew's part of the house.

Clare turns the doorknob deliberately, rattles it.

"Hello? Hel-lo?" She dares to raise her voice, as a reckless child might do.

But there is no response of course. Gerard is nowhere near—she is certain.

Yet she tries the doorknob another time. Emphatically rattling it.

"It's me, Uncle Gerard. Aren't you waiting for me?" Clare dares to laugh.

Presses her ear against the door. She recalls that one of Gerard's ears is mangled—in the car crash no doubt. A cascade of fine, near-invisible scars across his forehead like slivers of glass.

Yes, Clare hears something within. Rapid-thrumming sound, barely audible.

Beat beat beat—what is it?

20.

"Oh, but Clare—you can't go *alone*, you know! You will be lost—"
    "—in all those gravestones, and mausoleums, you will need—"
    "—guides!—*us*."

But Clare manages to elude the great-aunts with an excuse that she will be waking very early, can't sleep beyond six a.m., will drive to St. Cuthbert's cemetery by herself, doesn't want to bother them.

There, she discovers that her family has been split between two distinct parts of the cemetery: the Donegals in the oldest section immediately behind the church, where grave markers date as far back as 1779 and the trees are towering, ancient elms; the Thrushes in a newer section on a scarified hill, where the trees are much smaller and sparser.

Many more Donegals in the cemetery than Thrushes, Clare notes. Larger markers, stone angels, Celtic crosses. A sandstone mausoleum shaped like a Quonset hut, housing the remains of the patriarch Albert James Donegal, 1801–1886; his wife, Catherine; and nine children, most of whom died very young.

Clare locates a large marble gravestone shared by Leland Ellis Donegal and Maude Mary Donegal, with smaller gravestones flanking it, including that of Conor Matthew Donegal, August 2, 1955–January 6, 1989.

It's a shock, seeing this (small) marker. Should not Conor Donegal's grave marker be much larger, and the carved words on it much larger, as it towers like a totem in her imagination? She feels a sensation of faintness, despair.

Of course, your father has been dead all along. You are such a fool.

Amazing how many times she has been surprised, even shocked, by the revelation that her parents are no longer living. A fantasy since childhood, that they might be reunited . . .

Since Lucius Fischer's telephone call to Clare in Bryn Mawr, the conviction had become stronger. Though irrational, absurd. As Clare knows.

As if the stubborn and defiant child-self were pushing through the composed adult mask.

Another strange development: since coming to Cardiff, Clare has given her adoptive parents virtually no thought, as if they have ceased to exist, far away in St. Paul, Minnesota, as in another life-time. As if her life as Clare Seidel has come to an end.

She has given virtually no thought to her residency in Bryn Mawr. The research in the museum archives that has occupied most of her waking hours for years. Her several friends there. How close she'd come to an intimate encounter with—Joshua Matthius? A fellow historian at the Bryn Mawr Institute.

You might have fallen in love with Joshua. He might have fallen in love with you. What have you done, throwing your life away for an inheritance in Maine!

Clare feels only mild regret, her lost lives radiating from her like a spider's broken web, irremediable.

She has been taking pictures with her iPhone. Close-up, medium-close, at a little distance. To establish context, pictures of the Donegal cemetery compound. Pictures of the sky. (Cavernous clouds, into which one might fall and fall.) What seems wrong about her father's grave is that it isn't freshly dug, as (somehow) she'd expected, but weatherworn, covered with flattened winter-bleached grass. Indistinguishable from other graves. A uniformity of graves. The notorious name—CONOR DONEGAL. Yet here, in this place of stillness and silence, in which the only sounds are the cries of birds and a liquidy soughing of wind in the trees, the name Conor Donegal evokes no more outrage than the names on surrounding markers.

Death, the great leveler.

Death, cruelest of jokes.

For a long time Clare lingers at her father's grave. If she were religious, perhaps she would kneel in the matted grass, hide her face, pray . . . But the catastrophe is long past, twenty-seven years.

Pray for yourself now. You are the one who survived.

Clare tramps through the sodden cemetery in search of the Thrush compound. How much easier to have brought the great-aunts to guide her, but she shudders to think of it, the great-aunts' bright, stabbing chatter ruining the solitude of St. Cuthbert's cemetery.

The elderly women are well-intentioned, Clare thinks. Yet—sometimes—they terrify her.

Like Gerard. "Bachelor uncle."

With a jolt of the heart Clare discovers the graves of her mother, Kathryn; her brother, Laird; her sister, Emma. Beautiful sandstone markers within the Thrush compound, though their surnames are Donegal.

Evidently the Thrushes had refused to allow Kathryn and the children to be buried in the Donegal plot. Believing that Conor had slaughtered them, naturally Kathryn's family wanted to claim them as their own. Clare can understand this. Still, if Conor was innocent . . .

In death as in life, injustice.

The earliest Thrush burials were in the first decade of the 1900s, the more recent just a few years ago. Again, Clare finds herself surprised that her family's grave sites are clearly old, weathered.

KATHRYN THRUSH DONEGAL, FEBRUARY 8, 1958–JANUARY 6, 1989

LAIRD JOSEPH DONEGAL, SEPTEMBER 12, 1980–JANUARY 6, 1989

EMMA MARY DONEGAL, JULY 11, 1985–JANUARY 6, 1989

Why, her brother and her sister would be adults now! Older than Clare.

No longer children. As her mother, a beautiful young woman in photographs, would no longer be young; though, Clare wants to think, Kathryn might still be beautiful.

How long she stands before the graves, she won't recall afterward. She is shivering violently, stunned with grief. As if until now—well, she has not been *convinced*.

My mother. My brother.

My sister . . .

Overhead the sky is raw, turbulent. By the damp, chill smell of the earth you would guess the season to be late winter, not early spring. Yet small green shoots are visible here and there in the sodden soil. Those tiny white flowers called snowdrops. Birds are singing excitedly in the trees on all sides as if there is no death, no grief. Only hope.

Here here we are (again) here

Never doubt us, have faith, we will be beside you

Clare stands mesmerized, listening to the birds' cries. And to the silence beyond the cries. In this mysterious place, the name of which she can recall only with effort, *Cardiff, Maine,* it is permanently present tense. In such a state one cannot look ahead, one can only look behind. Something is about to happen—but when, and where? And how? Clare stands poised in anticipation. About to put one foot in front of the other, about to turn, to return, to (re)discover—what?

Seeing that her feet in running shoes are wet from the sodden earth.

Seeing someone, or something, a fleeting movement in the periphery of her vision . . .

But no, Clare turns and sees nothing. No one.

Unless—but no . . .

The cemetery is a lonely place at this hour of the morning. If there is another mourner, Clare doesn't wish to acknowledge him or her, nor does she wish to be acknowledged. Quickly she retraces her steps through the sodden cemetery.

Don't look at me please. Don't speak to me please. I am no one you know.

21.

"Your inheritance, Clare! You will want to see it." Elspeth gives Clare's hand a sharp little squeeze.

"But I could drive by myself, I think. I could find my way using the GPS . . ."

No, no! Not likely that Clare, *not a native of Ashford County*, could make her way alone.

The great-aunts have persisted. Drawing Gerard reluctantly into the discussion to confirm that the GPS in Clare's car would be useless in northern Ashford County: "The country roads twist and turn, there are bridges that have been out for years, you would only get lost."

Gerard speaks with an air of grim resignation, like one who is obliged to tell the truth though it is not in his own best interest. As if he feels, for all his air of detachment, a measure of sympathy for Clare.

"Yes. I could drive her. If that is your wish." Gerard speaks with clenched jaws, in a strangely stilted manner.

Not looking at Clare. As if there is something very bright, blinding, where she stands. He cannot risk his vision.

What an ugly man Gerard Donegal is! How he must have hated his brother, Conor. *A beauty in his daily life that makes me ugly.*

It has been some time since Clare has seen the bachelor uncle close up. He has been a shadowy presence in the house, a figure in the periphery of Clare's vision that might be a wraith or real; he has avoided her, tactfully, as he seems to avoid the great-aunts as much as he can.

"That's very kind of you, Gerard!"

"*Very* kind."

Clare is forced to smile, in agreement with the sisters. As Gerard glowers, shifts his shoulders self-consciously, frowns.

How like a disfigured priest Gerard looks, in a black T-shirt, loose like a surplice, dark trousers with soiled cuffs. His face is long, lean, gaunt, ascetic; his skin coarse-pitted, ashen; his jaws carelessly shaven, like the jaws of one who shaves without a mirror. One of his ears shows scar tissue. One of his shoulders is hunched.

Clare stares at the bachelor uncle in fascinated revulsion. She sees how, from time to time, he glances at her with his dark, damp, evasive eyes, and then quickly away.

He knows that I know his secret.

But no—how could he?

Why would Gerard agree to drive Clare into northern Ashford County when he so clearly doesn't want to? Why does he continue to live in the Donegal house with the great-aunts when he so clearly dislikes them? As if the man has surrendered his personality. His soul. As in an act of self-discipline, self-punishment. Penance.

Clare guesses that Gerard's life is a sequence of such acts of penance. He hates the elderly aunts but will do their bidding, if they insist; he hates his life, but will continue to endure it, if that is how things must be.

Of course! He is in Hell.

No. It won't really happen.

Clare cannot believe that she has acquiesced to the great-aunts' request. Clare cannot believe that she will be alone with the bachelor uncle. After twenty-seven years.

It will not. No!

Clare laughs, the possibility is so absurd.

Yet that night, in stealth, Clare makes her way downstairs into the kitchen of the Donegal house to select a knife, not the longest or sharpest of the knives she can find, but the most practical, durable, with a six-inch blade and a short handle. This she might wrap in a cloth and carry in a jacket pocket, if in fact she finds herself alone with Gerard Donegal . . .

22.

"Tell me. What you can."

Clare is not begging, but Clare is speaking urgently, as a needy child might speak. Hands clasped before her on her knees, tight enough to ache.

"Anything you can remember. Please."

Gerard behind the wheel, silent. In profile his expression is subdued, severe.

How strange it is, Clare seated beside the bachelor uncle after all. As she would not have believed, yet—here she is.

If this is happening, it must be fated.

In the stolid steel-colored Mercedes Gerard inherited from his now-deceased parents. Driving through early-morning Cardiff, across a bridge, into the hilly countryside beyond. The journey is unfolding like a dream, yet not a dream of Clare's own: like massed clouds overhead of varying hues of pebble-gray, metallic-gray, powder-gray, blown ragged and ravaged from the Atlantic Ocean several miles to the east.

"Because I don't remember anything. Almost anything . . ."

In Clare's jacket pocket, snug against her ribs and below her hard-beating heart, the kitchen knife wrapped in cloth.

* * *

He is driving Clare because it's his *duty*. As well as his penance.

Well—he feels sorry for her, too. The orphaned niece. Which is why he can scarcely force himself to glance at her, to acknowledge her.

A misshapen person, Clare has thought. And his soul misshapen, within.

Hadn't Gerard Donegal withheld emotion from Clare from the first? Refusing to embrace her as a normal uncle would have done?

She'd been wounded by him, then. Now she detests him as the enemy.

Yet he is behaving politely toward her. Now that they are alone together in his car, away from the distracting banter of the great-aunts, you might almost think that Gerard, despite his reticence, which may be a kind of shyness, is behaving in a friendly fashion.

That is, he is not hostile. He is not ignoring her.

As he is a careful driver, perhaps excessively cautious, like one who has survived an accident, Gerard scrupulously obeys the speed limit at all times. As when he is walking, Clare has noted, he limps just perceptibly to avoid the sudden pain he knows is lying in wait for him if he brashly missteps.

Clare asks him about the Jesuit seminary in Portland. Elspeth and Morag happened to mention that he'd been a seminarian at one time in his life . . . What sort of courses did he study at the seminary? How many years are required to become a Jesuit? Is it true, Jesuits all earn Ph.D.'s and most of them teach? Why did he drop out?

Clare is determined to ask questions of the sort that might plausibly be asked by a young female relative who doesn't know

Gerard well and wants to know him better. Naïve questions, naïvely aggressive, impulsive-seeming.

A guileless young woman, intimidated by the severity of her uncle's manner, hoping not to be discouraged by his habit of frowning reticence.

But Gerard merely shrugs, not to be drawn into an intimate conversation.

Feeling rebuffed but wishing not to acknowledge it, Clare says (not quite sincerely) that she'd had religious predilections when she was younger, too. Of course, she hadn't considered entering a convent.

Smiling at the inanity of the phrase—*entering a convent.*

Or—*taking the veil.*

She'd never been seriously religious. She doesn't think so. Something has been left out of her, a capacity for the naïve hopefulness of belief.

Maybe it occurred when she'd been given up for adoption. Or earlier, crouching to save her life in the spidery place beneath the sink.

Unperturbed, Gerard continues his careful driving along a two-lane state highway leading out of Cardiff.

Next Clare dares to ask him about an automobile accident he'd had, of which the aunts have spoken more than once. Had the accident involved just Gerard, or was another vehicle involved? Had anyone else been in his car? Were others hurt, too? And when was this?

At this, Gerard does glance in Clare's direction, as if mildly shocked by her audacity.

"I'm sorry. I can understand that you might not want to talk about it . . . I've narrowly escaped accidents myself. I've been lucky, I guess."

As if they were having an ordinary conversation, Clare goes on to tell the unresponsive Gerard that she'd once been driven by a friend in Chicago, the car hit a patch of black ice on Lake Shore Drive and began to skid . . . Clare shudders, recalling.

A genuine memory of Clare's, long-forgotten but surfacing now, as the glinting-gray Mercedes crosses a high bridge above a turbulent river, taking her and Gerard out of the city. And what an abrupt change—across the river, the city has virtually vanished.

Thinking of the skidding incident, treacherous black ice, Clare feels an ache of nostalgia for that lost time. She'd been in her mid-twenties. She'd been seeing a young man (physicist, Chicago) whom she'd imagined she might love, as he'd seemed to love her, or at any rate to feel strongly about her. Then the skid on black ice, a violent slam against a guardrail that miraculously did not shatter, flame-flicker of panic that they might die together. Clare Seidel and the young man whose name, a few years later, Clare scarcely recalls.

Yet now, in Gerard Donegal's stiff presence, it isn't so much the panic Clare recalls as a sensation of triumph, escape. *For she had not died.*

Not that time. And not the other.

Clare is feeling giddy; she had not slept well the previous night.

Anticipating the drive with Gerard Donegal. Alone in a vehicle with Gerard. Miles into the countryside of northern Ashford County.

In a trance of excitement, apprehension. Seeing again her fingers selecting the knife with the six-inch blade, short handle.

Seeing her fingers carefully wrapping the knife in a cloth to protect them from the bare knife blade in her pocket.

Of course Clare is not going to use the knife. Ridiculous!

Never in her life has she killed any living thing except (perhaps) insects. Flies, ants, beetles. Less frequently, spiders.

Once, she'd swatted a moth fluttering against a lamp shade. That had turned out to be a beautiful creature with elaborate patterned wings. Feeling sick about what she'd done in a moment of careless exasperation . . .

You can't, of course. How could you.

The knife in her pocket is her protection, Clare thinks. It is not a weapon that will leap from its hiding place, seeking revenge.

Minutes have passed. Gerard continues his careful driving now on a near-deserted state highway, headed north. Here are steep hills, rock-strewn gullies, tall firs, deciduous trees (ash, birch, chestnut) just beginning to bud. The massed clouds overhead are starting to break like shattered ice.

It's a beautiful, harsh landscape. But here and there are ravaged-looking spaces in which trees lay heaped on one another on the ground, as in the aftermath of an earthquake.

Clare asks Gerard what has happened here. As if inadvertently, she calls him Gerard.

Gerard. Clare has dared to speak the name.

"Winter. Storms," he replies tersely.

If her question is impersonal, Clare thinks, Gerard will reply to her.

"If I were to live here in Cardiff, by the sea, I think that another self would emerge in me. My soul."

Clare wonders if she has ever uttered the word *soul* aloud in such a context. She has never been one to speak in a sentimental way about such subjects.

She notes a stiffening of Gerard's shoulders, indicating that he is listening.

"You believe in the soul—do you?" she says. "If you'd wanted to be a priest . . ." Her voice trails off; she is uncertain what she is trying to say.

Does she mean to provoke her uncle, or does she mean to intrigue him? Is she hoping for both?

"It doesn't matter if we 'believe' in the soul," he says. "If we believe in God. The soul, which is in God, is *there*. Like the ocean, whether some fool believes in it or not."

Clare is astonished by Gerard's blunt remarks. She has never heard him speak at such length. His voice exudes derision, contempt. Yet she doesn't feel that it is derision or contempt directed at her specifically.

Haltingly she says that she has not thought much about such things. She is an art historian, she puts her faith in what can be seen.

"My parents—my adoptive parents—aren't religious. No one I know well is religious. But I suppose, if you think about it, the only thing that endures in us, over time, might be called the soul. The body's cells are supposedly replaced by new cells every seven years. But the soul abides."

The soul abides. Clare is struck by the novelty of such a declaration, from her.

Not wanting to think that she is hoping to make an impression upon Gerard Donegal. The murderer!

Though seeing the man now, at close quarters, Clare is not so certain. In fact, she is not at all certain that Gerard has been, or could be, a murderer . . .

She confides that she has been advised by some people to sell the property on Post Road—"My inheritance."

Gerard seems to be considering this disclosure. But he says nothing.

"The lawyer said that I didn't have to see it. I could place the property with a real estate agent in town, and spare myself. As soon as the probate court assigned me the title." Clare laughs unexpectedly. "But I didn't come so far to *spare myself.*"

This does seem to impress Gerard, she thinks.

In forty minutes he exits the state highway onto a one-lane asphalt road. Within a mile or two this road becomes badly potholed, turning back upon itself in a series of switchbacks, in the direction of the Atlantic Ocean.

Clare has been seeing road signs: Ashford County Road, Hiram Road, Post Road.

Her heart leaps—*Post Road.*

Here are pastures, cultivated fields. Grazing cattle. Horses. A farmhouse, outbuildings. In the Maine countryside most farmhouses are painted white, stark white. Clare wonders why, when white is the most vulnerable of hues. Perhaps it's defiance. Bravado.

She is becoming nervous. For they are approaching the house that is Clare's inheritance.

As if they'd just been discussing this subject and Clare hadn't asked her impetuous question miles back, Gerard says unexpectedly that he'd withdrawn from the seminary after he'd been badly injured in a car crash. He'd been hospitalized for weeks; he'd been in rehabilitation in Portland, learning to walk again, to coordinate his muscles, to think again.

Clare thinks, *Yes, I know.*

I know a lot about you.

Casually he remarks that he'd shattered a kneecap, broken a few ribs, scarred his face. There were neurological deficits, as brain damage is called. Does Clare know what *proprioception* is?

Vaguely Clare thinks that proprioception is a function of the brain that has to do with being in the body, identifying with one's body. "Like maintaining balance? Not falling down . . ."

"More or less. Yes. Knowing that you are *you*. If the brain is injured, sometimes you lose this sense. Proprioception—locating the soul within the body."

Gerard speaks with an odd sort of satisfaction, like one who is thinking, *What I deserved.*

As the Mercedes thumps along the potholed road, Clare is feeling a mounting sense of dread. She understands that they are nearing the house in which her family died on January 6, 1989. She can feel a gravitational pull, irresistible.

Gerard says, "The house is just ahead. Are you sure you want to see it?"

"Y-yes. I've come so far. I can't turn back."

"You could, you know. You—we—could turn back right now, Clare."

"No."

Clare sees overgrown fields, a partially collapsed hay barn, concrete-block silo. A two-story farmhouse with a lopsided front veranda, faded-gray clapboards, shutters. Gnarled vines have grown over part of the house like skeletal fingers, and the dirt driveway is badly eroded, impassable.

Gerard brakes the Mercedes to a stop in front of the house. Clare sits for a moment, staring, as if she has forgotten where she is, why she has wanted so badly to be here.

Hellhole. Never got over it. Jesus!—those children . . .

Silently Gerard switches off the ignition. Comes around to Clare's side of the car as if to help her out, but she has quickly climbed out of the car before he can assist her.

Recoiling from his touch. The possibility of his touch.

The house is locked, Gerard says. Of course, he has the key.

Key in Gerard's hand, for Clare to observe.

Like a magician who shows you that he has no tricks up his sleeve.

Clare follows him to the front door, her feet sinking in the soft, sodden earth. Rotted floorboards in the veranda, Gerard cautions her to avoid.

An outer door with a torn, rusted screen. An inner door, which Gerard unlocks.

"No one has ever lived here? Since—"

"—since then. No."

Clare is smiling, inanely. Taking note of the faded-white clapboard siding, a decayed bird's nest behind one of the shutters. Gerard has managed to unlock the door and push it open. He is taller than Clare by several inches, but his shoulders tend to stoop. There is something shrinking about him, appalled.

Hellhole. Can't turn back.

These words are so vivid to Clare, it seems to her that one of them, Gerard or herself, must have uttered them.

"You were here, weren't you. That day. Because you found the bodies—you called for help."

Is this an accusation? Clare stammers slightly; she means simply to be stating a fact.

Evasively Gerard murmurs what sounds like *yes*.

"You walked into the house and f-found them. I've read the accounts. That must have been a—a terrible sight . . ."

Terrible sight. Flat, dull, inadequate words Clare should be ashamed of uttering.

Such hollow words, Gerard doesn't trouble to respond.

Inside the house Clare feels as if she might faint, the smell is so strong—mildew, damp, rot. And a particular smell, of rain-sodden curtains, furniture, carpets.

Scattered about the floor, skeletons of small creatures that crack beneath Clare's feet.

Nothing looks familiar. Everything looks familiar.

Clare moves blindly. Gerard reaches for her arm to steady her—the floorboards beneath their feet are about to give way.

At his touch, his fingers gripping her arm through the sleeve of her jacket, Clare recoils.

She is trembling badly. Her voice quavers when she speaks. She is treading into forbidden territory now.

"What was the reason you came here—that day?"

Speaking to Gerard's back, for he is preceding her into the interior of the house.

"That day—why did you come out here? Why were you *here*?"

Though Clare knows, or should know. Numerous times she'd read of the Donegal family event, a christening at St. Cuthbert's Church, a midday brunch at the house on Acton Avenue, and Conor and Kathryn who were expected to come to Cardiff with their three young children, but did not come.

And no one answered the phone at the house on Post Road, though the number was repeatedly called.

"I drove out to the house because there was no one else. We knew—we thought—that something might have happened. Because Conor hadn't been—happy . . . I was the person who volunteered to drive out to the house, and that is the person I have been."

Gerard speaks flatly, simply. Clare is chilled by the equanimity of these words.

Cobwebs, scuttling spiders. As Clare enters the second room, something brushes against her hair and frantically, she thrusts it away.

"Why did God let what happened in this house happen? If your God is so loving."

Your God is a reproach. Clare intends that Gerard understands.

"God is not loving. The God of the Holy Bible cares nothing for love. Obedience, blind subservience—that is what God demands, not love. Jesus Christ was the risk-taker, a *provocateur.* God punished Jesus to put Him in his place."

Clare is astonished that anyone should speak as Gerard does, with such certitude. "And what place is that?"

"That Jesus suffered in his physical body, that Jesus was reduced to being just a man. *That* was the punishment."

They are standing in the doorway of another room. Clare feels a clutch of horror—*the kitchen.*

It is not familiar to her, yet it is. Her eyes glance about, seeing nothing she recalls, yet if she shuts her eyes, it is this room she recalls—scuttling in terror across the floor, crawling into the hiding place beneath the sink.

Clare is very clever. To prevent her teeth from chattering, she clenches her jaws tight. In a pose of calm curiosity, asking Gerard, "Did the killer mean to kill the little girl, or did he relent and let her live? Or had he forgotten she existed?"

Gerard winces at the question. Clare feels her heart pound in the excitement and dread of the hunt.

His back to Clare, Gerard is setting upright a chair that was overturned on the floor. With the pointless scrupulosity of one intent upon establishing order amid chaos, he positions the chair at the table, confronting three other chairs. Their cushions are torn and filthy, the Formica-topped table so thick with grime that its original color is undetectable. Beyond is a window with a cracked pane, a discolored kitchen sink stippled with insect husks.

"Did you know that I was hiding beneath the sink? Or—had you forgotten that I existed?"

It is the single question Clare has most wanted to ask.

"What do you mean?" Gerard asks. "When I came to the house to see—what was wrong?"

"Yes. When you came to the house."

"It was like opening the door of a blast furnace—stepping into the house when no one answered the door, calling 'Hello'—then seeing—what my eyes saw . . ."

His brain had gone blank, Clare supposes. He hadn't forgotten. He hadn't been thinking at all. *She*, beneath the sink, had ceased thinking as well.

He'd found the phone, Gerard continues. Like an automaton, he'd dialed 911.

Like an automaton, he'd lived the years that followed.

In a state of stupefaction. In a state of nullity. Brain blank—blasted clean. He would never remember what he'd said, done. He hadn't known, he hadn't realized—or seen—that the little boy, his nephew, Laird, was dead too, like the little girl Emma and the adults—Conor, Kathryn. He'd forgotten to look for Laird. As he'd forgotten to look for Clare.

Though he doesn't remember (he claims), he'd made the call, must have made the call. Stumbled out of the house and waited to hear sirens, outside in the driveway.

"I do remember, I didn't pray. I didn't address God. I understood—there was no God *there*. Like pushing open a door—and there's nothing there."

In Gerard's face, a crucifixion. Scarcely can he bring himself to look at her, as Clare is looking searchingly at him.

Clare listens, entranced. She understands that her uncle is telling the truth, as the truth has been revealed to him.

What is the clinical term—*temporary insanity.*

"We should leave now, Clare. You don't need to see more of the house."

Clare. She wonders when he has begun calling her by her name.

"Yes. I need to see more."

"I don't think so."

"I've come so far, I can't turn back now."

"Don't be ridiculous. You *can* turn back. We can."

Wanting to shout at him—*But you were the one! Not my father.*

Gerard stands hesitant, as if expecting Clare to obey him, to leave the house.

You! You're the one, with your hateful God.

Clare stoops to open the little door beneath the sink. The forbidden place, yet here it is—not forbidden at all. Twenty-seven years have passed, only weather has been perpetrated upon the (abandoned) (accursed) house.

Such a small, cramped space! Such a filthy space! Covering the floor, badly discolored, rotted paper. Aged Brillo pads, reduced to rust. Cloaking the drainpipes, spiderwebs as thick as gauze. You would not think a child could fit into such a space.

Even a terrified child, a child behaving with the instinct of a panicked rat, you would not think she could fit in such a cramped space, as you would not think that an adult woman, on her knees on the filthy floor, leaning her head and shoulders into that shadowy space, could push so far into it, cobwebs in her hair, in her eyelashes, gagging from the odor . . .

"Clare! What the hell are you doing!" Gerard pulls at her shoulder, shocked.

But Clare intends to refute Gerard. Confound Gerard. It is the profound fact of her life, *she has come so far.* Out of sheer perversity, pushing halfway beneath the sink, managing to make herself small, smaller, arms folded over her face, and her face hidden, heart swinging like a pendulum.

Curled and coiled in that filthy place like an infant not yet born. As if she is drifting, not in this cramped space beneath a sink, but in interstellar space.

If there is a God, perhaps He will have pity on her.

As at a distance, she hears the man calling her name, appalled and disbelieving—"*Clare! Clare Ellen!*"

*   *   *

In the dark, smelly place beneath the sink. Behind the drainpipes. She has made herself small enough to hide here.

Strands of a broken spider's web sticking to her skin. Her eyes wet with tears. Hunching her back like a little monkey. Arms closed tight around her knees raised against her small, flat chest.

She is just a little girl, small enough to save herself. Small enough to fit into the spider's web. Smart enough to know that she must not cry.

Must not breathe. So that no one can hear.

So that he *can't hear.*

*But the door to the hiding place is opened, she sees a man's feet, legs. She hears him calling her name—*Clare! *Out of her pocket she has taken the blunt compact knife, a razor-sharp blade she draws swiftly across the exposed throat. She is only protecting herself—it is the single act of a lifetime. At once blood spurts, vivid as color in a sepia print, serpentine, joyous, as the stricken man cries out in pain and terror and staggers away, clutching his throat.*

Much later, when she is strong enough, she rouses herself from a deathlike stupor. And when she crawls out of the hiding place and manages to stand upright, she sees the blood trail meandering and drunken across the filthy linoleum floor into an adjacent room and beyond. Following this, out of the house. And in a trance of fascination and horror, she follows the blood trail across a patch of muddy earth where puddles as sharp as knife blades glitter with sunshine. Beyond this, the ruined orchard where the trail will end.

23.

The man walking in the ruined orchard.

Long she has dreamed of the man walking in the ruined orchard. His back is to her, his face is hidden.

He is moving away from her. She will run after him, calling to him—*Wait! Wait for me.*

The pear orchard has been neglected for twenty-seven years, but not all the trees are dead—that is the surprise. And even those trees that appear to be partially dead are partially in blossom, misshapen boughs stippled with small white blossoms, like clumps of damp snow.

Stubborn, grim, piteous beauty. But beauty.

"Breathe. As deeply as you can."

He has walked her forcibly out of the house. He will see to it that she recovers in the open air.

He'd knelt in the kitchen and pulled her out of the cramped space beneath the sink. Half lifting her, ignoring her protests, deflecting her fists and her curses.

At the back of the house, Clare struggles to remain standing as strength dissolves in her legs like melting ice. Overhead the sky is glowering white, oppressive.

And her head, her brain in a delirium of emotion—it is all she can do, it requires the most enormous effort, to maintain consciousness.

Gerard stands a little apart, not touching her.

"Keep it up. Deeper. Oxygen to the brain."

Clare obeys. Tries to obey. She is determined to remain upright. It is humiliating to her that Gerard has had to steady her.

The air is fresh and cold and thrilling to inhale deep into her lungs.

About her, glittering mud puddles, splotched sunshine.

Gerard is scolding, as a relative might scold: "I told you. It wasn't necessary. Those old women put us up to it. You can sell the property without examining it. Anything you can get for it—sell. It's accursed—you must know that."

Accursed. A ridiculous word!

She does not believe in such antiquated words.

And *God*: of all words, the most antiquated and absurd.

"You! You with your hateful God."

Out of nowhere these words spring. Yet Gerard does not appear to be surprised.

"Clare, God isn't hate any more than God is love. God is what precedes hate and love."

"*You* killed them—did you?"

Gerard shakes his head curtly—*no.*

"Then—who did?"

"You know who did."

"No. I do not."

Clare's voice lifts in a childish scream. Raging, impotent. In a hallucination she sees herself rushing at the man, stabbing at his head, his face, a six-inch blade to the heart . . .

She has been hearing a curious wheezing noise close about her head. At first she thinks it must be a large insect, a moth beating frenzied wings. Then she thinks it must be wind in the trees, though the pear trees in the orchard are stunted and have virtually no leaves so early in the season.

"That's you. Your breathing. Hyperventilating. Try to calm down."

Clare tries. Filling her lungs slowly with air. Careful, cautious.

She stands at the edge of a precipice—does she? Madness.

(The knife in her pocket, still. Wrapped in a cloth. She has forgotten it, or nearly. Yet the knife remains close against her rib cage, beneath her heart.)

By slow degrees Clare's strength returns. She can almost feel strength rising through her body, an impersonal force from the sodden earth. And how startling to her, a marvel, how her feet are firm again on the earth.

The man she fears and despises has helped her regain her balance.

Proprioception.

With a measure of caution and disapproval, Gerard regards Clare as one might regard a bright-feathered bird with a savage, unpredictable beak. She wants to laugh in derision: her behavior in the house was genuinely shocking to her uncle. Her remarks, her accusations —deeply wounding, unfathomable to a former seminarian.

He has touched me. My body, his hands. Try to forget that!

"You're upset, Clare. You don't know what you've been saying. It was a very poor idea, coming out here. It was never my idea. My advice is, file your claim in probate court, make an arrangement with a real estate agency in Cardiff, and go home. I can help with the transaction. You don't need to stay in Cardiff. This isn't a place for you."

Clare wants to protest angrily, *But this is my place. I want to live here.*

"Unless you're thinking you want to move here. Live here. Fix up the abandoned house. Is that what you're thinking?"

"N-no. Of course not."

"The house is not redeemable. Who would want to live here, where people have died? I told my mother not to hang on to it—to sell it or give it away. Especially, not to leave it to you in her will."

But then I would not be here. I would not know all that I know.

Seeing the expression in Clare's face, Gerard relents.

"It's beautiful here, yes. The countryside. Your parents were drawn here at the wrong time in their lives. You don't need to repeat that. And don't let my aunts talk you into living with *them.* They would devour you alive."

"Why do you live with them, then?"

"Because they need me. As my mother needed me."

"And that's enough to give up your life, for them?"

"There isn't much life to give up. Frankly."

Clare is astonished to be speaking so openly with her usually sullen-faced uncle. The two have been walking behind the house, scarcely aware of their surroundings, in the general direction of the ruined orchard.

Five acres of pear trees, Clare has been told. Never very prosperous and now badly neglected.

Accursed. Yet this is Clare's inheritance.

She will not sell the property, Clare thinks. But she will not live here. Not alone. Not *here*.

She will not live with the great-aunts either. But she may remain in Cardiff. For a while.

She sees that Gerard is limping. She feels a powerful wave of pity for him, the afflicted man, and regrets that she has hated him and wished him dead.

She thinks, *He is the one. With his hateful God, he will need solace.*

24.

A rain-lashed April morning after a night of rain-lashed dreams.

Phone rings: Who can be calling?

It's the phone, not Clare's cell phone, but the landline, which Clare rarely uses and has come to disdain as a vehicle for telemarketers, robot calls.

If it were her cell phone, of course she would be prepared to answer. Intimate as a stent in her brain, Clare's cell phone.

But this is the other phone. The old phone. A fixture in the (rented) duplex on Abington Street, Bryn Mawr. Out of curiosity, or loneliness, or heedlessness, Clare is about to lift the receiver when she sees that the caller ID isn't one she recognizes.

That evening, she will be meeting a friend in Philadelphia. A man whom she doesn't know well, for whom she has felt an unmistakable stirring of sexual desire, yet also apprehension, even dread. She is not certain that she wants to dismiss a friend, and risk a lover. A one-way transaction she has regretted in the past.

It isn't this person who is calling Clare, she sees. *L. Fischer*—no one she knows.

She deliberates: Should she answer the call?

Rain pelts against the windows of wherever this is. Clare Seidel is living at the present/fleeting time. A delirium of raindrops, like spiderwebs, sliding down the panes.

Should she answer?

Clare feels a jolt of joy suddenly, a shot of heroin to the heart that (she guesses: she has not yet had the experience) either transports you to paradise or slams you to the floor, dead.

MIAO DAO

1.

Like a crazed bat careening at her face. Couldn't duck in time.

As carefully her mother said, "It has nothing to do with you, Mia."

Pausing then. Drawing a shaky breath. For Momma had been locked away in the bedroom much of the day while Mia was in school, all that rainy afternoon locked away, drinking dark wine that stained her teeth and turned her breath sweet, and now her words were slurred. Mia had to lean forward to hear while trying not—trying so hard—not to smell Momma's breath.

Repeating: "Nothing at all to do with you."

So that Mia thought—*Nothing. Me.*

The news was stunning. Like walking on a floor that begins to shift and slide.

Her father (who'd been away for twelve days, traveling on business, she'd been told) was moving permanently out of the house, moving out of the family. *But why?*

Evasively her mother said, "Your father needs to be by himself right now. He will explain to you in person . . ."

But Daddy was not here to explain. Mia had not seen Daddy for almost two weeks, and even then, on the last day, he'd returned home late from work and missed dinner and had seemed distracted when Mia tried to tell him about a project she was doing for her social studies course on "indigenous tribes" who'd once lived in the Allegheny Valley. *Shouldn't you be in bed, sweetie? What the hell time is it?*

Unmistakable look of guilt, impatience. The look in a man's eyes of wishing very badly to be elsewhere.

Up too late, don't you have school tomorrow? Sure you do!

Wanting to object, she wasn't a *silly little girl*. She was twelve, and mature for her age. (Everyone said.)

And a smart girl—one of the smartest and most perceptive students in seventh grade, though (oddly) Mia had somehow failed to perceive, unless she'd perceived but chose not to acknowledge, that Daddy had moved his things from the big upstairs bedroom into the "guest room" at the rear of the house, with its own door leading outside.

When had Daddy moved into the guest room?—truly Mia could not have said.

As she hadn't seemed to notice, Daddy's coats and jackets had been gradually disappearing from the front closet. Well, possibly Mia's eyes had perceived that there was beginning to be more space in the closet, but her brain, no. Not exactly.

"Married too soon. A mistake."

The mother could not help herself, such words escaped her lips like deranged bats. Even as her hands fluttered about Mia as if to shield her. Grip her tight.

The calm, still, stony voice came to Mia frequently: *You are the reason they married too soon. You are the mistake.*

You are the reason Daddy is moving away.

* * *

"Don't think of *him*. Think of *us*."

Brightly and resolutely Mia's mother spoke. For there were the younger children to console—Mia's little brothers.

Neither Randy nor Kevin seemed to understand that Daddy was *gone*. Exasperating that, though they'd been told, and Daddy himself had tried to explain to them, Daddy was not coming back.

Stunned, slow-blinking. Sniveling, snuffling. Then bawling, throwing tantrums. Kicking the sofa. Stomping on the stairs.

Oh, Mia felt sorry for the boys!—but avoided them.

She was twelve, almost an adult. (She believed.) Runny-nosed little brats of six and four were far below her radar.

At least Mia had her own room and could shut her door (if not lock it). Randy and Kevin shared a room. Through the wall she could hear them chattering and squabbling nonstop, like small rodents.

"Try to be nice to your brothers, Mia. Daddy leaving us is very hard on them."

Mia stiffened, hurt. But did not protest. *Hard on—them? What about me?*

Resolving that she would never trust her mother again. For her mother did not care about *her*.

Still, Mia and her mother prepared meals together. The kitchen was the bright-lit place. Warmth emanated from the pumpkin-colored counters, the russet-red Mexican tile floor. Warmth from overhead lights. Shining copper pans on display, her father's expensive Japanese knives. Bright-colored plates from Italy, glittering stemware visible through the glass panes of cupboard doors.

"Married too soon. You came too soon."

The mother often spoke in a dazed voice. As if she were alone and the daughter not close beside her.

Then, seeing the look of shock and hurt in the daughter's eyes, the mother quickly amended: "Of course it was not *your fault*."

"Has someone been fooling with my knives?" The question struck fear in the hearts of the children.

Though certainly, none of the children had touched their father's expensive Japanese knives. (Had Momma? If so, Momma wouldn't have failed to return the knife to its proper place on the magnetic rod.)

This past year Mia had begun to notice that her father was often distracted, restless. No sooner returning home than he had to make an "urgent" phone call—couldn't sit down for dinner just then. He complained of "clutter" in the house but objected to Mia's mother "disturbing my things" where he'd flung them down. Especially he disliked items out of place in the kitchen: he could detect if one of his Japanese knives was just slightly askew, as this might mean that someone had been using it who had no idea how it should be used, thus endangering the razor-sharp blade.

Mia did not like to look at the dazzling knives; the razor sharpness seemed to hurt her eyes. But there was comfort in the beautifully carved ebony handles.

All that Mia had dared, with no one to witness, was to close her hand around one of the knife handles without removing it from the magnetic rod. A strange sensation!—the carved ebony felt warm, as if another person had just been holding it.

When Mia's father returned for the rest of his possessions, he was furious to discover one of the expensive knives missing. He accused Mia's mother of misplacing it, and Mia's mother protested, saying that he'd probably misplaced it himself. So Mia's father went away, for the last time, in a mood of bitterness and animosity.

When Mia returned from school that day, this was the first thing she noticed—the glittering Japanese knives gone from the kitchen; where they'd hung, now a terrible emptiness.

Mia could not remember when she'd first learned of the "wild kitties" in the vacant lot beside their house. Possibly she'd heard someone speaking of them—"wild kitties who don't have homes."

Later, Mia would hear the more precise term—*feral cats.*

A colony of feral cats living in the dense underbrush in land no one seemed to own, called a cul-de-sac.

In the beginning, not many feral cats had lived in the cul-de-sac. Eventually, their numbers increased.

It had become Mia's secret, stopping to visit the feral cats on her way home from school. For her father disapproved of the cats and was particularly incensed that several persons in the neighborhood fed them regularly. To him they were *dirty strays, diseased. At risk for rabies. Someone should call animal control, have them trapped and euthanized.*

The word *euthanize* was chilling to Mia. When she'd first heard it, she had not known what it meant and so asked her mother, but she mispronounced the word—*youth-in-eyes.*

"Oh, Mia. I think you mean—*eu-than-ize.*" Her mother laughed at Mia, not meanly but in a way to make her blush and want to run out of the room. For years afterward, having to endure both her parents telling their friends how as a little girl Mia had mistaken *euthanize* for *youth-in-eyes* and wasn't that hilarious?

No, Mia thought. *Not funny at all.*

And now, in the year her father abandoned his family, Mia was certainly old enough to know what *euthanize* meant.

Fancy term for murder. What they'd like to do to me.

Her father objected to "strays" trespassing on his property, even when the cats were (as Mia could see) very beautiful. Sleek-black, taffy-colored, white with multiple markings. Brindle cats, steel-gray cats. A thick-furred orange tiger with a wonderful crooked plume of a tail.

Except when you saw the cats close up, they were not usually so beautiful—their eyes were likely to be sticky with mucus, their fur matted and mangy, their bodies so thin that the impress of ribs showed through their fur. Seen at close range, the orange tiger, which looked so fierce from Mia's bedroom window, had bitten ears and one blind eye.

"Oh! Poor kitty."

In secret Mia put out food for these cats at the back door of her house. But the food was soon gobbled up by squirrels.

The feral cats were solitary hunters. Sometimes Mia glimpsed one behind the house, nearly hidden in the dusk. How slowly it moved, crouching, tensed, about to spring. Scarcely breathing, Mia would watch.

If she were a huntress, she thought, that was how she would move through the grass.

Yet in the next moment, for no reason Mia could determine, the feral cat might bolt away, disappear.

Calling *Kitty, kitty, kitty!* in a friendly voice made no difference. The feral cats did not trust human beings, and so did not trust Mia.

During the past year her father had called the township to complain: Why did property owners pay exorbitant taxes if diseased stray animals were allowed to breed one hundred feet from a house, like his house? Why wasn't he allowed to fire a rifle at feral cats to protect his property?

Zoning laws forbade hunting within the township. Discharging a firearm—this was a crime.

Their backyard bordered the empty lot, and so feral cats often crossed warily through the property on their way from and to the lot. Mia would hear her father yelling at the cats—*Dirty vermin! Get the hell out of here!*

It was not like Mia's father to be so excitable, usually. Some terrible change had begun.

Returning home one evening, turning into the driveway. Mia's father was driving, Mia's mother was in the passenger's seat, and Mia, Randy, and Kevin were in the back. Suddenly her father accelerated as a blurred white shape slunk in front of the car. Everyone —except Daddy—cried, "No! Don't!"

There came a muted *thud*—an ear-piercing caterwaul—but when Mia and her mother searched for the creature, they failed to find it. Nor were there bloodstains on the driveway or in the grass.

In the shrubbery beside the house, in the backyard, in a wooded area beside their property—no animal.

Mia's father insisted that he'd only intended to scare the God-damned thing, hadn't hit it, but Mia didn't believe him, and she went away weeping.

Crawled off to die. All alone.

Especially it exasperated Mia's father that several "softhearted busybodies" in the neighborhood set out food and water for the feral cats, which, he said, would only cause them to multiply faster and attract other vermin, like rats.

He went to investigate. He saw no cats. But there were aluminum pans and plastic bowls that he kicked into the underbrush.

Well, maybe the glimpse of a cat. Beneath a pile of tree debris that had formed a natural shelter.

A neighbor, a woman named Mrs. Hansen, was carrying a bag of dry cat food to pour into the pans, and when she and Mia's father saw each other, they exchanged words.

Mia's father was not accustomed to others, especially women, confronting him, disagreeing with him. Mrs. Hansen did not back down as Mia's father scolded her for "aiding and abetting" a public nuisance; when he raised his voice, Mrs. Hansen raised hers. In Mia's house, she and her mother were listening to the escalating voices, chagrined.

Mia's mother said, with a nervous laugh, "Thank God your father doesn't have a rifle!"

When Mia's father returned to the house, furious and muttering, Mia hid away in her room. She did not want to hear her father speaking harshly and threateningly of the beautiful homeless cats; she did not want to see his flushed face. Especially she did not want to hear her mother speak soothingly to her father, trying to reason with him. Or Randy and Kevin saying excitedly that if Daddy bought them a BB gun, they could scare away the cats for him.

"Thanks, guys. Maybe I'll take you up on that, someday."

But Daddy disappointed the boys, in the end. Went away without a thought of the feral cats, and when he returned on (alternate) Saturdays to pick the children up for the day, he never asked about the cats, or anything much to do with the household he'd left behind.

* * *

It was Mia's secret from her mother, too—visiting the feral cat colony. For Mommy would not have approved.

Often now, Mommy was in an irritable mood. On the phone, sobbing. Or suddenly angry, slamming the receiver onto the hook. Scolding Mia's brothers, who bickered, left their toys underfoot, turned the TV up too high. Glaring at Mia, who returned from school suspiciously late.

"Where the hell have *you* been? Hanging out with—who?"

Mia was becoming stealthy, cunning. She brought the cats water and food from the refrigerator—things her mother wasn't likely to miss. One day daring to take lamb chops from the freezer— originally purchased for her father and left behind in a lower drawer—to leave on the ground, to defrost. When she returned from school hours later, the meat was entirely gone—not even bones remained.

Several cats peered at Mia suspiciously. The more she looked, the more cats she saw, all poised to flee back into the underbrush if she made a sudden move. "Kitties? Don't be afraid, I'm your friend . . ."

Hiding behind a fallen tree limb, camouflaged by desiccated leaves, was the tiger cat with a clouded eye, bitten ears. His sand-colored fur was matted and tufted.

Why would we trust you? We don't trust you.

Suddenly she saw, only a few feet away, a skinny black cat crouching in the grass, amber eyes of startling beauty staring at her with (it seemed) a look of hope—until Mia made a move as if to pet it and the black cat shrank away, baring its teeth.

"Oh, I'm sorry! I wasn't going to hurt you . . ."

But the skinny black cat was gone. The others were gone in a heartbeat.

The cul-de-sac was becoming a place where people dumped things. Amid the underbrush and debris were old rotted newspapers, cardboard boxes filled with trash, broken bits of Styrofoam and plastic. It seemed sad to Mia that the feral cats had to make their home in such a place, with little protection from cold weather, rain, and snow.

"Wish I could bring you home with me. All of you . . ."

At least, now that Mia's father was gone, the cats would be safer. Mia tried to take comfort in this.

2.

"Hey there! Bbbbs."

Like hyenas, they laughed. Soon after her thirteenth birthday, brushing against her in the school halls, on staircases, and in the cafeteria as soon as she stepped inside.

At first Mia thought it had to be an accident. Accidents.

Not boys in her grade (which was eighth grade), but older boys. Taller boys. Boys whose names she didn't know, whose faces were not familiar to her.

"Hi there Bbbbs. How's it goin'?"

In her confusion and embarrassment, Mia had no idea what the boys were saying. She was too surprised at first to comprehend that they were brushing against her, colliding with her on purpose. And there was the juvenile-hyena laughter, sniggering and breathless.

"Lookit her—Bbbbs! Where're ya goin' so fast?"

As she turned an astonished face to them, her tormenters were delighted. As she betrayed a glimmer of hurt, fear, embarrassment, mortification, they only brayed louder. One of them, the oldest, the tallest, dared to elbow Mia in the softest part of her chest so that she cried out in pain and the surprise of pain—"Scusa me, Bbbbs!"

Ninth-grade boys whose names Mia didn't know. Running through the eighth-grade corridor, colliding with others and laughing uproariously as they fled.

Mia stood hunched against a row of lockers, stunned. Her heart beat rapidly; she could not comprehend what had happened, so quickly. Her chest, her small, tender breasts, ached where she'd been bumped.

Why were the boys singling her out? Could they see in her face that her father had ceased to love her?

Went away cringing, eyes downcast. She didn't cry—not the first time.

Too embarrassed to report the boys. Too ashamed. Mia reasoned, *It will only make them hate me worse.*

For there seemed to be a kind of anger in their faces as they swooped upon her. They must have been lying in wait, they must have known where Mia would be. There was laughter and jeering, but something else Mia could not comprehend—resentment, anger. But why, why anger at *her*?

And always it happened so quickly. Once, twice, three times— in a single week. The boys appeared out of nowhere, hooting with laughter, bumped against Mia, and were gone.

Others students, with whom they collided in their haste to escape, shouted after them. At least one teacher noticed but did not intervene.

Mia went away dazed, each time. She'd learned the name—the last name—of the loudest boy: Dempster. She remembered how other girls had been subjected to this sort of torment from boys like Dempster in the past and she'd tried not to notice. Girls who slunk away self-consciously as a small gang of boys teased, jeered, laughed at them, dared to brush against them or jostle them, while younger girls like Mia avoided even looking at them, hoping to be spared. And of course they *were* spared, at the time.

That fierce sidelong look the boys cast at certain girls—the more "mature" girls. Mia was slow to realize that the same thing was happening to her now.

Often now, other girls avoided her. Not her closest friends, but others. Even her friend Janey seemed embarrassed for Mia, though she made it a point to walk with Mia between classes and into the cafeteria, as one might accompany a very young, naïve child, as if to protect her.

Not that Janey could protect Mia much if the boys ganged up on her. Janey herself was jostled roughly, jeered at.

After one of the assaults, when the boys emerged out of nowhere to collide with Mia, laugh at her, chortling *Bbbbs!* as they ran away, Mia sobbed to Janey, "I hate them! What are they saying?—*Bbbbbs . . .*"

Reluctantly Janey whispered in Mia's ear, "*Boobs.*"

Of course. You knew. Should have known.

No more embarrassing word than *boobs.* Mia felt her face heat with shame just to think of it.

Boys often swore, said nasty things. *Fuck, shit* were frequent. *Asshole* was frequent. But *boobs* was a different sort of word, not a swear word, not obscene, more of a comical word, to make people laugh.

*Hey there—Boobs! Yeh—*you.

Wanting to text Janey. So lonely!

Just to say—she wasn't sure.

Hate them. Wish they were dead.

Where were you after school . . .

But Mia knew, since sixth grade, that she couldn't exactly trust Janey not to share texts or emails with other friends. And lately she sensed how they talked about her, felt sorry for her, but (maybe) laughed at her behind her back.

Boobs.

"Mia? Let me look at you, sweetie. Stand *still*."

That concerned smile. Assessing eyes.

Mia's mother would not dare touch her—would she? Not actually bring the flat of her hand—lightly—against Mia's chest?

No. Wouldn't dare. Mia steeled herself. *Do. Not. Touch. Me.*

Her mother was surprised, it seemed. As if, these past several months, the past year in fact, she hadn't been noticing Mia, too much else in her life now (as a single, divorced mom) to distract her, distress her. (Dating sites? Was she, actually? Mia cringed to think so.) Most of her mother's attention was channeled into fury like a laser blade. *That son of a bitch. That bastard. I trusted him! And he lied, lied—about money, about the property, about this "girl" he's been "seeing"* . . .

Matter-of-factly saying, with not a clue of how stiff, how still Mia was holding herself, "Next thing we know, you'll have to wear a bra. Yes. I guess so. After all, you're thirteen."

Like a curse, it sounded. *Thirteen.*

"Why on earth are you looking at me like that? What—"

Mia twisted away from her mother's hands. Weak hands that could not keep her.

She'd been preparing all that day to tell her mother about the boys at school. She knew the term—*harassing*. But now, no.

Thinking how, when she'd been a little girl—her body small and as smooth as a doll's and the "nipples" on her chest so tiny you would hardly know they were there—Daddy had loved her. Daddy had loved her a lot. And Mommy had loved her much more than Mommy loved her now.

For now, Daddy was *away*. And Mommy's life had been changed.

Mia's little brothers were frightened, Mommy shouted at them, which she had not ever done before, and told them, *Go away, you're giving me a headache.* Mia knew to keep her distance from their angry mother.

Overhearing Mommy on the phone—*So distracted and exhausted by that bastard's lies, can't sleep without sleeping pills and can't get through the day without antidepressants, sometimes I think I just—want—to—DIE . . .*

Yes. Should've known. Staring at herself in the bathroom mirror naked (a word she hated: *naked*) staring with narrowed eyes at her breasts (another word she hated, though not so much as she hated the word *boobs*), which were taking shape as if of their own volition, against her wishes. Fleshy, soft-skinned, pale. With particular repugnance Mia stared at the small rosy nipples she knew were meant for a baby to suck—knowledge that filled her with dismay, disgust.

Only a short while ago her chest had been thin and as flat as a boy's. Her collarbone was still prominent, her skin as pale as white candle wax, but unmistakably she was putting on weight, stomach and hips, upper thighs—and she was growing taller.

Taller she did not mind. Taller would protect her from the boys. But gaining weight, that Mia dreaded.

The worst thing anybody could say about a girl was that she was fat. Worse even than *boobs* was the derisive—*fat-ass*.

All the girls shunned fattening foods, or tried to. Every girl Mia knew was in terror of gaining weight. Still, there were girls not so thin as other girls, and there were girls who were frankly overweight. Mia was still slightly underweight, according to online charts she'd consulted, but she wasn't so thin as she had been, and there seemed to be nothing she could do about it.

Just as there was nothing she could do about hairs sprouting in her underarms, on her legs, and between her legs . . .

Tried not to eat fattening foods. Tried not to eat everything on her plate and not have second helpings. No more sugar on her cereal!—no more sugar-coated cereal. No more whole milk, only nonfat milk and only nonfat yogurt.

The only good thing about her father leaving them, and her mother so agitated and distracted, Mia could skip entire meals without her mother taking much notice. She could get through an entire day at school not eating anything at all, just drinking Diet Coke—but then she was so hungry when she got home, she could not stop eating.

She wished she could wake up in her old body. Flat chest, flat hips. As smooth and hairless as a doll's skin.

Dreaded Daddy knowing. Any of it.

Especially how the guys were teasing her. Tormenting her. Ernie Dempster—that was his name. But there were others. Just the way they looked at Mia sometimes—even the nicer boys. Maybe it was punishment Mia deserved. Not sure what she'd done, but it had to be something.

So naïve, not realizing that the contours of her body were so visible through her clothing. Nothing she'd even considered in the past.

It seemed to Mia unfair: her breasts weren't really big, yet. The size of (medium-size) apples. And maybe the boys thought she was good-looking—"sexy."

If so, Mia wasn't trying. Couldn't help her face, hair.

In eighth grade, maybe she was "mature" for her age. Why boys' eyes snagged onto her.

Dreading to think that her breasts would continue to grow to the size (maybe) of her mother's—big, heavy, and spongy, like foam rubber. *No! I would rather die.*

"Mia, are you even listening to me? Hello?" Mia's mother snapped her fingers in Mia's face, exasperated.

What had Mom been saying? Mia had no idea.

"I was asking you—"

"Oh, leave me alone!"

Running away to hide in her room. Suddenly could not bear to be around her mother.

Waiting for Mom to follow, knock on her door. *Oh honey, I'm sorry. I didn't mean . . .*

(This seemed to be happening often lately. Mia's mother would speak sharply to her, Mia would run away upstairs. Some sort of apology to follow.)

But now the phone was ringing. Mia couldn't hear her mother answer, but the ringing stopped and Mia was left alone.

189

Hate you. Never want to turn into you.

Not crying, for what was the use?

Undressing for bed, eyes averted from the mirror. Loose night-gown, like a sack. And in bed lying on her right side so that her tender, fleshy breasts were protected by her arms, her arms like folded wings. Hoping she would dream of that other, lost time.

In the underbrush, a dark, furry shape. Moving so swiftly it is scarcely visible.

But if you stand very still and stare long enough, you will see the feral cats emerge.

Wary, watchful, glittery eyes. Ears pricked in alertness.

Learn to disguise. Camouflage.

Hiding in plain sight.

Soon, she'd perfected her strategy. *Hide in plain sight!*

At school, slumping her shoulders. Hunching her shoulders to make her chest concave. Shielding her breasts with her upper arms. Holding her books against her chest when she could, when it didn't look weird, in the corridors between classes, which was the dangerous time when guys could brush against her, bump into her. Instead of wearing her backpack, carrying it in her arms against her chest. Like a shield.

No more sweaters. No T-shirts. Loose-fitting shirts like boys' shirts, not tucked into her loose-fitting jeans. Better yet, a loose-fitting T-shirt and over that, a loose-fitting shirt. Maybe, over both, a loose-fitting jacket.

Mia smiled. The layered look. So clever!

She had not the courage or the nerve to stare down the boys. The feral cats taught *flight not fight.*

As it happened, other eighth-grade girls were beginning to "mature" as well. One day you glanced up—half of your friends had *boobs.*

It wasn't just physical maturity, but behavior as well. A way (some) girls had of presenting themselves, to be seen, admired.

Lipstick, even eye makeup. Eye-catching clothes.

Mia had no interest in being eye-catching. No lipstick for her. Not only were her clothes loose-fitting, they were likely to be dull, drab colors—khaki, mud-brown. Not bright-colored sneakers with garish laces, but the most ordinary running shoes.

It was amazing to Mia how other girls, particularly older, high school girls, so avidly sought the attention of boys. Some of these the very boys who'd tormented Mia. Why would anyone want to attract *them?*

Pierced ears, pierced eyebrows, noses, upper lips. Overnight it seemed, many had tattoos. Streaks of neon color in their hair. Very short skirts! Halter tops like bras.

There were Jacky, Dana, Thalia in eighth grade: girls who squealed when boys collided with them accidentally on purpose. Teasing in the cafeteria, in the parking lot behind the school. Girls who ran after boys, incensed and scolding, thumping them with their backpacks. Girls who actually wrestled with boys, slapping and pummeling. Mia shrank away, not wanting even to be a witness to such stupid behavior.

And then one afternoon there was Janey, of all people, involved in a silly confrontation with a ninth-grade boy named Rocco. And

Janey running to join her friends, flush-faced and eyes shining with indignation. "What an asshole! I hate him."

But Janey was so thrilled, she could speak of little else but Rocco.

How pathetic, Mia thought.

And how lonely she was.

. . . thanks for asking but not great, pretty terrible in fact but I am not going to kill myself or anything crazy like that, certainly I am not, wouldn't give that bastard the satisfaction, anyway the kids are OK, I want to think they see through their father's bullshit, but at least my daughter doesn't go to school dressed like a hooker. I mean, at least!

3.

"Kitty! Kitty-kitty-*kitty*!"

It was the happiest time in Mia's day. Visiting the colony of feral cats in the vacant lot next door. So little else in Mia's life she could depend on as she could depend on the feral cats. They might hide from her in the underbrush, but she knew they were there.

And if she waited long enough, if she was patient and quiet, some of them might appear.

Like a few neighbors, Mia sometimes left food for the cats. No matter how much, it never seemed to be enough. The aluminum pie pans, water bowls—usually empty. Mia supposed that other animals ate the food, too: raccoons, squirrels, rodents.

She'd bought a few packets of dry food for the cats, but these were expensive. To save money, you had to buy cat kibble in bulk, in large bags, but Mia couldn't afford these. And if she took leftovers from the refrigerator, her mother might become suspicious.

Slipping out of the house when no one would see her. After school, just before dusk was the best time. She didn't want her mother to know that she was still visiting the cats, and she didn't want her little brothers to know, they'd have followed her.

Mia recalled how her father had hated the feral cats. How he'd said half seriously that if he had time, he'd set out traps for them, or poison. *The only good cat is a dead cat.* Mia wanted to think that he hadn't meant it, exactly.

To Mia, the feral cats were consoling. They kept their distance in the underbrush, wary and watchful, but they did not react in panic when Mia spoke to them.

Calling *Kitty-kitty-kitty!* in a lowered voice was Mia's announcement that she was there. Unlike domesticated cats, the feral cats would never come when called, but eventually, if you waited long enough, several might appear. Or rather, if you waited long enough, you would see cats in the underbrush regarding you with wary eyes and realize that they'd been there all along.

If Mia remained very still, patient, and quiet, the more adventurous cats would approach the food plates she'd set down for them and begin eating hungrily.

How happy this made her! Watching the beautiful, lithe creatures, she forgot school, and she forgot her father. Forgot *boobs*.

Once, after school, on a day when Mia had avoided her friends, or her friends had avoided her, she was waiting for the feral cats to appear when a sensation of extreme sleepiness came over her and she lay down on the ground, her head resting on her backpack, and fell into a light sleep.

This day, in autumn, approximately eight months after Mia's father had left the family. Just three weeks since he'd shocked Mia and her brothers by announcing that he'd been transferred to Seattle and wouldn't be seeing them as often as he'd have liked . . .

Not that he saw Mia all that much. Every third weekend, or less. She didn't miss him, really. Didn't think so. It was harder on the boys. They missed their father.

Through closed eyes (it seemed), Mia could see the feral cats regarding her from their hiding places. A sleek black cat lifting its head to sniff, a thick-furred tiger cat squinting at her with one good eye. A mangy tortoiseshell with a crooked tail. A younger cat, with a predominantly white coat and glaring green eyes.

Mia lay very still on the damp ground, keeping her eyes closed. Scarcely daring to breathe, wondering if the cats understood that she was their friend, and that they could trust her.

Wondering if the cats were communicating with one another about her and she could not hear them. Their silence was uncanny, like gauze that shields, protects.

The glittery eyes moved over Mia, suspicious, wary. She held herself very still—she would make no sudden moves.

By degrees, one of the cats approached her. The thick-furred tiger cat with one sighted eye, one blind eye. Through her tight-shut eyes Mia could see, or believed she could see, the cat's single eye, as tawny as amber glass, fixed upon her.

Slowly, the cat approached. Slow and taut-muscled, as if it were hunting.

So close now, Mia could see the bristling white whiskers. The uplifted tail that looked as if it had been injured.

I will not hurt you. I love you.

Please let me pet you . . .

Then, Mia couldn't help it, her eyes opened of their own volition, and she saw that the burly tiger cat was within inches of her face, crouched low, ears laid back and teeth bared in a soundless warning snarl—*Don't! Don't touch.*

Mia sat up, confused. In an instant the feral cat scrambled away, vanished in the underbrush.

All the cats had vanished in that instant. Mia was alone.

Not certain at first where she was. Shivering with cold, clothes soaked through from the damp ground where she'd been lying on rotted leaves . . .

There was her backpack on the ground. Vaguely she recalled the desire to sleep so strong that she could not withstand it. How strange this was! Nothing like this had ever happened to her.

Her secret, no one must know. Her girlfriends would tease her, or feel sorry for her. They did not seem to like her so much lately. Even Janey.

Her mother would be furious—such *asinine behavior.* Her father would be disgusted and wish never to see her again, and who could blame him?

Mia picked up the backpack. Brushed at her damp clothing. It would appear that she was alone in the vacant lot, yet she felt the glittery eyes upon her, invisibly.

"Please trust me! I am your friend."

But it was time to leave. The sky was darkening with storm clouds, and already there came a distant rumbling sound, as if from the underside of the earth.

That night in her bed holding herself very still as she'd held herself still in the woods in secret in cunning dreaming of making herself small, as small and sleek and deceptive as a cat, crawling into the underbrush to hide with the feral cats who were her true friends and companions. The feral cat colony was a labyrinthine place, like the interior of a castle, a place of refuge, a warren of small chambers linked by small doorways, as warm as the interior of a beating heart. And here Mia was able to sleep as she could not sleep in her own bed. For here she could curl into a ball among the others, pressing against their furry sides, snug together in this secret place where there was solace and comfort and protection as thunder rumbled far away overhead.

4.

"What d'you think, kids? Like it?"

Mia's mother had had her hair cut, styled, lightened to a brassy-gold color that winked and flashed like a machete. Mia was dismayed, her mother looked so young.

Nor did Randy and Kevin know what to think. Staring at their mother. Was this glamorous, grinning woman *Mommy*?

Ten months had passed since the father had left them. Mia never uttered the word *Daddy* any longer. The divorce was said to be *final*. The father had moved to the West Coast; contact between him and Mia, Randy, and Kevin was tenuous and unreliable. Mia's mother had a new job (real estate), and a new car (Prius). She wore designer jeans, tight-fitting suede trousers and matching jackets, high-heeled boots. A fleece jacket, a gorgeous faux-fox coat. Her face was heavily made up, as a face on a billboard. Her fingernails that had been broken and neglected were now meticulously filed and polished. She'd borrowed money for the car and for the clothes and what she called "maintenance" (hair, face, nails), but it was money from a new friend, at a very low interest.

Recently, Mia's mother had been going out on dates. Mia couldn't imagine anything more pathetic, her mother (who had to be in her late thirties at least) meeting men on *dating sites*.

And soon, then: "Kids, come here! Mia, come downstairs! I'd like you to meet . . ."

The name was weird, Mia hadn't understood at first. Later she would learn that it was Pharis.

As she would learn that Pharis Locke was a self-styled *entrepreneur* and *consultant*. He had his own start-up company, involved in some way with the most advanced computer technology.

How they'd met—oh, this was comical!—Mia's mother dissolved into laughter explaining, something to do with Match.com, and a misunderstanding about a dinner date, and Pharis Locke grinned and snatched up her hand and kissed it and Mia could only scowl in embarrassed silence.

"Some things feel like fate, y'know? Destiny."

Mia's mother was sober, suddenly. Wiping at her eyes.

"It's true, some things *are* fate. The universe is predetermined. Living in the present tense, we can't see, but when we look back at our lives, often we can. In my own case . . ."

Pharis Locke spoke in a deep-baritone voice like a man on TV. You wanted to think a man with a voice like this is to be trusted.

Pharis Locke's head was big and blunt and near bald except for a fringe of kinky grayish-ginger hairs at the base of his skull. His eyes were unusually small, wide-set in his broad face, like the eyes of a pit bull. He had a mustache, and a wispy beard that gave him a rakish appearance at odds with his thickset body. Had to be older than Mia's father, and not nearly so good-looking, though he had a kindly-seeming smile.

Mia was trying very hard to like Pharis Locke. Certainly she wanted to be happy for her mother, now that her mother had a new friend, but her face felt stiff, her mouth refusing to smile.

Looming over her, baring his gums in an eager smile, Pharis Locke asked Mia which grade she was in, the most banal, boring question you could put to anyone, but Mia did not roll her eyes, did not snigger or scowl, but tried to answer politely, in such a lowered voice that Pharis could not hear, and Mia's mother had to repeat, in a bright voice, "Eighth grade."

"Ah, eighth grade! Well."

At this Mia did roll her eyes, or nearly. (No! Mia was determined to be very good, not to embarrass her mother.)

"Yes, it goes fast. Time. When you're a parent . . ." Mia's mother faltered, hadn't meant to say exactly this but couldn't think how to change the subject. ". . . it seems the kids grow up while you remain the same—the same age."

"I know just what you mean! So true."

Mia had all she could do to keep from laughing in the adults' faces. Each trying to impress the other. Why was her mother teetering in ridiculous open-toed high heels and what's-his-name wearing a striped purple shirt of some satiny, glossy fabric and ill-fitting designer jeans that looked brand-new? Every word uttered by the two of them was false, phony.

Later, Mia would recall how Pharis Locke's small, beady eyes fixed smilingly on her face as her mother was speaking—*as if not listening to her mother at all.* And then, the small, beady eyes glanced downward to Mia's (shapeless) shirt, to her legs (in jeans) and grimy running shoes, as if Pharis was surprised to learn that Mia was in eighth grade and not in a lower grade; that she was at least twelve or thirteen, and not younger. For Mia did not dress like a girl her age, or like a girl at all.

Perplexed, Pharis Locke seemed. Bemused.

Still, he didn't keep asking his silly questions. As if he respected Mia's stiffness, shyness.

Randy and Kevin were shy also but flattered by the adult male's interest. It had been a long time since their father had turned such attention upon them. Pharis Locke seemed wholly sincere, asking where they went to school and if they liked school. Which grades were they in? What did they want to do when they grew up? And Pharis Locke did seem to be listening to them as they answered excitedly.

Mia thought, *Don't fall for it. He's a phony. Just pretending to care about us.*

Yet she had to concede that it was touching, the little boys were so eager to receive a stranger's attention, like a warm, bright light shining on their faces.

As Mia's mother looked on, her eyes glimmering with tears. *Pathetic*—Mia didn't want to think.

How their father would sneer at their mother's *new, dear friend.* He would disapprove of their mother's seeing a man, bringing a man home, introducing a man to her children so soon after the children's father had left.

Unfair, but that's how men were. Mia was beginning to see.

Half consciously, she'd learned to please and placate her father in order that he would smile at her and love her and not (ever) sneer at her. For how painful it was to see that look come into her father's face, the subtly uplifted lip, the cold, mocking eyes turned upon some object of disdain and disapproval.

She'd learned to dread the sneering faces of boys. Quickly looking away, knowing she must not lock eyes with them.

Anything to do with sex provoked the boys to hyena laughter. As if sex were a threat to them. Anything to do with softness, tenderness. *Boobs.*

Still, Mia's brothers seemed to be getting along very well with Pharis Locke. Their faces glowed as they listened to his accounts of white-water rafting in Wyoming, hang gliding and bungee jumping in Australia, mountain hiking in Peru, hunting for elk in Montana, shark fishing in the Florida Keys. Exasperating to Mia to see how eagerly the boys believed these tales, and even Mia's mother seemed willing to overlook the man's boastfulness.

Mia's mother, who claimed to have *seen through that bastard's bullshit* in reference to Mia's father, now falling for this bullshit, from a man named Pharis Locke.

"Someday, maybe—we'll all go on an adventure together, how'd you like that?"

Pharis spoke almost wistfully. Stroking his wispy graying-gingery beard.

But Mia was already slipping away, heading upstairs with the excuse of homework, no need even to murmur under her breath, *Count me out.*

Here was a surprise: Pharis Locke wasn't going away.

Maybe not such a surprise: Mia's mother seemed to like Pharis so much, she was seeing him several times a week. No matter that Mia distrusted him, Mia's mother trusted him.

He's very nice. He's a gentleman!

He's much, much nicer than any other man I've ever met. (And that includes you-know-who.)

He thinks you kids are "terrific"—isn't that wonderful? Says he'd always wanted to have kids. And now he can afford them.

Mia gathered that her mother had gone out with other men she'd met online, that these dates had not turned out so well. But Pharis Locke was different, somehow.

Repellent to think of her mother having sex with a man, and certainly with this man, but Mia was beginning to wonder if she'd been too quick to judge Pharis Locke. Clearly, her mother did seem happier since she'd met Pharis, and being happier, she was nicer to Mia and her brothers, that was a fact. And maybe Mia's mother deserved to be happy, even if there was something pathetic in Pharis Locke providing happiness for her.

Mia recalled how her father had often interrupted her mother, or talked over her as if not hearing her. Much of the time he'd scarcely listened to her. But Pharis Locke listened to her, and he seemed intensely interested in whatever she said.

He says we're such a beautiful family. His actual words—"beautiful."

If you didn't listen to their actual words, Mia thought, it was—maybe—not so pathetic. Two adults who were maybe lonely, at any rate not-married and not-young, trying to—well, whatever they were doing.

Taking a chance on love. Once more!

Pharis Locke didn't just take Mia's mother out; often he took the family out: dinner, movies, Treasure Island Park. When Mia stayed home, she felt a pang of jealousy, envy. Wondering if they missed her. Hoping that her mother would call her on her cell phone just to check on how she was, but her mother didn't call, and Mia had too much pride to call *her.*

And Pharis Locke brought them presents.

For the boys, a spaceship video game suitable for younger boys—Junior Astronaut.

For Mia, an exquisite little locket on a silver chain—"Authentic mother-of-pearl."

Reluctantly, Mia thanked Pharis. Reluctantly, Mia smiled.

Not that she approved of her mother's man friend. She did not approve. But still, if her mother had to have a man friend, Pharis Locke wasn't the worst.

"Pray for me, Mia. I want so badly for this to work." The words spilled from Mia's mother with such urgency, Mia couldn't scowl or turn away in embarrassment.

For maybe, after all, it was all what Mia wanted: her mother to be happy. Her brothers to be happy. At least, not as unhappy as they'd been.

5.

And Mia had her own (secret) happy time. Except.

One afternoon in late winter, hurrying to the feral cat colony after school and seeing to her horror that something had happened—everything had changed . . .

Seeing to her horror that the underbrush had been cleared away. In the partly thawed earth were heavy tire tracks. The aluminum-foil pie plates and plastic bowls had been crushed, mangled.

"Oh no. Oh—*no*."

Mia stood unmoving. Unable to comprehend. The feral cats were—gone?

It was as if she had been dealt a blow to the chest. In the region of the heart. She heard her breath come quickly, hoarsely.

Could not believe it. A sensation of faintness suffused her body. She was afraid to give in to tears. If she began crying, she might not be able to stop . . .

That had happened a few times. Since Daddy. Not often. Not for a while. Crying, giving in. Mia had it under control. Mostly.

But now. *No.*

Someone in the neighborhood must have called animal control. Someone like Mia's father, who'd hated the feral cats and wanted them destroyed . . .

In a trance, Mia stood, staring. She could not breathe at first. Waiting for—what? A movement in the devastation, a flash of orange, or black, or white—a muffled cry . . .

Except for the calls of birds, it was very quiet here. Far away overhead, a droning aircraft. If you listened very closely, the sound of wind in the trees.

"Kitty? Kitty-kitty . . ."

The vacant lot covered an area of about three acres. Much of the land was impassable, dense with trees, underbrush. Mia had never ventured far into the woods. She had to wonder if some of the cats had run away, fled in terror, and were hiding.

The canny thick-furred tiger with just one good eye that had approached Mia when she'd fallen asleep, the sleek black cat that kept its distance, warily, the slender white cat with marblelike markings and glaring green eyes: surely one of these had escaped? At least one? So badly Mia wanted to believe, she'd begun to tremble with anticipation.

But it was terrible to see how a heavy vehicle, a bulldozer, had been driven into the lot from the road, flattening and uprooting bushes, young trees, brambles, and thistles, creating a kind of primitive roadway, gouging the earth. There'd been beauty in the uncultivated land; now all was broken, ugly. Mia felt a pang of sheer rage for the adults who'd perpetrated such cruelty.

It was so unfair, Mia thought. So cruel. The cats were beautiful creatures, condemned because they were homeless. It was not their fault that they lived in the wild. That they had no "homes"—"owners."

They'd rarely left their territory except at night. They harmed no one. Few people even knew they existed. And yet . . .

Mia thought of how, in the derisive world of school, such a loss would be ridiculed. She would be ridiculed. It filled her with horror to think of the coarse boys at school who'd tormented her discovering the vacant lot, the feral cat colony, and making the cats' lives miserable. At least that had not happened.

And at least the boys had stopped singling her out. Other girls had caught their eyes, better-looking girls. More "mature" girls. Mia had learned to hide her body from the gaze of predators, as the feral cats had learned to hide. Disguise, camouflage. *Hiding in plain sight.*

How she hated the crude, cruel boys! Thinking of them, she felt her heart begin to beat rapidly. That sensation of being trapped, jeered at. She'd have liked to be a slender young cat, to escape her tormenters . . .

"Kitty? Kitty-kitty . . ."

Calling in a forlorn voice, as a child might do. But she was tired now, and feeling hopeless.

Her feet were wet. She'd lost her gloves. Her hands were stippled and bleeding from thorns. Her breath was beginning to steam.

It was late afternoon. She had no choice, she'd have to give up her search. A wave of loss swept over her, a feeling of angry despair.

And then she saw—what was it?—a small dark body, motionless in the tall grasses . . .

To her horror, a cat's body: a corpse.

Not one of the feral cats she recognized. She didn't think so. A cat twisted on its side, eyes open, unseeing. A cat of about medium size, with mangy gray fur, a stubby tail. It had crawled into the underbrush to die, Mia thought. Maybe it had been injured by the bulldozer.

Her eyes welled with tears, spilled over with tears, and suddenly she was sobbing.

Hate hate hate hate hate—whoever had done this.

Leaving the ravaged lot, Mia encountered an older woman in a hooded jacket, trousers, and boots, who was just arriving. She'd witnessed the raid of the cat colony by the township animal control unit that morning, she said; she'd been checking back every few hours to see if there were any cats remaining that she might rescue.

This had to be Gladys Hansen, one of the neighbors who'd fed the feral cats for years, with whom Mia's father had had a disagreement.

Bitterly Mrs. Hansen told Mia that another neighbor had called the township animal control department to arrange for a raid on the colony that morning. She'd hurried over to try to prevent them but arrived too late, and anyway, they'd outnumbered her. "There was nothing I could do but scream at them."

They surrounded the cats and captured them in nets, Mrs. Hansen said. Then they bulldozed the underbrush. A more humane way would have been to trap them, but that would require too much time. If any cats had escaped the nets and were in hiding, they didn't seem to care if they'd injured them or killed them.

"And all in the name of 'public safety'! The pretense is that the township is doing this for the cats' well-being because cats in the wild sometimes get feline leukemia and other illnesses. But of course all they're going to do is euthanize the cats—they are not going to help them. Not even the kittens. It's easiest to kill them all and not be bothered with treating any of them. Feral cats usually can't be adopted, but kittens . . ." Mrs. Hansen paused, breathing heavily. Tears shone in the woman's eyes, and Mia was in dread of seeing an older woman cry. "Those beautiful creatures have as much right to live as anyone. As much right to live as we do."

Politely Mia excused herself. The last thing she wanted to do at the moment was commiserate with another person.

Returning home, she managed to avoid her mother, who was on the phone speaking animatedly. (With Pharis Locke? Or with a woman friend, about him?) Later, Mia's mother knocked on the door of her room to ask her what on earth was wrong. "You scared your brothers, Mia. They said it looked like you'd been crying."

"Well, I am *not crying*. I am doing homework."

It was true. Mia lay sprawled on her bed, her math textbook and notebook spread about her.

Her mouth was dry, her heart beating hard in fury. She had not been able to calm her rushing thoughts since she'd returned home. Who had taken the time to complain about the feral cats? And why—out of pure meanness? Her father would be satisfied now, if he'd known.

Mia stood at her window gazing out into the gathering darkness. Sometimes in the past she'd seen small, fleeting figures in the grass—feral cats?—so quickly they appeared, and disappeared, she couldn't be certain. But now, nothing.

Soon, Pharis Locke arrived downstairs. The jocular, booming voice greeting Mia's mother and Randy and Kevin, filling Mia with a sensation of dismay—it was becoming so familiar.

Is he going to move in, Mom? He's here all the time now.

No! Pharis is not going to move in—not here.

Something about her mother's intonation, Mia hadn't wanted to hear more. No no *no*.

The evening meal passed in a haze of misery for Mia. She could not keep from thinking about the feral cats trapped in nets. She could imagine their terror. And then, the terrible bulldozer. The mangled body, as lifeless as debris.

Resenting Pharis Locke's ebullience at dinner, which jarred so with her mood. She could not concentrate on the conversation, such as it was. Pharis spoke, Mia's mother listened adoringly. Randy and Kevin listened adoringly.

Mia wondered what was wrong with *her*? She'd been hurt to think that her brothers had been frightened of her.

Aware that Pharis was asking her something. Vaguely she replied—she had a math test the next morning, she was distracted thinking about it.

The kindly gaze drifted onto Mia. Lingered on Mia. The mouth smiled.

She could not respond. Her heart was broken.

"Mia? Is something wrong?"—Pharis spoke gently.

Mia shrugged. *No.*

"She's moody all the time. She doesn't mean to be rude. It's a phase she's going through—as people say." Mia's mother laughed, to show that she wasn't concerned.

"Ah, yes! Phases. I remember them well, when I was Mia's age."

You were never my age. Go away.

After dinner, as Pharis and the boys watched a video Pharis had brought over, Mia helped her mother clear away dishes and clean up in the kitchen. The magnetic board where Mia's father's fancy Japanese knives had been displayed was empty, Mia's eye was drawn to it.

Waiting for her mother to scold her for being rude to their guest, but her mother said only, in a lowered voice, "Please, will you just try, Mia! For my sake. You don't have to love him."

"Love him? Why would I love him?"—Mia was indignant.

"If—if Pharis comes into our lives. More permanently."

"*More* permanently? What does that mean?"

But Mia's mother turned away. To keep from crying? To keep from smiling?

As soon as she could, Mia ran upstairs. Laughter wafted to her from below. Family laughter. She did not belong in this family.

It was understood that Pharis Locke stayed overnight on evenings he came for dinner. No one seemed surprised any longer. Mia could see that Randy and Kevin were not dismayed, but rather relieved. Their mother's friendly, flushed-faced friend wouldn't be abandoning them that night.

Sleeping together. Disgusting!

Mia had a difficult time concentrating on schoolwork. She had a difficult time trying to sleep. When the house was still and darkened and it was nearing one a.m., Mia threw on clothes, located a flashlight, and made her way outside, back to the vacant lot.

It was daring to step outside in the night. How surprised her mother would be, and upset! And embarrassed, if Pharis Locke knew.

Fresh, cold, damp air. Overhead a faint moon like a half-closed eye. Mia felt a stab of excitement. Following the flashlight beam. Shining light on ugly gouged tire tracks. Broken and shredded trees. Somewhere close by a hoot owl called, an eerie, floating cry that

211

made hairs stir on the nape of Mia's neck. Sharp, pungent smells of thawing earth, rotted leaves and branches. Making her careful way, staring at what the flashlight revealed. It looked so different from the way it looked in daylight: all color seemed to have been bleached away. Here was a twilight world of uprooted trees, gnarled roots.

Her breath steamed faintly; it had to be below freezing, but Mia had thrown on only jeans and a light jacket.

Silence. The hoot owl had ceased. Mia was some distance from the roadway, in an area beyond the devastation.

Then she heard a faint mewing from a few yards away, almost inaudible. In an instant she was alert, hopeful. She stooped, peered. "Kitty? Where are you?"

On her hands and knees, Mia crawled into the underbrush, awkwardly wielding the flashlight. Lifting debris, she was astonished to see in the beam of light a single small kitten, ghostly white, mucus-sticky eyes enormous in its face. An adult feral cat would have arched its back, bared its teeth, hissed, and fled from an intruder, but the little white kitten only stared at Mia and mewed piteously. The sound resembled *Miao*.

"Like my name. Mia."

Mia managed to capture the kitten, which hissed silently at her and made a feeble gesture as if to scratch her with its miniature claws, but Mia was wearing gloves and long sleeves, the kitten's tiny claws were harmless. Mia laughed in delight. The kitten weighed virtually nothing in her hand—a squirming bit of white fluff, a twitching tail, eyes that appeared to be entirely black, all pupil.

The only living creature amid the terrible devastation. And Mia had rescued it!

She would bring the stricken kitten back to the house with her; there was no question about that. She would save its life, for clearly it was starving, lost without its mother.

As soon as Mia lifted the kitten to hold against her chest, it ceased struggling, but it continued to make the tiny bleating sound as Mia carried it back to the house—*Miao, Miao, Miao . . .*

"Poor kitty! But you are safe now."

6.

That night it was revealed to Mia in a dream that the true name of the white kitten was *Miao Dao*. And that it was no accident that Miao Dao had come to dwell with Mia and sleep beside her on her bed.

The promise was that, from that night, Mia would never be alone. Even when she was away from the house, and away from the white kitten, the spirit of Miao Dao accompanied her, and the memory of Miao Dao's soft, feathery-white fur and deep purr and eyes glittering like black marbles remained with her.

In school, when Mia felt awkward or lonely or self-conscious, she would only have to recall Miao Dao snuggling against her in the night, sleeping against Mia's arm or side, or sometimes on Mia's pillow, to feel secure, safe, loved.

Naïvely Mia had hoped to keep the feral kitten a secret from her mother, but of course within a day or two Mia's mother discovered the kitten in Mia's room, where she'd set down bowls of food and water and, in a closet, a makeshift litter box fashioned out of sand and bits of dirt. Mia had been trying to clear the kitten's eyes of mucus as well.

"Mia! This is one of those feral kittens, isn't it? You've brought it into our house?"—Mia's mother was more exasperated than angry.

She'd heard about the raid on the feral colony, she said. She'd heard that the animal control unit had arrived early in the morning before anyone was aware of what was happening, so that they could clear out the underbrush and take away the cats without interference.

"Did you call them, Mom?"—Mia spoke with barely concealed sarcasm. She'd picked up the little white kitten, to shield it in her arms from her mother.

"No, I did not. I didn't know anything about it until afterward."

Mia supposed that that was so. Her mother wasn't the sort of person to complain to the township.

"But I think the raid was necessary. The feral population was increasing. Wild cats have all sorts of diseases that can spread to pets, and they have short life spans."

"Not this one. I intend to take care of Miao Dao myself."

Mia's mother didn't quite hear. "*Miao*—what?"

"Miao Dao. That's her name. You can't take her away from me, she belongs here." Mia's voice lifted stubbornly, excitedly. She'd determined that Miao Dao was female.

"I don't think so, Mia. This is such an unsettled time in our lives . . ."

"That's why she belongs here."

"If your father knew . . ."

"Well, he doesn't have to know. He's *gone*." Mia spoke bitterly, yet with an air of satisfaction.

". . . and then there's Pharis . . ."

"What has Pharis got to do with it? He doesn't live in this house. He doesn't have jurisdiction over me. That's ridiculous."

Boldly Mia continued to oppose her mother. With the instinctive cunning of a girl of thirteen she understood that her mother was faltering, out of guilt; she must not falter herself.

Finally Mia's mother gave in. Mia could keep the kitten—for the time being. As long as she cared for it and was responsible for it.

"Of course I will care for Miao Dao. I love her already."

Love was such a defiant word. Mia saw with satisfaction that her mother winced, just perceptibly.

"Well, it will have to be taken to a vet. It will need shots. Its eyes are infected. If it's a female, as you seem to think, it will need to be spayed." Mia's mother spoke doubtfully, as if she might rescind her permission at any moment. "And I think it should be kept in the basement, not in your room. Or, not only in your room. That won't be healthy for either of you."

Mia murmured in agreement. Thinking, *Miao Dao will sleep with me every damn night. See if you can stop us.*

"Well. It—she—is very beautiful, despite the runny eyes. So *small*."

The little white kitten had been fearful at first of Mia's mother's raised voice but had begun to relax in Mia's arms, flexing her tiny claws into the fabric of Mia's sweater, on the brink of purring. But when Mia's mother reached out to pet the feathery-soft top of the kitten's head, Miao Dao suddenly hissed at her and swatted at her hand.

"Oh!—what?" Mia's mother snatched her hand away.

Mia laughed, the sight of the tiny kitten hissing and clawing at an individual so much larger than herself was comical. The alarmed expression in Mia's mother's face was comical.

The kitten claws were much too small to break the surface of Mia's mother's skin, but quickly Mia said that Miao Dao hadn't meant it—"She's just nervous around anyone else but me."

Mia's mother was looking chagrined, wounded.

"Well! Tell Miao—whatever her name is—she's on probation in this house. Tell her that."

7.

A few weeks later Mia's mother and Pharis Locke were married.

A small private wedding ceremony. Not in a church, but in the local courthouse, in the office of a justice of the peace. Quasi-secret, as Mia's mother wanted it.

"Now, you kids have a new dad. One who really cares about you."

Was this so? Mia hated to think *yes,* maybe. For the original dad—Daddy—had faded in their lives like one of those sunsets that begins slowly, emblazoning the sky with a fiery light, but ends abruptly, a sudden dimming—then *out.*

Mia's father was always promising to fly east to spend some time with his children, whom he said he was missing "like crazy." Or suggesting that the children fly to Seattle to spend some time with him and the (new) wife. Except there was never the right time *convenient for everyone.*

(For a while Mia had haunted the [new] wife's Facebook account, fascinated that the [new] wife with the silly name ["DeeDee"] resembled Mia's mother as she'd looked, judging from photos, twenty years ago. But she'd lost interest. DeeDee was just too boring posting reports of her pregnancy.)

(And if/when DeeDee had a baby, was this baby supposed to be Mia's half sister or brother? Mia's lip curled in disdain.)

Embarrassing as a half sibling might be, it was more embarrassing that Mia's mother was getting (re)married—Mia couldn't bring herself to tell her friends at school. One more reason why she was drifting away from her friends. Or maybe her friends were drifting away from her.

Why do you need them? You don't. You have me.

Warm against the side of Mia's leg, or her arm, sometimes curled up on the pillow beside her head, the little white feral kitten slept every night in Mia's bed. She would have been lonely with her mother away on her honeymoon—a week in Sarasota, Florida, on the Gulf of Mexico—except for Miao Dao, who purred even in her sleep to comfort Mia.

Why do you need them? You don't. You have me.

All this while Miao Dao was growing rapidly.

Twice a day, sometimes more frequently, Mia made sure that Miao Dao was fed, with cat food purchased with Mia's allowance. Soon Miao Dao was no longer a kitten, but a lean, lithe, sleek young cat with wary eyes, pricked-up ears, a switching tail. Her fur was snowy white, without a blemish—no stripes or spots anywhere on her body. Like the interior of her mouth, the pads of her feet were pale pink. Her whiskers were unusually long and stiff, like the hairs in her ears.

Soon Maio Dao ceased to use the litter box in Mia's closet, mewing to be let outside.

Mia was sorry: she'd hoped that Miao Dao would be an indoor cat. The veterinarian who'd examined Miao Dao had strongly advised this, but it soon became impossible for Mia to restrain the restless young cat.

She compromised by putting a collar with an ID tag and a little bell around Miao Dao's neck, to curtail her hunting. But Miao Dao was always slipping out of the collar, and sometimes she brought back to the house, for Mia, little gifts of prey—mangled mice and birds, frogs, once even a wounded garter snake.

Often now, Miao Dao was gone, sometimes for hours, and each time, Mia was anxious that she wouldn't return. But Miao Dao always returned.

Sleeping in the crook of Mia's arm. Snuggling against her. The quiet purring deep in Miao Dao's throat as consoling as a lullaby. But sometimes Mia wakened with a start to discover that the warm, furry figure was gone.

At the rear door of the house, calling *Kitty-kitty-kitty!* Holding her breath until the white cat appeared, trotting to her.

Rubbing against Mia's legs. Butting Mia's legs with her head. Purring!

Mia adored the sleek young white cat that belonged to *her*. She'd never had a pet before, though she'd wanted one for years. Her father had joked that he preferred dogs to cats but no animal at all to either dogs or cats. Randy and Kevin had pleaded for a puppy, but no. *Who would do the work? We know who would do the work: M-O-M.* Mia's mother had laughed to soften her sharp words.

Mia noted that Miao Dao didn't seem drawn to anyone else in the family. When her little brothers sighted Miao Dao, they eagerly approached her, but Miao Dao coolly eluded them. No matter how they pleaded with her, she seemed scarcely to see or to hear them.

But if they tried to corner her, she bared her teeth and hissed at them.

"Don't scratch them, Miao Dao! They're just children; they don't mean any harm."

Miao Dao allowed Mia's mother to feed her, sometimes even to stroke her fur, but Miao Dao never rubbed against Mia's mother's legs or purred audibly in her presence. Pointedly, Miao Dao avoided Pharis Locke, who stooped over her, wanting to "tickle" her beneath the chin. "Pretty kitty! What's your name—Meow Dowie—" Pharis laughed, as if the name was ridiculous to him, unpronounceable as a foreign name.

Mia began to notice that: when Pharis entered the house, Miao Dao slunk away. If she'd been purring and pressing against Mia's hand, she went very still at the sound of the man's jocular voice— "Hel-lo! I'm home! Where is everyone?"—and soon disappeared.

Once, Mia happened to see, or imagined she saw, the man who was her stepfather giving a little kick at Miao Dao as she fled past him through a doorway. When Mia opened her mouth to protest, Pharis said quickly, "Hey, we're just playing around—Meow Dowie and me."

Soon after this incident Miao Dao stayed away overnight. Mia was anxious, searching outside the house, calling *Kitty-kitty-kitty!*

Randy and Kevin helped Mia look for Miao Dao. Mia's mother offered to drive her around the neighborhood. Only the stepfather seemed indifferent, if not ironic. "Cats run away, dear Mia. This was a feral cat. Cats have no loyal genes in their bodies, unlike dogs."

Tearfully Mia told her mother that she thought Pharis had hurt Miao Dao. Maybe he'd taken her away somewhere, left her by the side of the road. She wouldn't put it past him, to take revenge on Miao Dao because Miao Dao didn't like him.

"That isn't true, Mia. Pharis wouldn't do such a thing. He has told me he thinks the cat is a great beauty. He just wishes it was more civil to him—which is what he says about you, too."

Another day, and a night. And still Miao Dao was missing.

Mia rang doorbells in the neighborhood. No one had seen a young white cat—"If it was one of the feral cats, it probably just ran away. You can't domesticate them, they're wild like chimpanzees, and sooner or later they turn against you."

Politely Mia listened to such remarks. Bit her lower lip to keep from crying. Thanked whoever it was, left her name and telephone number behind, along with a photo of Miao Dao gazing up at the camera with widened eyes.

Certainly is a beautiful cat, people said. Though some stared at the photo, frowning.

For was it natural, a snowy-white cat with black eyes? Didn't white cats usually have blue or green eyes?

Of course Mia returned to the vacant lot several times. Though knowing it was probably useless, tramping to the rear of the property and back again through the underbrush. Pleading, "Kitty-kitty-*kitty!* Miao Dao! Oh please—come back . . ."

Nothing Mia could do, she knew. If Miao Dao preferred to live in the wild, and not with her.

Still, the ugly tire tracks remained in the earth. A turmoil of uprooted trees and bushes. A devastation of storm debris, litter. Even the smells were sharp, unpleasant. A sour, rotted odor underfoot. The beautiful feral cats were gone.

Mia would have liked to curl up and sleep with the feral cats, as she'd done when she'd been younger. When the feral cats had allowed her. Or Mia had dreamed of sleeping with the feral cats, but had not, actually. (Had she?)

Mia stayed in the vacant lot for an hour or more. Not wanting to return home. Through the trees she could see lighted windows in the distance. Her own house, the houses of neighbors. How petty human life seemed to her, how banal. Her mother and the new stepfather were altogether banal. It frightened Mia that she disliked them so. For they were all she had of family now that Miao Dao had abandoned her.

If she could run away, as Miao Dao had run away . . . But where had Miao Dao gone? Mia felt a clutch of panic, thinking that just possibly Miao Dao had been taken in by another family, another girl Mia's age, and slept with this girl on her bed now and not with Mia, who loved her so.

Not wanting to think—*He has killed her. Run her over in the street. Poisoned her. Because Miao Dao didn't love him, as the rest of us are supposed to love him.*

8.

Soon after the return from the honeymoon, soon after Pharis Locke moved into Mia's mother's house, it became clear that Pharis Locke was *master.*

Of course, no one called him master. Not even Mia.

Though noticing that, now that he and her mother were married, Pharis wasn't so—would you call it gracious?—patient?—thoughtful?—willing to listen as he'd once been.

A gentleman—Mia's mother's word.

For it seemed that, in any discussion, Pharis had to get his way. Whether the subject was X, Y, Z. "He just pretends to listen to you, Mom. He just lets you *talk.*"

Of course, Mia's mother's new husband wasn't as rude and impatient to her as Mia's father had been; but then, he'd been her husband for only a few weeks.

Nor did Pharis seem nearly as interested in Randy and Kevin as he'd once been. No time for the boys' chatter, impatient when they clamored for his attention—"Don't you two have homework to do? I'm sure you do." He chided Mia's mother for spoiling her sons, he chided the boys for not respecting their mother.

With Mia, he was more circumspect. Cautious. Seeing the expression in Mia's face of wariness and disdain for him, the intruder in the household.

"Now you have a stepdad, you know you are *protected*. Anything anyone says to you, does to you—just let me know, honey."

Mia bristled. *Honey!* Her father had sometimes called her this; she'd basked in her father's attention like a cat. But not Pharis Locke's.

And did Pharis have as much money as he'd boasted of before the wedding? This wasn't so clear.

The nature of Pharis's business was mysterious, unpredictable. He didn't seem to be selling any actual "product"—any computer or electronic device you could see. He didn't seem to own a building, a factory, even a suite of offices; he'd been working out of his condominium in a high-rise building, which he'd subsequently sold. Vaguely, he spoke of profits, losses. Fluctuations of the market. Yet he owned, or was, a corporation, for Mia had seen mail addressed to Pharis Locke Consultants, Inc., but she had no idea what this could be. And what did *consultant* mean, anyway? Couldn't anyone be a consultant, on any subject?

When Mia asked her mother about Pharis Locke Consultants, Inc., her mother told her irritably that it was none of her business. Mia had the impression that her mother didn't know much more than Mia knew.

True, Pharis Locke seemed to have money. He boasted that he'd sold his condominium for more money than Mia's mother's house (four bedrooms) was worth. He'd repaid loans Mia's mother had taken out during the months of the divorce, as well as her legal fees.

How grateful Mia's mother had been for Pharis's generosity! Mia was thinking that her mother might have confused gratitude with love.

9.

Hate hate hate them.

Lying in wait for another girl, after school. The Dempster boy and two or three others. A girl who wasn't Mia, but this girl must have known that they were there and avoided them, and there came Mia, unwitting and oblivious, and even her loose-fitting clothes did not spare her from their derision, vulgarity.

Panicked, Mia ran. The boys hooted with laughter, pretended to be pursuing her but soon lost interest.

Making her way home, hands over her ears. How Mia hated their braying laughter . . . She had to be grateful that they didn't jostle against her, actually touch her as they'd done in the past. Grateful that other, "sexier" girls usually drew their attention.

If she'd told her mother, possibly her mother would drive to school to pick Mia up. But it was likely that her mother would also insist on speaking to the school principal, and Mia would be questioned, and Mia would be forced to say that she didn't know who the boys were, didn't know any of their names, for if she told on them, if she uttered the name *Ernie Dempster*—it would only be worse for her. She knew.

Almost Mia was tempted to tell Pharis. *Stepdad. Protect you.*

But no, not a good idea. Anything Mia did would only involve her in a way she didn't want to be involved. And *stepdad* might offer to pick her up from school, and she didn't want that.

Mia was unhappy, missing Miao Dao. It had been weeks since the beautiful white cat had disappeared.

Mia's mother offered to drive her to the animal shelter to bring home a rescue cat, but Mia refused, indignant. "I only want Miao Dao. I told you—I love her."

"But Mia, she's gone. We've looked everywhere . . ."

"She might come back. She knows where we live."

If stepdad overheard, he might say, insufferably, "Cats run away, Mia. That's how cats are. Especially, that's how feral cats are." As if meaning to console Mia but maddening her instead.

That's how assholes are. You said it!

In the night, Mia woke from dreams of agitation and loneliness. Pursued by jeering boys. Desperate to hide, to squeeze herself into—what was it? Underbrush, the devastated cat colony.

Struggling to breathe, Mia reached for Miao Dao in the bed beside her and woke despondent. Miao Dao was not there.

But there was another dream that came to Mia sometimes, a lovely dream in which Miao Dao came silently to sleep in the crook of her arm, against her heart.

And then, the most palpable dream, a dream of being smothered by Miao Dao clambering onto her chest. No longer the young, slender white cat, but a muscled, mature cat with large paws and sharp upright ears, like those of a fox. Glittering black eyes. And what a purr! Low, guttural rumble, like a panther's.

*Did you think that I would leave you? I would never leave you.
Have faith.*

In an instant Mia wakened. Sitting up in bed confused and excited, but another time, Miao Dao had vanished.

Still, in Mia's bed, in the air about the bed, a smell of wet earth, rotted leaves and grass, something dark and viscous, like blood.

10.

"Okay, sweetie: call me Dad."

Smiling. Baring damp teeth. Not adding *please*.

His eyes lingering on her. When she was feeling sad, as if to console.

Not that Mia smiled back or remained in his view for very long. No.

Yet: the way he smiled at her as her brothers chattered. Signaling it was *me and you* and not the boys—they hadn't a clue.

The way he winked, a playful wink, a half wink, as Mia's mother spoke in a bright, glib voice to which neither the stepdad nor Mia was listening.

"Where's your locket, sweetie? The one I gave you? How come you never wear it? Did you lose it?" Stepdad pretended to pout.

Mia protested, she hadn't lost the locket. Just didn't wear necklaces all that much. Face warm, confused-feeling, was he calling her *sweetie* now?

As her father had, but not for a long time.

Honey. Sweetie. Had to be silly, if not pathetic, Mia felt comforted by such names. Beginning to see why her mother fell for Pharis Locke, such kindness in his manner.

230

Following this, Mia remembered to wear the locket at such times and in such places when Pharis was likely to notice. Actually she'd been somewhat hurt, stepdad had thought she might have lost it.

"Pretty"—murmured so that only Mia could hear. Though Mia pretended not to hear.

Pretty necklace, or—pretty Mia?

At school she had to be vigilant. For when she chided herself—*You're just imagining it, don't be ridiculous. They are not looking at you*—often she turned out to be mistaken, and in fact yes, the jeering boys were looking at her.

Also on the street. At the mall. Especially if she happened to be alone. Not with other girls whose laughter, clothing, makeup drew the attention of observers—for other girls didn't so much mind, or seemed actually to enjoy, basking in the attention of (male) strangers. (Though Mia's friends could be shocked, offended when a guy or guys said something really crude, gross, obscene to them. Suddenly the attention wasn't so welcome.)

But when Mia was alone, no protection. That sensation of eyes drifting onto her. Snagging on her like burrs. Though she continued to wear shapeless T-shirts, pullovers. Not skintight jeans like the other girls. No.

As if the boys saw through Mia's disguise. Her desperation. As predators can perceive a wounded animal, very slightly limping.

Trying to console herself—*They don't mean anything. It isn't personal.*

Her body, they were interested in. Not Mia herself. And so it was *not personal.*

231

Except today they call after her *Mi-a! Miii-ahhh!*

They know exactly who she is. They are waiting for *her*.

Embarrassed, ashamed. Walking quickly, shoulders slumped, head down. Her heart is beating crazily, almost she feels that she will faint.

Cuts through an alley. Blindly running, staggering.

Then, at an intersection, she finds herself crossing a street, looking neither to the right nor to the left—desperate to escape the boys. There comes the sound of a horn, very loud, close by—Mia panics, freezes. *Watch where you're going!*—an impatient (male) voice. Mia manages to get to the curb before a wave of dizziness sweeps over her.

She is gripping a railing. So important not to faint, to fall. Her breath comes swift and shallow, and she has no idea where she is, what time this is, who has been pursuing her, and why she is so frightened—but why also the fear has begun to lessen, like a tourniquet being slowly unwound.

Makes her way home, where, that night, in her bed, Miao Dao awaits her.

11.

Next morning, news was that a ninth-grade local boy had died in what was being called a vicious assault.

The body was found in the early morning amid trash cans in an alley near his school. Head wounds, deep lacerations in the scalp, throat violently slashed by some sort of clawed instrument or serrated knife. The fifteen-year-old victim was believed to have bled out while trying desperately to crawl on his belly out of the alley to the street twenty feet away.

Like wildfire, this news spread through school. Mia was as astonished as anyone, hearing. Having to ask several times—*who was it?*

No one in their class. Last name Dempster.

"Oh, my God! Who did it?"

"How did it happen? When?"

"What was Ernie doing there—in the alley?"

As others marveled at the news, shocked, thrilled, shaking their heads in awe, Mia hung her jacket in her locker, quietly. No questions for anyone.

Afterward, in her first class, recalling the welcome surprise of the white cat snuggling beside her in the night. How thrilled Mia had been that Miao Dao had returned, wet-muzzled, smelling of something dank, earthy.

For no reason she could have said, Mia smiled.

"Is this kid somebody you knew, Mia?"—Mia's stepfather was frowning at the lurid headlines on the front page of the newspaper.

Mia shook her head, *no*.

"Sounds like he was practically decapitated. Christ!"

Mia's mother came to lean over Mia's stepfather in a way that offended Mia—resting her arms on the man's shoulders, nudging her chin alongside his head. Mia saw that the stepfather didn't take much notice, only continued reading.

"Ernest Dempster—fifteen. Ninth grade. Not in your class, eh?"

Mia shook her head, *no*.

"Did he belong to a gang? Maybe that was it."

"There aren't gangs in schools here!"

"Mia, there aren't gangs at your school, are there? Or in the high school?"

Mia shook her head, *no*.

"Maybe it was a pervert. Picked up the kid, slashed his throat. Has to be something sick like that."

Glancing around for Mia. But Mia had vanished from the kitchen, as silent as a wraith.

12.

For her fourteenth birthday, a silver bracelet engraved *Mia*.

Birthday cake. Fourteen candles. Having to blow them all out, shutting her eyes in the effort.

Mom had meant well. (Mom always meant well.) Devil's food cake, chocolate fudge frosting, which was, anyway used to be, Mia's favorite frosting.

Glasses of wine for Mia's mother and Mia's stepfather at dinner. Glasses refilled. Singing "Happy Birthday" to Mia, adults and Mia's brothers, and Mia's face burned with embarrassment, an abashed sort of pleasure.

The bracelet was a joint present, Mia's mother said. She and Pharis had picked it out together.

Mia thought—*Daddy wouldn't have bothered. Daddy wouldn't have had time.*

Dreading the birthday for weeks. Wishing she could skip the birthday.

The last birthday she'd been happy had been her twelfth. Wishing time would stop. If her father returned now, seeing Mia taller, older, what Mom called *filling out on top*, he'd be disgusted.

The stepfather urged Mia to sip a half glass of wine. Hadn't wanted to, but always you had to give in. Pharis kept coercing, easier to give in than to keep saying no, Pharis never accepted *no*. Mia winced at the strong, tart taste of the wine at first, but the second sip was easier, her tongue seemed to be warming, thrumming.

Sensation of warmth in her throat, chest.

Slipping on the silver bracelet. Pharis urging her to say thank you, thank you with a kiss, laughing as Mia shrank away. Sliding his arm around her waist so she hadn't any choice.

Mia giggled, uneasy. Hot wine kiss, a smudge of a kiss against her cheek, somehow lurching in the direction of her mouth. *Her mouth.*

So surprised, she hadn't pushed him away. Just stood there. If his fat tongue had tried to enter her mouth—(it had not)—she'd have been unable to keep it out, and somehow (she knew) he must know that.

Mia's mother, fussing with Kevin. Eyes averted.

The hand drifting across her hips. Light as a caress—not heavy. In fact, had her stepfather exactly *touched* her?—it was like the kiss. Couldn't be sure.

Electricity in that touch. Hairs stirring on her arms and at the nape of her neck.

Sadness. Resignation. Sudden fit of giggling.

Anger: Daddy had abandoned her, to the *stepdad*.

"Mia? Where're you running to?"

Nowhere. Upstairs. Homework.

Miao Dao.

* * *

236

Mia is astonished. Too surprised at first to be upset.

She has just stepped into the bathroom, is about to close the door—confused to see that the door is being pushed open, not hard but firmly against her arm.

In the crack of the door, the ruddy, flushed face—"Hey. Sorry."

He's drunk. He's laughing. Can't be an accident, Mia thinks. The stepdad must have been watching for her to enter the bathroom in the upstairs hall close by her room. Must've moved swiftly, hadn't given her time to shut the door, let alone lock it.

"What—do you want? Go away . . ."

Mia's mouth is dry. Mia's heart hammers in her chest. Away from the house she wears shapeless clothes, but sometimes in the house the stepdad has seen her in just a T-shirt with jeans, shorts. His eyes crinkling at the corners, lingering on her like crawling ants.

No plausible reason for Pharis Locke to be using this bathroom when there is a bathroom attached to the large bedroom he shares with Mia's mother, which none of the children use.

In fact, Mia has never seen Pharis Locke use this bathroom.

Mia is uneasy. There has been a change in their relations after the smudge-kiss on Mia's mouth on the evening of her fourteenth birthday.

What Mia remembered afterward is that the fat tongue had tried to push into her mouth. At the time she'd been too confused to know what was happening.

In panic Mia had shut her jaws tight. Teeth tight. Fear contending with disbelief, outrage—*But my mother was three feet away. My mother was right there. He would not have done that with Mom right there . . .*

Yet: change is in the air. *He* has changed.

Late winter, dripping eaves. Gusting wind, melting snow. Sudden splotches of sunshine. A sense of wildness, restlessness. Cries of spring birds.

Mia returning home from field hockey practice. Mia peeling off the shirt she wears over her T-shirt. Mia in shorts.

He has seen, the stepdad. Out of the corner of his eye.

Evenings at mealtimes. Something is different. Stepdad is drinking more than he used to—beer, mostly. Often the stepdad is resolutely *not looking* at Mia. Where previously he'd talked with Mia, talked and laughed, as he did with the boys. Now, *not-looking*.

Though when he does, he asks about the silver bracelet. ("Why aren't you wearing it, Mia? Haven't lost it, have you?") His tone is both bossy and wistful. The bully is always the one who has been *hurt*.

Mia's mother urges her to wear the bracelet *and* the locket. At least when stepdad will notice.

Mia objects; she doesn't wear jewelry, much. Especially a silver bracelet that rattles when she's typing.

"Please," Mia's mother begs. "Please *try*."

He's your husband. Not mine.

Mia doesn't know whether to feel relief or annoyance or concern, or—hurt. The sudden alteration in the stepdad. As swift as a blind yanked down. Even when Mia remembers to wear the bracelet —or the locket—Pharis keeps his eyes averted from her and turns his attention on Kevin and Randy, who compete with each other to impress him. When he can't avoid acknowledging Mia, he is inanely polite. ("Would you please pass the salt, Mia. Thank you!")

Mia wonders if her mother notices this excessive politeness but decides no, her mother does not notice.

To be a mother with a new husband, Mia thinks, you must learn to *not-notice* much.

A shock to Mia when her mother steps out of the room and the stepdad turns his hungry gaze on Mia, rushing like a dog released from a kennel.

The boys don't matter. The boys won't notice how stepdad is suddenly smiling at Mia. Stroking his beard in that way Mia hates, caressing himself. Tip of a fat pink tongue glistening between his lips.

Dirty girl. Sure you are. Think I don't know you!

Mia is astonished. She looks away, face burning.

And that night, in the upstairs hall. At Mia's bathroom door.

His skin seems coarser. More flushed. Swollen nose riddled with broken capillaries that Mia has not noticed before.

Stepdad mutters an apology that doesn't sound very apologetic. "Hey. Said I was sorry. Don't be so touchy, Mi-a." Retreats to the adults' bedroom at the farther end of the hall. Mia presses against the door to hold it shut. She is trembling, disbelieving.

After using the bathroom, Mia hurries to her room, shuts the door. But cannot lock it.

Thinking—*Maybe it was an accident. He wouldn't come into this room . . .* Not with Mia's mother in the house.

Mia drags a chair to the door, positions it so that the door can't be opened.

Each night she leaves her window open a few inches. Even in cold weather. For when she goes to bed, if she lies very still, after a while, Miao Dao might come to her.

Silently. Through the window. Not every night, not most nights, but Miao Dao will come only at night and only when Mia lies very still beneath the covers breathing calmly and evenly.

Her secret! Precious.

How the beautiful white feral cat uses her sharp claws to climb up a tree beside the house and leaps from a limb of the tree to Mia's windowsill. Lowers her head, pushes through the narrow space and into Mia's room.

With a muted little cry—*miao!*—the white cat leaps onto the bed. Burrows beneath the bedclothes, presses against the side of Mia's body. Her purring is thunderous. Into the crevice beneath Mia's arm, Miao Dao's hot breath, the solace of her soft, thick fur, quick-beating heart.

Mia smells the sweet-sour aroma of damp blood on the cat's breath, for (of course) Miao Dao is a huntress.

Falling asleep to the deep, guttural purring that takes on the rhythm of Mia's heart.

Sometimes Mia wonders: *Is* this the Miao Dao she'd rescued as a tiny kitten?

Hardly a year has passed, and Miao Dao is a large cat, still lithe but solid and muscled, weighing at least twenty pounds. Nothing kittenish about the shining dark eyes, sharp, glistening teeth, steely claws. Almost, Mia thinks that this beautiful white creature isn't the original Miao Dao but another who has taken Miao Dao's place.

Your stepfather murdered the kitten. Stomped her to death with his feet. You know this, or should. I have been chosen to take her place. He will not murder me.

240

13.

On the stairs. In the upstairs hall where it seems he is always lying in wait.

As he passes Mia, passes close by Mia, seeming not to mind if she hears his quickened breath, trailing a hand across her back—just a touch! Small of Mia's back—a phantom touch. She flinches from him, sees that look in his (heated) face. Suet-colored eyes, like flies alighting on something rotted and delicious.

He makes her feel ashamed. Just—being herself.

For Mia has become strangely weak, tentative. Telling herself she is not afraid of him—the *stepdad*. She is afraid of her mother.

Afraid for her mother. Afraid that her mother will be devastated if Mia tells her what is happening.

Mia has overheard sharp words between her mother and the new husband. For the new husband, Mia's mother is learning, is not so very different from the previous husband.

Mia doesn't want to notice. Mia doesn't want to care. She cared too much in the past and doesn't want to care now.

In recent months, since the honeymoon in Sarasota, Pharis doesn't try so hard to please Mia's mother. He is away from home more frequently. His laughter is often jarring, mirthless.

Mia wonders if something has gone wrong with Pharis Locke Consultants, Inc.

She remembers how anxious her mother was when her father had first become estranged from them. Worries about money, about *keeping the house*. She wonders if her mother is beginning to have such worries again.

Wanting to accuse her mother—*Why did you marry him? Why did you bring a stranger into our house? And now—does the stranger half own our house?*

Returning home from school to discover in her room, on her bed, a magazine that appears to have been casually dropped onto the coverlet. Pulp magazine with a naked, ludicrously big-breasted woman on its cover—*Hot Eye Kandy*.

Mia laughs aloud, this is so—tacky.

Stupid, silly. *Gross.*

With averted eyes she picks up the magazine. *Does not* glance through it, as the stepdad wants her to. Instead she quickly slips the magazine into her backpack. Goes downstairs, takes care that her mother doesn't notice where she is headed, disposes of the magazine in the big green trash container in a corner of the garage.

Not the recycling bin for magazines, paper. Where the magazine might somehow be discovered.

Another day, Mia discovers in her math textbook small drawings in red pencil. Crude cartoon drawings. (Female body? Breasts?) She is astonished that an adult man would go to such lengths to harass her, take such time.

Rubbing at the small red drawings, trying to erase them. Tearing pages. Finally Mia scribbles over the drawings with a red pencil of her own. If anyone saw how her math text has been defaced, they would be utterly perplexed.

But then, Pharis keeps his distance. Avoids Mia. Misses dinner with the excuse of a "business meeting."

"Where is Dad," the boys ask their mother. When did her brothers begin calling *him Dad*, Mia wonders.

She is/is not afraid of him. All she has to do is scream. All she has to do is run away. All she has to do is confess to her mother how he is harassing her.

That look of sick yearning. Resentment, anger beneath.

Slack lips. Wet smile. Meat-smile.

In the upstairs hall, where suddenly he appears—again. His shirt falling open, exposing the rounded, fatty stomach covered in gray hairs. Matted hair on his chest, nipples like little buttons.

Male nipples! Mia wants to laugh wildly.

And another time, pushing open the bathroom door. When Mia would have sworn Pharis wasn't home.

"Go away! Leave me alone! I hate you."

Red-faced, the stepdad mutters his lame apology—*Sorry*. Clumsily backing away, guessing that this time he has gone too far.

As Mia has gone too far, past a point of no return. Instead of shrinking away as she has in the past, this time declaring *I hate you*.

A relief, Mia flees the house. Across the backyard into the shadows at the edge of the property.

Into the adjacent woods where the feral cats once lived.

"Miao Dao? Are you here? Kitty-kitty . . ." Her voice is hopeful, pleading.

Here is a mangled landscape. Overgrown even where the bull-dozer razed trees and underbrush; and now trash is being dumped in the lot—rotted newspapers, plastic soda bottles, cans.

Bitterly Mia thinks—what a loss, the feral cats' home was razed for *this*.

It is quiet here. No one knows that Mia is here. If she stands very still and looks carefully, she can see ghost cats in the shadows, watching her warily.

". . . I am your friend. I love you."

Out of the shadows the beautiful white-furred cat appears, the size of a lynx. Big-pawed, with a plume of a tail. Shiny dark-marble eyes fixed upon Mia. *Here I am. Did you think I had abandoned you?*

As Mia stares, Miao Dao makes her way through the under-brush. Unerring, scarcely hesitating, as graceful as a wraith. Not daring to breathe, Mia leans forward to pet the cat, but just as she is about to touch Miao Dao's head, there is a clumsy, clattering sound behind her, there comes a loud voice—"Mi-a? Hey—where are you?"

Pharis Locke has followed her into her secret place.

She is stunned. Resentful. In an instant, Miao Dao has bounded away and is gone.

Pharis Locke has been drinking. Eyes like crawling ants. How Mia hates him and fears him! He is a bully, yet there is something weak, yearning about him. Stroking his bearded chin, tugging at the skimpy hairs. Mia can hear him breathing as if he has become winded.

"This is our secret, eh? Your mother doesn't know where you go every night. How you're prowling out here at night. Just what the hell are you doing, Mia? Meeting a boyfriend here? Boys?"

Stepdad leers at Mia. He has been advancing upon her, and now he stops, calculating. (Should he reach out? Touch her? Take hold of her? And if he does, what will Mia do? He knows how quick the girl is, how rapid the reflexes of a girl of fourteen. He knows how she can turn against him, scream at him—*I hate you.* Must calculate the risk of terrorizing her against the possibility of overpowering her. If he can manage it, he believes that Mia will cease resisting.)

Yet it is quite possible that the (concerned) stepfather feels responsibility for the stepdaughter. It is possible that he is genuinely bewildered. For why would a fourteen-year-old girl tramp out here into a scrubby woods? What can draw her to this desolate place gouged with tire tracks, litter?

"All right, Mia. Let's go back home . . ."

Stepdad speaks familiarly. As if he has the right.

But Mia shrinks away. Muttering that she can find her own way home. Thanks!

To stepdad's surprise Mia breaks into a run, as a defiant child might. Ignores the man calling after her as she runs through the woods, along the narrow path through the brambles. Mia is thrilled, as if she's on the hockey field, running with a stick gripped in both hands, outdistancing her opponents.

Stepdad is left behind, thwarted and panting. Stepdad has come into the vacant lot from the street, can't navigate the path through brambles. By the time he returns to the house, Mia is upstairs in her room.

Thinking—*Is it my fault?*

That Pharis Locke has so altered. This past year, since he has married Mia's mother and moved into their house. Now that Mia is fourteen and "older"—not a child.

He has become crude, obstinate. Scratching roughly in the area of his groin, as if unconsciously but then, gradually, with un-mistakable crudeness when Mia has no choice but to pass close by him. And the simpering sounds emitted from his mouth for only Mia to hear—"*Dirty girl! Mi-a.*"

Playing with Randy and Kevin. Pretending to be listening to the boys' chatter. Then, suddenly upstairs, standing outside Mia's room, belt undone, trousers open. Obscene motions with his hand. Mia is utterly shocked, taken by surprise—her eyes shift downward, she is unable to look away.

At first she is stricken with shame. Then hears herself laugh. Wild snort of laughter.

"What's that?" she says. "You've got to be kidding."

Instantly the stepdad ceases the obscene motions. Flinches away from Mia's jeering eyes, mortified.

So quickly it has happened. Mia would never have expected this: a thrill of power. That the man can be assaulted in a way particular to him, his maleness.

She realizes: the man's power is to intimidate, to make you ashamed. But your power over him is the power of laughter.

For (Mia sees) it is very funny. The man's penis, the flabby thighs of the middle-aged man, the stubby flesh between the thighs brandished as a kind of weapon but limp now, slack and defeated. Laughable.

Mia slams the door to her room. Not in fear but in laughter.

14.

Bad Mia! As Pharis glumly predicted, she has lost the silver bracelet engraved with her name.

Reporting to her mother, reluctantly. Guiltily. After Mia has enlisted Kevin and Randy to help her search for the bracelet upstairs and downstairs, with no luck.

Mia's mother is stricken: "But, Mia—how on earth could you lose a bracelet with a clasp like that?"

Mia shrugs a shoulder. "No idea."

"Did you wear it to school?"

Mia considers. "Not sure."

"If you did, it might turn up in the lost and found. Did you look there yet?"

Mia frowns. "Not yet."

"Your stepdad will be so—disappointed. So upset. If he finds out . . ."

Mia agrees. "Better not tell him."

Another day. Alone in the kitchen together. As if she has just thought of it, Mia's mother lowers her voice to ask Mia if—Pharis has "touched" her—ever?

Mia is stunned by this question. Yet she has no idea how to reply.

Realizing what courage has been summoned by her mother to ask such a mortifying question. Mia sees the dread in her mother's eyes.

Shakes her head mutely. *No.*

No? He hasn't touched Mia? Or—threatened to touch her?

"N-no."

Eyes averted, voice lowered, Mia assures her mother that there is nothing to tell her.

Mia's mother persists, fearfully. "Mia, are you sure?"

Flushed with anger, Mia laughs. "I told you, Mom—*sure.*"

Has to be a coincidence—for Mia's mother and Mia's father are not in contact—that Mia's father calls her the following day, the first call from him in weeks, and asks her, in a casual way, what it's like to live with a "new dad." Mia can't think how to reply in a way that would not incriminate her mother or call attention to Mia's unhappiness and worsen their lives. Mia understood: her father does not (really) want her and her brothers to be happy without him in their lives. Though of course Mia's father does not (really) want the children of his first marriage in his life any longer, for he has a "new family" now—new wife, new baby (girl). Mia bites her lip, feeling a stab of jealousy, that her father has a new daughter, replacing her.

Especially, Mia's father does not want his ex-wife to be happy without him. All this, Mia knows. It makes her sad to know, but she knows.

So, assuring her father that the new dad is "terrific" and Mom "a lot happier" now than she'd ever been in Mia's memory.

At the other end of the line, silence. Mia's words are a rebuke, an insult. Stiffly Mia's father murmurs: "Great news! Just great. Thanks."

Soon after, the conversation ends. Mia has a premonition—*It will be a long time before he calls again.*

15.

Stunning, the animosity between Mia and the adult man legally related to her as her *stepfather*.

The thrill of it. A greater thrill, because it's at close range, more intimate than the animosity Mia felt for her tormenters at school.

No one torments Mia at school any longer, since the death of the Dempster boy, which has never been satisfactorily explained.

Throat slashed. As if with a large, serrated knife, a clawed instrument. Neither weapon ever found, and no suspects.

At Mia's school, people still speak in hushed voices of the death, the murder. Mia's friend Janey has heard—from a family friend whose brother-in-law is an officer on the local police force— that Ernie Dempster may have been involved with drugs, selling drugs at the school, and was killed as punishment or as a warning.

"No news?—about the kid with his throat slashed?" Pharis sometimes asks Mia at mealtimes, in an ironic voice. The mysterious, unexplained death seems to intrigue him. With Mia's mother, Randy, and Kevin looking on, listening—Mia has to report that there is no news, not that she knows.

Pharis makes a *tsking* sound as if, in some way, the death of Mia's older classmate is a symptom of something gravely wrong with the culture of youth to which his obstinate stepdaughter belongs. (Yes, Pharis has discovered that the silver bracelet is missing. And yes, Pharis has declared himself, bluntly and curtly, *pissed*.) Stroking the stupid wispy beard, twisting his mouth in a grimace, showing the moist tip of the snake-tongue, just fleetingly, so that no one else at the table will see, only Mia.

My fault, Mia thinks. *Dirty girl*.

The tense, drawn look in her mother's face reminds Mia of the tense, drawn look in her mother's face at the time of the divorce. But now Mia's mother tries to disguise it with makeup, not very successfully.

(Is Mia's mother drinking again? Mia has reason to think so.)

(Secret drinking. But Mia can guess.)

If Pharis has been out, this means that Pharis has been drinking. There is a pretense of business meetings—"conferences." Pharis Locke Consultants, Inc., is (primarily) an online business, Mia has gathered. Not sure if it has an office anywhere except inside Pharis Locke's console computer, now established in the downstairs guest room, where Mia's father once slept.

His footsteps on the stairs after the house has darkened. His presence outside Mia's bedroom door. As if the man is brooding, contemplating. What he would like to do to her. What he will do to her. When he can. When she can't stop him. Soon.

Mia is fully awake, trembling. She has dragged a chair against the door in such a way as to prevent it being opened.

Beginning to sweat with the possibility that if he's drunk enough, Pharis will repay her for laughing at him. The unforgivable insult—laughter. A rebuke of the maleness of the man, unbearable to him.

If he is determined enough, Pharis can push open the door. Send the chair flying. If he is angry enough. Insulted.

Mia can scream for help. Of course.

Yet screaming for help will only madden Pharis. If Mia's mother comes to her, Pharis will be furious at *her*.

He has yet to touch either of them in anger or impatience. He has (yet) to discipline the young boys, though Mia can see how at times he would dearly like to, and possibly will, soon.

He is far heavier than Mia. Far stronger.

He has been drinking, which is a kind of strength. If he wishes, he can force himself into the room and cause Mia to scream in a way she has never screamed.

Dirty girl. This is what you like.

The boys at school loved it, that Mia was terrified of them. Ernie Dempster's ecstatic face. She'd seen the face astonished with a splattering of blood, the eyes dulling . . .

Mia stands very still in her nightgown, barefoot. The window has been left open a crack to let in Miao Dao. But it may be one of those nights that Miao Dao does not push her way into the room to sleep beside Mia but remains outside in the woods. If Mia wants Miao Dao, she may have to seek the cat in the woods.

Outside her door, Pharis has moved on. She is fairly certain that he has moved on. Thank God! Perhaps she'd imagined him outside her bedroom door. She is faint with relief. Laughs aloud. Another night, and the stepdad has spared her.

16.

A raincoat over the nightgown, feet thrust into sneakers. Mia is too excited to go to bed. The air in her room is stultifying.

Slips from the darkened house. Runs across the lawn through damp, tufted grass into the shadowy wooded lot next door, where Miao Dao and the other feral cats await her.

A hazy night. A night like gauze. Mist. Objects melt together, their boundaries unclear.

Mia is thrilled to be here. She can breathe here. She is very happy. Mia wants only to curl herself up here. She would like to shrink to a size not much larger than Miao Dao. She will burrow into the underbrush, protected by the feral cats who love her and would never wish to hurt her.

"Hey! Mi-a!"

A crude chortling. Clumsy stumbling in underbrush. A flashlight beam jerks over Mia, blinding her. She tries to shield her eyes with her hands, provoking derisive laughter in her pursuer. She is in despair. Pharis has followed her to this secret place and defiled it.

She is sick with dismay. The feral cats will flee now. Miao Dao will never appear, out of revulsion for Pharis Locke.

Pharis is laughing at her, the look in her face of shock, alarm, mortification. But Pharis is also irritable, menacing. His words are slurred, mean: "Where the fuck are you going, Mi-a? Jesus! It's a jungle here . . ."

In this beautiful quiet place, the shock of the man's voice. His heavy footsteps, panting breath. He has followed her here—how? She is certain that he'd gone to bed, certain she was safe from him that night.

Laughing, in cruel delight. For indeed Pharis is drunk. And wanting to punish.

"Little bitch. What the fuck d'you think you are doing . . ."

Rudely the blinding light pokes at Mia's face. At her chest, her belly. Drops to her groin. Pharis is very close to Mia now. She seems incapable of running from him, she is suffused with dismay, regret. She has betrayed Miao Dao and the feral cats—has she? She has led this terrible person into their secret place.

Pharis grabs at Mia. She throws off his hand, which is a mistake. For Pharis is easily angered. He is sensitive about being respected, disrespected. Mia whimpers in pain; he has struck her face with the back of his hand, not on purpose—unless yes, he has struck her on purpose. His intention is to intimidate her, overpower her, reduce her to terror so that he can run his hands over her, throw her onto the marshy ground and push himself between her legs, defeat her.

"You—goddamn—*dirty girl*—"

Out of the shadows, a flash of white. A white-furred creature leaping, sharp teeth bared.

There is a strangled scream. With both hands the man tries to push away the furious creature that has attached itself to his throat.

It is the size of a large cat, or a lynx, snarling, growling. As Mia stares in horror, Miao Dao leaps down from the man's shoulders, releasing him to stagger blindly, fingers pressed against his neck in a futile effort to staunch the outpouring of blood.

But the man is helpless. The man falls heavily. All his strength is draining from him. Mia is transfixed. She sees but cannot stop what is happening: the slashed carotid artery, the geyser of dark blood.

Is there a moon? A clouded moon? The flashlight has fallen into the underbrush and is lost.

Mia whimpers in fear. She laughs, a wild cry of a laugh. Mia rouses herself. She rouses herself to run toward the (darkened) house. She has been cunning, she has not locked herself out of the house but fixed the lock so that the door, stealthily shut behind her, did not lock.

How quiet the house is! Like a house in a dream, or at the bottom of the sea.

Only Mia's sharp breathing, the pounding of her heart.

Must call 911. Emergency. Ambulance . . .

In the kitchen, fumbling for the phone against the wall. Hesitant to switch on the overhead lights. Mia is shivering and whimpering to herself as a small child might, in a state beyond terror, of pure emotion, sensual, near to unbearable . . .

"Oh, Mia."

Mia has been very quiet, she is certain. Yet Mia's mother has awakened and has come downstairs into the kitchen in her nightclothes, wraithlike but unflinching and determined. As if Mia's mother has sensed a seismic shift in the night. The very foundation beneath the house shuddering.

Mia's mother switches on a single bright light above the sink. This single light is all that is required, for there is Mia at the sink, in a trance, eyes dilated, wearing a raincoat over her nightgown, running hot water from the faucet, scalding-hot water, desperate to rinse the razor-sharp Japanese knife, to remove all stains.

"Give it here, Mia."

The knife is taken from her fingers. Mia has failed to wash it thoroughly. Blood traces would remain on the blade and on the carved ebony handle.

Deftly Mia's mother gives the knife another swipe or two beneath the faucet, then places it in the dishwasher, which is two-thirds full of dishes and silverware. No problem for Mia's mother to rapidly punch in the controls, SANITIZE, EXTRA RINSE, set the dishwasher thrumming.

Returning then to the upstairs of the darkened house, to their beds. Preparing for the next day, and the next. In the kitchen, all surfaces gleaming. When they are questioned, as of course they must be questioned, there is not much useful information to impart: an utter surprise, shock, no possible explanation, yes he'd been drinking, yes he was often away until the early hours of the morning, no his wife knew nothing of his financial affairs, yes he did seem to have "enemies"—the wife thought they might have been business associates, but she wasn't certain, for he'd kept such information to himself.

No, the stepdaughter had scarcely known him.

No need or wish for the family to move to another house. Why?

Whatever had happened to the stepdad had not happened in the house.

Whatever had happened to the stepdad had not happened to *her.*

Which is why Mia's sleep is a deep, dreamless sleep. Which is why, close beside Mia, Miao Dao sleeps through the night and why, through all the years of Mia's adolescence, Mia and Miao Dao will be inseparable.

PHANTOMWISE:
1972

Out of the steep, snowy ravine. Clutching at rocks, her hands bloodied. And all the while, snow falling, temperature dropping to zero degrees Fahrenheit.

How still the soft-falling snow amid rocks! The yearning, the temptation to lie down, sleep.

He'd wanted her to die. He'd wanted to kill her with his hands. But she has escaped him, he will not follow her. (She vows) he will not find her ever again.

1.

By the time she allowed herself to think *It has happened*—*to me*, it was already too late.

So unexpectedly it had begun. Almost, Alyce would think afterward, as if someone else had acted in her place. She'd stared in astonishment from a little distance.

She hadn't been *drunk*. Except so excited, so elated, so—*exhilarated*.

That he'd even noticed her. Invited her to come with him after the reception. After the lecture. He'd known the speaker, a visiting professor from the University of Edinburgh. Before the lecture she'd seen him speaking with the distinguished white-haired professor, she'd seen them smiling, shaking hands.

A theory of language. Theories of language. How does language originate?—Is consciousness a blank slate (as it had been once thought by philosophers like John Locke) or is consciousness something like a field of shimmering possibilities generated by the particularities of the human brain?

If consciousness can be dis-embodied, is there the possibility of consciousness persisting after physical death? Is there the possibility of *hauntedness*?

He'd asked what she had thought of the lecture, and Alyce said she could give no opinion, she had not enough knowledge. And he'd said what sounded like—*Well, you will. You've only just begun.*

How flattering to Alyce Urquhart, at nineteen.

They were crossing the darkened campus. Afterward she would realize how subtly he was guiding her—a light touch to her arm, an indication. *Yes, this way. Here.*

Afterward she would recall how at dusk the old Gothic buildings of the campus took on a sepulchral air. And how a light mist seemed to radiate from streetlamps, as if the very air had become blurred.

Tall, straight fir trees rose out of sight. Entering the region of trees was like entering an enchanted forest marking the western edge of the campus.

Her heart swelled, she felt such happiness. If she were to die—if she had already died—it would be this moment she would remember most vividly: the fir trees that were so beautiful and the young philosophy professor at her side who had singled her out for his attention that evening.

But she did not know him, her instructor, well enough to exclaim, *Oh, how beautiful! Look.*

Whatever Simon Meech said to Alyce Urquhart that evening, Alyce would not recall precisely. Even in the presence of persons whom she knew, Alyce was inclined to shyness, and she did not know Simon Meech at all. Yet suddenly he meant much to her; she had not guessed how much. And only vaguely would she recall how, without seeming to do so, he led her away from her residence hall. Away from the bright-lit, over-warm, and buzzing dining hall, where at this hour of the evening she'd have been pushing along a cafeteria tray in the company of other girls and listening or half listening to their chatter in a pleasantly neutral state of mind— mindlessness—and not required to think *But who am I to be doing this? And what will come of it?*

What will come of it: the steep, snowy ravine, bloodied hands grasping at rocks, the determination to haul herself up, not to surrender and not to die.

A misty and rain-lashed autumn. Her second year at the college she'd envisioned as a sort of floating island, an oasis-island amid the rubble of her familial life.

And what will come of it. Of me.

Alyce's most cherished class was a creative writing poetry seminar taught by an elderly visiting poet from Boston. Once, Roland B___ had known Edna St. Vincent Millay and Robert Frost, Ezra Pound and T. S. Eliot, Wallace Stevens, William Carlos Williams, and Marianne Moore. He counted himself a friendly acquaintance of Robert Lowell, Elizabeth Bishop, Anne Sexton. He'd known Sylvia Plath—"for a teasingly short while."

A smooth, hairless dome of a head that seemed too large for the narrow shoulders. Suety eyes, deep-sunken like a turtle's, yet luminous. Roland B___ seemed always cold, though dressed for the upstate New York winter: Harris tweed jackets with leather elbows, sweater-vests, woolen scarves slung cavalierly around his neck. The backs of his delicate hands were unusually pale, the skin seemed soft, flaccid. Alyce had the idea that if she were to lean across the seminar table and press a forefinger into that skin, the indention would very slowly fill in.

Aloud, in a hoarse, reverent voice, the elderly poet read, or sometimes recited poetry as if he were alone and the students were privileged to overhear, straining to listen. Alyce complained that her neck ached after three hours in the seminar, leaning forward, not wanting to miss a syllable.

This was not an actual complaint of course. Her heart beat with awe for the distinguished poet, so blissfully self-centered, he seemed a very Buddha basking in his own divinity.

At the first class meeting Roland B___ asked each young poet to recite a favorite poem—"a poem of unqualified greatness." The request was a total surprise. No one was prepared.

Alyce recited a little-known poem by William Butler Yeats—"To a Friend Whose Work Has Come to Nothing." Technically the poem was fascinating to her: harsh, percussive, accusatory, with a formal rhyme scheme, rage tempered by art. As a first-year student, she'd unconsciously memorized the poem out of her English literature anthology; one day, she'd realized that she knew it by heart.

Liking the quiet rage of the final lines. *Amid a place of stone / Be secret and exult, / Because of all things known / That is most difficult.*

Whatever Roland B___ might have expected from an undergraduate at the university, it was clear that he hadn't expected this impassioned poem by Yeats. "Well! A unique choice, Miss—" squinting at the class list as Alyce provided her last name in an embarrassed murmur: "Urquhart."

"Ah, Urquhart"—as if the name might mean something to him. Roland B___ gazed at Alyce with an expression of wonder.

Clearly, Roland B___ did not know what to make of her, just yet.

2.

This season of reversals. A balmy autumn followed by an abrupt snowstorm in early November. Leaves ripped from trees, the pale sky mottled with clouds, a dank air in the "historic" eighteenth-century buildings modeled (it was said) after Cambridge University.

Not a season for romance. Not a season for sentiment. If others in the residence hall could have guessed that Alyce Urquhart was newly pregnant, they would have been astonished, speechless. For God's sake—*how?*

No one had seen Alyce Urquhart with any man or boy publicly. Her lover was her Philosophy 101 quiz section instructor, but each was discreet in the presence of the other, and Alyce took care to match Simon Meech's aloofness with her own.

Still, Alyce would sometimes raise her hand in class to answer a question Simon had put to several rows of students, which no one else knew how to answer or answer adequately.

"Yes? Miss—" Just perceptibly, Simon might smile.

But Alyce did not mistake the gesture as an invitation to smile back.

It was in this way that she'd attracted Simon Meech's attention, of course. *Always* the bright young schoolgirl determined to be impressive to her teachers.

As a young instructor, Simon inclined toward haughtiness, disdain. A kind of Kinch—James Joyce's notion of himself as Stephen Dedalus, a brilliantly unhappy young man in his mid-twenties, vain and uncertain, insecure, eaten up with pride. Yet, in his way, wanting to be *good*.

Before coming to the university to earn a Ph.D. in philosophy, Simon had been a seminary student for three years. He'd intended to be a Catholic priest, a Jesuit, but as he'd told Alyce, his plans had not worked out.

Another girl would have asked, *But why not?*—but Alyce understood that Simon did not want to be asked such a question.

Nothing personal, private! Nothing that pried into the young man's soul. Alyce understood for she did not want to be asked such questions either.

Through lowered eyes she observed him at the front of the classroom—her lover. Though she did not consciously think *lover*.

Was love involved? She had not heard *love*—the word—uttered between them.

In class Alyce took careful notes. Or it appeared that she took careful notes. Leaning over her notebook in a trance of concentration, hair falling across the side of her face as she moved her pen quickly across the page.

Now her feverish note-taking had a singular theme. What could not be uttered aloud took shape beneath her pen. *I am afraid, Simon . . .*

But no. Why should she announce that she is afraid.

Instead, she would say, *Simon, I think . . .*

But this too was weak, craven. Why should she say merely *I think!*

Bravely she would say, *Simon, I am . . .*

But her resolve faded. Her courage melted away, a puddle at her feet. How could she bring herself to tell her sardonic Kinch lover *I am pregnant.*

The words would not come. She could not choke up such words that were both banal and terrible. Her tongue had gone numb, a chill suffused her body.

Hurrying away from the classroom even as the bell clanged. If Simon glanced after her with something like surprise—that she should be so eager to leave the classroom even as other students lingered to speak with him—she didn't want to notice. *Away, away. Must get away.*

Desperate to hide in the women's restroom, beneath the stairs. To check another time. To determine *if.*

Though knowing—*No. Don't be ridiculous.*

In less than a week she'd become compulsive about checking her underwear to see if the bleeding had begun. Though knowing that it had not.

In the morning, after troubled sleep, checking her nightgown, bedsheets. *But—is it? No.*

Haunting to her now, the dark menstrual blood that refused to appear. Like a shadow that, when you glance up, startled, has vanished—has not been there at all.

He'd tried to pull out of her at the crucial moment, Simon had.

Tried, but had not, or had not exactly. Not *entirely.*

A groan of something like pain, anguish. The hawkish Kinch face contorted for a long moment, the teeth bared.

She'd scarcely seen him. His lower body. His penis that was (she would try to recall afterward as one might try to recall a frightening dream, to master the dream) blunt and hard, hot with blood and angry-seeming.

Yet soft-skinned. Astonishingly soft, flaccid. When they'd lain together, panting and sweating, and whatever had passed through them like an electric current had vanished as if it had never been, she'd felt it—felt *him*—against her belly, sticky with mucus.

For this was love, was it? Naïvely she'd wanted to think, *It's a promise. Love will come.*

The truth was, she'd hardly known what was happening. What Simon was doing to her, or trying (awkwardly) to do to her, that yielded no pleasure for her, only just a sharp-piercing, shocking hurt between her legs that had felt like an evisceration.

Clumsily they were lying together on a sofa in Simon's apartment, much too narrow for them. The sofa was not very clean, and now it would be less clean, a patina of grime on a nubby beige fabric. Without wishing to, Alyce had noted the frayed carpet, stains in the hardwood floor and in the faded wallpaper. A smell of cooking odors from the floor below. The apartment was furnished, Simon had said with a smiling shrug, as if to absolve himself of responsibility for it.

It was an interim life, Simon said. A between life. Neither here nor there. Not yet.

She hadn't known what he meant. Much of his speech, airy, witty, self-conscious, Alyce didn't quite understand, but she understood that she was expected to react with a smile, laughter, admiration.

In their lovemaking Simon had panted like a creature that has been hunted down, not like a hunter. Yet, Alyce would recall, he had hunted, pursued, chased down, all but coerced *her*.

Not rape. Nothing so physically coercive. Instead he'd made her feel shame, that she had caused him to misunderstand her.

"Why did you come back here with me, then? Why are you being disingenuous now?" He'd professed surprise, reproach when Alyce had seemed to resist him.

Disingenuous. She knew what this word meant, though she guessed he might assume that she did not know.

"I—I don't know . . . I'd thought—you wanted to . . ."

Spend time with me. Talk with me. About linguistics, philosophy of mind . . .

She'd been confused. Her brain wasn't functioning with its usual precision. Like a fine mechanism into which static has been introduced, to befuddle.

Simon had shocked her by addressing her with an air of disdain, sarcasm that was totally unlike the way he'd behaved at the reception, or the way he behaved in the classroom. Oh but didn't he *like* her?—she'd thought he had liked her.

Like a child, she was abashed, wounded. Naïvely wanting to say, *But I'd thought you liked me . . .*

But then, hearing the petulant edge in his own voice, Simon smiled and was friendly again, and charming; holding her hand, stroking her arm, her shoulder. Telling her that she was very beautiful, he'd seen from the first day in their class that she was very beautiful, and quick to understand what others were slow to understand or never understood at all. He had seen that she was special. It was rare that any undergraduate had such an instinctive grasp of philosophy, especially a female undergraduate. (Had Simon been about to say *girl*? But he had not.) He'd had trouble looking away from her, he claimed, paying proper attention to the other students. He'd shown her first short paper, intriguingly titled "Zeno's Paradoxes and Our Own," to the professor who lectured in the course, who'd been impressed as well. Both had agreed on a grade of A.

He was leaning very close to Alyce and breathing audibly, hotly, like one who is not accustomed to such intimacy yet believes it to be his due.

Still, Alyce held herself stiff and unyielding. Her heart was beating rapidly, as the heart of a creature that is trapped, yet has not quite acknowledged it is trapped.

"Well. We can leave. We don't have to stay if you're not comfortable here, Alyce." Simon's voice was flat, dismissive. The enunciation of *Alyce* was not flattering.

"I—I think—yes, I would like to l-leave . . ."

Her voice trailed off. The misunderstanding had been hers, that was clear. Yet she had no idea what to say. Apologize? Simon saw how she was hesitating, trying to smile, and he put his hands on her and his mouth against her mouth, and so a kind of fury passed over them.

Not rape. Not—precisely.

Though her body tensed against him, unmistakably. Stiffening in sheer physical panic, dread. Another man, a truer lover, would have relented, drawn away. Would have soothed the frightened young woman, comforted her, spoken to her. But not this man, who'd lost awareness of Alyce except as a physical being, in opposition to him but weaker than he, unable to withstand his greater strength.

"*Oh Christ. Jesus!*"—the cry was torn from him.

Not pleasure, such intensity of feeling. Convulsive, anguished.

Not guessing, at the time, that he would blame *her*.

Afterward she'd dressed quickly in the bathroom of his apartment, a space so cramped she could barely move without colliding with the sink, the toilet, a wall. Clumsily washing herself, not meeting her dazed and bloodshot eyes in the mirror, dragging wetted fingers through her straggly hair.

He'd walked her back to the residence, mostly in silence. Long Kinch legs, eager to stride ahead of her. The air was colder, the mist had thickened. The tall, straight fir trees were near invisible. She would recall—her pride would insist—that Simon had clasped her hand for at least part of the walk, but in fact he'd only just gripped her arm at the elbow from time to time, not so much to comfort as to hurry her.

"I'll let you go, from here. It's not a great idea for us to be seen together." He'd stopped at the sidewalk leading to her residence and was already backing away.

No kiss. No final squeeze of Alyce's hand. She would tell herself, of course, he was concerned for her, for her as well as himself.

She would not see him again. She would stay away from his class, which met late on Thursday afternoons. He'd had so little awareness of her in that moment; he'd forgotten her entirely in the very instant of penetrating her body.

Hating him. So very ashamed that she had not been able to withstand the man.

She *would not stay away from class*. Certainly not!

Why should she deprive herself of philosophy? She loved and revered the texts she was reading for the first time—Plato, Aristotle, Marcus Aurelius, Spinoza, Locke, Hume. John Stuart Mill. Ridiculous for her to stay away from class because of the man and risk a failing grade.

And she would see Simon Meech again. If he summoned her, she would come to him.

In all, five times. In the furnished apartment, arriving by stealth, after dark. On that sofa. As winter deepened. As dark came earlier each day and snow muffled the stone walkways and there were more of Alyce's clothes to be tugged off by the man's impatient hands. And afterward, clumsily washing herself, her raw and chafed and heated body, avoiding her reflection in the mirror—*Is this me? Alyce? Doing such things?* The wonderment in it, dread and pride commingled.

Touching her mouth, tenderly. Lips swollen from being kissed, sucked.

Yes. It is you. No one else.

3.

And then Roland B___ interceded in her life.

No one could have anticipated. (Alyce could not have antici-pated.) How, crossing the snow-swept square in front of the uni-versity library a few days after she'd had no choice but to realize that she must be pregnant, she'd heard a familiar voice calling her name—"Alyce?"

Blindly she'd been making her way. Head lowered, thoughts abuzz with alarm, fear—*No. Can't. Not possible.*

The surprise of her name in this public place like a burst of music.

She turned and saw—who was it? A gentlemanly older man—in a brown winter overcoat with a sealskin collar, pumpkin-colored knit cap pulled down over his head—crinkling his eyes at her in delight. "Miss Urquhart? It *is* you."

Startling Alyce, the gentleman reached for her hands. She was too surprised to shrink back shyly.

"Alyce—I believe? Hel*lo*."

"H-hello . . ."

It was an astonishment to be greeted this way by the visiting poet who was so formal in his speech in the seminar. Rarely—indeed, never in Alyce's memory—had Professor B___ called any student by a first name. She wouldn't have dared to assume that the poet even knew her first name—or that, outside the seminar room, he would recognize her.

"Have you seen the Poet's House, Alyce? No? Come, then. You will be my first visitor."

"I wish that I could, Professor—but . . ."

"It's close by. In this direction. My dear, come!"—linking his arm through Alyce's arm in a display of mock gallantry.

How playful Roland B___ was in the bright, open air! Not a small, tentative man as he'd appeared in the seminar room, but as tall as Alyce and quite forceful.

The Poet's House, as it was called, was a handsome old faded-redbrick Edwardian residence that looked as if it were held together by the thick-clustered ivy that covered its walls. Set back behind a wrought iron fence and gate, it had the air of a quaint period piece; in its small front lawn was a statue in black marble of the Presbyterian minister who'd founded the college in 1847.

In the foyer, a brass plaque noted that such distinguished poets as Robert Frost, Amy Lowell, Theodore Roethke, and Galway Kinnell had been residents in the house. The interior exuded an air of faded opulence: antique furniture, musty brick fireplace, French silk wallpaper, Steinway grand piano with several (muted) keys that Roland B___ cheerfully struck as he led his visitor into the drawing room.

"Let me take your coat, dear. You will stay awhile, I hope."

"I—I can't stay long. I was on my way to the library . . ."

"And would you like tea, dear? I was going to prepare tea for myself."

No, no! I must leave.

"Y-yes. Thank you."

Roland B____ was standing somewhat close to her, smiling.

She could see just his lower teeth, which were somewhat small, uneven, stained.

Roland B____ was observing her with a smile. The flush in his cheeks and glisten in his eyes made Alyce wonder whether he'd been drinking in the afternoon.

No doubt it was lonely for him here, away from friends and companions in Boston. In the seminar he'd several times spoken of Boston with a wistful air.

"Your choice of tea, dear: green, Darjeeling, Earl Grey, Lapsang?"

Whatever Roland B____ was having, Alyce said she would have.

"You are very agreeable, dear Alyce! In our seminar, you are not so easily persuaded."

This seemed to Alyce a remark as provocative as a nudge in the ribs. As if, through the weeks of the semester, the poet had been hoping to persuade her—of what?

How little he knew of her, or could guess! Alyce herself could not bear to think of her predicament, what grew in her belly like a tiny acorn, unstoppable.

Leading Alyce along a corridor into a rear bedroom with elaborate white molding at the ceiling. A four-poster bed with a brass headboard, threadbare Indian carpet, tables piled with books and magazines. A small chandelier hung from the ceiling, also brass, in need of polishing.

"Here you have a glimpse, my dear, of a bachelor's stoical life. When I was young, I yearned to be alone, and I got my wish. And now I am older, and the danger is past."

Seeing that the faded quilt on the bed was crooked, Roland B__ deftly smoothed out the wrinkles.

The four-poster bed was not large, an old-fashioned double bed, but you could see that the occupant used just one half of it, with large square pillows propped up against the headboard; on the bedside table, a notebook and a stack of books. There came to Alyce's nostrils a faint, musty smell of bedclothes not freshly laundered.

"D'you read in bed, Alyce?"

Alyce nodded *yes*.

"D'you write in bed? In a notebook?"

Alyce nodded *yes*.

"Reading poetry, scribbling poetry, dreaming poetry. Yes, I'm sure that you do."

Roland B__ was standing uncomfortably close to Alyce. She laughed nervously and edged away.

In all the rooms of the Poet's House that Alyce had seen, the poet kept books, papers, worksheets. You could see that wherever he went, Roland B__ had to have a book at his fingertips, and he had to have his work. He'd positioned an antique writing desk in a bay window so that he could sit and gaze out at the brick-walled courtyard, which was filling up with snow.

"My dear Alyce, sit! Sit here."

Roland B__ urged Alyce to sit at the desk, his hands on her shoulders. Then, leaning over her, his chin grazing the top of her head.

Very peculiar, Alyce thought this. As if Roland B__ were imagining he might see through her eyes.

Alyce would have liked to throw off the poet's hands, leap to her feet, and escape. But a sensation of lethargy came over her, as if her limbs had lost their strength. She could barely move.

He sees that I am unhappy. An open wound.

"You are welcome, you know. At any time."

In the courtyard, snow was falling steadily now. A swirl of white, mesmerizing. Soon the old, faded brick would be obscured by powdery white. Footsteps would be muffled. Voices would be muffled. Within the movement of the snow flurrying to earth all was still. Alyce Urquhart and Roland B___ might have been alone together in a remote place, in a remote time. The elderly poet standing behind Alyce, his hands on her shoulders, silent, staring out the window at the foreshortened view filling up with snow.

In that way it began.

All things begin in innocence.

That is to say—ignorance.

4.

God help me. Even if You don't love me.

5.

Feverishly her brain worked. Like a cornered rat, she thought herself. Scrawling lines of poetry until her fingers ached.

Yet she did nothing. Like one waiting for—what?

Each morning, after a feverish night. Choking back waves of nausea she could not bear to think was morning sickness.

So banal! Shameful.

What had taken root inside her without her awareness? What grew darkly, flourished. That tough, rubbery little slug not to be named, still less confronted.

What she could not acknowledge, had revealed to no one. And could never, to her lover.

For he was Kinch, he would be repelled by her.

Futile pounding at her belly with her fists, as a child might pound, biting back tears of anger and self-derision. Each morning checking her nightgown, the bedsheets. So desperately did she wish to see coin-size spangles of blood, streaks of blood, her eyes blurred with moisture almost saw these in the rumpled sheets.

God help me, just this once. I will never doubt You again.

It's your baby too, Simon. We are equally responsible. Therefore you must help me.

Could not bring herself to approach the man. Certainly not in the classroom or in the university office he shared with another young professor.

Nor could she envision herself walking (slowly? briskly?) across campus, making her way to the weathered Victorian house in which the man she loved (for she did love Simon Meech, that was the shameful fact) rented a furnished apartment. A lone figure in a film, dark-clad against snowy white. Climbing stairs, lifting her fist to knock on a door. Dear God, *no*.

Haunted by the thing inside her, in the pit of her belly, in her *uterus*, that was so tiny! Surely something might happen to it. How frequent were miscarriages? If Alyce continued not to eat, not to sleep, dazed and uncertain descending staircases, crossing busy streets . . .

The fact was, Alyce had no idea how to procure an abortion, and she had no money to pay for an abortion, nor even any idea how much money would be required for an abortion. One hundred dollars? Five hundred? A thousand? In high school she'd heard rumors . . .

Unexplained disappearances of girls, deaths.

What she did know: abortion was illegal. There was no region of the country in which abortion was legal. Simply to inquire about an abortion might be illegal—might be enough to get her expelled from the university. She dared not risk assuming that another girl would take pity on her and help her. And not report her to authority.

There was only Simon with whom she might plead. And yet there was not Simon.

He would stare at her in disbelief, dismay. Revulsion.

He'd seemed to praise, in certain of his remarks, the "celibate" life. The life that "transcends" the merely personal, trivial, the biological self that is a refutation of the spiritual self. The priestly life far superior to the conjugal life. Several times he'd expressed impatience with Alyce when she tried to discuss such issues with him, as if there might be two sides to a question and not just his.

Like a candle flame extinguished by a single rude breath, the man's feeling for her. Erotic longing could not withstand such raw need. Alyce could not risk that.

How do you "abort" a fetus, yourself? Not easily.

There were drugs, Alyce knew. Powerful abortifacients, available only to physicians, for provoking miscarriages when something has gone wrong with a pregnancy. But these could be lethal if not administered by a doctor. And they were not available, in any case.

Wire coat hanger: the most common remedy. Possibly, ice pick, long-bladed knife, chopstick . . . Alyce began to feel faint, dazed at the thought.

6.

So lonely, could not say *no*.

Astonishing to Alyce to learn, in time, that Roland B____ wasn't old—not *old*. Just sixty-one.

Old enough to be Alyce's father (of course) but (possibly) not old enough to her grandfather . . .

She was recalling: Sylvia Plath, patron saint of lost souls, had been only thirty at the time of her suicide.

Despite the bald dome of his head and the formality of his public manner, Roland B____ was a surprisingly youthful person. His face gave the impression of being unlined, though (as Alyce saw close up) his skin was a network of creases as fine as cobwebs. His pebble-colored eyes were heavy-lidded at times, like a turtle's, though at other times alert and curious. What appeared to be a scattering of liver marks on the backs of his hands were freckles. Guarded and muted in the seminar, he was capable of quick, spontaneous laughter in the privacy of the Poet's House, especially if he'd had a drink or two.

Red wine, occasionally whiskey. Alyce accepted a drink but (usually) left it untouched.

In the seminar, when Alyce spoke, Roland B___ regarded her through half-shut eyes, as if it wasn't her words, but her voice that fascinated him. She reminded him of someone—did she? She'd wondered at first if he even knew who she was—which of the names on the student roster was hers.

And in the Poet's House, Alyce wondered if he knew who she was among the many women and girls with whom he'd been intimately acquainted in his lifetime.

From his poetry Alyce knew that Roland B___ had had lovers. He spoke of a stoical bachelor's life as if with regret, but his had not been a bachelor's life, and probably not stoical. Only first names were attached to the wraithlike presences that had drifted in and out of the poet's life when he'd been a younger man.

But he never forgot Alyce's name once he'd learned it. Very carefully he pronounced the name—"Alyce."

Telling her that he'd once met the original Alice: "Alice Liddell."

Alice Liddell? For a moment Alyce didn't recognize the name. Then she recalled: of course, the child Alice, model for the Alice of *Alice's Adventures in Wonderland* and *Alice's Adventures Through the Looking-Glass*. The dark-eyed, dark-haired, dreamy little seven-year-old whom the Oxford mathematician Charles Dodgson (Lewis Carroll) had photographed in poses of extraordinary tenderness and intimacy, in a way that would be outlawed in the present time.

"Alice Liddell's family banished 'Lewis Carroll' finally—no one knows exactly why, but we can imagine. His heart was broken."

Poor Alice Liddell, forever haunted by "Alice"—the child she'd never really been and could not escape; as an elderly woman she'd been brought to the United States by her ambitious son, who'd wished to peddle a book he'd written about her. She'd been obliged to meet with the press, pose for photographs, sign copies of the son's book. Roland B___ had been a young man at the time, newly arrived in New York City, and at a gathering at the National Arts Club he'd actually—for a fleeting moment—shaken the hand of the "original" Alice.

Still an attractive woman, he'd thought, despite being exploited by her son and his publishers. The following year, 1934, she'd died at the age of eighty-two.

Nineteen thirty-four! Alyce was astonished, this was so long ago.

Roland B___ said thoughtfully, "All her life she'd had to endure seeing pictures of herself growing ever older, set beside Lewis Carroll's notorious photographs of her as a child—the dark-eyed, dark-haired little beauty, a precocious seductress with one bare shoulder exposed. Newspaper reporters fawning over her, to her face, then writing ironic profiles of her as an aging adult woman."

Precocious seductress. How old had the child Alice been in those photographs? Seven, eight? Alyce recalled that Alice had been made to resemble not a little English girl from a staid middle-class academic family, but a Gypsy child wise beyond her years.

How painful that would be, Alyce thought. Haunted by your own child-self. Forever young as you grow older.

Alyce told Roland B___ she'd thought the *Alice* books were frightening when she was a child. Even the illustrations by John Tenniel frightened her. So grotesque!—and Alice so often looking pained, grown too big, or shrunken, made to carry freakish creatures in her arms, fleeing from a shrieking mad queen—*Off with her head! Off with her head!*

She recalled the Alice of the books as a child very different from herself. Rather, the British girl had seemed somewhat adult to Alyce. And an orphan.

An orphan? Roland B___ was curious.

Well, Alice had no parents in the *Alice* books. Down the rabbit hole into Wonderland, and through the mirror into the looking-glass world—Alice wanders entirely alone, lost, without even a last name.

"I suppose you are right, dear. I'd read the books so long ago, I scarcely remember details. It never occurred to me that, as you've said, Alice was *alone*."

Roland B___ began to recite:

"A boat beneath a sunny sky,
Lingering onward dreamily
In an evening of July—

Children three that nestle near,
Eager eye and willing ear,
Pleased a simple tale to hear—

Long has paled that sunny sky:
Echoes fade and memories die:
Autumn frosts have slain July.

Still she haunts me, phantomwise,
Alice moving under skies
Never seen by waking eyes . . ."

The poet's voice trailed off with an air of melancholy, regret.

Alyce was feeling uneasy. In the poet's overheated drawing room, a sense of chill.

287

She was being made to recall fragments from the *Alice* books as one might recall fragments of disturbing dreams. Like bats with fluttering wings, these beat about her head. "Curiouser and curiouser"—"'Twas brillig, and the slithy toves"—"beat him when he sneezes"—"six impossible things [to believe] before breakfast." The mad twins Tweedledee and Tweedledum screaming at each other. The elderly white king sleeping beneath a tree, dreaming of Alice, and if he wakes from dreaming of her, she will vanish. Oh, terrifying! The Walrus and the Carpenter, strolling along the beach and devouring baby oysters *one by one*. Alice is herself going to be eaten—it's only a matter of time. Alice is only protected by remaining entranced in Wonderland and in the looking-glass world, by the game of chess in which the (unlikely) promise is that she will become a queen. Recalling the elderly White Queen disappearing into a soup tureen, about to be eaten by a leg of mutton, and candles rising madly to the ceiling—*Something is about to happen!*

Alyce shuddered. She'd hated and feared the *Alice* books and had had bad dreams about finding herself captive inside their pages. She was only realizing this now.

On his fingers Roland B___ calculated how old he'd have been when Alyce was seven: "Fifty, at least! More than the difference in years between Charles Dodgson and Alice Liddell."

But why was Roland B___ telling her this? And why, with such a strange smile?

The poet dared to take her hands, to comfort her.

"'Still she haunts me, phantomwise.'"

Alyce tried to smile, embarrassed. The poet held her hands with surprising strength.

"You are an unusually beautiful girl, Alyce—I mean, your beauty is unusual. It is not at all conventional, and some might say—those lacking a discerning eye—that you are not conventionally attractive at all. You remind me of the child Alice Liddell, actually —those dark, melancholy eyes."

Alyce drew a sharp breath. "Well. I am not Alice Liddell, Professor. And I think I will leave now."

And so the comforting hands released hers, startled. The eyelids hooded like turtles' eyelids fluttered in alarm. Alyce rose to her feet, smiling to think, *Enough of goddamned dark, melancholy eyes. I have shocked you at last, haven't I.*

7.

Each morning, the tiny slug held firm. Deep inside the dark-haired, dark-eyed girl who'd once been—no had never been—Alice Liddell.

No loosening of menstrual blood, no fresh dark stains in the bedclothes. No.

God help me. Even if You don't love me.

And the blunt and unassailable answer came at once to her: *Die, then. The power is in your hands.*

The possibility of killing herself.

In the early hours of the morning, suicide appeared to be more feasible than abortion, certainly more convenient, as it didn't involve others and would incur no expense.

Preposterous even to consider. A pregnancy would last only nine months, and nine months is not long in a normal lifetime. *Yes, but there would be no normal lifetime remaining after the pregnancy.*

Steeling her courage to ask one of the older girls in the residence if Alyce could speak with her in private about something serious, something private, rehearsing the faltering words she would say, but her weak courage failed, she could not bring herself to so expose herself, for she could not trust anyone. Could not.

Throwing oneself from a height, from a bridge, would be an effective means. Stepping in front of a speeding vehicle, preferably a truck or a bus. Alyce tried to imagine summoning such courage if she had not even the courage to approach someone to speak of her predicament.

Later in the pregnancy, when she became desperate. Maybe then. If desperate, fanatic, and obsessed, maybe you don't need courage.

Certainly Alyce would become desperate when others began to notice, to suspect. When her stomach swelled out and her clothes no longer fit.

How long did she have? Weeks? A death sentence—the pregnancy growing like a tumor that could not be stopped.

Slashing her wrists. All she would require was a razor or a sharp knife, and the act could be executed in the night, without detection if she acted sensibly. In a bathtub with running water, to dilute the flow of blood, carry it away to oblivion. In one of the bathrooms in the residence that was single occupancy, equipped with a bathtub and not a shower stall; a room that could be locked, where no one could interrupt, and Alyce could sedate herself with aspirin and lower herself into hot, steaming water, shut her eyes, refusing to see, for she was a coward and could not bear to see streams of blood in water rushing down a drain. As her heart beat slower with the loss of blood, a sweet comfort would come over her at last . . . But—would she have removed her clothes, as if for a bath? Or—would she be dressed, or partly dressed, in her flannel nightgown perhaps? For she would not (oh, she *would not*) want to be discovered both naked and dead.

And how would *dead* be accomplished, exactly? Only one wrist could be slashed by the badly trembling right hand, not both wrists. The left wrist, or rather the inside of the left forearm, the tender flesh there would have to be cut (deeply, swiftly, unerringly) before pain overcame her and the razor or knife fell from her fingers into the splashing water . . .

Overdose of pills? Which pills? Alyce had no prescription pills, would have to buy pills at a drugstore, and what pills would these be?—sleeping pills? She had no idea. If she were at home, she'd have access to the medications in her parents' medicine cabinet— pills for high blood pressure, angina, kidney trouble, arthritis. But if she swallowed enough pills to kill herself, that might cause her to vomit, for she was not accustomed to swallowing pills. Had no idea how her stomach would react. And if she didn't vomit enough, she would sink into a sweaty stupor but not die, her heart continuing to beat like a stubborn metronome, waking hours or days later in her own vomit and excrement, taken by ambulance to an ER where her stomach would be pumped—whatever "pumped" meant. It did not promise romance or dignity. Hospitalized for psychiatric evaluation, parents contacted, discovery of pregnancy, removed from the university, possibly brain-damaged, possibly "vegetative state" . . .

Alyce laughed. Three twenty a.m. and she was standing flat-footed on a cold hardwood floor, having heaved herself up from the bed in which she'd failed to sleep since turning out the light several hours before.

Deciding, *Goddamn, she would not.*

Would not kill herself, nor even make the attempt.

* * *

Returning from morning classes to discover a folded note in her mailbox, a phone message. Something like a sliver of glass piercing her heart at the thought that this was Simon summoning her to him at last. In fact, as her fluttering eyes barely made out through a scrim of tears, the note was a phone message for her: *Dearest Alyce, Please call this number. R.B.*

8.

In this way, her life was decided.

The gift of her life. So Alyce would think, at the time.

Returning to the Poet's House. Her heart beating eagerly as Roland B___ opened the door with a playful bow.

"Dear Alyce! I have missed you. Come in."

It was decided, Alyce would act as Roland B___'s assistant and archivist. For that would be the formal title of her role in his life and (as she might have anticipated at the time) in his posthumous life—*assistant, archivist*.

"I will pay you, of course, Alyce. I don't expect you to give up your precious time for nothing."

And, "Please do call me Roland, dear. Will you at least try?"

It was touching to Alyce, that the poet so readily forgave her for her rudeness to him. Brushing aside her embarrassed apology with a dismissive gesture—"Don't be absurd, dear. An old man is well advised to be put in his place when he oversteps boundaries. Good to remind me."

"Oh, but, Professor—you're not *old*."

The words leaped from Alyce. She had no idea that she would speak at all in response to the poet's rueful remark.

She'd spoken laughingly, out of nervousness. Like Alice in the looking-glass world, in which all things are reversed, comical.

But she saw how it was true. Roland B____, in his solitude, loneliness. At the university he was admired, often invited to receptions, luncheons, dinners, but he went everywhere alone and returned to the faded-brick Poet's House alone. In the antique-furnished bedroom, in the four-poster bed alone.

And Alyce in *her* solitude, loneliness. Surrounded by others her age, swarms of others on the university walkways, yet alone.

For Simon Meech had not contacted her, and in the classroom he seemed now scarcely to glance in her direction and to take no notice that she departed immediately when the class ended.

All the colors of the drawing room in the Poet's House seemed brighter to her, richer and more beautiful than she recalled. Crimson velvet pillows on a dove-gray velvet sofa, a deep russet-brown Chinese vase on the fireplace mantel, portraits of stern-looking eighteenth-century gentlemen on the walls.

How comical, these portraits! As if, long dead, long forgotten, they were playing the roles now of ancestors.

"Come in, dear Alyce! Your hands are cold. Will you have tea?"—drawing her into the overheated interior where, on the beautiful old grand piano, a crystal vase of red roses pulsed with vivid color—*For me? Those roses are for me.*

Here was someone who cherished her. Would not repudiate, hurt her.

Strange, since Alyce's previous visit there'd come to be a new mood between her and Roland B____ that was lighter, more playful, and (just perceptibly) erotic.

She'd dared to speak sharply to the professor. She'd pushed away his hands and left him. Astonishing him, as she'd astonished herself, and now they were beginning anew.

He'd bought back from a local bakery delicious flaky-buttery scones. Serving these to his visitor, with Lapsang tea in Wedgwood teapot and cups. Though she'd been stricken with nausea only a few hours earlier, Alyce felt now a wave of hunger powerful enough to make her tremble.

"You do look pale, dear. I was noticing in our class the other day. You were very quiet while the others chattered so self-importantly. Is something troubling you? Or is it—'*Time's winged chariot, hurrying near*'—?"

An obscure reference, surely to a poem. But not a poem that Alyce knew.

"But you're too young, I think, to be troubled by the rapid passing of time as we others are . . ."

At this Alyce laughed again, spilling tea from the dainty Wedgwood teacup. As if *time passing* wasn't as painful to her as an abscess. As if such rituals as tea mattered when a few hours ago she'd been crouched over a toilet, dry-heaving.

"If there is something in your life that troubles you, I hope that you can confide in me, dear. I realize that at your age, so much is undecided, undefined. Recall what Paul Bowles said—'Things don't happen, it depends upon who comes along.'"

Alyce had no idea who Paul Bowles was, but from the tone of Roland B___'s voice, she gathered that he was a visionary of some sort.

How shaky Alyce was feeling, yet how elated in the presence of this kindly man. The gleaming dome of a head, across which feathery strands of gray hair lay lightly. The pouched eyes, crinkling at their corners. The hopeful smile, exposing yellowed teeth. Alyce felt how brittle her composure, that could be broken by a tender word from this man, a caress.

But what had he asked her? Hungrily she'd devoured an entire scone and emptied her cup of Lapsang tea. Her hands were still trembling.

"Well, dear. Perhaps in time you will confide in me, as your friend. From your poetry, I believe that I know you—inwardly. Please think of me as the friend of your soul."

On a mahogany table in the drawing room were manuscripts, drafts of poems, letters both handwritten and typed. On the floor, boxes of papers. Much of this was new since Alyce's most recent visit.

"I've had these boxes sent to me so that I can begin working on my archive here. D'you know what an archive is, dear?"

Alyce thought so, yes. Only the estimable merited archives.

"Virtually everything in a writer's life. But I've saved only papers, documents, publications, letters—hundreds of letters. Out-of-print books, limited editions. I've delayed for years—never answered inquiries from Harvard, Yale, Columbia—as I've delayed making out a will. It's damned difficult, you see, for those of us who fantasize that we will live forever, to think of ourselves as mortal, let alone posthumous . . . But if you could help me, dear, I think I could face the challenge."

"Of course, Professor. I can try."

Again she spoke without thinking. So yearning to please the elderly poet, so lonely, so desperate she could barely contain herself in the presence of someone so seemingly kind.

"Please, I've told you—Roland. *Professor* is for *les autres*."

"Roland." The name sounded unreal in Alyce's voice, unconvincing.

"Rol-*land*. Give it a French inflection, *s'il vous plaît*."

"Rol-*land*." Like an overgrown child, Alyce was blushing with embarrassment.

"Well. That's an improvement, at least. *Merci!*"

Outside the drawing room windows, daylight was rapidly fading. In the chipped Wedgwood pot Lapsang tea cooled, forgotten. In a hearty mood, Roland B__ poured whiskey into shot glasses for his visitor and himself and insisted that Alyce drink with him: "We have much to celebrate, my dear."

Soon, a fever came into the poet's face; he was laughing happily. By the end of the evening, when Alyce prepared to return to her residence, Roland B__'s words had begun to slur and his fine-creased skin was deeply flushed. It was touching to Alyce, how in her presence the poet seemed to warm, even to glow.

Insisting, of course he would pay her. He would pay her very well. But she must tell no one else about their arrangement, none of Alyce's classmates in the seminar, not anyone, for fear that *les autres* would misunderstand.

Not wanting Alyce to leave. Please no! Not just yet.

She had a curfew, Alyce tried to explain, laughing. All undergraduate women who lived in university residences had midnight curfews.

Ridiculous! Alyce should move out of such a confining place to a place of her own. *He* would help her pay for it.

9.

How happy Alyce was in the Poet's House! *It* did not have the power to paralyze her here.

That interlude of days nearing the winter solstice, when Alyce arrived breathless and hopeful at the redbrick residence between four thirty and five p.m. Bringing her schoolwork, anthologies and texts she had to read for courses, papers she had to write, her notebook in which she kept drafts of her poems, in the interstices of helping Roland B___ organize the archive.

"My dear, we are making progress! I'm proud of us."

By the time Alyce arrived, Roland B___ would have had a whiskey or two, a glass of wine or two, or three. Grateful to see her. Trying to maintain dignity. Kissing her hand, hands.

Sometime between eight and nine they would eat a meal together, which Roland B___ ordered and paid for, delivered to the Poet's House from one of a half dozen restaurants in town. By the time the food arrived, Roland would have had another whiskey or begun another glass of wine, and Alyce would have left the worktable to set the dining room table with beautiful, if chipped and cracked, china she'd discovered in a sideboard, tarnished silverware, white linen napkins, cut-glass water goblets. Candlestick holders, candles. Their food was delivered in Styrofoam packages, transferred by Alyce to platters set in an oven at three hundred seventy-five degrees Fahrenheit. The aroma of heating food made her mouth water; she'd never been so ravenous.

Interludes of nausea were behind her now, mostly. Her center of gravity was settling in the region of her pelvis, closer to the ground.

Five days a week Alyce came to the Poet's House. Soon, then six days a week. Seven. For always there was much to do that was thrilling, and in addition, Roland B___ paid her generously as he'd promised, often in twenty-dollar bills, hastily, scarcely troubling to count out the bills, as if paying were embarrassing to him, as *being paid* was embarrassing to Alyce. "You need not report this income, you know, dear," Roland B___ said quietly, "as I shall not. What passes between us, the IRS *shall not know.*"

On Roland B___'s sturdy old Remington typewriter Alyce typed ribbon copies of poems as well as numerous drafts of poems along with personal letters of Roland B___'s that she was entrusted with critiquing and even correcting.

Telling herself, *I am doing this for him, he is my friend. The more I do for him, the more he is my friend.*

Only when she left the overheated Poet's House to return across the snowswept campus to her residence a quarter mile away did reality sweep in upon her, as jarring as a clanging bell.

What was happening to her! What must she *do?*

Out of compulsion checking her underwear, her nightgown. Bedclothes. Hardly recalling what it was she sought—smears of blood, barely recalling it was menstrual blood, which had begun to seem to her remote, like an imperfectly recollected dream.

Yes but: the swell of her belly. Definitely. She could feel.

No longer losing weight out of anxiety and nausea, but gaining weight. Five pounds, six . . . Eight pounds.

Roland B___ remarked how beautiful Alyce was. How smooth her skin, how shining her eyes . . . She wasn't so thin as she'd been. Definitely she was looking healthier.

"You see, you are *my* Alice. Come into my life when Alice was required, like magic."

Alyce laughed, embarrassed. Did Roland B___ really mean such things, or was he being fanciful? Poetic?

She wondered if, in his vanity, the elderly poet might have thought that his undergraduate assistant was falling in love with him.

It was becoming ever more difficult for Alyce to politely decline Roland B___'s offers of drinks. Possibly, she would take a few sips of wine. But whiskey—*no*.

Pointing out, primly, "You know, Professor—I'm underage."

Roland B___ protested: "My dear, this is a private residence. No one can intrude here. The state has no authority here. My domicile." Pausing, slyly considering: "*Our* domicile. *Our* Wonderland. Without a warrant, no officer of the state can cross the threshold, and certainly no office of the state can arrest *me*."

Soon, too, wanting Alyce to stay the night.

And what were you thinking, Alyce? That it would just—go away?

As one might be fascinated by a lump in a breast, a thickening tumor. A kind of paralysis. Sleeping heavily, her limbs mired in something soft, like mud. Warm mud.

Recalling overhearing her mother and an aunt speaking in lowered voices of a friend's daughter who'd had a six-months' miscarriage when no one including (allegedly) the girl had even known that she was pregnant. A stocky girl, wearing loose-fitting shirts, overalls, not a very attractive girl (so it was said, an important detail), utterly astonished the family had been, disbelieving, scandalized. It had seemed improbable at the time that the girl hadn't known she was pregnant, yet now Alyce understood. It was very easy not to think about *it*. Anxiety about the future was replaced by a sudden need for a nap.

A swoon of ignorance, the most refreshing of deep sleeps.

That somehow it would go away. Cease to exist.

And you would wake to discover that it was all a bad dream—like Alice waking from her nightmare.

"My dear, unavoidably, I must be away for the rest of the afternoon. But I will hurry back, I promise!"

It was flattering to Alyce that Roland sometimes left the Poet's House while she remained behind. The poet had come to trust his assistant, deferring to her out of respect for her good judgment or out of a cavalier wish not to be bothered with details. Yes, yes!— those were letters from T. S. Eliot, who was plain "Tom Eliot" to anyone who knew him, indeed yes, as Robert Lowell was "Cal." Alyce was correct, such precious archival material needed to be kept in plastic binders, but—where would you get such binders? The university bookstore? Huge, ghastly place with racks of insipid bestsellers, dour textbooks, T-shirts, and sweatshirts, couldn't bring himself to step inside a second time . . .

Of course Alyce would acquire the binders. Far more capably than Roland B____, Alyce did such mundane tasks.

Mesmerizing to Alyce, to lose herself in hours of close, exacting reading, deciphering handwritten letters to Roland B____ , faded carbon copies of Roland B___'s letters, handwritten manuscripts by the poet himself, annotated galleys. Hundreds of letters from individuals whose names were known and individuals whose names were unknown. In the 1930s Roland B___ had begun publishing verse; by 1954 Roland B___ had become poetry editor of *The Nation* and would correspond with dozens of poet friends. You could see—Alyce could see—how the young, ambitious poet had made his way, not unerringly, but erratically, haphazardly, sending poems to whoever would receive them and offer comment or publication, grateful for any attention, encouragement, acceptance from any editor, like one who is climbing a wall of sheer rock, grasping at slippery surfaces.

Often Alyce brought letters to the window to read carefully. Small, crabbed handwriting, faded typewriter ink. A letter from John Crowe Ransom, editor of the *Kenyon Review*, praising and accepting several poems. A short, scribbled letter from the poet Delmore Schwartz thanking Roland B___ for some favor. A letter from Elizabeth Bishop on hotel stationery, a sequence of dashed-off sentences, rueful complaints about "Cal." In these letters there was an air of intimacy, intrigue, and gossip that fascinated Alyce, who had nothing like this in her life.

Very easily she could fold up such letters—some of them were paper-thin blue airmail stationery. Slip them into her book bag. Roland B___ would never know, for Roland B___ was a very careless custodian of what was his.

Especially the poet's early limited-edition publications, what Roland B___ called chapbooks, carelessly crammed together in boxes.

One of the these was *Phantomwise and Other Poems*, published in 1936, beautifully printed on stiff white paper with a mother-of-pearl cover and, on the title page, Roland B___'s youthful, grandiloquent signature.

According to the copyright page, there'd been just fifty copies printed. In the box were three copies, each water-stained and torn.

The epigraph was familiar to her:

Still she haunts me, phantomwise.

What was this: a line from *Alice in Wonderland*? Charles Dodgson looking back at the seven-year-old Alice, suffused with yearning.

Leafing through the water-stained little book, which was just twenty pages. A half dozen poems by Roland B___ that Alyce had never seen before and did not fully understand. Probably forgotten now by the poet himself.

Quickly she returned the copy of *Phantomwise* to the box. Even if her eccentric employer never knew that the book was missing, even if no one would ever care that it was missing, Alyce would not behave so dishonestly. She could not steal.

It would be a betrayal of Roland B___'s tender regard for her. Her regard for him. Their mutual respect that was unlike anything else in Alyce's life.

"Which of these do you prefer, Alyce?" The poet was revising poems originally published years ago, in 1953, in preparation for a *Selected Poems*. With the tactlessness of the young, Alyce said, "The older version. It's much stronger."

"Really? The *older version*?"

"Yes."

The poem was a clever imitation of a Donne sonnet. Alyce, who knew only a few poems by John Donne, knew this. The harsh rhythms, masculine accents. By adding lines, Roland B___ had softened the poem.

Her remark had surprised him. As she'd surprised him, yes, and pleased him enormously, entering the Poet's House with the little cracked opal ring on the smallest finger of her right hand.

The look in Roland B___'s face! Like a candle, lighted.

My dear. You have made me so happy.

But now he'd gone away, not so happy.

In the kitchen she heard him clattering about. Seeking a glass.

Often, Alyce washed dishes after their meals. Liking the feel of hot, soapy water. If she had not, the elderly poet would have left dirtied dishes in the sink, in a pool of scummy water, awaiting the cleaning woman on Wednesday mornings. He seemed incapable of washing even teacups and coffee mugs. Whiskey glasses, wineglasses accumulated, out of an impressive store in the Poet's House cupboards, until Alyce washed them and left them sparkling on the shelves.

Of course, Roland B___ was getting a drink now. To soothe his jarred nerves.

Returning at last, whiskey in hand, and to Alyce's relief no whiskey for her.

But he also had a gift for her—"In gratitude for your astute insight and your honesty, dear Alyce. A collector's item—supposedly."

It was a copy of *Phantomwise*, the slender chapbook with the mother-of-pearl cover. Alyce felt her face burn, as if she'd been exposed as a thief.

But Roland B___'s face was crinkled in a wide smile, without irony.

Holding the water-stained little book out to her opened to the title page—"*For my dear Alyce, who brings the light of radiance into my life. With love, Roland.*"

Alyce took the book from Roland B___'s fingers. Tears leaked from her eyes. It was not possible to keep from crying, he was so kind.

"Oh Alyce, what's wrong? Why are you crying?"

Heard herself telling him, at last: she was pregnant.

That word, blunt and shaming: *pregnant.*

How long, how many weeks exactly, she didn't know.

Didn't want to know. Had not allowed herself to know.

Stammering, sobbing. Like a child. A broken girl. Her composure shattered as backbone might be shattered. Roland B___ tried to comfort her.

Later Alyce would realize that the elderly poet had not been so very surprised. Must have known, suspected—something . . .

Of course he was very kind to Alyce. Sitting beside her on a sofa, gripping her hands to still them. Letting her speak in a rush of words, and letting her fall silent, choked with emotion. Such kindness was terrible to her, obliterating. She could not recall when anyone had been so kind. So sympathetically listened to her.

"My dear. My poor dear. This is not good news for you, is it?"

No. Not good news. Alyce laughed, wiping her eyes.

He was holding her. As an older relative might hold her.

Assuring her he would help her. If she would allow him.

In his arms Alyce wept. Heaving sobs, graceless. Her pride had vanished. She was exposed, helpless. The posture she'd so rigorously maintained in her classes, within the gaze of others, abandoned. Suddenly a pregnant creature, helpless.

"Marry me, dear. Make me your husband. I will take care of you and your baby. It will be 'our baby.'"

Roland B___ spoke urgently, his words slurred from the whiskey.

Alyce laughed nervously. No, no! She could not.

"I know you don't love me—yet. I can love enough for both of us. You know, you are *my Alice*."

Alyce wanted to push away. She wanted to snatch up her dignity, what remained of her dignity, and flee the Poet's House. Yet there she was, weakly huddled in the poet's arms. As if shielded from a strong wind. Scarcely recalling the man's name. Yet her mind was working rapidly—*He will help me. He has saved me.*

In the four-poster bed, in the dimlit bedroom. An antique bed with a hard mattress that creaked beneath their weight. It was too absurd, Alyce thought. This was not happening! The elderly man breathing loudly, panting as if he'd climbed a flight of stairs. Tenderly holding her, kissing her mouth, her throat. Feathery-light kisses that became by quick degrees harder, sucking kisses that took her breath away.

"No. Please. Don't." Alyce pushed at him, frightened.

"Sorry!"

The elderly lover would make a joke of it, if he could.

Still, he was breathing hard. Harshly. Excused himself to go into the bathroom, swaying on his feet.

There came a sound of faucets, plumbing. Alyce sat up, swung her legs off the bed. What was she doing, why was she here? She would leave before he returned. Or—she would wait for him in the drawing room, in her coat. For it would be rude, unconscionable, to rush away without speaking to him.

She would ask him for financial help. Please would he help her!

All she wanted was her old, lost body. The *not-pregnant* body. A girl's slender body with narrow hips, small, hard breasts, flat belly, and nothing inside the belly to make it swell like a balloon.

How happy she'd been, in that not-pregnant body. Wholly unaware, oblivious. And now.

She had no doubt, Roland B___ could put her in contact with someone who could help her. Roland B___ could provide the money.

An abortion. A doctor who could perform an abortion.

These blunt words had to be uttered. She, Alyce, would have to utter them.

After some minutes Alyce returned hesitantly to the bedroom. But Roland B___ was still in the bathroom. Something fell to the tile floor, clattered. Alyce came closer to the door, not knowing what to do. She had not wanted to think that something might be wrong with the elderly poet, that his breathing had been harsh and laborious almost as soon as he'd urged her into the bedroom and onto the bed.

Alyce had balked like an overgrown girl. She had given in, but stiffly. She had not returned his kisses, except weakly, out of a kind of politeness. For a man of his age he'd been surprisingly strong. He'd been surprisingly heavy. But then, he was not *old*. She knew that.

Her face was wet with tears. Hair in her face. At last daring to call, "R-Roland? Is something wrong?"

How the name *Roland* stuck in her mouth! She could hardly bear to speak it. Like playacting this felt, speaking a name in a script.

The panicked thought came to her—*Is he ill? Is he dying? Am I to be his witness?*

Alyce approached the bathroom door. Leaned her ear against it. "Hello? Excuse me? Is—something wrong?"

In poetry you chisel the most beautiful words out of language. In life you stutter words. It is never possible to speak so beautifully as you wish to speak.

Inside, a response she could not quite hear. Maybe it was a reply, *no, yes, I am all right, go away.* Or maybe it was a groan. A cry. A muffled plea. *Help me, I am not all right. Do not go away.*

A terrifying thought, that the elderly poet was ill. At the very moment of his declaration of love for her, his wish to help her, to marry her . . . Alyce had long suspected that Roland B___ was not entirely well: hearing him breathing laboriously, moving with unnatural slowness at times. Wanting to think at the time, *Oh he's been drinking. That's why.*

Like seeing a spark fly out of a chimney and fall onto a carpet.

In the next instant the spark may become a flame. The flame may become fire.

Is he dying? He doesn't want to die alone . . .

Then, suddenly: the door was opened. Roland B___ emerged, trying to smile.

A ghastly smile. His skin pale, as if drained of blood. And his eyelids fluttering. His hand pressed against his chest.

She would call 911, Alyce told him. They could not wait any longer.

Roland protested *no*. Not yet. His heart "played tricks" on him —sometimes . . .

No. No longer. Alyce would call 911 and save the poet's life.

10.

"He is expecting me. He needs me."

At the ER, insisting that yes, she was Roland B___'s assistant, a student at the university enrolled in the professor's course. For she could not bring herself to say that she was the elderly poet's *friend*.

Still less, that she was the poet's *Alice*. The girl he'd offered to marry.

"He needs me, he expects me. I would have ridden with him in the ambulance, but there was no room . . ."

A nurse led Alyce into the interior of the ER. She could not stop from glancing into small rooms with doors ajar—dreading to see what, who was inside. Smells assailed her nostrils; her eyes filled with tears. She thought, *Oh God, if he dies. If he has died.*

Barely could she recall her own condition. What was growing, flourishing in her belly. Her aching and oddly full breasts. How she'd confessed to the poet and how he'd taken hold of her hands, his kindness. His wish to help her.

. . . *love enough for both of us.*

The nurse was handing Alyce—what? A half mask of white gauze. Slipped a half mask onto her own face. Explaining to Alyce that until blood work confirmed that the patient didn't have a contagious illness, they must proceed as if he might have one, and that the contagion might be spread by airborne germs or viruses.

Contagious? Illness? Was this possible? Alyce fumbled affixing the mask to her face, and the nurse adjusted it for her.

Before the door to room eight. Preparing for what was inside as the nurse opened the door.

And there was the elderly poet in bed, in a sitting-up position, bare-chested, partly conscious, staring and blinking at Alyce as if he couldn't see her clearly or was failing to recognize her in the mask. Without his glasses he looked much older than his age—disheveled, distraught. The pale dome of a head, shockingly bare.

"Oh, my dear . . . What have they done to *you*?" he said.

Bravely Roland B___ was smiling at his visitor. Quickly she came to him, took his hand. Fingers as cold as death.

Her first impression was one of shock, yet relief—Roland was alive, that was all that mattered.

Thanking Alyce for coming. Begging her not to leave him.

How misshapen, Roland B___'s body in the cranked-up hospital bed! He might have been a dwarf, with foreshortened legs. Alyce had never glimpsed the elderly poet unclothed, always he'd been quite formal; in the Poet's House, when he'd removed his tweed coat, he wore long-sleeved shirts beneath, often sweaters, vests. Scarcely had Alyce thought of the poet as a physical being.

Until he'd urged her into his bedroom and onto his bed, she had not once thought of him as a sexual being—such a thought repugnant to her.

Now, with dismayed eyes, Alyce saw folds of flesh at the poet's chest and stomach, of the hue of lard. Sloping, knobby-boned shoulders. The flabby chest was covered in a frizz of gray hairs, and amid these a dozen electrodes, wires connected to a machine. Was this an EKG? Monitoring his heartbeat? An IV dripped fluids into his right arm: antibiotics? medication to slow and stabilize the rapid heartbeat? Oxygen flowed into the patient's nostrils through plastic tubes. Like clockwork, every several minutes a blood pressure cuff tightened on the patient's left upper arm with an aggressive whirring sound, then relaxed, like an exhaled breath. Alyce stared, entranced, at the monitor screen. The numerals meant nothing to her—84, 91, 18. Green, blue, white. During the course of this first visit Alyce would surmise that the numerals in the high 80s measured the patient's oxygen intake.

It was explained to her that Roland B___ would have a CAT scan and an echocardiogram in the morning. He would have further blood work after eight hours of antibiotics. The rapid heartbeat wasn't tachycardia, but fibrillation, which was more serious. Possibly, the elderly man had a viral infection, which had precipitated the attack. Possibly, he had pneumonia. Alyce tugged at the mask, which fitted over her mouth and nose uncomfortably.

It alarmed her, how Roland B___ was coughing. (Had he been coughing at the Poet's House? She didn't think so.)

"They don't know what is wrong with me, I'm afraid," Roland B___ said with an attempt at his old gaiety, "but I'm sure it's nothing to worry about, dear. I hope it won't be a cause of worry to you."

Alyce insisted that she wasn't worried. Even as she felt sick, disoriented with worry.

Wondering if, in his physical distress, the elderly poet remembered what she had told him. If he remembered what he'd told her.

. . . *love enough for both of us.*

313

For hours that night, sitting with Roland B__ in the small room, much of the time holding his hand.

Even when he drifted off to sleep, eyelids fluttering and lips twitching, holding his hand.

At eleven thirty p.m., when the ER was closing to visitors, Alyce was told that she could remove the mask on her face. Blood tests had established that the patient didn't have a communicable disease.

Removing the damned mask, which the nurse directed her to discard in a bin labeled MEDICAL REFUSE.

Removing the mask so that Roland B__ could see her more clearly and unmistakably identify her: "My dear—Alyce."

"Yes—Alyce . . ."

"You are looking so—pale, dear. Please don't worry! I feel so much better already, just knowing that you've been here and that we—we have—we will settle matters between us as soon as I am back home. Won't we, dear? As we'd discussed?"

"Y-yes."

"Kiss me good night, dear. I'm not contagious now. And will you promise to see me in the morning?"

Alyce promised. How exhausted she was, and how badly she wanted to escape the stricken man, to burrow into sleep in her own bed.

But Roland was blinking at her, his eyes forlorn without his glasses. The blood pressure cuff jerked to life, squeezing his upper arm as if in rebuke.

Lowering his voice, Roland B__ asked anxiously, "You are—I mean, you *are not*—my wife yet? I think—not yet? No."

Was he joking? Alyce wanted to think so.

* * *

The patient in room eight did not survive the night. We had no number to call and we regret to inform you . . .

In fact, when Alyce returned to the ER the next morning, trembling with fear, she was informed that Roland B___ had been moved out of the ER to a room on the fifth floor. His heartbeat had been stabilized: his condition was "much improved." Yet he would probably remain in the hospital for several days, undergoing tests.

In relief, Alyce bought him a small bouquet of fresh flowers from the hospital gift shop. It was heartening to see how his face lighted when he saw her and the bright yellow flowers in her hand.

"My dear! You've come back. Thank you."

Leaning over the hospital bed to kiss his cheek. Resisting the impulse to shut her eyes in a delirium of relief. *He is alive. Alive! That is all that matters.*

She'd scarcely slept the previous night. Many times reliving the shock of the poet's collapse, even as he'd vowed to protect her.

Marry her, and they would have a child together . . .

It was clear to her now. Nothing mattered so much as Roland B___. She had to be with him, at his bedside. For he had no one but Alyce, whom he loved and had promised to protect.

She'd ceased thinking of the other. The man who'd impregnated her and now shunned her. She did not even hate him, who'd so wounded her.

Roland had not asked Alyce about the father of the unborn baby. Alyce seemed to understand that he would not.

Saying to her only, in a discreet, lowered voice so that no one might overhear, "And you, dear? *You* are all right, also?"

"Yes! Oh, yes."

It was a relief to Alyce. Roland B___ did seem to have improved since the previous night. He was still inhaling oxygen through tubes in his nostrils, but the numbers on the monitor were higher, in the 90s. IV fluids were still dripping into his veins, but his color was warmer, his eyes more alert. With a droll gaiety he showed his visitor his poor bruised arms from which "pints of blood" had been drawn.

As Roland B___'s assistant, Alyce had much to do. She must notify his closest relatives, whose names he provided her; she must notify the English Department that he would be postponing his seminar for a week. Alyce did not want to say, *But are you sure, Roland? One week?*

Clearly, he had a serious cardiac condition. Still, there was a possibility that he had an infection, for he was running a slight temperature. Though he was eager to be discharged from the hospital, he tired easily, several times dropping off to sleep while speaking with Alyce; once while explaining to her what she should say to his relatives, to keep them informed but discourage them from visiting him.

As it turned out, Roland B___'s relatives, who lived in the Boston area, were not very keen on visiting him. On the phone with Alyce they expressed surprise, alarm, concern—but said nothing about visiting him in the hospital. ("Is Roland out of the ER? Not in intensive care? That's a relief!") Alyce wanted to ask sarcastically why didn't they come to see him now, before he might be in intensive care again? Wouldn't that be more sensible?

Roland had said that he didn't want to speak with his relatives just yet. Nor did the relatives express much urgency about speaking with him.

Often when Roland slept he woke disoriented, frightened. A nurse suggested to Alyce that she remain close by, to assure him—"Older patients need reassurance that they haven't been abandoned."

Abandoned! Alyce was determined that this should not happen.

If she missed more than a few classes, she would fail her courses, Alyce was warned. She would have to apply for extensions through the dean's office, and even then such applications might be denied.

But Roland was dependent upon her for tasks he could not do from his hospital bed. Letters he must write, or believed that he must write, which he dictated to Alyce, who dutifully typed them out on the Remington in the Poet's House, brought them back to him for proofreading, and addressed and mailed them. There were telephone calls Roland couldn't bring himself to make, which Alyce must make for him; he'd grown to hate the phone because no one spoke loudly or clearly enough any longer. Since the shock of his collapse and hospitalization, Roland seemed determined to show how alert, energetic, and assertive he was, how *well*—though he was still a hospital patient attached to monitors beside his bed and dependent on Alyce or a nurse to help him make his faltering way to the bathroom when he needed it.

He'd been insistent that the damned catheter be removed from his penis. No more! A man's pride would not allow that insult.

Especially, Roland wanted to display for Alyce his returning vitality, his good humor. He wanted the medical staff to see, his physician to see, how well he was becoming, in order that he might be discharged soon.

Wanting to suggest to Roland that she might spend fewer hours at the hospital so that she could return to her classes, catch up on her work. That she might write poetry of her own again, to read to him.

But she could not force herself to utter such words—*I need more time to myself, Roland. I am afraid that I will fail my courses . . .*

He would be hurt, she knew. Since his collapse he'd become extremely sensitive, thin-skinned and suspicious. If Alyce was late coming to the hospital by just a few minutes, he wondered where she'd been; if he dropped off to sleep and woke startled, not knowing at first where he was, he might stare at her almost with hostility, as if not recognizing her.

But then, when she spoke his name, it was wonderful to see awareness and recognition flowing into his face again—"My dear! Dear Alyce. It is you, isn't it?"

"Yes. Of course."

"I love you, Alyce. You know that, I hope."

Alyce was deeply embarrassed. Could not bring herself to say *Yes. I know.*

"When I am discharged—which will be next Monday, I've just been informed—we will make our plans, dear. We—have—many— plans—to make . . ."

It was the pregnancy to which he was alluding, Alyce supposed. Yet he could not quite name it.

Soon after their nighttime meal, Roland fell asleep with a book in his hand, which Alyce extricated carefully from his fingers and set aside, with a bookmark to mark his place. She stooped and kissed the poet's high forehead, with its faint creases that felt cool against her lips; she listened to his shallow but rhythmic breathing, as comforting to her as a baby's breathing might be. Love for the man suffused her heart, but how vexing, just as she switched off the bright overhead light, preparing to leave the hospital for the night, a young nurse entered the room and switched it back on, rudely waking Roland, who fluttered his eyelids, confused.

Alyce watched as the nurse poked for a vein in his right arm, which was already discolored. "Be careful!"—Alyce spoke sharply.

It was new to her, this sharpness. As if she were already the poet's young wife, destined to outlive him and to bring up their child by herself, the renowned poet's literary executrix whose life would be closely bound up with his.

Afterward, she kissed the poet good night a second time, switched off the overhead light a second time. In the corridor outside, the nurse was waiting for her with a quizzical smile. "Is he your grandfather? Somebody said he's a famous professor."

It had been Roland's third full day in the hospital, unless it was the fourth.

11.

In Alyce's mailbox when she returned late from the hospital, a folded note with the terse message. *"Please call me. S."*

Clutching the note, her heart pounding. A rush of sensation came over her, of dread, apprehension, and yet such excitement, she felt for a moment that she might faint. She had to lean against the wall, her head lowered, as a struck animal might lean, uncertain what has happened to it.

No. Go to hell. It's too late, I hate you.

And yet she could not say no.

Asking Alyce to meet him the next evening at a Greek restaurant some distance from the university, a place to which he'd never taken her, dim-lighted, near deserted, where no one from the university was likely to see them together.

He'd heard, Simon said bluntly, with no preamble, two things about the visiting poet Roland B___: the man was in the hospital, and Alyce, one of his students, was visiting him daily.

Evasively Alyce said yes.

"And why would you do such a thing?"

"Why?—I'm his assistant."

"Assistant? Since when?"

"And archivist."

"*Archivist?*" Simon stared at Alyce, incredulous. "You're an undergraduate, you know nothing about library archives. Why would anyone hire *you?*"

Alyce's face burned with resentment and unease. This question had occurred to her too, more than once.

"Did you know this Roland B___—before?"

"Before—"

"When you—when we—when we first met . . ."

"I told you, he's my professor."

"I mean, were you his assistant then? His archivist? I hadn't been under that impression . . ."

Alyce had never seen Simon Meech so discomforted. He was not so eloquent now, his manner not poised, aloof, as it was when he stood before a classroom. When she'd approached the booth in the restaurant in which Simon was sitting with a drink in front of him, she'd seen his eyes glide over her with something like surprise, as if he'd forgotten, or had wished to forget, what she looked like. He had not, it appeared, even shaved that day, or he had shaved carelessly.

It had been five weeks since Simon had last brought Alyce back to his apartment. Five weeks since he'd spoken to her. In the interim she'd missed several philosophy classes, she'd neglected to hand in an assignment. He might have been concerned for her, her health, her welfare, what was happening in her life, but in his frowning face Alyce saw that his concern wasn't for her, but for himself.

A waiter approached. Simon jerked his head irritably, without glancing at the man, to signal, *Go away, this is a private conversation.*

"When did you start seeing this Roland B___ outside of your class with him? That's what I'm asking."

"Why are you interrogating me, Simon? Why does it matter to you?"

Even her naming of him—*Simon*. This was startling to him, for she'd scarcely dared to call him any name at all, previously.

"Let's leave here. We should talk in a private place."

"In your apartment? No."

"Not—not there. I have a car . . ."

Simon was almost pleading. She wondered what he knew, or could guess.

How hard it was for him to speak. And amazing to Alyce, to hear the man utter words she might have fantasized hearing weeks before, when he had mattered to her.

Reaching for her hand. Squeezing her hand. As rarely he'd done when they were alone together. In a faltering voice telling her that he'd missed her. He had thought it was wisest—for her, for them both—not to continue to see her, but—"I've wanted to call. I haven't really known what to do, Alyce."

But—did Simon love her? Soon, in her dazed state, Alyce would imagine she was hearing the word *love*.

Staring at their hands. Badly wanting to extricate her hand from his. Yet he was gripping her hand hard. As Roland B___ had sometimes gripped it, as if in desperation.

What a charade this was! Telling Alyce now that he missed her, when she no longer missed him.

"I didn't think you cared for me, Simon. I didn't think you even liked me." Almost spitefully she spoke, childishly. Those hours of hurt, shame, despair, when she'd wished indeed that she could

322

die, cease to exist without the effort and pain of suicide—the man must pay for it all.

"That's ridiculous. Certainly you could tell—I felt strongly about you. I'm not accustomed to spilling my guts the way poets do."

Poets. The word was a sneer in Simon's mouth. Alyce was surprised that he remembered she was a poet, or hoped to be. Fortunately, she'd never dared to show him any of her (love) poems, nor had Simon asked to see any.

She had to leave, Alyce said. She had to return to the hospital. She'd been there for much of the day and had only returned to the campus briefly to get Roland B___'s mail and other items . . .

"Jesus, Alyce! What are you to that man? He's—what? Seventy years old? You're being used by him—exploited."

"He is not seventy. He is sixty—barely."

"Oh, ridiculous! You are doing this out of spite, to hurt *me*."

Simon spoke angrily, resentfully. His face flushed as if with fever. This was a new, rough familiarity between them that would have been astonishing to Alyce if she'd had time to contemplate it.

Stubbornly she said, "He's all alone. He doesn't have anyone else."

"Of course he has someone else! He probably has a wife somewhere, and grown children. He's just taking advantage of you."

Alyce didn't want to say, *Yes, but he loves me too. I am taking advantage of his love.*

It seemed that they would not be having a meal together at the Greek restaurant. A waiter hovered nearby, ignored by Simon, who was becoming increasingly distracted.

Not a meal, not even drinks. Unless Simon had had a drink before Alyce arrived.

He began to plead. He apologized. He was very sorry for his poor judgment. Would Alyce forgive him? Try to forgive him? See him again?

No. Not ever.

Goodbye!

Preparing to leave, extricating her hand from his (sweaty) hand and taking pity on him, the look in his narrow, pinched face, his broken Kinch pride, almost Alyce might have gloated—*Now you know what it is like to be rejected, and humbled.*

Simon was asking if he could drive her to the hospital, at least. They could talk together during the drive. She owed him that much, he would have thought.

Owed him! No.

Seeing the look in Alyce's face, quickly amending: "I mean—since—since we've meant something to each other . . . At least I thought we did."

Alyce felt again that rush of pity, sympathy for the stricken man. He had not meant to hurt her, perhaps. He had not thought of her, but of himself—not her weakness, but his own.

Simon was a young man: not yet thirty. Several years in the seminary had kept him immature: he knew little of the fullness of life. Before Alyce, he had not had any lover. He seemed awkward at touching and being touched. Yet Simon was older than Alyce Urquhart by at least ten years. A (male) faculty member at the university, improperly involved with a (female) undergraduate.

Alyce had the power to sabotage his career, she supposed. If she reported him to the dean of students, if she described his sexual coercion of her, as she saw it now, her shyness and intimidation by him. *And the pregnancy. If she told anyone!*

Relenting yes, all right. He could drive her to the hospital if he wished. And they could talk—"Though I don't really think we have anything to talk about, Simon."

This was bravely stated. Never in the raging despair of the previous weeks had Alyce imagined such a statement made to the man who had impregnated her, and abandoned her.

They were standing beside the booth. Still, the restaurant was near deserted. Simon seemed about to embrace her, but he hesitated.

On the way to the car along a windy, snowswept street, Simon thanked her. His voice was elated, excited. She had forgotten his height—he was taller than she by several inches. She had forgotten the intensity of which he was sometimes capable, so very different from his calm, cutting eloquence.

He was considering returning to the seminary, Simon said. His contract at the university was being negotiated for the following year. In fact, there was the possibility of a three-year contract, and tenure. But he was no longer certain that he wanted tenure, a career at the university.

"The lay world, the civilian world, is—thin. Everything seems flat. Bleached of color."

Simon spoke with bitterness that was a kind of wonder. Glancing about, as if seeing in this very place, which to Alyce looked so solid, how flat and two-dimensional the world was, how empty. She tried to see the world as he might see it, but could not.

"It's God that has drained away. The meaning of my life."

In the car, driving. Alyce was deeply moved that Simon Meech would speak to her in this way. Thinking out loud. Baring his soul.

The streets had been plowed recently. The air was very still and cold, and what Alyce could see of the night sky was beautifully illuminated by a partial moon, but Simon, behind the wheel of his vehicle, which rattled and shuddered, did not seem to notice. Belatedly she realized that he'd (probably) been drinking before she'd met him; he had hurriedly settled a bill on the way out of the restaurant.

"I think that I can regain it. Him. By returning to where I was before I left the seminary. The person I was."

Him. What a curious way in which to refer to God. As if this *him* were a fellow creature with whom the seminarian would be on particularly good terms.

"Not everyone wants to live in the secular world. Some of us require a different air."

Alyce heard herself murmur "yes." Perhaps she was disappointed. Simon didn't love her after all. There was no room for earthly love in his priestly heart.

"I think we need to talk, Alyce. I think there is much you have not told me."

Calmly he spoke. But Alyce could hear the rage quivering beneath.

Instead of driving Alyce directly to the hospital, Simon was taking a longer route, which involved crossing a bridge over a wide, dark river edged with serrated jaws of ice.

Weakly Alyce protested, but Simon promised he wouldn't keep her long.

Driving away from the city. Into the countryside. Simon's foot on the gas pedal erratic, aggressive.

Very still Alyce sat, staring at the rushing road.

Beginning to understand that (possibly) she'd made a mistake.

Leaving the restaurant with Simon instead of walking quickly away. Accompanying him to his car parked on a side street. Stepping into the car, into which she'd never stepped before, out of a (vague, apologetic) wish to placate the man whom (she'd been encouraged by him to think) she had hurt.

"You're pregnant, aren't you? That's why you've been avoiding me." In the darkness of the countryside, asking her almost casually, glancing at her, a smirk of a smile.

Alyce was stunned, speechless. That Simon had asked such a question. Never had she imagined that Simon Meech would be even capable of uttering the word aloud—*pregnant.*

"N-no . . ."

"What do you mean, no? You are *not pregnant*, or you haven't been *avoiding me?*"

Still, Alyce stared ahead at the rushing road. Her thoughts beat frantically. She could not think how to reply.

"Well, are you? Look at me. Answer me."

"I—I am n-not . . ."

Realizing now, she had not wanted the man to know. Not this man.

Not because he would cease to love her. He did not love her now. But because he would wish to harm her, as his enemy.

"How long? How pregnant are you?"

Just short of jeering. Furious. In the restaurant, he'd kept glancing at her furtively. And now with that look of reproach and disbelief.

Rapidly Alyce's brain worked. She must find a way to answer him, to placate him. A raging man beside her, a vehicle hurtling her into the snowy countryside.

327

Simon's foot on the gas pedal alternately pressing down, releasing, and pressing down again. Several times he asked her how long, how long *pregnant*, and Alyce managed to stammer that she was not, not *pregnant*. And still he asked her, *how long*.

She had not calculated. So long as the duration of the pregnancy was imprecise, not marked on any calendar, it had not seemed altogether real to her, even as her belly was swelling, thickening. Even as her breasts were becoming the fatter, softer breasts of a stranger.

How many miles Simon drove into the countryside, away from the lighted city, Alyce had not a clear idea. Seeing his hands on the steering wheel as tight as fists.

She hadn't even known that he owned a car. Perhaps this wasn't Simon's car, but one borrowed for the night.

At last turning into an area cleared partially of snow. Long swaths of snow left by a forked plow. A small parking lot, it appeared to be, a rest stop with shuttered restrooms, beside the state highway and overlooking the river.

Had he planned this place? Alyce wondered. It did not seem to her by chance, Simon's car turning into this remote place.

He has brought other girls here. It was his intention all along.

Telling Alyce that he knew what the situation was, but he wanted to hear it from her. In her own words.

"No accident, is it? You knew. You wanted it."

She had no clear idea what he was talking about. But there was no mistaking his anger.

"Did you? Purposefully? Use me? To trap me? Or—for some reason of your own that you're too stupid even to know?"

328

Alyce licked her lips. To deny this, to cry *no*, would be a confirmation of his suspicion, a mistake.

She would not beg him to drive back to the city. She would not beg him. Desperately calculating how quickly she must act to get out of the car before it was too late.

"I don't intend to let you ruin my life, Alyce. No one is going to do that. If—"

Alyce grasped the car door handle, managing to open it before Simon could stop her. Surprising the man, she was so quick and so strong, pushing away his flailing hand.

Because she'd seemed mute, passive. Because she had not resisted. He had underestimated her, had no idea of her cunning.

Outside, cold, wet air against her face. Running, slipping on icy pavement as the man pursues her, thudding footsteps, surprisingly fast, faster than Alyce would have thought the priestly Kinch capable. Coming up behind her, furious and cursing, and suddenly near enough to strike her with his fist, a glancing blow that would knock her down if she were not in motion, ducking instinctively from him, silent, teeth gritted, knowing she must not infuriate him more by screaming, and she must not squander her breath.

And now she is down, falling heavily onto the freezing ground. And the man above her, his face white and contorted. Kicking her. Grunting, cursing. As she tries to shield her face, her head. Kicking her back, her sides, her thighs. Trying to turn her over, to kick her belly. "*Bitch. Whore. Did it on purpose. I will kill you.*"

So quickly it has happened, the man's fury. As when he'd first touched her weeks ago. She'd felt the sudden flaring up of the man's desire, like flames that ran over each of them, each of them helpless to thwart it. Thinking, *But this can't be happening. He would not—no . . .*

In fury the man is sobbing. Oh, he had not meant to *kick her*.

Her fault, the woman's fault. Provoking his feet to kick. Not his fault, but hers. Making a beast of him when it is she, the female, that is the beast, the bestial thing. How can he forgive her!

Seeing that Alyce lies very still in a paralysis of terror, he ceases kicking her. Exhausted, panting—he relents. But blaming her nonetheless—"You! You did this. Goddamn your slut-soul to hell."

Simon will think that she has died, possibly. Or, no—Simon wipes tears from his eyes and can see that she is breathing, just perceptibly.

Backing off from the fallen girl in disgust. Alyce can hear him muttering to himself—"Jesus, Mary, and Joseph!" It is a plea, the most succinct Catholic prayer for help, forgiveness.

Alyce groans, racked with pain. The man has returned to his car. He will drive away now, he will abandon her in this freezing place.

Her head is throbbing, her eyesight blotched. Later she will discover that the cartilage of her nose is broken; blood flows freely. Close against her face, rivulets of ice, like veins. The warm blood—not hot: lukewarm—will freeze against the ice if she gives in, if she allows herself, as she so badly wants to do, to sleep.

Lying on the ground. Trying to breathe. Lying where he has flung her. Where he stood above her kicking her, her belly, her chest. She can scarcely draw breath, the pain is so strong. Ribs cracked, broken. Massive bruises on her chest, belly. The bleeding face, broken nose. Broken tooth crushed into the gum. Wanting to kill her, but he has not killed her. Whatever is growing inside her, the living thing, the *baby*, he has wanted to kill, but did not.

330

Ruining his life. It is the *baby* that will ruin his life.

All this Alyce thinks. Calmly and almost coolly, as if (already) she were floating some distance overhead, observing the abject fallen figure (her own), the figure crouched over her (Simon Meech) and then backing away.

Very still she lies, in the cunning of desperation. Willing the man to drive away and leave her. Willing the car engine to flare into life, the foot pumping the gas pedal.

But then she hears his footsteps—staggering and wayward in the hard-crusted snow, like the footsteps of a drunken man. Is he returning to her to murder her?

By this time Alyce has managed to rise from the ground. She is dizzy. She is on her knees. Her stunned face is smeared with blood; she has no idea she has been cut. No idea her tooth has been smashed into her gum, for there is no sensation in her lower jaw. A fist in her face, the heel of the man's boot in her face. *Her face* that has been so precious to her.

The man, infuriated, past all restraint, is returning to her. He is the priestly Kinch, he cannot help himself. Like one who must crush a beetle beneath his feet, cannot trust the badly wounded beetle to expire of its own volition, a filthy thing he must grind into oblivion. And Alyce fumbling to seize a rock too large for her hand, fist-size, a rock covered in ice, as the man stoops over her, panting audibly, to strike her, to take hold of her, close his fingers around her neck.

Doesn't know what he is doing. Fingers around the girl's neck to squeeze, squeeze. Not planned. Not premeditated. There is innocence to it, almost. But Alyce slams the rock into his face in desperation. Somehow this has happened. Scarcely able to clutch the rock in her hand, yet Alyce summons the strength to slam the rock into the jeering face. Into the eyes and the bridge of his nose, and she feels the *crack* of the bone and feels—or imagines she feels—the man's wet, warm, rushing blood against her fingers. Against her face. Hears him cry out in rage, disbelief.

Running from him, limping. In triumph.

In triumph, carrying her life as one might carry a torch, shielded against the wind. Her life, and the precious life within her, a torch, a tremulous flame shielded from the wind by her crouched and running body.

And behind her the man calling to her. Pleading, "Aly-ce! Aly-ce! Where are you, come back, I wasn't serious. Aly-ce!"

Suffused with strength. Where moments before, she'd been weak, paralyzed. Weak, as if the tendons of her legs had been cut. As if the vertebrae of her upper back had been broken. As if her carotid artery had been slashed by an invisible knife wielded in the murderer's hand, but new strength flows into her. Running into a snowy field beyond the parking lot. Thick-crusted banks of snow. Pathways through the snow, trampled by myriad feet. But the surface of the snow is icy-hard, treacherous. There has been a thaw and refreezing. Melting and immediate refreezing. Alyce is slip-sliding down a hill into a ravine of rocks, boulders. She imagines she hears trickling water amid columns of ice.

Fainter now, the man's uplifted voice. An attempt at laughter— "Aly-ce! I was only joking!"

In the ravine she hides. A steep ravine filled with snow. But beneath the snow, cast-off household things—broken chairs, sofa, stained carpet. The skeletal remains of a small creature—raccoon, dog. The man will drive into the interior of the park along a winding road, calling to her— "Aly-ce! Darling! I love you, I was only joking! Come back!" *Sees, or thinks she sees, the headlights of the vehicle on the road, until finally the lights have vanished and the wind is still.*

Out of the steep, snowy ravine. Clutching at rocks, her hands bloodied. And all the while, snow falling, temperature dropping to zero degrees Fahrenheit.

How still the soft-falling snow amid rocks! The yearning, the temptation to lie down, sleep.

Five miles back to the city. She will stagger to the highway, she will limp along the highway facing oncoming traffic. Blinded by headlights, her eyes aching where he'd kicked and punched and pummeled her, until at last a motorist stops to pick her up.

Call ambulance? —but no, Alyce insists no.

She is going to the hospital, no need of an ambulance.

Call police?—but no, Alyce insists no.

Trickle of blood between her legs. Not a sensation of heat, but cold. Begins high in her belly, higher still in the region of her heart. Between her thighs, clamped together tight, sticky clots she hopes won't leak out and through her clothing onto the vinyl seat of the stranger's car.

Thinking—*I am alive. That is all that matters.*

Elated to think so. Elated, thanking the motorist for the ride.

Saying to the driver—"Thank you. We owe you everything!"

At the hospital, it is nearing midnight. At such an hour the front entrance of the building is locked, the foyer is darkened, and you must enter by the ER at the side of the building.

On foot, in light-falling snow. Lucky Alyce is wearing boots. These hours she has been walking, trudging, staggering in snow that has accumulated to a depth of four or five inches. On her hot skin, snowflakes melt at once. Laughing to see, as a child might see, how, behind her, there are no tracks in the fresh-fallen snow leading from the curb to the ER entrance.

"Hello? Hello? Hello? Hello? Let me in, please!"

A surprise to Alyce, the automated doors refuse to open. Locked from inside? She peers through the plateglass window, baffled.

But yes, this is the ER. The reception area of the ER. Where they'd brought Roland B___ on a stretcher. An interior Alyce had not realized she'd memorized as one might memorize a poem unconsciously.

But at last someone comes to open the door. A medical worker in white nylon shirt, trousers. Alyce has no ID—she has left her book bag, her wallet, miles away. Fallen onto the floor of the man's car, or out onto the frozen ground when she'd fled in terror of her life, to be discovered by a snow removal crew in the morning.

At first they will not admit her into the ER. But then the decision comes to admit her.

Carefully it is explained to Alyce that she must take a back stairway to the fifth floor, to where Roland B___ awaits her.

"You are his—granddaughter?"

"Yes! I am his granddaughter," Alyce says, laughing. "He is expecting me. He won't have gone to sleep without me."

When she'd been alive, she would have been deeply embarrassed. And the seeping-cold sensation between her legs, deeply embarrassing if anyone had seen.

Now, grateful to be here. For nothing else matters, Alyce sees that now. The elderly poet awaits her. They will be together, he will cherish and protect her.

On the fifth floor. She is breathless from the stairs; there are no elevators at this hour. She is breathless from hurrying. The corridor is deserted. Where is the nursing staff? The doors to several rooms are ajar. And the door to room five twenty-six is open, there is a blinding shaft of sunshine inside.

"Alyce, my dear!—my darling. Where have you been? My beautiful ghost-girl, I have missed you."

On the morning of December 11, 1972, the body of a young woman was found by hikers in a snow-filled ravine in a wooded area of Tecumseh State Park, five miles north of Bridgewater. The young woman was initially believed to have been strangled to death, for there were multiple bruises on her throat, as well as elsewhere on her body, but the Tecumseh county coroner has ruled the primary cause of death to be hypothermia. Subsequently identified as nineteen-year-old Alyce Urquhart of Strykersville, New York, a sophomore at the university, the victim is believed to have been left unconscious by her assailant or assailants in a ravine, to freeze to death when the temperature plummeted to a low of zero degrees Fahrenheit during the night.

If there were tire tracks on the roadway and in the parking lot near the ravine, a five-inch snowfall had covered them.

The deceased young woman had been an undergraduate in the College of Arts and Sciences at the university. Residents in her dormitory were reported to be shocked by the news of her death and spoke of her with respect and admiration. Saying, You could see that Alyce was a very serious student. The rest of us would goof around, but not Alyce. She was always in the library. (At least, we thought she was always in the library. We'd see her rushing off after class, she'd say she was going to study in the library where it was quiet, then she wouldn't return until midnight.)

No, Alyce didn't have a boyfriend, or a man friend. Never saw her at frat parties or anywhere with a guy.

During her freshman year at the university Alyce Urquhart had earned high grades and was on the dean's list. Her current instructors have testified that the young woman was an outstanding student until mid-November, when with no explanation she ceased attending classes regularly and failed to complete assignments.

Her philosophy instructor, Dr. Simon Meech, testified to police that Alyce Urquhart had done "usually very good" work in his section of Introduction to Philosophy.

No, he had not had any personal contact with the victim. He'd realized that she was one of his students only when he'd seen the "shocking and tragic" article on the front page of the local newspaper and checked the name against his class list to discover Alyce Urquhart on that list.

Dr. Meech had begun to notice that Miss Urquhart was missing classes when she failed to turn in a written assignment in early December. She had not offered her instructor any explanation, and there had been no contact between them. "Our undergraduates are adults, whom we treat accordingly," Dr. Meech said. "They must be responsible for attending classes and for completing their coursework."

Yes. The deceased had turned in work of unusual quality for an undergraduate in philosophy, and especially for a young woman.

Bridgewater police officers are investigating the death, which has been classified as a homicide. At the present time there are no suspects. Anyone with information that might prove helpful to the case is asked to call the Bridgewater Police Department at 518-330-2293.

THE
SURVIVING
CHILD

1.

The surviving child, he is called. Not to his face—of course.

The other, younger child died with the mother three years before. *Murder, suicide* it had been. More precisely *Filicide, suicide.*

The first glimpse she has of the surviving child is shocking to her: a beautiful face, pale and lightly freckled, darkly luminous eyes, a prematurely adult manner—solemn, sorrowful, wary, and watchful.

As sharp as a sliver of glass piercing her heart comes the thought—*I will love him. I will save him. I am the one.*

"Stefan! Say hello to my friend—"

No comfortable way for Stefan's father to introduce her, the father's fiancée, to the surviving child. Presumably Alexander has been telling Stefan about her, preparing him. *I am thinking of re-marrying. I have met a young woman I would like you to meet. I think you will like her, and she will—she will like you* . . . No way to express such thoughts that is not painful.

Seeing the apprehension in the child's face. Wondering if, since the mother's death, the father has introduced Stefan to other women whom he has invited to the house, or if Stefan has chanced to see his father with a woman, one who might be expected to take the mother's place.

But Elisabeth is not jealous of other women. Elisabeth is not envious of other women. Elisabeth is grateful to have been plucked from obscurity by the gentlemanly man who is her fiancé, the widower of the (deceased) (notorious) poet N.K.

Stooping to shake the child's small-boned hand. Hearing herself say brightly, reassuringly, "Hello, Stefan! So nice to meet you . . ." Her voice trails off. She is smiling so hard her face hurts. Hoping the child will not shrink from her out of shyness, dislike, or resentment.

Stefan is ten years old, small for his age. It is terrible to think (the fiancée thinks) how small this delicately boned child had to have been three years earlier, when his mother had tried to kill him along with his little sister and herself.

Alexander told her how the boy stopped growing for months after the trauma. Very little appetite, sleep disturbed by nightmares, wandering the house in the night. Disappearing in the house in broad daylight so that the father and the housekeeper searched for him, calling his name—*Stefan! Stefan!*—until suddenly Stefan would appear around a corner, on a staircase, in a corridor, blinking and short of breath and unable to explain where he'd been.

Almost asphyxiated by the mother. Heavily sedated with barbiturates as well. Yet somehow: he'd been spared.

Stefan had not cried in the aftermath of the trauma, or not much—"Not what you'd expect under the circumstances."

Under the circumstances! Elisabeth winced at Alexander's oddly unfeeling remark.

The fiancée has been introduced to the child as Elisabeth, but the child cannot call her that name of course. Nor can the child call her Miss Lundquist. In time, when Elisabeth and the child's father are married, the child will learn to call her—what? Not Mother. Not Mom. *Mommy?* Will that ever be possible?

(Elisabeth has no idea what the child called his mother. It is very difficult to imagine the elusive poet N.K. as any child's mother, let alone as *Mom, Mommy.*)

Those wary, watchful eyes. How like a fledgling bird in its nest Stefan is, prepared to cringe at a gliding shadow—a parent bird, or a predator that will tear him to pieces? The fledgling can't know which until it is too late.

Yet politely Stefan murmurs replies to questions put to him by the adults. Familiar questions about school, questions he has answered many times. He will not be asked questions that are painful to answer. Not now. When he'd been asked such questions in the aftermath of his mother's death, the child had stared into a corner of the room with narrowed eyes, silent. His jaws had clenched, a small vein had twitched at his temple, but his gaze had held firm and unswerving.

Later the father would say that he'd been afraid to touch the child's chest, or his throat, at the time—*I was sure Stefan had stopped breathing. He'd gone somewhere deep inside himself where that terrible woman was calling him.*

It is months later. In fact it is years later. *That terrible woman* has disappeared from their lives and from the beautiful old shingle board house in Wainscott, Massachusetts, in which Alexander and N.K. lived during their twelve-year marriage.

Lived "only intermittently"—Alexander has said. For frequently they lived apart, as N.K. pursued her own "utterly selfish" life.

Not in the house, but in the adjoining three-car garage, a converted stable, which the fiancée has not (yet) seen, the poet N.K. killed herself and her four-year-old daughter, Clea, by carbon monoxide poisoning.

And no suicide note. Neither in the car nor elsewhere.

It is true, Alexander acknowledged having found in her bedside table a diary N.K. kept during the last fevered weeks of her life.

His claim was that he'd had to destroy the diary—without reading it—knowing it would contain terrible accusations, lies. The ravings of a homicidal madwoman, from which his son had to be spared.

For he could not risk it, that Stefan would grow up having to encounter in the world echoes and reflections of the sick and debased mind that had tried to destroy him . . .

Despite the trauma, Stefan has done reasonably well at the Wainscott Academy. For several months after the deaths he'd been kept at home, with a nurse to care for him—he'd had to repeat third grade—but since then he has caught up with his fifth-grade classmates, Alexander has said proudly. All that one might have predicted—fits of crying, child depression, "acting out," mysterious illnesses—seemed not to have occurred or were fleeting. "My son has a stoical spirit," the father has said. "Like me."

The fiancée thinks, seeing the child, *No. He is just in hiding.*

Elisabeth has calculated that there is almost exactly the identical distance between Stefan's age and hers as there is between hers and Alexander's: eighteen years. (Stefan is ten, Elisabeth is twenty-eight. Alexander is in his late forties.)

Elisabeth will brood over this. It is a very minor fact, yet (she thinks) a way of linking her and the child, though (probably) the child will never realize.

If she were alive, the sick and debased N.K. would be just thirty-six. Young, still.

But if N.K. were alive, Elisabeth Lundquist would not be here in Wainscott in her fiancé's distinguished old family house, smiling so hard her face aches.

It is impressive: Stefan knows to stand very still as adults speak at him, to him, above his head. He does not twitch, quiver as another (normal?) child might. He does not betray restlessness, resentment. *He does not betray misery.* His smile is quicksilver, his eyes are heavy-lidded. Beautiful dark brown eyes. Elisabeth wonders if those eyes, so much darker than the father's eyes—as the child's complexion is so much paler than the father's ruddy skin—resemble the deceased mother's eyes.

Elisabeth has seen photographs of the dramatically beautiful N.K. of course. She has seen a number of videos, including those that, after N.K.'s death, went "viral." It would have been unnatural if, under the circumstances, she had not.

The Guatemalan housekeeper, Ana, has overseen Stefan's bath, combed and brushed the boy's curly fair-brown hair, laid out clean clothes for him. Of course at the age of ten he dresses himself. On his small feet, denim sneakers with laces neatly tied. Elisabeth feels a pang of loss. The child is too old for her to help him with his laces—ever.

It will be a challenge, she thinks. To win over this beautiful, wounded child.

"Mr. Hendrick?"—Ana appears, smiling and gracious, deferential. It is time now for the evening meal.

Supper is in a glassed-in porch at the rear of the house, where a small round table has been set for three people. At its center, a vase of white roses fresh-picked from the garden.

As they enter the room, Elisabeth feels an impulse to take the child's hand, very gently—to allow Stefan to know that she cares for him already though they have just met. She will be his friend.

But when Elisabeth reaches for Stefan's hand, her fingers encounter something cold and clotty, sticky like mucus—"Oh! Oh God." She gives a little scream and steps away, shuddering.

"What is it, Elisabeth?" Alexander asks, concerned.

What is it, Elisabeth has no idea. For when she looks at Stefan, at Stefan's hand, small-boned and innocent, entirely clean, lifted palm-outward before him in a pleading gesture, she sees nothing unusual—certainly nothing that might have felt cold, clotty, as sticky as mucus.

"I just felt—cold . . ."

"Well! Are your hands cold, Stefan?"

Shyly Stefan shakes his head. Murmuring, "Don't know."

Elisabeth apologizes, deeply embarrassed. Must have imagined—something . . .

Alexander has no idea what is going on—(unless Alexander has a very good idea what is going on)—but he chooses to be bemused by his young fiancée, eighteen years his junior: the young woman's fear of harmless insects, her fear of driving in urban areas, her fear of flying in small propeller planes used by commuters from Boston to Cape Cod.

Elisabeth manages to laugh, uneasily. She reasons that it is better for Alexander to express bemusement, impatience, irritation with her than with the sensitive Stefan.

Quite a beautiful room, the glassed-in porch. White wicker furniture, a pale beige Peruvian woven rug. On a wall a Childe Hassam Impressionist seascape of the late nineteenth century.

As they are about to sit, Stefan suddenly freezes. Murmurs that he has to use a bathroom. Over Alexander's face comes a flicker of annoyance. Oh, just as Ana is serving the meal! Elisabeth is sorry about this.

"Of course. Go."

At the table, Alexander pours (white, tart) wine into the adults' glasses. He is determined not to express the annoyance he feels for his son, but Elisabeth can see his hands trembling.

Elisabeth remarks that they have plenty of time to drive to the concert in Provincetown for which they have tickets. "It's only six. We have an hour and a half for dinner . . ."

"I'm aware of the time, Elisabeth. Thank you."

A rebuff. Alexander doesn't like his naïve young fiancée even to appear to be correcting him.

Gamely Elisabeth tries again: "Your son is so—beautiful. He's . . ."

Unique. Unworldly. Elusive.

Alexander grunts a vague assent. Somehow managing to signal *yes* and at the same time *Enough of this subject*.

Elisabeth is one of those shy individuals who find themselves chattering nervously, for conversational silence intimidates them.

It is hard for her to remain silent. She feels (she thinks) that she is being judged. Yet she has discovered to her surprise that it is not difficult to offend Alexander Hendrick inadvertently. A man of his stature, so thin-skinned? She worries that even a naively well-intentioned compliment about Stefan may remind him of the other child, Clea, who died of carbon monoxide poisoning wrapped in a mohair shawl in her mother's arms . . .

Terrible! Elisabeth shudders.

"How is this wine? It's Portuguese—d'you like it?"

Wine? Elisabeth knows little about wine. "Yes," she tells Alexander, who is frowning over his glass as if nothing were more important than the wine he is about to drink.

"I'm wondering if I should have bought an entire case. Might've been a mistake."

Is wine important? Elisabeth supposes that it must be if Alexander thinks so. Her fiancé, to her a distinguished man, director of a wealthy arts foundation established by his grandfather, has a habit of weighing minor acts, innocuous-seeming decisions, as if they were crucially important, and might turn into *mistakes*. At first Elisabeth thought he was only joking, since the issues were often trivial, but now she sees that nothing is trivial to her fiancé. The mere possibility of a mistake is upsetting to him.

Driving to Wainscott, bringing Elisabeth for her first weekend visit to the house on Oceanview Avenue, Alexander had said suddenly, "I hope this isn't going to be a mistake."

Elisabeth had laughed nervously. Hesitant to ask Alexander to explain, for he hadn't actually seemed to be speaking to her, only thinking aloud.

They are waiting for Stefan to return to the table. Ana has lighted candles that quaver with their breaths. Why is the boy taking so much time? Is he hiding from them?—from his father? At Alexander's insistence, Ana serves the first, lavish course—roasted sweet peppers stuffed with pureed mushroom. On each Wedgwood plate, a red pepper and a green pepper perfectly matched.

Not the sort of food a boy of ten probably likes, Elisabeth thinks.

"Well. Let's begin. We may run into traffic on the highway."

Heavy silver forks, knives. Engraved with the letter *H*. Virtually everything in the house, as well as the house itself, is Alexander's inheritance; N.K.'s things, which were not many, were moved out after the deaths, given away. Even the books. Especially books with *N.K.* on the spine.

Not a trace of her remaining. Don't worry, darling!

Wondering once more if Alexander has brought other women to Wainscott, to meet Stefan. To see how they reacted to the surviving child, and the house. Young women, presumably. (Now that he is middle-aged, Alexander isn't the type to be attracted to women his own age.) Wondering if, initially drawn to Alexander Hendrick, these women have fled?

When you see the house, you'll understand—why it means so much to me. And why I am not going to move out.

Rarely did Alexander speak directly of N.K. Usually obliquely and in such a way that Elisabeth was not encouraged to ask questions.

In itself, suicide would be devastating. The suicide of a spouse. But conjoined with murder, the murder of a child—unspeakable.

The dead must present a sort of argument, Elisabeth thinks. The argument must be refuted by the living. The dead who have taken the lives of others, and their own lives, must especially be refuted by the living, if the living are to continue.

After several minutes Alexander says sharply to Ana, who has been hovering in the background, "Look for him! Please."

Elisabeth winces. The way Alexander gives orders to the house-keeper is painful to her.

Ana hurries away to call "*Stefan! Stefan!*"

Elisabeth lays down her napkin. She will help look for the child . . .

"No. Stay here. This is ridiculous."

Alexander is flush-faced, indignant. With his fork and knife he slides something onto Elisabeth's plate. At first she thinks it is quivering with life, slimy like a jellyfish; then she sees that it is just pureed mushroom, seeping fragrantly from the roasted peppers.

Ana is on the stairs to the second floor. A short, stout woman, heavy-thighed. Out of breath. "Stefan? Hello?"

They listen to her calling, cajoling. If only Stefan will answer!

But Ana returns, panting and apologetic. Can't find him, she is so sorry—not in his room, not in any bathroom. Not in the kitchen or the back hall or—anywhere she could think of.

"Goddamn. I've warned him, if he played this trick one more time . . ."

Alexander lurches to his feet. Elisabeth rises also, daring to clutch at his arm.

"Maybe he's sick, Alexander. He was looking sad—maybe he just doesn't want to see anyone right now. Can't you let him—be?"

Alexander throws off her hand. "Shut up. You know *nothing.*"

He stalks out of the glassed-in porch. Elisabeth has no choice but to follow, hesitantly. Hoping that Ana has not overheard

Alexander's remark to her. Not the first time her fiancé has told her to *shut up.*

Stomping on the stairs, calling "Stefan? Where the hell are you?"

Elisabeth follows into the hall. Not up the stairs. Not sure what she should be doing. Weakly calling, "Stefan? It's me—Elisabeth. Are you hiding? Where are you hiding?"

Where are you hiding? An inane remark, such as one frightened child might ask another . . .

Desperate minutes are spent in the search for the child. Upstairs, downstairs. Front hall, back hall. Kitchen, dining room. Living room, sitting room. And again back upstairs, to peer into closets in guest rooms. In the master bedroom, where (Alexander says grimly) the boy "wouldn't dare" set foot.

Finally, there is no alternative. The distraught father must go to look in the forbidden place: the garage. Telling Elisabeth and Ana to stay where they are. By this time Alexander is very upset. His face is ruddy with heat, his carefully combed hair has fallen onto his forehead. Even the handsome blue silk necktie has loosened as if he'd clawed at it.

Elisabeth hears the man's impatient voice uplifted at the rear of the house—"Stefan? Are you in there? You had better not be in there . . ."

That place. Where she died. And your little sister died.

Anxiously Elisabeth and Ana wait in the hall for Alexander to return. It is not likely (Elisabeth thinks) that the father will easily find the son and haul him back in triumph.

"Stefan has done this before, I guess?" Elisabeth asks hesitantly, and Ana, protective of the child, or not wanting to betray a family secret, frowns and looks away as if she hasn't heard the question.

Saying finally, choosing her words with care, "He is a good boy, Stefan. Very sweet, sad. There is something that comes over him—sometimes. Not his fault. That is all."

To this Elisabeth can't think of a reply. She is steeling herself for Alexander's reappearance. The loud, angry voice like a spike driven into her forehead—she must make every effort not to acknowledge that it gives her pain.

And then, almost by chance, Elisabeth happens to glance back into the glassed-in porch, which she knows to be empty, which *has to be empty*, and sees at the table a child-size figure, very still—can it be Stefan? In his chair, at his place?

Elisabeth hurries to him. So surprised, she doesn't call for Alexander.

"Oh!—Stefan. There you are."

As if he has been running, the child is out of breath. Almost alarmingly out of breath.

His face is very pale, clammy-pale, coated in perspiration. His eyes are dilated with excitement, his lips seem to have a bluish cast. And there are bluish shadows beneath his eyes.

Oxygen deprivation? Is that it?

Even as she is profoundly relieved, Elisabeth is astonished. She would like to touch the child—hug him, even—but does not dare. A faint, subtly rancid smell lifts from him, like a sour breath.

Ana hurries to tell Mr. Hendrick that his son has returned safely.

Elisabeth approaches the child calmly, not wanting to overwhelm him with her emotion, dares to grasp his hand, and this time the small-boned hand is pliant and not resistant, a child's hand, slightly cold, but containing nothing repulsive, to terrify.

So relieved to see him, Elisabeth hears herself laugh nervously. She will not allow herself to wonder why he is so breathless, and so pale.

Nor does she accuse the child, except she must ask where he has been—hadn't he heard them calling him for the past ten minutes or more?—hadn't he heard his father?

Evasively Stefan mutters what sounds like "Here. I was here."

Nothing sly or mischievous, nothing deceitful about the child, Elisabeth is sure. But how strange!—where had he been? And how had he slipped past her and Ana to return to the dinner table on the porch?

In the pale, freckled face there's a look of adult anguish, cunning. And the skin is still clammy-cold, with the sweat of panic.

As the angry father approaches, footsteps loud in the hall like a mallet striking, Stefan cringes. Elisabeth holds his small, weak hand, to protect him.

"You! Goddamn you! Didn't I warn you!"—for a terrible moment it seems that Alexander is about to strike his son; his hand is raised for a slap; but then, like air leaking from a balloon, Alexander's anger seems to drain from him. His eyes glisten with tears of frustration, rage, fear. He drags out his chair to sit down heavily at the table.

"Just tell me, Stefan: Where were you?"

And Stefan says in his small, still voice what sounds like "Here. I was here . . ."

Alexander snatches up his napkin to wipe his eyes. "Well. *Don't* do anything like this again, d'you hear me?"

2.

Bollingen Prize Poet N.K., Child Found Dead in Wainscott, MA
Asphyxiation Deaths "Possibly Accidental"

Bestselling Feminist Poet N.K. Takes Own Life
Four-Year-Old Daughter Dies With Her
"Shocking Scene" — Wainscott, MA

Always Elisabeth will remember: the shocked voice of a colleague rushing into the library at the Radcliffe Institute.

". . . terrible. They're saying she killed herself and . . ."

Lowered (female) voices. Solemn, appalled. Disbelieving.

Glancing up from her laptop as talk swirled around her.

Who had died? A poet? A woman poet? *And* her daughter?

Wanting to know, not wanting to know.

That evening, at a reception at the institute for a visiting lecturer, all talk was of the suicide. And the death of the child.

Asphyxiation by carbon monoxide poisoning.

". . . wouldn't have done it. I don't believe it."

". . . herself, maybe. But not a daughter."

". . . not possible. No."

How shocking the news was! The voices were embittered, in-credulous. How demoralizing for women writers, women scholars, women who declared themselves feminists. Nicola Kavanaugh—N.K.—had been a heroine to them, defiant and courageous and original.

"... murder, maybe. Someone jealous ..."

"... that husband. Weren't they separated ..."

"... but not the daughter! I know her—knew her. N.K. would never have done *that.*"

Of course they had to acknowledge that N.K. had written freely, shockingly, of taboo subjects like suicide—the *unspeakable bliss of self-erasure.*

Elisabeth listened. Grasped the hands of mourners that clutched at hers in anguish. She had not been a fellow at the institute several years before, when N.K. came to give a "brilliant"—"impassioned"—"inspiring" presentation on the "unique language" of women's poetry, but she'd heard colleagues speak admiringly of it, still.

At the institute, Elisabeth was researching the archives of the Imagist poets of the early twentieth century. She'd read no more than a scattering of N.K.'s flamboyant, quasi-confessional poetry, so very different from the spare understatement of Imagism; she wouldn't have wanted to acknowledge that she found N.K.'s poetry too harsh, discordant, angry, *unsettling.* Nor had she been drawn to the cult of N.K. that had begun even before the poet's premature death.

What is a cult but a binding together of the weak? So it seemed to her. The excesses of feminists she hoped to distance herself from. A certain physical/erotic posturing, needless provocations. Not for her.

Soon then, reading an obituary of N.K. in the *New York Times*, Elisabeth discovered that N.K. had allegedly named herself, or rather renamed herself, as "N.K." in homage to the Imagist poet H.D.; she'd wanted a pseudonym "without gender and without a history."

Names are obscuring, misleading. So N.K. argued. Surnames—family names—have no role in art. Artists are individuals and should name themselves. "Naming"—the most crucial aspect of one's life, the name you bring with you, as blatant as a face—should not be the province/choice of others.

Essentially, your parents are strangers to you. It is not reasonable that strangers should name *you*.

And so, Nicola Kavanaugh had named herself N.K. The poet's vanity would help brand her, help to guarantee her fame.

Soon after, Elisabeth found herself staring at a poster on a wall in Barnes & Noble depicting the gaunt, savagely beautiful N.K. in a photograph by Annie Leibovitz. The poet had been wearing what looked like a flimsy cotton shift—you could almost see the shadowy nipples of her breasts through the material—and around her slender shoulders a coarse-knitted, fringed shawl. Her thick, disheveled hair appeared to be windblown, her eyes sharp and accusing. Beneath, the caption: *"Live as if it's your life."*

3.

"And what did you say your name was, dear?—'Elizabeth?' I didn't quite hear."

"Elisabeth."

Gravely he laughed at her. Leaning over her.

"Is that a lisp I hear?—Elis-a-beth?"

"Y-yes."

By chance, months later, when the last thing on her mind was N.K., Elisabeth was introduced to Alexander Hendrick. A tall, gentlemanly man of whom everyone whispered—*D'you know who that is? Alexander Hendrick—N.K.'s husband.*

He was older than Elisabeth by nearly twenty years. Yet youthful in his manner, even playful, to disguise the gravity beneath, even as he had to shave (Elisabeth would learn) twice a day to rid his jaws of graying stubble, sharp little quills that erupted not only on his face but beneath his chin, partway down his neck.

She'd known something of the man's identity, apart from the disaster of his marriage: he was the director of the Hendrick Foundation, which had been founded by his multimillionaire grandfather in the 1950s, to award grants to creative artists at the outset of their careers.

Including, in 1993, the young experimental poet-artist Nicola Kavanaugh, as she'd called herself then.

Had Alexander Hendrick and Nicola Kavanaugh met before Nicola received the grant or afterward?—Elisabeth was never to learn with any certainty.

"Tell me you aren't a poet, my dear Elisabeth."

"No. I mean—I am not a poet."

"You're sure?"—Alexander Hendrick was grimly joking, unless it was his very grimness that joked, that made such a joke possible.

Elisabeth laughed, feeling giddy. Since adolescence she'd been waiting for such a person, who could intimidate her yet make her laugh.

4.

You tell yourself: the new life is sudden.

The new life is a window flung open. Better yet, a window smashed.

Sometimes it is true. The *new life* is flung in your face; you have not the capacity to duck the flying glass.

What was it like, to visit that house? Will you have to live there as his wife—permanently?

Can you—permanently?

Are there traces of her? Is there an—aura?

Oh Elisabeth. Take care.

The (civil) wedding in March is very small, private. Few relatives on either side.

Immediately afterward they leave for a week in the Bahamas. And when they return, it is to the house on Oceanview Avenue, Wainscott, where the surviving child awaits, looked after by the housekeeper, Ana.

Are you prepared for him? A ten-year-old stepchild whose mother tried to kill him?

In death, N.K.'s notoriety has grown. Articles about her appear continuously in print and online. An unauthorized video titled *Last Days of the Poet N.K.* goes viral. An unauthorized "Interview with the American Medea, N.K."—in fact, a pastiche of several interviews—appears in *Vanity Fair*, with photographs of the starkly beautiful woman over the course of years. There are Barnes & Noble posters, T-shirts, even coffee mugs—a cartoon likeness of N.K. with an aureole of fiercely crimped dark hair and a beautiful, savage, unsmiling mouth.

Of these outrages Alexander never speaks—perhaps he is not aware (Elisabeth wants to think). The posthumous cult of N.K. is like a cancer metastasizing—unstoppable.

Sylvia Plath, Anne Sexton, and now Nicola Kavanaugh—N.K. For each generation of wounded and angry women, a deathly female icon.

At first the mainstream media contrived to believe that N.K. had been mentally ill—to have killed her daughter as well as herself. It was known that she'd "struggled with depression" since adolescence; she'd tried to kill herself several times in the past. But then, newer readings of N.K.'s poetry suggest that her horrendous act had been deliberate and premeditated, a "purification" of the self in a rotten world.

It seemed clear that she'd meant to kill Stefan as well, initially. She'd given the seven-year-old a sedative, as she'd given the four-year-old a sedative, and brought him into the garage with her and into the Saab sedan; then, for some reason, she'd relented and carried him back into the house and left him and returned to the car with the motor running, filling the garage with bluish smoke for the stunned Alexander to discover hours later.

The dead woman lying in the front seat of the car with the little girl, Clea, in her arms, the two of them wrapped in a mohair shawl.

Was there a suicide note?—Alexander saw nothing.

It would be his claim: he'd seen nothing. Emergency medical workers, law enforcement officers, investigators—no suicide note discovered in the car.

Yet it came to be generally known that there'd been "packets of poems" scattered in the back seat of the car. (As well as the left sneaker of a pair of sneakers—belonging to Stefan.) Not new poems by N.K., but older poems, among her more famous poems, that quickly took on on a new, ominous prescience. The posthumous cult of N.K., so maddening to Alexander and his family, quickly fastened upon these poems—*the small bitter apples of extinction*.

Ana had been given the entire day off by Nicola. The housekeeper hadn't been expected to return until eight o'clock in the evening, by which time Nicola and Clea had been dead for several hours.

Stefan, missing, was eventually found by searchers inside the house, partially dressed and shoeless, at the rear of an upstairs closet. (The mate to the child's sneaker in the rear of the Saab would be discovered in a corner of the garage amid recycling containers, as if it had been tossed or kicked there.) He was curled into a fetal position, so deeply asleep he might have been in a coma. His blood pressure was dangerously low. His skin was deathly white, his lips had a bluish cast. Emergency medical workers worked to revive him with oxygen.

The surviving child was slow to come to consciousness. Not only carbon monoxide poisoning but barbiturate would be discovered in his blood. He would remember little of what had happened.

Except—*Mummy gave me warm milk to drink, that made me sleepy. Mummy kissed me and told me she would never abandon me.*

Yet the child's mother must have changed her mind about killing him with his sister. A short time after she'd started the Saab motor, when the seven-year-old was unconscious, but before she herself had lapsed into unconsciousness, she'd pulled him from the back seat of the car, dragged or carried him all the way upstairs to a hall closet . . .

Elisabeth ponders this. Why did N.K. relent, allowing one of her children to live? The boy, and not the girl? *Did* in fact this happen as it's generally believed?

Elisabeth wonders if the seven-year-old might have crawled out of the car and saved himself. Yet why would he have hidden upstairs in a closet? And he'd been deeply unconscious when his father discovered him.

More than three years after the deaths, the Wainscott police investigation is closed. The county medical examiner issued his report: homicide, suicide. Carbon monoxide poisoning. Heavy barbiturate sedation. Still, no one knows precisely the chronology of events of that day. The surviving child cannot be further questioned. The surviving husband has declared he will never speak again on the subject publicly.

And privately? Elisabeth knows only what Alexander has chosen to tell her, which she has no reason to disbelieve. N.K. had suffered from manic depression since early adolescence; she'd been a "brilliant poet" (Alexander had to concede) afflicted by a strong wish to harm herself, and others unfortunate enough to be caught up in her emotional life. She'd been coldly ambitious, Alexander said. Always anxious about her reputation, jealous of other poets' prizes, publicity. Ultimately she'd cared little for a domestic life—though, for a few years, she'd tried. Perversely, the children had adored her, Alexander said bitterly.

And yet, what is it we cannot know? Though the heart breaks, the great sea crashes, crushes us. We must know.

Since becoming Alexander's wife, Elisabeth has resisted reading N.K.'s poems. Yet it is difficult to avoid them, for often lines from the poems, even entire poems, are quoted in the media. Quickly Elisabeth looks away, but sometimes it is too late.

. . . crashes, crushes us. We must know.

Very still Elisabeth has been sitting, fingers poised above the laptop keyboard. How many minutes have passed she doesn't know, but her laptop screen has gone dark, like a brain switching off. By chance she hears a quickened breath behind her—turns to see, in the doorway, the beautiful child, her stepchild, Stefan.

"Oh—Stefan! Hello . . ."

Elisabeth is so startled by the sight of him, something falls from the table—a ballpoint pen. Clattering onto the floor, rolling.

"H-have you been there a while, dear? I didn't hear you . . ."

Rises to her feet, as if to invite the elusive child inside the room, but already Stefan has backed away and is descending the stairs.

Like a wild creature, she thinks.

If you reach out for a wild creature, it shrinks away. Oh, she is so crude!—so yearning, the child sees it in her face and retreats.

5.

"Certainly not! We live here. We are very happy here. It's *ordinary life* here." Declaiming to visitors, Alexander laughs with a sharp sort of happiness.

A steady procession of visitors, guests at Hendrick House. In the summer months especially, on idyllic Cape Cod.

No aura. Not her. That one is dead, gone. Vanished.

On the wide veranda looking toward the ocean, in the long summer twilight. Drinks are served by a young Guatemalan girl who is helping Ana tonight, crystal glitters and winks. Elisabeth is the new wife, shy among her husband's friends. He has so many!—hopeless to try to keep their names straight.

Perhaps these are not friends exactly. Rather, acquaintances and professional associates. Visitors from Provincetown, Woods Hole. Houseguests from Boston, Cambridge, New York City, connected with the Hendrick Foundation.

In summer the house on Oceanview Avenue is particularly beautiful. Romantically weathered dark brown shingle board with dark shutters, stone foundation, and stone chimneys. Steep roofs and cupolas, a wraparound veranda open to the ocean on bright, windy days. Fifteen rooms, three stories, the converted stable at the rear. Not the largest but one of the more distinctive houses on Oceanview Avenue, Wainscott. Originally built in 1809 and listed with the National Register of Historic Places. Beside the heavy oak front door is a small brass plaque commemorating this honor.

Of course, Alexander has an apartment elsewhere, on Boston's Beacon Street, near the office of the Hendrick Foundation. In the years of his marriage to N.K. he was obliged to rent an apartment in New York City, on Waverly Place, to accommodate her.

". . . well, yes. We 'took a chance' on her at the foundation—though after Allen Ginsberg, that sort of wild, feckless quasi-confessional poetry was fashionable—riding the crest of the 'new feminism' . . ."

Elisabeth marvels at the coolness with which Alexander is able to speak of N.K. at such times. So long as the subject is impersonal; so long as the subject is poetry and not *wife*.

Coolness and condescension. (Male) revenge on the (female) artist. Yes she is, or was, brilliant—"genius." But no, I am not so impressed.

Elisabeth gathers that most of these guests had known Nicola Kavanaugh. You see them frowning, shaking their heads. Pitying, condemning. Allowing the widower to know that they side with him of course—the bereft, terribly wronged husband.

Monstrous woman. Deranged and demented poet.

". . . yes, I've heard. It will be unauthorized—of course. The last thing we need is a biography of—her. Fortunately, copyright to her work resides with me, and I don't intend to give permission for any sort of use—even *the—and—but* . . ."

Laughter. As he is famously stoical, so Alexander is very witty.

A *biography?* This is the first Elisabeth has heard.

Not from Alexander, but from other sources Elisabeth has learned how the poet Nicola Kavanaugh was reluctant to marry—anyone. How she'd suffered since early adolescence from mania, depression, suicidal "ideation"—and suicide attempts. Love affairs with Nicola were invariably impassioned, destructive. And then, at last, after a most destructive relationship with a prominent woman artist living in New York City, to the astonishment of everyone who knew her and against their unanimous advice, Nicola suddenly married the older, well-to-do Alexander Hendrick, who'd been one of her ardent courters for years.

She'd married for solace, it was said—for financial security, and to pay for therapists, prescription drugs, hospitalizations; as a stay against the wild mood swings of manic depression; for peace, comfort, sanity. *Because a sexually rapacious young woman took advantage of a besotted, well-to-do older man with literary pretensions.*

In her poetry, N.K. scorned the conventional life of husband, children, responsibilities, bourgeois property, and possessions, yet in her life she'd behaved perversely, taking all these on.

Elisabeth has heard that Nicola loved the house in Wainscott—at first. A romantically remote place on Cape Cod to which she could retreat. A place where she could be alone when she wished, in solitude.

And she'd loved her children as well—at first.

Yet it would turn out that the poet wrote some of her most savagely powerful poems in this house, in the final year of her life. Sequestered away in an upstairs room, barring the door against intruders—her own children.

Terrible things Elisabeth has heard about the predecessor wife. Terrible things she is reluctant/eager to believe.

In her extreme emotional states, N.K. mistreated, abused both children. Screamed at them, shook them. Locked them in a closet. *Sight of babies appalls. Doubling myself. Sin of hubris. Stink of pride. Bringing another of myself into the world: unforgivable.*

And *How will they remember their mother?—little lambs of sacrifice, shall their eyes be opened?*

Alexander would testify at a police inquiry into the deaths that his wife had wanted children to save her life, and then, after their births, she'd resented them. She'd loved them excessively (it seemed) but had been fearful of hurting them. She couldn't bear them around her often, but claimed not to trust nannies or the housekeeper. She didn't want them near windows for fear they would fall through the windows, piercing themselves on the glass. Didn't like to take their hands to lead them upstairs or across a street; there was the terror of losing her grip of their hands. Could not bear to bathe them for fear of scalding them or drowning them. Several times she'd wakened Alexander in the middle of the night (in Alexander's bed: for the two did not share a room), crying that she'd cut the children's throats like pigs, tried to hang them upside down but couldn't, they fell to the floor and were bleeding to death . . . Alexander had to take the sobbing, hysterical woman into the children's rooms to show her that they were untouched, and then for a long time she stood disbelieving by their beds, until saying at last in a flat voice—*All right then. For now.*

Is madness contagious? Elisabeth shivers in the perpetual wind from the Atlantic.

". . . Stefan? Reasonably well. Thank you for asking. There's a girl looking after him tonight, upstairs."

"How has he adjusted, in this house? It must be . . ."

"No. Stefan is very happy here. I've told you. He cries if he's made to leave even overnight."

"Really! Is that so?"

"Yes. Strangely so. As I think I've told you—all of you."

"He must be very happy then, with his new stepmother . . ."

New stepmother. Elisabeth has been only half listening as talk swirls about her head, but she hears this, distinctly.

A rude remark, cruel and insinuating—or an entirely sincere remark made by an old friend of Alexander's who wishes him and family well?

"Really, we are all very happy here. Elisabeth has been 'settling in'—wonderfully. She and Stefan are making friends. So far, the summer has been . . ."

Feeling the visitors' eyes on her. Sensing their disappointment in her, so plain-faced, dull, and so *ordinary* after Nicola Kavanaugh.

Like a dun-feathered bird holding herself very still not to attract the attention of predators. Very still among these strangers, seeming to listen to their sharp, witty voices while hearing in the wind from the Atlantic the throaty voice, as intimate as a whisper in her ear.

But you know that I am not gone, Elisabeth. You know that I have come for you and the boy.

6.

"This house is not 'poisoned'—not by *her.*"

Not to Elisabeth has Alexander uttered such words, but she has overheard him on the phone, speaking with Wainscott relatives. His tone is vehement, contemptuous. *Who has been spreading such rumors of—hauntings . . .*

He will not be driven away from this property, he has said. Hendrick House will endure beyond individual lives. It will endure long after *her.*

Elisabeth never has to wonder who *her* is. Sometimes, the contemptuously uttered pronoun is *she.*

Bitterly Alexander says, "Nicola came here with a pretense of wanting a 'quiet' life, and she never made a home here. Her clothes were in suitcases. Her books were in boxes. Ana did most of the unpacking, shelving books. Nicola couldn't be bothered. She was immersed in her poetry, her precious career. She had her lovers, women and men. She'd promised that she had given them up when we were married, but of course she lied. Her entire life was a lie. Her poetry is a lie. When she was sick with depression, her lovers abandoned her. Where were they? Hangers-on, sycophants. And her 'fans'—they were waiting for her to die, to kill herself.

The promise of the poetry. But they hadn't anticipated that their heroine would take her own daughter with her. *That*, they hadn't expected."

Alexander speaks defiantly. Elisabeth listens with dread. Like holding your breath in the presence of airborne poison. She doesn't want to breathe in hatred for the deceased woman. She doesn't want to feel hatred for anyone.

How beautiful the house is, Elisabeth never tires of marveling.

But beware. Beauty's price.

Sucking your life's blood.

Strange, wonderful and strange, and uncanny, to live in a kind of museum. Classic Cape Cod architecture, period furnishings. Especially the downstairs rooms, flawlessly maintained.

Of course such maintenance is expensive. Much effort on the part of servants and on the part of the wife of the house. Polished surfaces, gleaming hardwood floors. Curtains stirring in the ocean breeze. High, languidly turning fans. (No air-conditioning in any of the landmark houses of Wainscott, so close to the Atlantic!) Long corridors, with windows at each end looking out (it almost seems) into eternity.

Rot beneath, shine above. Rejoice, love. Lines from one of N.K.'s chanting poems, "Dirge"—Elisabeth hadn't realized that she'd memorized it.

Does the door lock? No?

Still, the door can be shut. Though no one is likely to follow her here, except (perhaps) the child, Stefan, who is at school on this rainy, windy autumn day.

Alexander is in Boston for several days, and even if he were home, it isn't likely that he would seek her out in this part of the house, in which he has little interest.

On the third floor, up a flight of steep steps, Elisabeth has discovered a small, sparely furnished room in what had been, in a previous era, the servants' quarters.

Here there is no elegant silk French wallpaper as in the downstairs rooms. Not a chandelier, but a bare-bulb overhead light. A single window overlooking sand hills, stunted dun-colored vegetation, the glittering silver of the Atlantic.

In the room is a narrow cot, hardly a bed. A bare plank floor. No curtains or shutters. Not a closet, but a narrow cupboard opening into the wall, rife with cobwebs and a smell of mildew.

At a table in this little room, at a makeshift desk, Elisabeth sits, leaning on her elbows, which have become raw, reddened. Much of her skin feels windburned. For here at the edge of the ocean there is perennial wind: gusts rattling windowpanes, stirring foliage in tall pines beside the house. Elisabeth has brought her laptop here, but she often leaves it unopened. Her work on the Imagist poets beckons to her, as if on the farther side of an abyss, but—she is afraid—she is losing her emotional connection with it. Reading and rereading passages of prose she'd written with conviction and passion as an eager young scholar at the Radcliffe Institute, and now she can barely remember the primary work, let alone her enthusiasm for it . . . The spare impersonal poetry of H.D. seems so muted set beside a more impassioned and heedless female poetry.

Elisabeth strains her eyes, staring toward the ocean. Wind-stirred waves, pounding surf frothing white against the pebbly shore. Overhead, misshapen storm clouds, and in the pines beside the house, what appear to be the arms, legs of struggling persons—naked bodies . . .

Promiscuous life rushes through our veins. Unstoppable.

An optical illusion of some sort. Must be.

Elisabeth can see the thrashing figures in the corner of her eye, but when she looks directly at the agitated foliage, she can't decipher the human figures, only their outlines. The impress of the (naked) bodies in the thrashing branches, where they struggle like swimmers in a rough surf.

Turning her head quickly to see—if she can catch the figures in the trees.

"No. You can't catch them."

Behind her, beside her, a throaty little laugh. It is Stefan, who has crept noiselessly into the room.

Very quietly, though very quickly, like a cat ascending the steep steps to the third floor of the house, Stefan must have come to join her. Hadn't she shut the door to the little room? He'd managed to open it without her hearing.

Elisabeth is startled but tries to speak matter-of-factly. For she knows children do not like to see adults discomforted.

"Catch—what?"

"The things in the trees. That never stop."

Stefan speaks patiently, as if (of course) Elisabeth knows what he is talking about. "You can see them in the corner of your eye, but when you look at them, they're gone. They're too fast."

But there is nothing there. In the trees, in the leaves. We know that.

Elisabeth's heart is pounding quickly. Almost shyly she regards the stepchild who so often eludes her, seems to look through her.

Stefan seems never to grow, has scarcely grown an inch in the months since Alexander first introduced them.

My new, dear friend Elisabeth. Will you say hello to her? Smile— just a bit? Shake her hand?

Oh, Stefan's curly hair is damp from the rain! Elisabeth would love to embrace him, press his head against her chest.

Droplets of rain like teardrops on his flushed face and on the zip-up nylon jacket he hasn't taken time to remove. Something very touching about this. Has Stefan hurried home from school, to *her*?

"Stefan! You're home early . . ."

Stefan shrugs. Maybe he hadn't gone to school at all but simply hid in the house somewhere, in one or another of the numerous unused rooms. Or in the forbidden place, the garage.

Stefan ignores his stepmother's words, as he often does. Knowing that the words that pass between them are of little significance, like markers in a poem, mere syllables.

He is at the window, peering out. Wind, rain, thrashing pine branches, an agitation of arms and legs almost visible . . .

Convulsed with something that looks like passion, we tell ourselves, Love.

Whose words are these? Elisabeth wonders if Stefan can hear them, too.

It is true, she thinks. The convulsions in the trees. Our terrible need for one another, our terror of being left alone. To which we give the name *Love*.

"She taught me how to see them—Mummy. But they always get away."

Elisabeth isn't sure she has heard correctly. This is the first time that Stefan has uttered the word *Mummy* in her hearing.

"Now Mummy is one of them herself. I think."

For the remainder of the long day, feeling both threatened and blessed.

The child had come unbidden to *her*.

A wraith may not be approached, for a wraith will retreat. But a wraith may approach you. If he wishes.

Stefan darling. Try to forget her. I have come to take her place, I will love you in her place. Trust me!

7.

Certainly it is true, as Alexander has said, there is nothing poisoned or haunted about the Hendrick family house.

For how could there be anything wrong with a house listed in the National Register of Historic Places and featured in the fall 2011 issue of the sumptuous, glossy *Cape Cod Living* . . .

Yet things *go wrong* in the house. Usually these are not serious and are easily remedied.

For instance: sometimes after a heavy rain, the water out of the faucets tastes strange. There is a faint metallic aftertaste; in full daylight you can see a subtle discoloration, like rust. And there are mysterious drips from ceilings, actual pools of water, bulges in wallpaper like tumors. Unsettling moans and murmurs in the plumbing.

The water is well water, claimed to be "pure"—"sweet tasting." The well is a deep natural well on the Hendrick property that has been there for generations, fed by underground springs.

Ana tells Elisabeth that perhaps she should make an appointment with the township water inspector to come to the house for a sample of their well water. To see what, if anything, is wrong.

Drips in the ceilings, bulges in wallpaper, groaning pipes—Elisabeth should call the roofer, the plumber as well. Since the fancy silk wallpaper in the dining room has been discolored, she had better call a paperhanger too. And there are several cracked windowpanes, after a windstorm, that will have to be replaced—sometimes shards of glass litter the downstairs foyer, though no (evident) windowpanes have been broken. Ana can provide local numbers, for (Elisabeth gathers) these repairmen are frequently called.

"All the old big houses in Wainscott are the same," Ana says adamantly. "All my friends, they work in them, they tell me. It is nothing special to this house."

Nothing poisoned or haunted in this house. We know.

It has fallen to Elisabeth to make such appointments since Alexander is often in Boston on business. Indeed, Elisabeth is eager to shield her husband from such mundane tasks, for he is easily upset by problems involving his beloved house, and it is increasingly difficult to speak to him without his taking offense.

Also, Elisabeth is the wife of the house. As Mrs. Alexander Hendrick, she feels a thrill of satisfaction. She is sure that her emotionally unstable predecessor took no such responsibility.

The new wife is nothing like—her! Alexander didn't make a mistake this time. This Elizabeth—"Elisabeth"—is utterly devoted to him and the child and the household, she is a treasure . . .

Listening, but the voice trails off. Always she is hoping to hear *And Alexander is devoted to—her!*

Methodically, dutifully calling these local tradesmen, and (oddly) no one is available to come to the house on Oceanview Avenue just then. All have excuses, express regret.

374

"But we can pay you—of course! We can pay you double."

Calling a local plumber, and the voice at the other end expresses surprise—"Hendrick? Again? Weren't we just there a few months ago?" and Elisabeth stammers, "I—I don't know, were you? What was wrong?" and the voice says, guardedly, "Anyway, there's no one available right now. Better try another plumber. I can give you a number to call."

But it is a number Elisabeth has already called.

"Try Provincetown. They'll charge for coming here, but . . ."

None of this Elisabeth will mention to Alexander. It is only results he cares to be informed of.

So much to do each day. Like a merry-go-round that has begun to accelerate.

Vague thought of *having a baby of my own, someday, a little sister for Stefan*. About this she feels excitement, hope, dread, guilt.

So many distractions, Elisabeth has (temporarily) set aside the scholarly work she'd been doing at the Radcliffe Institute. Research that once fascinated her. As elusive and shimmering as a mirage in the desert, her Ph.D. dissertation on the experimental verse of H.D. and H.D.'s relationship to Ezra Pound and T. S. Eliot. She has written drafts of the (seven) chapters but must revise, add footnotes, update the already extensive bibliography.

No end to fascinating research! But she must be careful that she does not stray from H.D. to N.K. She does not intend to *snoop*.

It is uncanny, some lines of poetry by H.D. echo lines of poetry by N.K. Or rather, some lines of poetry by N.K. echo lines by H.D.

A case of plagiarism? Or admiration, identification?

I have had enough.

I gasp for breath.

When they were first married and Elisabeth came to live in her husband's family home in Wainscott, it was with the understanding that she would return to her scholarly work when things "settled down." The director of the Hendrick Foundation is a feminist—of course. In the past most Hendrick fellowships went to male artists, but no longer.

No one has urged Elisabeth to complete her Ph.D. at Harvard more enthusiastically than Alexander. When Stefan is older and doesn't require so much attention, Elisabeth might find a teaching position at a private school on the Cape . . .

It is true, Stefan requires attention. The fact of Stefan, the surviving child. Elisabeth knows that she must be indirect in watching over the elusive child, not obvious and intrusive. She must never startle him by a display of affection. And she must never intervene between father and son.

If Alexander is chiding Stefan, for instance. It is painful to Elisabeth to hear, but she must not intervene.

As she sometimes overhears Alexander speaking harshly on the phone, so she overhears Alexander speaking harshly to Stefan. Chiding him for being dreamy, distracted—*other-minded*. For sometimes Stefan is surprisingly clumsy—slipping on the stairs, spraining an ankle; falling from his bicycle, badly cutting his leg. Objects seem to twist from his fingers—cutlery, glassware that shatters on the floor. He is often breathless, anxious. Nothing annoys the father so much as an *anxious* child who shrinks from him as if in (ridiculous!) fear of being struck.

At such times Elisabeth bites her lower lip, straining to hear. She should not be eavesdropping, she knows. If Alexander caught her . . .

She rarely hears Stefan's reply, for the boy speaks so softly. If there is any reply.

Yet it is true, as Alexander has boasted: Stefan appears to be happy in the house on Oceanview Avenue. At least, he is less happy elsewhere.

Indeed, he is reluctant to leave on short trips, even to Provincetown. It is all but impossible to get him to stay away overnight. If forced, he will protest, sulk, weep, kick, suck his fingers. Even Ana is shocked by how childish Stefan becomes at such times.

The house is an epicenter, it seems. Stefan will allow himself approximately a mile from this center before he becomes anxious.

From her third-floor aerie Elisabeth has observed Stefan pedaling his bicycle to the end of the block, turning then to continue around the block. Though he quickly passes out of her sight, Elisabeth understands that Stefan must keep the house at the epicenter of his bicycling. Soon he will reappear, coming from the other direction along Oceanview, pedaling fast, furiously, as if his life were at stake.

Once, waiting for Stefan to reappear, waiting for—oh, how long?—an hour?—an *anguished hour?*—Elisabeth can bear it no longer. She hurries downstairs, rushes out onto the front walk to look for him, and stands in the avenue waiting for him—*where is he?* Until finally she glances behind her and sees Stefan hovering at the front door, watching her.

She is embarrassed, and blushes deeply. When she returns to the house, he has disappeared—damned if she will look for him.

8.

Convulsed with something that looks like passion, we tell ourselves, Love.

A high, skittering sound, as of glass shards ringing together. Unless it is laughter. Elisabeth steps back, and in the next instant the cut-glass chandelier in the front hall loosens, falls from the ceiling, crashes to the floor, narrowly missing her.

In the aftermath of the shattering glass, that high, faint laughter—so delicious, you want to join in.

Surfaces, and beneath. Elisabeth is learning not to be deceived by the elegant polished surfaces of the house.

A place of sickness. Don't breathe.

Walls look aslant. Doors stick or can't be closed. Doorknobs feel uncomfortably warm when touched, like inner organs.

Light switches are not where Elisabeth remembers them to be—where Elisabeth *knows* them to be. Fumbling for the switch in her own bedroom.

You will never find the light nor will the light find you but one day the light will shine through you.

Finally, her fingers locate the switch. Blasting light, blinding.

In the mirror, a blurred reflection. Wraith-wife.

No: she is imagining everything. In the mirror there is nothing.

For several days her skin has felt feverish. A sensation of heaviness in her lower belly, legs. No appetite and then ravenous appetite and then fits of nausea, gagging. The worst is dry heaving, guttural cries like strangulation.

The most peaceful blue sleep. Hurry!

As Elisabeth stands in the shower in her bathroom fierce sharp quills springing from the showerhead turn scalding-hot with no warning. Elisabeth cries out in surprise—and pain—and scrambles to escape before she faints . . .

A previous time, the shower had turned freezing cold.

Slipping and skidding on the tile floor, whimpering in pain, shock.

In fear of her life—almost. Hearing, in the pipes in the walls, muffled derisive laughter.

Safer to take a bath. Always in the morning and (sometimes) before bed as well if she is feeling *sullied, bloated.*

Fortunately, there is, in another adjoining bathroom, an enormous bathtub in which she might soak in hot (not scalding) sudsy water, curling her toes in narcotic pleasure, letting her eyelids sink shut.

Tub is too crude and utilitarian a word for such a work of art: a marble bathtub. Faint blue veins in the marble, like veins in flesh. Ancient, stately, six feet long, and deep. Eagerly Elisabeth tests the water, lowers herself into it, taking care not to slip, not to fall. It is such pleasure, pure sensuous delight. Almost at once she begins to sink into a light doze. Her hair straggles into the steamy water, her pale, soft, startled-looking breasts begin to lift . . .

Hurry! We have been waiting.

Finds herself thinking of an Egyptian tomb. Mummified corpses of a young wife and her baby wrapped in swaddling laid solemnly in the tomb side by side.

Sinking into the water, the enervating heat. Her mouth, nose beneath the water . . . Too much effort to breathe . . .

I have had enough.

I gasp for breath.

Waking then. With a start, in shock. No idea where she is or how much time has elapsed in this place.

Hovering above the naked female body. The body is white, wizened. The fingers and toes are puckered, soft. In panic she must return to this body . . .

The bathwater has turned cold and scummy and smells as vile as turpentine. The marble has become freezing cold, and slippery. In her desperation to climb out of the deep tub, Elisabeth's feet slip and slide; her strength has been sucked away. Loses her balance and falls onto the floor, nearly striking her head on the marble rim.

Oh!—pain has returned, and humiliation. For she is trapped inside the wizened white naked female body again.

In the winter, many nights Alexander is away. Bravely, Elisabeth is the *wife of the house.* Elisabeth is the *stepmother* of the surviving child.

Dining together, evenings by the fireplace. Animated, the child will speak of school, books he is reading or has read. Safe topics for stepmother and stepchild to navigate, like stepping-stones in a rough stream.

The father forbids television in the house on Oceanview Avenue. No internet for Stefan. No video games! He will not have his son's mind (he knows to be a brilliant and precocious mind, like his own at that age) polluted by debased American culture.

(Alexander watches television in his Beacon Street apartment, but the sort of television Alexander watches is not debased.)

As if he has just thought of it, Stefan says, "That room—where you are—that was Mummy's, too."

Elisabeth is surprised. *That room?*—she'd chosen it because it is so spare, so unattractive. Two flights of stairs, the second flight to the old servants' quarters steep and narrow.

She'd assumed that N.K. had worked in another room. *Her* room shows no signs of human occupancy.

"Oh, Stefan. I—I didn't know . . ."

"Mummy wouldn't let us in, mostly. Not like you."

Is this flattering? Elisabeth wants to think so.

But who is us, she wonders. Little Clea, also?

The remainder of the meal passes in silence, but not an awkward silence, and when Elisabeth undresses for bed that night, she finds herself smiling, a frothy sensation of uplift in the area of her heart.

Not like you like you like you. Not!

And later, as she is sinking into a delicious sleep—*Live like it's your life.*

Solemn ticking of the stately old Stickley grandfather clock in the hall.

Yet Elisabeth begins to hear the ticking accelerate and hesitate; a pause and a leap forward; a rapid series of ticks, like tachycardia.

(She has had tachycardia attacks since moving into the house, but in secret. Never will she voluntarily confide in her husband that she has what is called a heart murmur.) In the night she hears the clock cease its ticking, and she lies in a paroxysm of worry that it is her own heart that has ceased. A whisper consoles her—*Quick if it's done, is best. Most mercy. Blue buzz of air, the only symptom you will feel is peace.*

Ignores the whisper. Very quietly descending the stairs barefoot to check on the clock, to see why it has ceased ticking; why the silence is so loud in the interstices of its ticking.

The clock face is blank!—there is no *time . . .*

It has already happened, Elisabeth. That is why time has ceased. It is all over, and painless.

But no: when she switches on the light, she sees that the clock is ticking normally. (Elisabeth is sure: she stands barefoot in the hallway shivering, listening.) And there is the clock face as always, stately roman numerals, hour hand, minute hand, a pale, luminous face with a lurid smile just for her.

The wife of the house.

The well water has been diagnosed by the township water inspector: an alarmingly high degree of organic and fecal material. Decomposing (animal?) bodies. Excrement. Contaminated water leaking into the well, and until the well can be dredged and the water "purified," it is recommended that the Hendrick household use only bottled water for drinking and cooking purposes.

Informed of this humiliating news, Alexander flushes angrily. Elisabeth steels herself to hear him declare *This house is not poisoned.* But he turns away instead, as if it were Elisabeth who has offended him.

9.

The next evening meal with Stefan. Elisabeth has given Ana the day off, wanting to prepare the meal herself.

She takes care to prepare only a variation of one of the few meals that Stefan will consent to eat—with no chewy, pulpy meat in which muscle fibers are detectable or anything "slimy" (okra, tomato seeds) or small enough (rice, peas) to be mistaken by the child for grubs or insects. To Ana's vegetarian egg casserole Elisabeth has added several ingredients of her own—carrots, sweet peppers, spinach.

But Stefan isn't as talkative as he'd been the previous night. When Elisabeth brings up the subject of her third-floor room and the view of wind-shaken trees outside the window, Stefan says nothing. Almost, Elisabeth might wonder if he'd ever spoken to her about the struggling figures in the trees or if she'd imagined that remarkable exchange . . . Just slightly hurt, that Stefan is suspicious of the casserole she has prepared, examining forkfuls before lifting them to his mouth. And he is taking unusually small bites, as if shy of eating in her company or undecided as to whether he actually wants to eat the food she has prepared.

Yet he'd once nursed. Imagining the child as an infant nursing at the mother's breast.

Or at Elisabeth's breast.

She feels a flush of embarrassment, self-consciousness. What strange thoughts she has! And she is not drinking wine with the meal, as Alexander often urges her to do, to keep him company.

Tugging at the breast of life we must devour.
Helpless otherwise, for dignity's not enough.
Surrender dignity and in return royally
Sucked.

In person, when N.K. read this abrasive poem or recited it in her smoky, throaty voice, audiences laughed uproariously. (Elisabeth has seen videos.) The enormous wish to laugh with the woman declaiming such truths, like a tidal wave sweeping over them.

Since Alexander has been spending more time in Boston, Elisabeth has been on the internet, watching videos of N.K. Doesn't want to think that she is becoming obsessive. Knows that Alexander would disapprove, and so has no intention of allowing him to know.

Fear of being sucked and fear
Of sucking.

Stefan's silence is not hostile nor even stubborn, but (Elisabeth thinks) a consequence of shyness. Stefan may have felt that at their last meal he'd revealed too much to her and betrayed his mother.

No betrayal like loving another.
No betrayal like love of the Other.

Distracted by such thoughts, Elisabeth has taken too much food into her mouth. Trying to swallow a wad of clotted pulp. Her casserole is lukewarm and stringy, unlike Ana's. Something coarse-textured like seaweed—must be the damned spinach. Chewing, trying to swallow but can't. Horribly, strands of spinach have tangled in her teeth. Between her teeth. Can't swallow.

Trying to hide her distress from Stefan. Not wanting to alarm the child. (Oh, if Alexander were here to witness such a sight! He'd have been dismayed, disgusted.) A deep flush rises into Elisabeth's face. She can barely breathe. This clump of something clotted, caught in her throat—horrible! The harder she tries to swallow, the more her throat constricts.

"Excuse—"

Mouth too full, can't enunciate the word. Desperate now, staggering from the table, knocking something to the floor with a clatter. With widened eyes Stefan stares at her.

Must get to a bathroom, thrust a finger down her throat, gag, vomit violently into a toilet . . .

And then you die. And then

it is over.

So much struggle so long—why?

At last in a bathroom, no time even to shut the door behind her as she manages to cough up the clotted, pulpy mash, stringy spinach, in a paroxysm of misery, gagging as she spits it into the toilet bowl. Though able to breathe again, she is distressed, agitated. Too weak to stand, she sinks to her knees. Her face is flaming hot, the heaviness in her bowels like a fist.

A sound of faint laughter in the aged plumbing.

Then Stefan is standing beside her. Without a word, he soaks a washcloth in cold water from the sink and hands it to Elisabeth to press against her overheated face.

Too frightened, too exhausted even to thank the child. His small-boned hand finds hers, his fingers in her fingers clasped, tight.

Oh Stefan thank you. Oh I love you.

10.

Impossible to sleep! Bile rising in her throat. That which she has bitten off, she cannot swallow. The muscles of her throat gag involuntarily, recalling. Cannot believe how close she'd come to choking to death.

What an awful death—gagging, choking. Unable to swallow and (at last) unable to breathe.

Days have passed. Nights. She is losing track of the calendar.

Her eyelids are unnaturally heavy. Yet she cannot sleep. Or if she sleeps, it's a thin, frothy sleep that sweeps over her like surf. Briefly her aching consciousness is extinguished and yet flares up again a moment later.

A brain is dense meat. Yet a brain is intricately wired, billions of neurons and glia. The wonder is, how do you turn the brain *on*? How do you turn the brain *off*? An anesthesiologist can put a brain to sleep, but can't explain why. And only the brain can make itself conscious.

Falling on the stairs, stumbling. *But the stairs moved. It was not my foot that tripped, stumbled. The stairs moved.*

Finds herself at the rear of the darkened house where the throaty voice has brought her. Not sleepwalking, but there is a numbness encasing her that suggests the flotation logic of sleep. Hand on the doorknob. Why? She has no wish to look into the garage—the forbidden place. Still less to step into the garage, where it is perpetual twilight and smells still (she believes) of the bluish, sweetly toxic gas that killed the mother and daughter.

Alexander has said, *Stay away. No need. Do you understand, Elisabeth?*

Yes, she'd said. Of course.

I will be very, very unhappy with you if.

Briefly he'd considered (he said) shutting up the garage, securing it. But then—*why?* Whatever danger the garage once threatened is past.

Yet the door to the forbidden place is opened. Elisabeth stands in the doorway, as shy as a bride

Dry-eyed from insomnia. Aching, oversensitive skin.

Shadowy objects in the gloom. One of the household vehicles —an older BMW, belonging to Alexander but no longer used.

Like any garage, this garage is used for storage. Dimly visible lawn furniture, gardening tools, flowerpots, shelves of paint cans, stacks of canvas. Shadowy presences in the periphery of Elisabeth's vision.

The Saab in which the deaths occurred is gone of course. Long banished from the property. Elisabeth has never been told, has never inquired, but surmises that it was towed out of the garage, hauled away to a junkyard.

For no one would wish to drive, or to be a passenger in, a *death car.*

(Would the interior of the car continue to smell of death, if it still existed? Or does the odor of death fade with time?)

In the doorway Elisabeth stands. It is strangely peaceful here, on the threshold. Gradually her eyes become adjusted to the muted light, and she has no need to grope for a switch to turn on overhead lights.

The garage door is closed of course. You can see light beneath it; obviously you must stuff towels along the entire length of the door to keep the sweet-poison air in and the fresh air out.

Blue buzz of air. The only symptom is peace.

Come! Hurry.

She is hurrying. She is breathless. On her knees on the bare plank floor in front of the narrow cupboard in the third-floor maid's room, she reaches into the shadowy interior. Cobwebs in hair, eyelashes.

Wrapped inside a beautiful heather-colored mohair shawl that is riddled with moth holes.

Her hands shake. This must be one of N.K.'s diaries, unknown to Alexander!

The diary he'd found after her death, he'd destroyed. *To spare my son.*

Feminists had angrily criticized the husband's actions, but Alexander remained unrepentant. Insisting it was his right—the diary was disgusting and vile (though he'd claimed not to have read it), and it was his property. His right as a father to spare his son echoes and reflections of the mother's *sick and debased mind.*

But Alexander is not here now, Elisabeth thinks. Alexander will not know.

The diary appears to be battered, water-stained. It is only one quarter filled. The last diary of N.K.'s life.

At the makeshift desk Elisabeth dares to read N.K.'s sharply slanted hand, in stark black ink. The low, throaty voice of the poet echoes in her ears, as intimate as a caress.

fearful of harming the children
fearful of harming the children entrusted to her
begins with "the"—not "her"
telling herself they are not THE children, they are HER children

she does not want to carry the new baby on the stairs
fearful of dropping her slipping, falling
fear of injuring loving too much

(not the husband's child)
(does he know?—must know)

of course the husband knows a man must know
pillow over my face, he says so the children will not hear
will win custody you will never see them again
your disgusting poetry will be my evidence in a court of law
you are not a fit mother
not a fit human being

he has struck me with his hand. the back of his hand. hits me on the chest, torso, thighs where my clothing covers the bruises. he says he will take the children from me if I tell—anyone. if I tell my doctor. I must say, I am clumsy, I drink too much, take too much medication (even if I do not—not enough).

I must declare legally, I have invented these accusations against him. I am a poet/ I am a liar/ I am sick & debased/ I have loved others, not him/

I am one who makes things gorgeously up.

days of joy, now it is a dark season
days of happiness I can hear echoing at a distance
he says I am not the beautiful young woman he married
I am another person, I am not that woman

to be a mother is to surrender girlhood
to be a mother is to take up adulthood

he says I am sick, finished unless I slash my wrists I am of no
interest to anyone

knowing how I am vulnerable, wanting to die (sometimes)
welcomed me back, forgave me (he said) even as I forgave him
(his cruelty)
his lies, he'd so adored me
but then it has been revealed, he has not forgiven me he will never
love the baby he guesses is the child of another

as in Nature, the male will destroy the offspring of other males

(why does this surprise me? it does not surprise me)
a mistake to have confided in him, in a weak mood my fear of
harming the children & he pretended to sympathize
then later, laughed at me in his eyes, hatred like agates

last night daring to say do it & get it over with

Elisabeth is so shocked she nearly drops the diary. For a long time she sits unmoving, staring at the page before her.

At last, hearing a sound outside the room, a tentative footstep. It is Stefan, is it?—the surviving child.

Stefan enters the room though Elisabeth has not invited him nor even acknowledged him. Asks her what is that, what is she reading, and Elisabeth says it is nothing, and Stefan says, his voice rising, "Is it something of Mummy's? Is that what it is?" and Elisabeth starts to reply, but cannot. Wraps the diary in the shawl to hide it, leans over the makeshift desk, and with her body tries to shield it from the child's widened eyes.

11.

So very easy. Sinking into sleep.

Position yourself. Behind the wheel of the car, so calm.

First, you swallow pills with wine. Not too many pills, enough pills for solace. And the child, you must tend to him.

Dissolved in milk. Warm milk. Who would suspect? No one!

Start the motor. Lay your head against the back of the seat. Shut your eyes. The child's eyes. Wrap him in the shawl, in your arms.

Soon, you are floating. Soon, you are sinking. Soon, you are safe from all harm.

For days, unless it has been weeks, Elisabeth has been feeling feverish. Sick to her stomach. A fullness in her belly, as if bloated with blood. Gorged with backed-up blood.

One day, ascending the stairs, she loses her balance, slips. It is a freak accident. It is (certainly not) deliberate. A sharp, near-unbearable pain in her right ankle, which has twisted, sprained. In her lower belly a seeping of blood, then a looser rush of blood, hot against her thighs, clotted. At first she thinks she has wetted herself, in panic. She calls for help. Weakly, faintly, doesn't want to upset her husband, doesn't want to upset the child, so very lucky that

393

Ana comes hurrying—"Oh, Mrs. Hendrick!"—and in the woman's eyes compassion, concern.

You may warm yourself in the shawl. That is for you.

Just seven weeks old. The tiny creature—"fetus." Not a pregnancy exactly—you wouldn't have called it.

Elisabeth is astonished, disbelieving. She'd been *pregnant?* How was that possible?

When he learns of the miscarriage (which is what Elisabeth's doctor calls it), Alexander is stunned. His face is gray with shock, distaste. "That's ridiculous. That couldn't be. You *were not pregnant*. The subject is closed."

12.

In her *Paris Review* interview N.K. said in jest, *The best suicides are spontaneous and unplanned—like the best sex.*

No more should you plan a suicide than you'd plan a kiss, or laughter.

True of N.K.'s earlier suicide attempts, but not true of the actual suicide in a locked and secured garage in the house on Oceanview Avenue, Wainscott. *Life catches up with you, taps you on the shoulder.*

Towels stuffed beneath doors, a plotted and meditated death, motor of a car running, bluish toxic exhaust filling the air. Stink of exhaust, having to breathe it in order to breathe in precious toxic carbon monoxide; the child beside her sedated, too weak to resist; the child in the rear of the Saab less cooperative but too groggy to resist . . . Beautiful Clea, beautiful Stefan, children the mother hadn't deserved. In her deep unhappiness *calling us back, the kiss of oblivion.*

In the dimly lighted garage, Elisabeth finds herself groping her way like a sleepwalker.

A powerful curiosity draws her. As water draws one dying of thirst.

Though Elisabeth has never been and is not suicidal.

This BMW, the older of Alexander's cars, seems to have been abandoned in the garage. Elisabeth is concerned that the battery might have died.

She will see! She will experiment.

Elisabeth found the key to the BMW after searching the drawers in Alexander's bureau. Loose in her pocket is the key now, along with a handful of sleeping pills. Consoling!—though she has no intention of using the pills.

And in her hand a bottle of Portuguese wine she'd struggled to open.

And the moth-eaten heather-colored mohair shawl that is yet beautiful, like wisps of cobweb.

Envy is the homage we pay to those whose hearts we don't know.
Envy is ignorance raised to the level of worship.

Just to enter the (forbidden) garage. To sit in the (forbidden) car. To turn on the ignition—the motor is *on!*

(If the ignition hadn't turned on, that would be the crucial sign. *Not now not you not for you.* But the ignition has turned on.)

Just to listen to music on the car radio. (But all Elisabeth can get is static.)

Just to drink from the bottle. Solace of wine, that might numb the ache between her legs, where blood still seeps, nothing dangerous, no hemorrhage, but more like weeping. *Not a real pregnancy, not for you.*

Like a woman with no manners drinking from the bottle. Hardly the wife of the house on Oceanview Avenue.

Homeless woman. Reckless harridan. Alexander would be appalled, but in her distracted state she'd forgotten a—what, what is it—wineglass . . .

The BMW motor is quiet. Loud humming, could be a waterfall. Bees at a distance. Oh, but Elisabeth has also forgotten—in her pocket, a handful of green capsules.

Turns off the staticky radio. Leans her head back against the top of the seat. *A mood is music.*

Very sleepy, tired. Even before the drone of the engine, the smell of the exhaust, tired. Weight of the air. Can hardly move.

One day. You will know when.

In the mohair shawl she is warm, protected. Warmth like a woman's arms.

Airy lightness. Like a kiss, or laughter.

13.

Elisabeth?—*the first time the child has uttered her name.*

And the sound pierces her heart, so beautiful.

Small fists on the window of the car door, close beside her head. Her heavy-lidded eyes are jarred open. With the strength of panic, Stefan has managed to open the heavy car door, he is shouting at her—No! No! Wake up!

Pushing away her hand. Fumbling to turn off the ignition. Coughing, choking.

In that instant the motor ceases. Hard hum of the motor ceases.

Elisabeth is groggy, nauseated. Hateful stink of exhaust. The garage has filled with bluish fumes. Yet: Elisabeth wishes to insist that she is not serious, this has not been a serious act.

If she were serious, she would not have behaved in such a way in the presence of the child. (In fact, she'd assumed that Stefan was at school. Why is Stefan not at school?)

Only a single capsule swallowed down with tart white wine. Just to calm her rapidly beating heart. No intention of anything further.

Wrapped in the beautiful moth-eaten mohair shawl. Shivering in delicious dread, anticipation. But now comes the frightened child, crouching beside her. Pulling at her, clawing at her. With all the strength

*in his small being, dragging her out of the car. As she stumbles, he runs
to press the button to open the garage door.*

A rattling rumbling noise like thunder . . .

*Pulling at Elisabeth. On drunken legs, coughing and choking.
Pleading with her—*Get outside! Hurry!

*Together, staggering out of the garage into wet, cold, bright air
smelling of the ocean.*

Don't die, Elisabeth—*the child is begging.*

Don't die. I love you. *The child is begging.*

*Never has Elisabeth heard her stepson speak to her in such a way.
Never has she seen her stepson looking at her in such a way. Never such
concern for Elisabeth, such love in his eyes.*

*And now that they are outside in the fresh, clear air, Stefan will
tell Elisabeth a secret.*

The most astonishing secret.

*Not Mummy who'd pulled Stefan from the car three years ago,
carried him out of the poisonous garage and upstairs in the house to
(just barely) save his life. For Mummy had been unconscious, her head
back at an angle, as if her neck were broken, and little Clea unconscious,
wrapped for warmth in Mummy's shawl and Mummy's arms and no
longer breathing.*

Not the mother. Not her.

*Stefan will explain: it had been the father who'd come home, who
had saved him.*

*Alexander had entered the garage, he'd smelled the stink of the
exhaust billowing from the rear of the car. Seen the hellish sight, knowing at once what the desperate woman had done. And in that instant
made his decision to let her die.*

Do it! Do it, and be done.

There is no love in my heart for you. Die.

Alexander's decision not to rescue the mother and not to rescue the little girl wrapped in the shawl in the mother's arms. Only just the boy in the back seat of the Saab, who was his son.

Blood of my blood, bone of my bone. My son.

Choking, coughing as he pulled the semiconscious child out of the car. Seeing that the boy was still breathing, sentient. Not knowing if it was too late and the child's brain had been injured irrevocably, but frantic to save him, the son. His son. Gasping for breath as he carried the seven-year-old out of the garage and kicked shut the door behind him.

Upstairs and in a panic, hiding the boy in a closet. Not knowing what he was doing, but knowing that he must do something. And not understanding at just that moment that he would claim to have discovered the boy in the closet, in his search for his son. And not understanding yet that the story would be that it had been the mother who'd carried the son upstairs, laid him on the closet floor, and shut the door.

The father's hands badly shaking. Still, he'd have had time to return to the garage, to rescue the mother and the younger child if he had wished, but he had not wished. Had not even turned off the motor in his haste to save his son.

A brute voice urged, in terrible elation—Let them die, they are nothing to you. They are not of your blood.

Elisabeth will be stunned by this revelation. Elisabeth will grasp at the child's hands, to secure him.

You have never told anyone this, Stefan? Only me.

Only you.

And so it was murder, yet not murder. The father had only to wait, as the garage filled up with poisonous haze, until the death of the woman was certain.

His excuse could be, he was agitated, confused. He was not him-self. Had not planned—ever—to do such a thing. Never would he have murdered N.K. with his own hands. Never would he have wished the little girl Clea dead—though Clea was not his, but another man's daughter.

One of the wife's lovers. Forever a secret from Alexander for in her diary which he would discover and destroy there were codified names, obvious disguises. Would not know the identity of the little girl's father though he'd been rabid with jealousy for this unknown person and in his passion would have liked to murder him as well.

And so it had happened. The deaths that were (the father would tell himself) accidents.

Yet he'd taken time to arrange the towels beneath the door to the garage, as the woman had arranged them. For it was crucial, the poison-ing should not cease until it had done its work.

Gauging the time. Though his thoughts came careening and con-fused. How many minutes more before the woman he'd come to hate would be poisoned beyond recovery?

Twenty, twenty-five minutes . . . By then, he believed, the woman and the child must be dead, and their deaths could not be his fault. For the hand that had turned on the ignition was not Alexander's, but the woman's.

In astonishment, Elisabeth listens. Yet she is not so surprised, for she has known the father's heart.

Stefan has saved her. It is wonderful to Elisabeth to learn that he has loved her all along, these many months of the most difficult year of her life.

Returning from school to save his stepmother. Daring to enter the garage that was forbidden to him. Daring to yank open the heavy door of the BMW, to shut off the ignition. Daring to scream into her slackened face—No! No! Wake up.

In confusion and fright she'd flailed at him. Thinking at first that he was the furious husband.

Then he'd hurried to open the garage door. Like rumbling thunder above her. Tugging at her, urging her from the death car. Together, staggering outside into the bright, cold air of March.

In this bright, cold air Elisabeth will run, run. Strength will flow back into her legs, her lungs will swell. Never has Elisabeth run so freely, alone or with another. She is suffused with joy. Light swells inside her, in the region of her heart. In her throat, into her brain. Behind her eyes that swell with tears. It is not too late, the child has not come too late to save her. Running hand in hand away from the shingle board house on Oceanview Avenue. Hand in hand away from the Hendrick family house and along the coarse pebbly shore wet from crashing froth-bearing surf Elisabeth and Stefan run. Giddy with relief for the cold Atlantic wind has blown the poisoned air away as if it had never existed. Rising on all sides now are gray sand dunes beautifully ribbed and rippled into which they can run, run and no one will follow.